MOVE HEAVEN AND EARTH

CHRISTINA DODD

HarperPaperbacks
A Division of HarperCollinsPublishers

HarperPaperbacks
A Division of HarperCollins*Publishers*
10 East 53rd Street, New York, NY 10022-5299

This is a work of fiction. The characters, incidents, and dialogues are products of the author's imagination and are not to be construed as real. Any resemblance to actual events or persons, living or dead, is entirely coincidental.

ISBN 0-06-103000-7

Cover illustration by Doreen Minuto

First HarperPaperbacks printing: August 1995
Special edition printing: August 1999

Printed in the United States of America

Visit HarperPaperbacks on the World Wide Web at
http://www.harpercollins.com

❖ 10 9 8 7 6 5 4 3 2 1

To my in-laws Tom and Lou,
who gave the world three children:
a Girl, a Boy, and Perfection.

Thanks to Tom for being a rock.
And Lou—
I wish you were here to see this.
You would have enjoyed it more than anyone.

Move Heaven and Earth

Prologue

Somerset, England, 1420

"The babe is hale an' hearty, Yer Grace." The midwife handed Radolf the red, squalling, still-wet newborn wrapped in a linen cloth.

The woman's voice lacked enthusiasm and Radolf accepted the kicking child with dreadful anticipation. "Let me see," he commanded.

The midwife knew what he desired, and she turned back the cloth to reveal the baby's gender.

"A son!" Patton, Radolf's chief knight, leaned over his shoulder and stared with frank envy, then slapped Radolf on the shoulder as the great hall rang with shouts of masculine celebration. "A son at last, with your black hair on his head and your vigor in his breast."

A son. Disbelief mixed with joy inside of Radolf. He'd prayed, worked, schemed for this moment since the day the king awarded him Clairmont Court and the dukedom. For what good are lands and title without a son to inherit them?

Lifting the babe high, he spun in a circle and shouted, "Behold your future lord!"

The shouts of celebration shook the rafters, and the child screamed in answer. Carefully, Radolf lowered the child and handed him to the midwife, then tucked the cloth around his flailing limbs. "Swaddle him well. Keep him warm and dry, and get a wet nurse to suckle him until my lady's milk comes through."

Her face waxen, the midwife returned the howling child to the warmth of her ample bosom and pulled the edge of her cloak over him. "That should not be a problem, Yer Grace."

Accepting a tankard of ale, Radolf drank the first toast to his son's good health. He wiped his lips on the back of his hand and frowned. "I know Jocelyn wished to feed him herself, but we can't have my son go hungry."

"Yer wife won't be feeding him," the midwife said.

Radolf drank another toast and belched. "Did she change her mind?" Then he remembered of whom he spoke, and bellowed with laughter. "Surely not Jocelyn. She's as pigheaded a woman as—"

"As you are a man," Patton finished for him with a shout.

The smile faded from Radolf's face, and he glared at Patton. The big man shriveled beneath the fury in Radolf's blue eyes. When Patton had shrunk away, when he'd displayed sufficient respect for Radolf's fury, Radolf allowed himself to relax. "Aye, perhaps 'tis true." He cuffed Patton on the ear—a friendly cuff, knocking him only halfway across the room. "Jocelyn's as pigheaded as I. A toast!" He lifted his tankard high. "To

Jocelyn, bed partner, housewife, healer, and the one wife who's carried a son for me."

The men drank, but the midwife still stood there, holding the baby in tender hands and staring at Radolf as if he were more than pigheaded—as if he were a pig.

What was wrong with the old witch? Even an ignorant midwife ought to know this was a cause for jubilation. Irritated, he demanded, "What is it, woman? Haven't you got your instructions?"

"Aye, Yer Grace, that I have. But I thought ye might want t' know why yer wife'll not be feeding th' babe."

Something about the way she said it made Radolf remember the screams emitting from the solar an hour ago. The men had said all women screamed in labor—they knew what they were talking about, didn't they?

Radolf handed the tankard to a passing squire. "Jocelyn is fighting to get up already, isn't she?"

Silent, the midwife shook her head.

He caught her arm in his hand. "Is she ill?"

"Nay, Yer Grace."

"Well, then." He grinned. "Why the long face?"

"She's dead." The midwife delivered the words as she would deliver a stillborn—grimly, stolidly.

"You're lying."

Radolf knew she had to be lying. Jocelyn wasn't a big woman, but she was the first of his wives who had returned as good as he gave. She never backed down, never feared his shouting, never flinched at his scars or his temper.

She was the first wife who'd given him a son. "You're lying."

He wasn't hollering now, but the midwife shrank back as if he were. "The priest is wi' her now." She tucked the shrieking baby closer to her and sidled toward the solar.

"Ye can see yer lady wife's body when we've cleaned an' prepared her."

Radolf followed. "You're lying."

"Ye can't go in there," she said. "'Tis a sight unfit fer a man not o' th' cloth."

Behind her, the priest exited the solar with a long face, and Radolf turned to stalk him instead. "Tell me she's lying," he said to the priest.

He was an old priest, hard of hearing but apparently skilled at comprehending a husband's disbelief. "My son, we must resign ourselves to the will of God."

"Resign?" Radolf worked his fists, open and shut, open and shut. "Resign?" His voice rose, and he started toward the solar.

The priest flung himself at Radolf, grabbed his tunic by the neck and clung. "It would be better if you don't look!"

Radolf carried him along like a flea on a dog.

Inside the door, Jocelyn's sorrowful serving maids rushed toward him, blocking his view. "Yer Grace, you can't!" they cried in unison.

But he could. She was there on the bed, alone, cold, white, still, the gold hair he loved to stroke dulled with sweat.

Not true. Not true.

Crimson stained the sheets. The snapping blue eyes that had challenged and enthralled him were closed and sunk deep into her skull.

Not true.

Her shapely limbs lay twisted, as if the bones had broken from the strain of producing his son.

The son he had prayed for to the exclusion of all else.

Not true.

Something—someone—knocked him in the back,

buffeted him until he faced the door. Someone stood before him, dragging him back to the great hall. Through the mist before his eyes, Radolf could see him. Patton. His lips were moving, and from a distance he heard Patton's words of comfort. "You can always get yourself another wife. It's not as if you haven't had to court wives before. It's been your misfortune to wed ones so puny they couldn't carry a child to term, but Jocelyn produced for you, and your next wife will, too."

A shriek worked its way up from Radolf's gullet and burst forth with such power men cowered throughout the hall. "Nay!" His fist shot out. He knocked Patton to the ground with one blow to the face. "Nay!" Picking up a bench, he heaved it across the trestle tables, and pitchers and cups flew. The odor of bitter ale curled through the air. "Never again!"

His gaze lit on the midwife, and he marched toward her. Squeaking, she tried to make a shield for the child with her body. "Stupid cow," he said, contempt weighing his tone. Gently, he folded back the cloth over his son and stroked the black hair so like his own. "I wouldn't hurt the child. Jocelyn gave her life for this child, and that makes him doubly precious to me." Then, glaring into the midwife's eyes, he commanded, "Get him the finest wet nurse in England. Make sure the milk is pure and sweet. Tend my son well, for he is the only son I will have, and if he dies, you die."

"Aye, Yer Grace." The midwife bobbed a curtsy, then another, and when he gestured, she ran toward the solar, there to bathe the babe in the warmth of the fire.

Staggering to his heavy chair, Radolf began to collapse into it. Then he looked at the symbol of his lordship: the dark wood, the intricate carving, the tapestry cushions that protected his noble arse, and he remembered.

Remembered how Jocelyn had teased him about his consequence. Remembered how he'd wrestled her into his lap. Remembered how he'd promised he would have a noble chair made for her—if she gave him a son.

Not true. Not forever.

Grabbing the chair, he heaved it aloft. Cushions scattered. He carried it to the window. It wouldn't fit through the narrow opening, so he banged it against the stone wall until the legs broke off and the back collapsed. Shoving it through the opening, he listened for the satisfying crunch when it hit the ground.

Splinters. It was splinters.

True. Forever. Jocelyn was dead. She'd died for his son, for Clairmont Court and for him, and never would another woman be worthy of the position of the duke of Clairmont's wife.

Lifting his fist into the air, he swore the oath that would bind him. "For the good of my sweet Jocelyn's son, I'll move heaven and earth to keep Clairmont Court—forever."

1

Somerset, England, April 1816

"A ghost walks the halls of Clairmont Court at night."

Miss Sylvan Miles clutched her bonnet in one hand and a strap with the other as the two-wheeled open carriage climbed yet another hill. With a throaty chuckle, she responded, "I'd be disappointed if one didn't."

The coachman hunched his massive shoulders. "Aye, ye may laugh. A meager woman might do so—until she comes face-to-face with that awesome lord."

Jasper Rooney had picked her up at the Hawk and Hound Inn only two hours before, and she'd thought him a dour young man with no imagination. Now she wondered if he didn't suffer from an excess of imagination. Telling herself she shouldn't encourage him, she tried to ignore the prod of curiosity. Instead she looked at the rugged moor that rolled past the fashionable Stanhope gig. She smelled the scent of the ocean as they neared it and hunched her shoulders against the nip of the breeze. And she burst out, "Have *you* seen this ghost?"

"Aye, that I have. Thought myself mad when I saw him striding the grounds in his fancy suit. I told our Reverend Donald, and he said I wasn't the first to sight it. 'Tis the ghost of the first duke of Clairmont."

His voice throbbed with emotion, and he trembled, but Sylvan wasn't afraid.

She'd seen worse than ghosts in her time.

Briskly, she demanded, "How did you know that? Did you ask the ghost his identity?"

"Nay, miss. But he looks just like the portrait of Radolf. A fearsome man, tall and brawn. A warrior with mace and sword."

She grinned, secure in the knowledge the coachman couldn't see her. "If he's carrying a mace, I'll do my best to avoid him. Warriors exhaust me."

"Ye're not a very respectful miss," Jasper chided.

"You're not the first to remark on that," Sylvan agreed. Then the carriage topped the hill, and she cried, "Stop!"

Before Jasper had pulled to a complete halt, she leaped off the steps and onto the ground. A tangled madness of ancient forest and moor, cliffs and savage ocean stretched before her. She waded into the new green grass, absorbing the scent of it as she crushed it beneath her feet. Close at hand, heather and bracken rippled, and beyond that, the sea's surface undulated at the command of the wind. Far in the distance, she could see squares of brown dirt that had been cleared and plowed and perhaps planted, but that had not yet produced an inkling of a crop. On the sea, a few fishing boats, dwarfed by distance, bobbed among the rocks. Clasping her hands at her breast, she tried to contain the welcome ache inside her.

It was a homecoming, but she'd never been here before.

"'Tis a god-awful primitive place, ain't it?" The coachman sounded as if he hoped she would agree. "Most ladies react just like you. I've had some of them want to turn back right here, but they always go on."

"I've never seen anything like this." Her lungs filled with fresh, brisk air, and it intoxicated her. She wanted to run and dance, to find a high place and jump off, trusting to the wind to carry her—

"Willing to brave the horrors of Clairmont lands for the prestige and wealth of the duke."

—and then drop her gently to earth, there to rest and heal.

"'Course, you can't leave," Jasper said. "His Grace said you were the new nurse for Lord Rand."

Rest. God, what she would do for a good night's sleep.

"Told him it was foolish, I did. The other nurses were men—as is proper—and *they* couldn't deal with Lord Rand."

Jasper's derision jerked her focus to him. "Deal with Lord Rand? What do you mean?"

"The tantrums and the shouting and the swearing have sent four strong men running in eight months. How's a woman going to take it?" His gaze ran contemptuously over her. "'Specially a tiny thing like you."

Sylvan stood stock still, struggling with a sense of betrayal.

Garth Malkin, current duke of Clairmont, had claimed his brother was an invalid. He'd implied that ill fortune had crushed all spirit from Lord Rand. He had fostered the impression of a cowed man who needed careful handling. His Grace's reassurances were the only reasons she had allowed herself to be persuaded to come, for she had not escaped her last encounter with Lord Randolf Malkin unscathed.

But she had found she couldn't bear the thought of Rand's scalding blue eyes bleak with defeat, nor his vibrant figure wasting away. She had imagined herself gently coaxing him back to life, bringing a smile to his pale lips and lighting the spark of his soul once more. Yet Jasper was insinuating . . .

"Having second thoughts, miss?"

Second thoughts, indeed. Second thoughts were for cowards and ladies, not for Miss Sylvan Miles.

Squaring her shoulders, she looked up at Jasper on his perch and smiled. "You'll have to wait and see, won't you?"

He stared down, slack mouthed, then an answering smile crept over his sullen face. "Perhaps you'll do. His Grace is no fool, is he?" Climbing down, he offered his enormous hand. "Best get in the gig."

Sylvan didn't move. "Where's the house?"

"Through the village, around the hill and up. Four hundred years ago, Lord Radolf built it facing the ocean, so the windows rattle in the mildest breeze. When a storm blows up, we're lucky to keep the fires lit and the smoke out of the house. The first duke acted just like today's Clairmonts. Not interested in good sense and comfort, only interested in struggle and challenge. Whole damned family's dicked in the nob."

Ho, now that was interesting. "Why do you say that?"

"Best get in, miss. They'll be looking for you at the manor."

He wasn't going to answer. Evidently, he regretted his

disclosure, and she couldn't urge him further. She might not have the breeding of a lady, but her governess had taught Sylvan well. A lady didn't listen to a servant's gossip.

Sylvan had always thought it a waste of valuable information, but that was her vulgar ancestry coming to the fore. Placing her foot on the step, she bounded back into the carriage with no assistance.

Jasper sighed in ill-concealed forbearance and climbed back onto his perch. He really was an enormous fellow. He should have been a farmer—or a soldier. "Were you at Waterloo?" she asked.

"Aye, miss. I was Lord Rand's body servant." He spoke to the fine pair of matched horses as they traveled down the winding road. "Still am, for that matter. I change his sheets, care for his clothes, wash him, dress him."

"Drive him too, I dare say."

"He doesn't go out, miss."

"Really?" She sat forward in the seat. "How does he keep abreast of that which must interest him?"

"Like what?"

"Well"—she tried to think—"such as the events of world? Napoleon's exile and such."

"I bring him the London papers when they arrive."

"What about . . . oh . . . the events of the estate?"

"I tell him what he needs to know."

Perhaps Garth had justification for worry. Perhaps Lord Rand had slipped into a decline of sorts. She assessed Jasper again. "So he depends on you completely. You care for him when he has no nurse in residence. Tell me about his condition."

"He can't walk."

Jasper's bluntness bordered on rudeness, but Sylvan wasn't offended. If he had been at Waterloo, then he'd treated the wound that downed Lord Rand, and he knew more about his state than anyone else. Jasper had already proved he felt protective of the family. Perhaps the tale of the ghost had been nothing but a fiction to scare her away.

"What's that?" She pointed at a smudge of dark smoke that rose along the horizon.

"The mill."

"What mill?"

"The cotton mill."

"On Clairmont lands?" She stared at the smoke, tracing it until it dissipated in the high winds that tore the clouds to tatters. "Impossible. Dukes don't indulge in trade." Surely not the pleasant, handsome Garth. "Only merchants do. Then they buy a barony and put their daughter on the marriage mart, seeking a title to match their fortunes."

"Well, I don't know about that, miss. I only know about His Grace."

What a clam! she thought in exasperation. She might as well have indulged in curiosity. Jasper wouldn't tell her a thing.

The gig rattled along the rutted track. They drove through a cultivated hollow where men plowed the soil and pressed seed in place, then into a pleasant country village with a few shops and homes. It looked clean and prosperous, the kind of place Sylvan had imagined existed but had never seen.

The blacksmith examined her as they drove by, then raised a hand in welcome, and she waved back.

A homecoming.

"We're starting the ascent to the manor." Jasper pointed with his whip. "If ye'll look up as we go around this corner, ye'll catch yer first glimpse."

She did, and no etiquette could stop her exclamation of "Mercy!"

The house straddled the rocky hilltop like a Gothic battleship defying the elements. Each succeeding duke evidently had a different idea of style and good taste, and some of them must have been, as Jasper claimed, mad. The hodgepodge of chimneys, windows, and carvings tried but could not distract from the exterior jumble of gray stone, sandstone, and marble.

"It looks," Sylvan said in wonder, "as if a giant child kicked over its blocks, then tried to reassemble them."

"Most visitors are in awe." Jasper's spine straightened beneath the black coat.

"In awe." Immense stands of horse chestnut and mountain ash whisked past, then the hedges. They rounded the bend and the house showed itself in its full glory. Nothing about it resembled her father's new house, which had been designed and decorated by the finest craftsmen in England, but somehow Clairmont Court welcomed her—her, the daughter of a merchant. They pulled up to a series of broad steps that led to the terrace and then into the house, and she stared at the towering structure. "I *am* in awe. I have never seen anything remotely resembling this. It's chaotic. It's barbaric. It's—"

A wooden chair crashed through a tall, narrow ground-floor window and skidded across the terrace.

"Likely to get worse," Jasper finished for her. "He must have heard you were coming."

Boys ran to the horses' heads while a deep voice raged from within the house. "A woman? You got me a hen-hearted woman?" A glass statue followed the chair, but through a different window, and shards sparkled like rain on a cloudless day.

Jasper leaped from his perch and ran up the steps, forgetting his duty to Sylvan, but she didn't mind. All the better to get a grasp on the situation.

Bracing herself, she descended from the carriage. She pulled off her gloves and her cornet bonnet, ran her hands through her hair, and fluffed it out.

The ragged edges of one window broke in a series of shattering protests as a stick, probably a cane, punched it out. "What the hell do you think to accomplish with a woman?"

"Give me that!" The sound of a scuffle carried clearly through the open window.

"That's right, steal from a crippled man."

"If you'd wait to meet her . . ."

Sylvan recognized Garth's voice, but more than that, she recognized the other voice. When she had known it before, it had been lightly contemptuous, unwillingly attracted. Now the tone had changed, but she remembered it from her experience on the battlefield and in the hospital. She'd heard it in every soldier's voice as he was carried, screaming, to the surgeon for amputation.

Rage and pain, disgust and fear.

She didn't want to face those raw emotions again. She'd spent the last eleven months trying to forget, while knowing she never would.

Run away! her mind urged. *Run before your foolish compassion traps you here.*

But her feet moved forward.

Call Jasper and tell him you've changed your mind. Run away!

Slowly, she mounted the stairs, and all the while Rand's voice raged and Garth admonished. A vase full of flowers flew out the window and broke so close the water wet her shoes and splashed her dress. Lord Rand must have seen her and was aiming now.

It was a clear sign she should leave, but instead she picked up one of the fragrant wild roses and walked on, hiding her apprehension with a calm expression. The expression she had perfected on the battlefield.

At the door, Jasper gestured heartily. "Come in, miss. Hurry! I've never seen him like this, and maybe when he realizes what a lovely lady ye are, he'll remember his society manners."

Sylvan could have laughed at Jasper's naïveté, except it showed how little the invalid was understood.

Her appearance wouldn't calm the beast, it would provoke him, for no man liked to be weak and helpless before a woman.

She really ought to leave before she stepped inside the house, but as she hesitated, she again experienced a moment of warmth, of homecoming. Clairmont Court sucked her in, and she stepped across the threshold.

"Take your outer garments, miss?" A broad-beamed maid bobbed a curtsy as Sylvan removed her pelisse and handed over her gloves and hat.

"Thank you," Sylvan said. The wide marble entry stretched all the way to the stairs, and doors opened onto it. One doorway seemed to bulge as two men and three ladies peered at her. Sylvan's dragging feet slid to a halt.

An attractive woman of perhaps fifty years complained in high-pitched exasperation. "I told Garth this was a bird-witted idea. I don't know why he doesn't listen to me."

"Perhaps, Mama, because he's the duke and you're only a duke's sister-in-law."

Sylvan glanced sharply at the young man who stood patting his mother's hand as they stood in the doorway of a salon.

He grinned and winked. "James Malkin, at your service, and my mother, Lady Adela Malkin."

"Why shouldn't he have a nurse?" Sylvan asked the lady.

"We don't need a *female* nurse," Lady Adela corrected. "You're no doubt sweet-natured and gentle, but all the other nurses have treated him tentatively, when what he needs is some sense knocked into him. "

"He's not a bad boy. He's just having trouble adjusting." The whispery voice belonged to a soft-faced, silver-haired woman dressed in the height of fashion.

Another roar of animosity blasted down the hallway, and Lady Adela flinched. "If he doesn't gain control, he'll have to be put away."

"Put away! Oh, Adela, how could you?" The second woman—Rand's mother, Sylvan surmised—lost the battle for composure as two large tears rolled down her face.

"Is that really likely?" Sylvan asked James, rather than the two ladies.

"Not at all," James said stoutly. "But I have to agree with m'mother. We've all tried kindness and he just gets angrier. Perhaps a bit of a jolt would help."

A bit of a jolt. She thought about that and started walking again. Jasper's boots clomped on the polished floors, leading her to the corridor that turned to the left, then to a door that looked as if it belonged to a study—a study that had been converted into a downstairs bedroom. Taking an audible breath, he opened it and held it wide.

The door. When she entered, she would be committed. As she hesitated, a candle hit the edge of the door, followed by a barrage of six more that bounced off the opposite wall. Jasper dodged while counting, then pronounced, "That's all on *that* candelabra, miss. Ye're safe for the moment."

So Sylvan sailed in.

She ignored the books on the floor and the shelves that showed broken-tooth gaps. She ignored the overturned furniture and the remnants of every ornament that had formerly decorated the shattered room. She ignored the red-faced duke of Clairmont, who held a cane clutched in his fist and muttered apologies. She looked only at the occupant of the chair with wheels.

Rand's eyes gleamed with demonic intensity as he examined her. His black hair stood in clumps over his skull, as if he'd been tearing at it. The wheeled cane chair must have been built especially to fit his wiry frame and long legs.

She knew they were long, because he wore a black silk robe. A robe hemmed so it wouldn't drag on the floor as he wheeled himself around. A robe that tied at the middle and revealed, only too clearly, that he wore trousers and nothing else.

He flaunted himself. One side of the robe had slipped over his shoulder, showing the development of a man forced to use his arms constantly. His chest was similarly muscular, and when she jerked her gaze back to his face, she found him maliciously laughing at her.

Did he think she'd never seen a half-naked man before?

"By Jove, Rand, cover up." Garth rushed forward and tried to adjust Rand's robe over his chest.

Rand shoved him away, still challenging Sylvan with his gaze. Only his hands betrayed his true agitation, for they gripped the two large hardwood chair wheels with white-knuckled dedication.

She had no attention to spare for Garth. She had no attention to spare for anyone but the man who rejected himself by rejecting her. Handing him the prickly stemmed rose with a flourish, she said, "For a cripple, you're not a bad-looking fellow."

He accepted it, then flung it away. "For a nurse, you look almost normal."

She grinned.

He grinned back.

She wondered which of them bared their teeth with more challenge. "What obnoxious behavior," she marveled. "Have you been practicing it long?"

His smile dipped a little. "No doubt I shall perfect it in the short interval of your *visit*."

"This is not a visit," she said crisply. "If I wished to *visit*, I would stay with someone of breeding and good manners. Instead, I am an employee, and as such must earn my wages."

His nostrils flared, his mouth compressed. "I dismiss you."

"You cannot. You did not hire me."

In one violent motion, he picked up a book and sent it flying out of an upper window. It crashed. She flinched, and he chortled. The sound irritated her and confirmed her tentative evaluation. Adela was right. This man needed something. Something different. Something besides tender care and gentle handling, and if he didn't behave, she was the woman to give it to him.

In blatant challenge, Rand threw another book out an upper window, and this time part of the pane exploded into the room. Garth cursed and jumped backward. Rand shook it off like a dog shaking off water. Shards rained into Sylvan's hair, and when she brushed it with her fingers, one came away bloody.

"Oh, Miss Sylvan." Garth stepped forward, his boots crunching the glass into bits, his expression a mixture of mortification and disappointment. "Let me have Betty look at that."

"No!" By Rand's smirking face, she knew Garth was giving up already. "I just didn't realize what Lord Rand desired. Now I do, and I will never forget." She had the satisfaction of seeing Rand's smile slip. "Lord Rand, if you wanted fresh air, you had only to ask. Breaking out the windows seems excessive, but it makes my duties easier when you express yourself so eloquently." Determined, she walked toward him.

Warily, he backed up.

She effortlessly circled him and grasped the handles of the chair.

"What do you think you're doing?" he said with a snarl.

"Taking you out for air."

"Madam, you are not!"

He clutched the wheels with determination, but she jerked backward, then forward.

"Ouch!" He looked at his palms.

She pushed him toward the door, bumping over the books and crunching pieces of glass to dust. "You'll survive."

Grasping the wheels again, Rand held tight. The chair slowed to a crawl, but the spokes stubbed his fingers and the friction warmed his lacerated palms.

He couldn't believe that the woman would do this. He hadn't been outside for months. The doctors had suggested he should go out. His mother had coaxed, Aunt Adela had nagged, Garth and James had teased. But no one had dared treat him with such impunity.

Now this wisp of a woman pushed him out into the hall where everyone could stare at him. He clutched the wheels again, and they almost stopped. He could hear her panting behind him as she fought his strength. He could feel her warm breath in his hair and her chest against his back as she pressed her whole body against the chair, and he gloated.

She was failing. He would win, and the first battle counted most.

Then the chair jerked forward so hard it threw his hands into the air, and he slewed around.

Garth stepped away and dusted his fingers. "Go outside, Rand," he said. "I wish I'd thought to do this myself."

"Thank you, Your Grace." The woman pushed him forward.

"But Your Grace, Lord Rand doesn't want to go outside."

Jasper sounded alarmed, and conversely, that made Rand more angry. His dedicated body servant, the man who'd accompanied him into battle, was nothing but an overprotective old woman who thought he could direct Rand's life.

Everybody thought they could direct Rand's life, including his brother and this half-pint nurse. The pressure of her body had been removed from Rand's back, but Rand knew she was still there, still pushing. Pushing, pushing. Pushing him around the corner and into the main hall. Servants watched, peeking with phony discretion from corners and cubbyholes. His family watched openly, crowding together in the hall.

"Garth, dear. Rand, dear. Oh, dear." His mother babbled while smiling valiantly.

"Good to see you, cousin." James used that hearty, encouraging voice he'd used since Rand returned from war, a useless cripple. This was the first time Rand had ever disappointed him, and he had disappointed him bitterly. James hadn't looked Rand in the eye since the battle of Waterloo.

"Rand." Aunt Adela's proper, well-bred tones rang like a church bell pealing over his head. "Cover yourself. You're indecent!"

These days, nothing amused him so much as offending his aunt Adela, and her horror restored a bit of his equilibrium. He smirked offensively.

"There's no talking to you, I see," she scolded. "But at least think of Clover Donald and her saintly ways. She's shocked."

Rand saw the vicar's wife peeking at him from far inside the room. She was a mouse, too timid to do more than catch a glimpse as she stood behind his mother, Aunt Adela, James, and the Reverend Donald himself.

"She probably hasn't had such a good time in years," Rand retorted, and waved. "Greetings, sweetheart."

Tall, blond, and dressed all in black, Bradley Donald took his ministry seriously, especially as it concerned his cowering wife. Whirling, he clapped his hand over Clover's eyes. "Sinful," he declared.

Rand relaxed as they wheeled past.

That had been fun.

Then he saw Jasper, mouth puckered tight, holding the front door wide.

Dear God, he was really going outside.

He, who had loved to walk and ride, was going outside in a wheelchair. He was going out with a nurse, like some defenseless worm who needed protecting.

He, who had been the strongest of the brothers. He, who had been the fastest, the most energetic, the one on whom all familial hopes had been pinned. He was going outside, and everyone was going to see him. Laugh at him.

"Please," he muttered, gripping the arms of the chair.

She wheeled him through the door and into the sunshine as if she hadn't heard.

Maybe she hadn't. Maybe her hearing had saved him from sounding as pathetic as he looked.

The wind struck him sharply, but the sunshine felt good on his face, not to mention his legs and chest. Two of the hounds rose and stretched, then came forward to snuffle at his hands. Petting them was a forgotten pleasure, for they weren't allowed in the house.

And really, how many strangers could see him as he sat on the terrace?

"Please, bring me my outer garments," the woman instructed the hovering servants. "Then pick up the chair and, if you would be so kind, carry it down the stairs."

He looked around and realized she was referring to *his* chair.

"What the hell are you planning?" he said in a snarling tone.

"I thought we'd go for a walk." That woman took her bonnet from the maid and tied it under her chin. "I fancy a look at the Atlantic."

Garth didn't blink. He acted as if Rand regularly wheeled himself around the countryside, flaunting his helplessness so everyone could point and laugh. Rand's beloved brother betrayed him with a gesture to Jasper. "Take him down the stairs."

Rand waited for Jasper to object again, but he had the proper respect for the duke of Clairmont.

Gesturing to two of the footmen, Jasper said, "Each of ye take a wheel." He leaned forward. "I'll lift the footrest."

Rand knocked him with his fist.

Jasper landed on his rear on the stone. Rand shot backward from the impact. When he regained control, he saw Jasper clutching his mouth and the two footmen cowering.

Lowering his hand, Jasper examined his palm and

saw blood, then wiggled his two front teeth. "Haven't lost that punishing right, Lord Rand."

"Try to pick me up again, and you'll see my left."

Jasper spoke reproachfully through swelling lips. "Now, Lord Rand, I'm just doing me duty."

Rand could scarcely see through the red mist before his eyes. "Your duty is to obey *me.*"

Sylvan pulled on her gloves. "You're acting like a slavering dog."

"And you're acting like a bitch."

The wind sang with its elemental voice, the dogs licked themselves, but everything else fell silent.

At the door, Garth groaned. "Oh, Rand."

Rand loved his brother. He really did. He knew that Garth had only his best interests at heart, but Garth didn't—couldn't—comprehend the despair and mortification that trapped Rand.

No one understood, but Rand hated to humiliate Garth with such a breach of manners. In truth, he had humiliated himself. Yet he wouldn't admit it. Not and see that woman simper. "Well, she is," Rand snapped.

"I've been called worse." Apparently unperturbed, that woman donned her pelisse. "And by better men."

Did nothing rattle her?

Jasper reached out and touched the footrest of the wheelchair, and when Rand did no more than glare, he nodded to the footmen. Silent, they carried Rand off the terrace, across the driveway, and onto the path that wound to the sea.

"Just go that direction, miss." Stiff with disapproval, Jasper pointed toward the patch of blue that shone beyond the trees. "'Tis a fairly good path, so ye'll have little trouble, but don't drop too far down toward the beach or ye'll have a time hoisting Lord Rand back up."

She moved to her place at the back of the wheelchair. "Thank you, Jasper."

"You've charmed my brother, have you?" Rand asked sharply. "You'll not charm me."

"I doubt the effort would be worth the results." She shoved the chair forward with one violent push, then, despite her diminutive stature, kept it rolling along the track.

Through the generations, the dukes of Clairmont and their families had ridden along this path, their horses wearing a rut through the smooth lawn and around bright, blooming peonies. The wheels of the chair bounced along, straddling the groove, and Rand bounced with it, experiencing the discomfort with grim triumph.

Some nurse this woman was, treating her patient with such cavalier disinterest. She was probably nothing more than one of those hussies who drank their patients' whiskey, administered medicine when they remembered, and whored with the patients who had money.

Too bad she couldn't whore with him. He'd give a lot to get that smug little face on a pillow. He'd show her who was in command.

At least . . . he'd have shown her at one time.

They reached the top of the gentle cliff that led to the beach. He'd been climbing down it since he was a toddler. The first part of the path was nothing more than a dip, really, coming to a broad flat place where he had sat many a time. But after that the path descended rapidly, twitching to the left, then the right, in sharp curves that made the descent possible for those with the legs to walk.

He'd once loved this spot. Now he clutched the wheels and glanced fearfully around. The cliffs closed the beach off in both directions, baiting the trap for fools who ignored the tide. Boulders pocked the sand, beckoning him as a bloody sacrifice. The ocean licked eagerly at the beach, sucking up the land.

"How beautiful."

Her words were nothing but an exhalation, but he heard them. He gazed again, squinting against the glare of the sun. He'd seen it that way once.

She stepped up beside him. "I can see forever."

He looked at her, and realized he could see forever, too. The wind made that possible as it blew the fine blue cotton of her dress against her body, molding every curve. She looked as if some man-elf, far gone with drink, had put her together as his ideal. She was petite, short enough that her head would fit under Rand's chin—if he could stand.

But she wasn't skinny. Nice curves. She was pretty, too. Not beautiful, but striking. Even in repose, her face told him that she liked to laugh, for the fine lines around her wide mouth and wide eyes slanted up. But her hair—was that blond or white that slipped among the brown strands?

"How old are you?" he demanded.

"I'm twenty-seven years old." She answered his question coolly, and asked right back, "How old are you?"

Then he remembered he wasn't supposed to ask a woman her age. It had been so long since he was made to be polite to anyone, so long since he cared what anyone thought of him, that he had forgotten even that rudimentary rule. But he refused to apologize for such a minor infraction.

He'd done so much worse these last few months, and to people he loved.

"I'm thirty-six years old, going on one hundred."

"Aren't we all?"

The birds catapulted on the wind. She studied them,

and he studied her. So white did mark her hair. Her skin glowed like that odd-shaped pearl his mother wore on special occasions, and her big green eyes sparkled as if she'd laughed her whole life, but at some time, for some reason, tears had etched betraying lines into the delicate skin.

"Let's go there." She pointed to the flat place down on the first rise.

"No."

"We could lean against the rock and it'll protect us from the wind."

"You'd never get me back up."

She let her gaze linger on him. "With those muscles, *you* could get yourself back up."

Suddenly, he realized the wind revealed more than *her* shape. It revealed his, too. What he had brazenly flaunted in the house seemed flagrant exhibitionism now. What was he doing on the cliffs in a robe?

He wrapped the flaps over his chest and tugged the tie at his waist. Then the chair moved, headed down the path under her guidance.

"Don't!"

He reached for the wheels, but she returned quickly, "Don't! I'll lose control."

Lose control. Oh, God, that nightmare phrase. He froze as she guided him down the gentle dip, and they came to a stop on the flat stone. She backed him up so he rested in a hollow. Removing her pelisse, she folded it and placed it on the ground, then sat at his feet.

She didn't say a word. He couldn't say a word. He was in danger here, he knew it. It was too open, too wild. This exposure whipped his skin raw, dried up his lungs, and chilled his soul.

Yet Sylvan's wide mouth, which looked as if it should

be in a constant motion of smiling and speaking, remained serene. Her hands rested in her lap, palms up. The incongruous lines in her face smoothed, and she watched the Atlantic as if her salvation existed in its depths.

She'd placed herself to block his chair.

She was saving him from himself.

At one time, he had come here when life became too frenetic, when he needed to make peace with the wildness of his soul. Now the predictability of the breaking waves began to work on him. The seabirds' calls, the salt tang on his tongue . . . The tight knot in his stomach loosened. For the first time in months, he didn't think, he didn't feel, he simply was.

And what made it better was that his companion seemed likewise affected.

Yet when she looked at him, he realized she felt compassion for him.

He was sick of pity. "What the hell's your name?" he demanded.

"Sylvan."

"Sylvan what?"

"Sylvan Miles."

That sounded vaguely familiar, and he glared. "Do I know you?"

Light and shadow danced across her face as if it were the land beneath a cloud-specked sky. The very lack of expression in her voice told him much. "We danced once."

Remembrance hit him in the gut.

She had been in Brussels before Waterloo, like so many other English ladies. They'd made a mockery of the greatest battle in modern Europe with their parties and soirees, and Sylvan had been in the middle, flirting with every man, captivating them all, laughing and gossiping, dressing in the most stylish costumes, riding a fine steed, and . . . dancing.

Ah, yes, how well he remembered.

"By God." Rand struck the arm of his chair with his fist. "You were with Hibbert, the earl of Mayfield. You're Hibbert's mistress."

Her serenity shattered, she jumped to her feet. "Don't you call me that."

"Why not? It's true."

"No, it's—" She closed her eyes for a moment, then opened them. Quietly, she said, "No, it is not."

By Jove, he had her now. She was sensitive about her past, as well she should be. "You're the same as every other female nurse," he said with relish. "Loose with your morals. But you weren't a nurse when you were with Hibbert." Tapping the arm of his chair, he used his ugliest, most insinuating tone. "He wasn't married, and until you, he'd never kept a woman."

She lowered her head like a bull about to charge. "Hibbert was my dearest friend, and I'll listen to no slander about him."

"Why would I slander Hibbert? I liked him, and he died a hero on the battlefield of Waterloo."

"Which is more than you did." She made her own tone derogatory when she said, "Your brother has never married, either. He's a duke, he needs an heir, and he must be nigh on to forty years old."

Oh, ho. That explained everything. She was a fortune hunter, like every other woman who pretended interest in Clairmont Court. He reared back in his chair. "Did you come here to catch a duke? Because I warn you—"

"No, I warn you." She took a breath. "Don't say another word."

"I won't let you make my brother's life a misery. I'll

tell Garth the truth—that you're a whore of the first water."

Wheeling around, she started up the path, and he watched with savage satisfaction. He'd chased her off, the little tart, and—"Hey, wait!"

She turned back, a tight smile on her lips.

"You can't leave me here."

"Oh, can't I?"

"Dammit!" He maneuvered his chair in a half-circle. "I can't get back by myself."

"Can't you?"

"You know I can't."

"You should have thought of that before you insulted me." She twitched the material of her skirt. "I'll see you at the house."

Raw fury and fear bludgeoned him. "I'll see you in hell."

"I already know that territory." She nodded congenially. "If we must meet in hell, I'll run circles around you there, too."

He stared as she walked away. Walked away! His only consolation was the clear outline of her buttocks, molded by the wind, as she strode toward the house, and even that was no solace—or shouldn't have been. Without wanting to, he appreciated that trim outline.

And why not? If he did what must be done, it would be his last memory.

Turning himself again, he gazed at the sea.

After all, what better place to put an end to the one and only madman the Malkin family had ever produced?

2

Rand's gaze burned through Sylvan's gown as he used the assistance of the wind to see what should be hidden. She knew it was so, although she refused to look back. Instead, she whipped up her anger at his incredible rudeness. Rand had to learn, and immediately, that he couldn't treat her so offensively. No relationship could exist between them until respect prevailed, and she had seized the first opportunity to teach it to him. This wasn't cruelty, it was instruction.

But what if he really couldn't get up the slope?

She pressed her hands to her mouth.

What if he were so far gone he refused the challenge? What if he slipped backward and plunged . . .

She slowed and almost turned back, but she could still feel his animosity lapping at her. He was angry and hostile but surely not suicidal. No, she was doing the right thing. She strode into the sparse growth of trees on the manor house lawn.

She knew when Rand lost sight of her. The heat of his regard disappeared, and in its place the wind chilled her. She'd left her pelisse behind, and she hesitated. That would be a good excuse to return and check on him.

That would ruin all her progress thus far.

"Sylvan!"

She looked up with a frown and found Rand loping toward her.

Rand? No, Garth. She placed a hand on her suddenly thumping heart. She hadn't realized how much the brothers resembled each other.

Yet they didn't. Their height appeared to be much the same, but Garth sported a slight paunch which Rand, even with his forced inactivity, had avoided. Their features were almost identical, but Garth's brown eyes watched those around him placidly.

It had been that quality that convinced Sylvan to come to Clairmont Court. She'd never met a man who'd set her at ease so immediately, or who so intuitively saw her dilemma at home.

"Sylvan, I've been watching for you. Where's Rand? It's all uphill from the cliff. Weren't you able to push him back? I'll just go after him."

He chatted, this man who had impressed her with his quiet stolidity, and she realized his anxiety for his brother. Quickly, she moved to intercept him.

"I left him on the cliff."

"You what?" His slow smile faded. "You left him . . . on purpose?"

"He was rude and surly." She tucked his hand into the crook of her arm and tried to drag him forward. "He's got to learn he can't insult me."

Hanging back, he glanced down the path as if expecting

to see Rand. "He's always rude and surly since his injury. I did warn you—"

"No, you didn't." Looking him in the eye, she said, "You said he was a broken man, totally overcome by his injury."

His smile curved his lips just enough to be smug, and he pointed out, "I didn't exactly say that. You jumped to that conclusion, and I didn't correct you."

Remembering the interview between the two of them, she grudgingly conceded he was right. He had insinuated much and said little, leaving her imagination to do the rest. These were intelligent men, these Clairmonts, and she would do well to remember it in her dealings with them. "Very well. I jumped to conclusions, and you did likewise. You want your brother to overcome his bitterness, I think, and I will do what I can to return him to you as a normal, functioning human being. When you came to my home and convinced me to help Lord Rand, you gave me free hand, remember? You promised—"

"I know what I promised, but I didn't expect you would leave him exposed to the elements overnight."

"Neither did I, but desperate circumstances require desperate measures."

They stared at each other, neither willing to give way.

"I won't let you kill him," Garth insisted.

"But it would be such a tidy reprieve." Garth gasped, and she pressed him. "You wouldn't have to bear the tantrums and the rudeness and the disappointment of seeing your brother reduced to a cripple."

"How dare you? I want my brother regardless of his condition!"

His outrage revealed very clearly why he had resorted to deception to get her to Clairmont Court. He would have done anything to bring her, for he would do anything for his brother. She reminded him, "He'll be more agreeable when he's housebroken."

"But I'm not going to have him put down, regardless of our success!"

"Good," she said mildly.

His eyes narrowed as he realized how she had tricked him, and he rubbed his face with stained hands. "You're a clever miss."

"I'll need free rein to train Lord Rand, when he's been resourceful enough to train all of you." Garth chortled, not at all offended, and she asked, "How long until sunset?"

"Probably three hours."

"If he's not in sight in two hours, we'll send someone to get him."

"You mean you think he can get himself back up to the manor without help?"

"What do you think?"

"I think he . . . well, I think . . ." Garth paused. "I always said Rand could do anything he set his mind to. I guess it's a question of whether he'll set his mind to staying there, or coming home."

"I don't know your brother well, but my guess is he'll stay on the cliffs until he's chilled, then come back on his own schedule." She smiled. "Just to show me he can."

Garth scratched the back of his head. "You might be good for Rand."

She dipped in a curtsy. "Thank you, kind sir."

"You might be good for all of us."

She didn't appreciate that comment as she should. It recalled Rand's accusation on the cliff—that she'd come to win a duke. She stepped forward with determination. "He looks very strong."

"He is. He hates this helplessness, and he insists on doing everything possible for himself."

"Then *you* think he can make it back?"

"Oh, yes."

"And you don't think—" she hesitated, hating to put the thought into his mind, but she needed more reassurance than her own instincts, "he would consider throwing himself off the cliff?"

Garth laughed out loud. "Rand? Never. Rand thrives on a challenge, always has. As I told you when I met you before—and coaxed you here—I'm surprised he's still so disturbed about his condition. It doesn't seem consistent with his character, somehow, but I suppose none of us knows how long the process of recovery should take. Do we?"

She could see the manor clearly now. Someone had placed boards over the shattered windows in Rand's room, but even with that bizarre addition the structure no longer looked like an architect's experiment. It looked only like a place to rest. "I certainly don't."

A couple came out onto the terrace. Sylvan recognized the dark clothes of the vicar she'd seen inside, and she presumed the woman to be his wife. He held her firmly as she stumbled down the stairs, and Sylvan wondered if she drank.

Garth insisted, "You know more than anyone, so Dr. Moreland says."

When the couple gained the flat ground, the vicar shook his wife, then marched her down the drive with the firmness of a perturbed father. Sylvan didn't envy the wife—she'd dealt with her own perturbed father. "Dr. Moreland was a sneak to tell you that."

"He said he'd never seen a woman work so hard to heal the wounded, and he'd never seen anyone, man or woman, who had a better instinct for the workings of an amputee's mind."

The couple disappeared from sight, and Sylvan banished them from her thoughts. "Your brother's not an amputee. From what I saw today—and I saw quite a bit—he has everything he was born with."

Garth reddened from his chin to his hairline, and she saw one more difference between the brothers. Garth's forehead was quite a bit higher than Rand's—his hair had lost the battle of Waterloo, and now made its long retreat.

With a gulp, Garth said, "I'm sorry about his . . . ah . . . lack of proper clothing today. He loves to offend our aunt Adela with his outrageous behavior, and removing his shirt is his new tactic."

"From the little bit I heard from your aunt Adela, offending her would pleasure a saint." He stopped and stared at her, and she realized she'd overstepped the bounds of courtesy. "Forgive me, Your Grace. It was insufferably rude of me to speak so of your aunt. If you would make allowances for my travel-weary mind—"

He cackled. "Pleasure a saint, eh? I confess, it pleasures me, and I'm no saint. When we were boys, Rand and I used to have contests to see who could best offend Aunt Adela. Of course, I always won, for as duke, whatever I did counted more than whatever he did. And whatever James did, poor cousin, counted more than whatever I did, for he is third in line for the dukedom—and, most important, her son."

"That must be a difficult role to fulfill."

"It weighs on him. She would do anything to advance his cause, and he would do anything to make her happy and keep her from nagging." Abashed, he asked guiltily, "But you never properly met any of them, did you?"

"There wasn't time." Mounting the steps to the terrace, she kept one hand on the rail to steady herself.

He summed her up shrewdly. "You never changed from your journey nor took refreshment. Betty will have my head for this."

"Betty?"

"My . . . the housekeeper. She bosses us all—except Aunt Adela, of course. Aunt Adela knows what's proper, but Betty knows what's hospitable." Cupping her elbow in his hand, he led her up the stairs and tried to move her to the house, but she resisted.

"I think I would like to sit out here," she said. "Just until Lord Rand comes into sight."

"I'll watch for him," Garth volunteered.

"I think not." She sank into one of the chairs set about the terrace to take advantage of the afternoon sun. The light struck her directly on the face, and the warmth the seat had absorbed prowled through her gown until it sank into her bones. "You'd go after him, or at the least hover anxiously."

"I confess." He lifted his hands. "I am anxious."

"He's not a child." She leaned her head back and thought how pleasant it would be to fall asleep. Her anticipation at meeting Lord Rand had disturbed her the night before, and the night before that, she'd been awake anticipating the trip. "He shouldn't be spoiled like one."

"So I have repeatedly said." Lady Adela swept onto the terrace. Dressed as if she were attending a fashionable tea, she came to a halt before Sylvan. "I didn't greet you properly when James introduced us. I bid you welcome to Clairmont Court."

Garth's eyes narrowed, and he called, "Mother, come out so *you*, as duchess, can greet our guest."

It was the cut direct, but Lady Adela nodded. "Quite

right. I shouldn't have thrust myself before the dowager duchess."

"Not at all." Lady Emmaline Malkin stepped onto the terrace and shaded her eyes against the setting sun. "I don't mind, you know that, Adela."

"Emmie, you're the dowager duchess, and you have the right—"

"I know, but I don't want to thrust myself—"

"You're wrong, dear. You should—"

Garth cut them off with a gesture. "Ladies, if you would please let me finish—"

"Garth, our guest hasn't even taken tea yet." Lady Emmie, petite and concerned, bustled over. "You can't drag out these courtesies."

From Garth's shrug, Sylvan deduced the greetings were over.

Lady Emmie's gaze darted around. "Er . . . where is Rand? I didn't see you pushing him when you arrived."

Sylvan's worst suspicions were confirmed. The family had had their noses pressed to the windows the entire time she walked with Rand, and they hovered now in expectation of some further tragedy. Her failure to bring him back, she feared, would be viewed as catastrophic.

Garth stepped in before she could speak. "Rand's making his own way back, Mother. Sylvan thought it would be salutary for him to learn how much he can do."

Lady Emmie's mouth moved without a sound.

"Remember, Mother, we discussed this," Garth said. "Sylvan knows better than any of us what is right for Rand."

If only that were true. Sylvan hoped her dismay at their misplaced confidence didn't show.

But Lady Emmie recovered with all the grace of a true-born English lady. "Won't you come inside, dear Sylvan? May I call you Sylvan?"

"I'd be honored, Your Grace, but I prefer to stay out here, thank you." And cast fearful glances toward the sea.

"Then we'll stay with you."

"I'd rather you didn't, Your Grace. I hate to have Lord Rand think anyone is apprehensive about his ability to return."

As if she didn't hear, Lady Emmie sank onto a sofa-length seat, her ample bosom sloshing within the constraints of her low-cut bodice. Sylvan held her breath, waiting for the gelatinous creatures to lap over the edge, but the lady seemed to have them well-trained, for they settled as she did.

Sylvan tried again. "Really, Your Grace, I'd prefer—"

"I hear you say we've been spoiling Rand." Rand's mother touched the fichu that hung around her neck, then tucked it into her cleavage. "We haven't spoiled him. We just—"

"Emmie, don't be a fool." Lady Adela sat beside Lady Emmie. "You've spoiled him terribly."

"*I've* spoiled him? I think I'm not alone in this."

"You don't mean to insinuate I've spoiled him?"

"No, not you. You've always maintained a proper distance. But what about *your* son?"

"Oh." Lady Adela sighed so that Sylvan knew the despair of a woman whose son had failed her. "James."

"You called, Mother?" James sauntered out.

Malkin blood must run strong in the veins, Sylvan thought, noting the family resemblance between James and his cousins. But James displayed a freer quality, as if he'd escaped the burden of responsibility and reveled in his luck. He wore the finest tight pantaloons, tied his cravat in the most intricate knot, and had his brown hair cut into the latest style. His boots shone in the sun and a monocle hung from a chain around his neck. In town, he would have been a dandy. In the country, Sylvan had to wonder who the display was meant to impress.

"The nurse here, Sylvan . . . " Distracted, Lady Adela pursed her lips. "Young woman, where did you get that dreadful name?"

"My mother is a country girl living in London. She misses her home terribly, and when I was born she named me for a wood fairy."

Lady Adela sniffed. "Common."

"Yes," Sylvan agreed. "She is."

"That's nothing to be ashamed of," Lady Emmie said firmly. "Better good common English stock than some foreign material."

"It's the common stock which put the taint in Malkin blood." Lady Adela gestured at the horizon where the smudge of factory smoke hovered. "And you see the results."

"My son is not tainted," Lady Emmie snapped.

"His ideas are a disgrace."

"Enough!" Garth's cultured drawl could sharpen with anger, and anger edged it now. "We've gone over this before, and I hardly think we need discuss it in front of Miss Sylvan."

The ladies quieted at once, red staining both their faces as they stared stiffly out across the yard.

James broke the uncomfortable moment of silence. "Miss Sylvan, did you suggest we've spoiled Rand?"

Sylvan wanted to ask if the entire family listened at doors, but manners interfered. "I did."

"So we've spoiled him," James said. "Deserved it. Came back from Waterloo a hero."

Pride strengthened Lady Adela's spine. "So did you, my dear."

"Oh, yes," Garth said, sarcasm in his tone. "One of our national icons."

Lady Adela sounded shocked at Garth's cavalier comment. "James was very brave."

James shrugged as if he could brush off Garth's asperity. "Garth's right, Mama. Nothing but one of the lesser players. M' wound was slight."

"Slight!" Lady Adela leaned forward and touched Sylvan's knee. "He lost two of his fingers."

"An amputation?" she asked him.

"Easier than that." He wiggled the remaining digits on his right hand. "Shot off. Clean. No infection."

"Did I see you in hospital?"

"Yes." He grinned with diffident charm. "Glad to see I always make an impression on a lovely woman."

"Be glad you didn't." She looked down at her own ten fingers, twining and retwining in her lap. "You don't want to be one of the patients I remember."

"Rest assured, ma'am, that no patient you helped will ever forget." His fervent protestation brought her attention back to him, and he touched his brow in a salute.

His charming gesture warmed her, empty though she knew it to be.

"James is more guilty than any of us for spoiling Rand," Lady Emmie said triumphantly. "He always worshiped Rand."

"That doesn't mean he spoiled him."

"James always dressed like Rand. He took an interest in politics because of Rand. He even joined the army because of Rand."

James sighed in embarrassment, and Sylvan bit back a smile.

Lady Adela harumphed and said, "Well, James is eleven years younger than Rand. I suppose there might have been some hero worship."

"James wants to go back to London."

"He can go back to London any time he pleases," Lady Adela snapped. "Our fortune is ample to keep—"

"James can't be important if he goes without—"

James's stylish facade began to crumple beneath the vexation of their prolonged quarrel, and Sylvan interrupted in desperation. "No one has told me the nature of Lord Rand's wound." A silence followed, and she looked sharply at the ring of guilty, dismayed faces. She turned to Garth. "Lord Clairmont?"

He wiped his hand across his face, then looked toward the west. "I don't see him yet."

"Nor I," Sylvan agreed. "Therefore this is the perfect time to describe the wound which resulted in his paralysis."

"Did you say you wanted to wait for Rand alone?" Garth persisted.

"Yes, but—"

"We'll leave you, then, and have tea sent out. Come, ladies." Lady Adela and Lady Emmie jumped up with an obedience Sylvan found suspect, and when James would have remained, Garth said, "*Come*, James."

For a brief moment, James seemed possessed of an ugly mood. Then with a gesture of resignation, he entered the house on his mother's heels.

Garth lingered for a moment to promise, "You'll get the cooperation you require, I vow."

Then he whisked inside after them all, leaving Sylvan to wonder what they were hiding. She *had* seen most of Rand this day, and he'd looked whole and unscarred. Yet something had placed Rand in the wheelchair. What was it, and where had it occurred?

"Miss?" Sylvan turned to find the broad-beamed maid at her side. "I brought your tea. You have here a hearty supply of biscuits and cakes, made by our Italian confectioner."

Sylvan gave a gurgle of laughter. "An Italian confectioner?"

A slip of a smile escaped the maid as she placed the tray on the narrow table and pushed it close to Sylvan. "Aye, miss. Isn't that grand?"

"Grand enough." Watching gratefully as the maid poured, she added, "I'm glad my father isn't here, or we'd have to have an Italian confectioner working in our kitchen tomorrow."

The maid's quiet amusement died and she examined Sylvan with a keen eye. "You're quality, then."

"Oh, no." Sylvan spread a snowy napkin in her lap. "I'm only rich. My father's a merchant baron. By that I mean, he was a highly successful merchant, and he bought himself a barony."

"Have you quarreled with him, that you've hired yourself out as a nurse?"

Her outspoken curiosity amazed Sylvan, and she examined the maid as thoroughly as the maid had examined her. She saw a tall woman of perhaps thirty-five, with strong, handsome features and a way of carrying herself that one seldom saw in a servant. Indeed, many a fine lady would have been pleased to have this woman's bearing and dignity. "You must be Betty," Sylvan said.

"That I am, miss. Mr. Garth told you about me?"

"Only that you boss them all, and that your hospitality is impeccable."

Wrapping her hands in her apron, Betty smiled. Dimples creased her cheeks, and beneath the lace cap she wore an abundance of auburn curls that bobbed when she nodded. "Mr. Garth is ever free with his compliments."

Sylvan sugared the tea and drank with wholehearted enjoyment. "Why do you call him Mr. Garth?"

Now Betty blushed. "Forgive me, I should not, but we're of an age and we grew up together."

The Malkin family, Sylvan concluded, could rightly be termed eccentric. Their housekeeper treated the duke with familiarity; the dowager and her sister-in-law disagreed like two children; they had a cotton mill on their land and their own ghost.

But then, they were of an old, noble family of large fortune, and eccentricity was acceptable. Sylvan had no such cushion to fall back on, and she answered Betty's earlier query. "My father didn't want me to come as a nurse, but His Grace made me an irresistible offer. His Grace promised that no one would bemoan my lost reputation while I remained under his roof."

"You lost your reputation, miss?"

"I don't like to brag"—Sylvan leaned closer to Betty, and Betty leaned forward to hear—"but I'm one of the most infamous women in England."

Betty stared at her, round-eyed, then burst into laughter. "Perhaps so, miss, perhaps so."

Stupidly, Sylvan felt almost hurt by Betty's incredulity. "You don't believe me?"

"Ah, miss." Betty wiped her hands on her apron. "A lot of noblemen visit Clairmont Court during the course of a year, and I've learned the difference between a lost reputation and a corrupted soul." Betty nudged the plate of biscuits closer to Sylvan's elbow. "You've got a fineness about you I never sensed with those corrupted ones."

"Nevertheless, my reputation is gone. I'm no longer

invited to the parties of the ton, and any man who shows interest in me does so to sample the wares."

Betty piled thin slices of plum cake and a variety of biscuits onto a china plate and pressed it into Sylvan's hand. "So 'tis your father who mourns your reputation, miss?"

"Bitterly and often. He does everything bitterly and often." Selecting a macaroon, Sylvan tasted it with approval. "Do you know the nature of Lord Rand's wound?"

She thought she'd slipped in the query casually, but while Betty never changed expression, Sylvan felt the barrier go up. "He can't walk."

However eccentric the Malkins were, they obviously had the loyalty of their servants.

"But he can use that wheelchair," Betty added, pointing across the lawn.

Sylvan looked, and she saw Rand, struggling to push himself up the path. "Thank God." Her hand shook in a sudden palsy, and tea slopped onto the napkin in her lap.

Betty patted her shoulder, then she called, "Jasper!"

Jasper charged out the door so quickly, Sylvan knew he'd been waiting for their hail. She looked reproachfully at Betty, but Betty whispered, "He couldn't hear us talking, miss." Then, louder, she said, "The master'll need help getting up the stairs. Best bring around your helpers."

Jasper hastened to obey, and Sylvan said, "If you would, Betty, tell the family to play some cards, settle with a book, and greet Rand casually. He'll not like it if he's treated like a conquering hero for such a measly feat."

"Do you think he'll fancy having the family treat it casually, after months of having them jump at his every wish?" Betty demanded.

"Perhaps not." Sylvan smiled. "But I prefer he be angered by lack of attention, not more."

Betty placed her hands on her hips and looked Sylvan up and down. "Is nursing anything more than just common sense, miss?"

"No, but common sense isn't that common, is it?"

"We're going to get along fine, miss." Betty bustled toward the house. "Just fine."

Jasper and his crew reached Rand before he had wheeled himself across the drive, but with violent gestures he ordered them back. Sweat glued the strands of his dark hair together and dripped off his heavy eyebrows. It ran in trickles along the grooves of his frown and shone off his chest.

He ignored his state with imposing determination as he pushed himself across the driveway and to the bottom of the stairs. There he stopped and let Jasper and the footmen lift him. They carried the chair up to the terrace, then on his order, set it down in front of Sylvan.

If anything, his bitterness of spirit seemed to have deepened, and she would have sworn he hated her when he said, "I hope you're happy, woman. You've proved me to be a coward, too."

3

Mortification burned like a live coal in his soul.

He'd been too gutless to push himself off the edge of the cliff.

As if he had anything to live for! A helpless deranged cripple. What further proof did he require of his own uselessness, his own madness?

That prissy little woman sat on the terrace, eating cakes and sipping tea and examining him as if he were an oddity.

Carefully, Sylvan blotted her lips with her napkin and stood. "You've taken a remarkable amount of air. I'm sure it exhilarated you. We'll do it again tomorrow."

"Tomorrow?" Rand's voice hit a high note he'd never reached before. "To—"

But his rage proved no match for his exhaustion. He was just too damned tired to throw another tantrum.

He removed her pelisse from his lap and viciously threw it in her face. Her teacup toppled when the sleeve hit it, and he had the pleasure of watching her scramble out of her chair to avoid the stream of dark liquid. Then he pushed his chair toward the door of the manor. Toward sanctuary. He rolled over the threshold, into the entry, and looked around.

Where was his mother? His brother? James, even Aunt Adela? Where were the people who cared about him, protected him?

Hearing voices, he wheeled his way to the study—and saw them.

His wonderful family, always so concerned about him, were playing cards. Chips were strewn across the table. Aunt Adela sat on the edge of her chair, and Lady Emmie held her cards with haphazard care. Garth struggled to loosen his already rumpled cravat, and James rearranged his hand as if that would change the spots.

To judge by their disheveled appearance, they had been playing the whole time he was gone.

"What the hell are you doing?" Rand boomed.

Everyone jumped as if his arrival startled them.

"By Jove, Rand, why don't you take over for this numskull?" James asked. "He's as slow at cards as he is at marriage."

Garth reached over and cuffed his cousin. "At least I understand trump."

With a restrained smile, Aunt Adela said, "Such unsportsmanlike conduct just because the ladies are winning."

"La! A pleasure to win," Lady Emmie said, then everyone bent to the cards once more, concentrating on everything but Rand.

Resentment boiled inside him. While he was struggling up the cliff, they'd been playing cards. They'd probably had a celebration at their first chance to get rid of him, cheered when that woman returned without him, and laid odds on his ability to return.

They pitched some cards on the table, then his mother chirped, "How was your walk, dear?"

His fury exploded. "Walk? Walk? I didn't walk. Your legs have to work for you to walk." He pointed at the useless limbs that used to carry him wherever he wanted to go. "I can't walk."

"I think your mother knows that," said Sylvan's voice behind him. "You don't need to bludgeon her with the sorry facts of your life."

Rand wheeled around, ready to attack, when Garth said, "It's just a manner of speech, Rand. Mother meant—"

"I know what Mother meant."

"Then don't speak so rudely to the dowager duchess," Aunt Adela said. "It's not appropriate to her station, or yours."

"Really, Adela, I don't mind." Lady Emmie smiled weakly, ever the peacemaker between Adela and her sons.

"I mind enough for both of us. If it weren't for me, this family would fall into ramshackle practices and moral weaknesses." Aunt Adela stared down her nose at Garth. "And even I am not bastion enough to stem the depravities of the current duke."

"Oh, let's not start that again." Garth threw his cards on the table. "You know my reasons, Aunt Adela."

"I'm going to bed," Rand announced.

"That's nice, dear." Lady Emmie waved a feeble good-bye, all her attention concentrated on the developing quarrel.

Pointing at Rand as if he were an exhibit, Lady Adela said, "See, Garth, even your brother occasionally prevails over his demeaning infirmity."

Rand heard Sylvan suck in a shocked breath, then she

cried, "Demeaning? What's demeaning about an injury taken in the line of duty?"

"It's not as if he were actually hurt." Lady Adela dismissed Sylvan and turned back to Garth. "Surely you, as duke—"

"Not actually hurt?" Sylvan's fists clenched at her sides.

"Shut up," Rand muttered.

"He's in a wheelchair!"

"Just shut up."

Losing patience, Lady Adela said, "He wasn't wounded!"

Silence hit the room with a thud.

"For God's sake, Mother." James leaped to his feet and paced toward the window.

Lady Adela shriveled under everyone's concentrated fury. "Well, somebody had to tell her."

Sylvan shifted position subtly, but Rand could read her impatience. "So, somebody tell me."

"What should I say?" Rand asked. "I can't walk, and there's not a mark on me."

"Not true!" James whirled in anguish. "I saw you when you stumbled into Wellington's presence. Covered with blood and bruises."

Rand sneered. "Minor wounds."

"Led charge after charge. Had three horses shot out from underneath you. After you lost your regiment, you scrapped like a madman. I fought clear across the battlefield, and I heard about your valor. An inspiration!"

"But I can't walk." Rand pushed his way into the center of the room, and everyone moved back. "If I'm such an inspiration, why can't I walk?"

"You could if you just tried," James insisted. "I know if you just tried—"

"Do you think I haven't tried? Don't you know how much I want to walk?" Rand took deep breaths to combat the constriction of his chest. "I've seen doctor after doctor, let them prod me and pour their vile concoctions down me. I've taken their stupid herb baths, and for what? To be as useless as I was before!"

"Please, dear." Lady Emmie clasped her hands before her, crumpling the cards in her fists. "Don't say that."

"Useless?" Rand took a twisted pleasure in her pain. "Useless. Useless, useless, useless."

"Rand." Garth and Rand locked gazes. "The afternoon proved to be congenial without you. Don't tempt us to discover what further enjoyment your absence might bring."

Rand couldn't believe his brother—his brother!—would threaten him in such a manner.

He flashed a glance of hatred at Sylvan. It was her fault. This whole, horrible afternoon was her fault.

"Boys, let's not quarrel." Lady Emmie laid a hand on Garth's arm and lowered her voice. "Garth, we have to make allowances."

"We've made allowances," Garth said. "It's time for life to go on. He's hurt, he's my brother, and I love him, but I'm tired of having him turn this house upside down night and day. Can't we have some peace? At least until I've finished the mill? Can't we just have some peace?"

Garth's despair struck at Rand, building guilt where there had been only rage.

Is that what his injury had done? Driven his placid brother to the edge of control? Rand knew the burdens that the duke of Clairmont must bear. In addition, he knew Garth's ambitions for their people, their lands.

He knew because Garth used to talk to him, exchange ideas, dream dreams. How long had it been since he listened to Garth?

He looked at James, and James looked away. He looked at Aunt Adela, and her mouth was knit so tight he knew she wanted to agree. He looked at his mother, and she sat wiping her eyes.

The silence this time stifled all thought.

"Have none of you heard of wind death?" Sylvan's voice sounded calm, as if she saw theatrics such as this replayed every day.

"I—" James cleared his throat. "I have. It's an old-fashioned term for . . . ah . . . when a soldier has no mark on his body, yet he's dead."

Sylvan nodded. "Surgeons used to believe that the wind of a passing bullet sucked the air from the soldiers' lungs and they suffocated. Upon examination, it was proved that severe internal damage caused the deaths, leaving no external symptoms."

"Are you suggesting that's what happened to Rand?" Lady Adela asked.

"Not quite," Rand answered. "I'm not dead, yet."

"A trifling distinction, but important." Sylvan sounded solemn, but Rand wondered. "I am suggesting there may be injury to the spine."

Rand wanted to believe it. He wanted to, so badly, but he said, "Impossible. It wasn't until I went to give my report to Wellington that I collapsed. I was unconscious for two days, and when I woke—" He pointed at his legs.

"Perhaps it wasn't one particular injury which crippled you," Garth suggested. "Perhaps all the injuries, coming one on top of the other, proved your downfall."

"Or an accumulation of blood on your spine, and as time goes on, it'll wash away. Walk again!" James's excitement betrayed his desire.

"Anything's possible," Sylvan said gently. "But Rand

needs to adjust to the situation as it exists, rather than looking for a miracle that may never happen."

James still stared at Rand with those haunted, hungry eyes, and Rand felt the weight of his expectations chaining him to the chair. "Who's going to help me adjust?" He sneered at Sylvan. "You?"

"Yes, her," Garth said. "Rand—"

"Don't you know who she is?"

Rand said it so nastily, Sylvan knew what he was going to reveal. Damn him. Couldn't he have waited just one day? Couldn't he have waited until she'd had some sleep?

"Nursing, I'm sure you'll all agree, is one of the most disgraceful professions a woman can stoop to."

The women averted their gazes, acknowledgment contained within their silence.

"Rand, this is unnecessary," Garth said shortly.

"But for this woman," Rand continued with relish, "nursing was a move up from the world's oldest profession."

"Rand." Lady Emmie gasped. "You don't mean . . ."

"Sylvan was the mistress of Hibbert, earl of Mayfield."

He could have said much worse, Sylvan supposed. He could have claimed she walked the streets of Brussels, or that he had had intimate knowledge of her for a price. But the results were much the same.

Lady Emmie laid a hand on her heart, and Lady Adela drew herself away as if Sylvan's mere presence contaminated the air. For just a moment, James viewed her with a kind of half-slobbering anticipation. Then he cleared his features and reverted to his previous courtesy.

Color flooded Garth's face. Rand cast one triumphant glance at Sylvan, and she knew he thought he'd won.

"Why did you tell them that?" Garth stepped forward

as if he wanted to pummel his own brother. "Did she make you do what you didn't want to do? Did she make you realize what an ass you've been? Is that why you attacked her?"

Rand's smile faded, and he shook his head as if he didn't understand, and Sylvan knew he didn't. He'd thought Garth would be as shocked as the rest of his family. He didn't know that Garth had offered her sanctuary from just those accusations.

Rand said, "Aren't you shocked? Don't you think our mother has the right to know what kind of woman she's dealing with?"

"You never used to be a hypocrite." Garth put his hands on the arms of the wheelchair and leaned forward until his face was level with Rand's. "I know you, Rand, and I know your tastes. You were jealous of Hibbert. You're probably still jealous of Hibbert."

"How the hell could I be jealous of a dead man?"

"He might be dead, but when he was alive he had what you wanted—"

"Garth!" Lady Emmie said, shocked.

"—what you still want. You're nothing but a sniveling little coward."

Sylvan moaned and covered her eyes. Rand was stupefied by the unexpected direction of this attack, but she was humiliated. How had Garth guessed so accurately about the desire that had united her and Rand in one short dance?

She remembered it even now. The bright room, overheated with the light of candles and the crush of human bodies. The music, a perfect waltz. The warmth of Rand's touch on her back, the strength of his shoulder beneath her palm. Their two hands, clasped firmly. Their two gazes, brushing, meeting, avoiding and returning as the rhythm whirled them up off the floor and into a magic place where they were alone.

And when the waltz finished, his fingers lifting her chin, brushing her lips, promising her unknown delights.

He hadn't asked her to dance again. She hadn't wanted him to.

The contact had been so brief, none of the gossips had even noticed. No one had noticed except dear Hibbert, and he hadn't lived beyond the next day.

"You dare?" Rand shouted.

Sylvan jumped, but he wasn't shouting at her.

He jerked his chair from beneath Garth's grasp. "Call me a coward?"

"Oh, you went to Waterloo and killed Frenchies for the safety of England," Garth acknowledged. "But you're afraid of the consequences. You've lived your whole life challenging injustice and brutality and walked away every time, the victor. Well, you're the victor this time, too, but you had to pay a penalty. Get on with it, Rand! Stop wallowing in this self-pity and get on with it."

Rand cast one flaming glance at his brother and wheeled around. If Sylvan hadn't moved, he'd have run over her in his haste to flee, and she didn't think he even noticed.

Garth touched her arm. "Don't worry."

She stared at him, uncomprehending.

"I'll make it right with the ladies and James. They'll treat you with the respect you deserve, I promise."

She nodded stupidly.

Steering her toward the door and into the hallway, he said, "Betty will show you up to your room now."

Betty stepped forward and took her arm, and Garth disappeared back into the study and shut the door.

"What a fuss, eh, miss?" Betty chatted as she led Sylvan up the grand staircase, down a wide hall, and through double doors. "But don't you worry. Mr. Garth'll straighten it out. We put your trunks in here. 'Tis the best suite in the women's wing, except those which Her Grace and Lady Adela occupy, of course."

Garth obviously hoped her living arrangements would ease the sting of her labor, for the door opened off the hall into a lavish sitting room decorated in shades of blue and gold. Chairs and a couch circled a massive fireplace where even now a fire blazed. A burnished table held a setting of china, and the windows were hung with brocade curtains. Through the open door she glimpsed a bedroom with a high curtained bed, another fireplace, and carpets to ward off the chill of the floor.

When Sylvan smiled and nodded, Betty continued, "We need to know if we should make arrangements for your abigail. Is she following later?"

"No. No, my father refused to let me take anything more than my clothes." Betty set to work removing Sylvan's dress with an efficiency that proved her experience, and she sighed when Sylvan said, "My father claimed if I wanted to be a servant for some upstart noble, I could do it on my own."

Betty clucked over her like a hen with a chick. "Aren't men fools? But I'll take care of you personally, and if I'm running off to my other duties, I'll send Bernadette. She's a bright little thing, and she can sleep in your room with you."

"No!"

Betty gave her a surprised glance, and Sylvan tried to temper her rejection. "Please. I don't even allow my own abigail to remain in my room. I'm a restless sleeper."

"As you wish, Miss Sylvan." Although puzzled, Betty

clearly made no attempt to comprehend the minds of the gentry. "Go in and take your bath, and when you come out, I'll brush your hair and ready you for bed."

Sylvan glanced out the window. "But it's barely sundown."

"Aye, but it's spring, and the light stays late. You've had a hard day of traveling, followed by one unpleasantry after another. I'll bring you dinner on a tray, and you can go on to bed. You just trust Betty, miss."

Surprisingly, Sylvan did. She hadn't allowed herself to be so cosseted for years, nor had she placed faith in another's judgment since her return from Waterloo. She had a bath and then found dinner awaiting her.

Surveying the beautifully laid tray, Sylvan said, "There must be a French chef, as well as an Italian confectioner."

"Aye, miss." Betty pulled out the chair and Sylvan sat. Betty swathed Sylvan in the linen napkin, picked up the fork, and put it in her hand. "Eat, now. You look like you've missed too many meals."

Sylvan didn't answer.

Shrewdly, Betty said, "Your clothes weren't made to hang on you, I don't think. Seems like you and Mr. Rand suffer from the same malady."

"And what's that?" Sylvan tasted the oxtail soup.

"Memories."

Sylvan put down her fork. "You are a very intelligent woman."

Betty picked it up and put it back in Sylvan's hand. "I am. Try the pasties."

As instructed, Sylvan tried the pasties. They were an exceptional combination of beef, pork, onions, and turnips, with a hint of marjoram, wrapped in flaky pastry. Like everything else, they tasted exceptional, but

Sylvan thought perhaps the company influenced the flavor of the food.

After all, how often did a woman of her reputation get treated with respect, even by a servant? And especially by a servant of such discernment. Of course Sylvan realized that her opinion of Betty related directly to Betty's opinion of her.

Idly, Sylvan asked, "What do you know about the ghost?"

"The ghost?" Betty turned away, and in an elaborately casual voice asked, "What ghost?"

"The ghost Jasper told me about."

Betty grimaced. "That Jasper! He has ever had a flapping lip."

"So there is a ghost!" Sylvan leaned on her elbow, cupped her chin in her hand, and stared at Betty. "Have you seen it?"

"Me?" Betty laughed with false airiness. "Seen a ghost? Try the lamb."

Sylvan speared one tender slice. "You have, haven't you?"

Hunching her shoulders, Betty muttered, "Once."

"Once?"

"It's good lamb, isn't it?" Betty asked. Sylvan still stared, and Betty admitted, "All right, twice. Once in the house." Shivering, Betty went to the windows where night pressed in. "Once I saw it looking in the glass at me." She shut the drapes.

The room seemed cozier with the drapes closed, Sylvan decided. "*I* don't believe in ghosts." Then she thought of the specters which nightly disturbed her rest. "Or I didn't used to."

"I never believed in ghosts before either, and in the daylight, I still don't. There has to be another explanation,

His Grace says, and I know it's true." Rubbing her arms with her hands, Betty took a breath. "But at night when the wind howls and the moon drifts in and out of the fog . . . well, then I remember the stories my granny used to tell about the first duke and how he always walks when there's trouble afoot at Clairmont Court, and I hide my head under the covers."

Sylvan shivered, too. Betty had a way of speaking that raised the hair on the back of Sylvan's neck. "Has any of the family seen the ghost? Has His Grace?"

"No. The night it looked in the window, he . . ." Betty faltered, and Sylvan could have sworn a blush swept Betty's fair skin. But Betty leaned to the fire and built it up, then lit more of the candles around the room. "No, His Grace hasn't, but I think Lord Rand has."

"Lord Rand?" Sylvan thought of Rand's cynical, angry face, and shook her head. "Surely not."

"Aye, miss, I think so." Coming close, Betty squatted by Sylvan's chair and lowered her voice. "When Lord Rand came back all crippled, he was angry at the world, of course, and dejected a whole lot, but Mr. Garth—His Grace—he talked to Lord Rand about the estate and made him help with the planning of the mill, just like old times, and Lord Rand was getting better. He was adjusting to that wheelchair, and even joked about his useless legs. There for a while he knew he wasn't the only one his accident had hurt."

Sylvan straightened. This was interesting. This was *fascinating*.

"Then the night I saw the face at the window, I told Mr. Garth, and when he told Lord Rand—laughing at me, he was—Lord Rand just exploded with rage. We'd never seen him like that, throwing things and cursing. And it's been the same ever since. He'll get a little better, then he gets worse again. Like today." Betty rose. "What else am I to think, but Lord Rand saw that ghost and knows what it portends?"

"Trouble."

"Aye." Betty rubbed her palms up and down her ample hips as if to dry the sweat off of them. "Trouble."

The knock on the door took them by surprise, and they both jumped. Then, sheepish at her alarm, Betty answered it. Sylvan couldn't see who stood without, for Betty blocked her view, but she heard a man's rumble.

"What is it, Betty?" she called.

Reluctantly, Betty answered, "'Tis Jasper. He wants a favor, but I've told him it's after ten o'the clock, and you're not to be disturbed."

"A favor?" Sylvan stood. "Is someone ill?"

"'Tis Lord Rand," Jasper called. "He needs you."

Sylvan's heart thumped in her throat. Had he done too much today? Had she pushed him too hard? Knotting her dressing gown, Sylvan strode to the door and pulled it away from Betty. "What's wrong with Lord Rand?" She walked down the hall and the stairway, never looking to see if the servants followed. The candles burned brightly in the entry as she passed through. "Is he having spasms? Coughing blood? Unable to speak?"

"No, miss."

Jasper trotted beside her and Betty trailed them both, muttering imprecations.

"He has a sliver."

Sylvan stopped so quickly Betty walked into her.

"A sliver."

"Aye, miss."

"Is this a joke?"

"Nay, miss." Jasper shuffled his feet but still looked her straight in the eye. "He pulled slivers off his wheel when he tried to stop himself today, and one's fair deep. I could have got it, but he just up and says he wants ye to do it."

That was interesting. "I wonder why."

"Could have knocked me over with a owl-wing feather, miss, but I don't know why."

"Let's go back to your room," Betty urged. "There's no need—"

"I think perhaps there is."

"At least get dressed!" Betty set her jaw. "Your reputation—"

"Can't be hurt." Sylvan smiled and turned back to her room. "But I will dress."

When she stepped out again, looking neat in a simple muslin gown, Betty still clung to her heels, protesting, "Miss, I don't like this."

Trying to surmise Rand's motive, Sylvan answered, "Perhaps he's testing me. Perhaps he's truly in pain, but won't admit it. Men are like that, you know."

"Aye, they are. Fools all," Betty grumbled, but she started down the hall to Rand's room. "And whether you worry about your reputation or not, I'll be there to protect it."

Jasper opened the door and half ducked. Apparently Rand routinely threw things at those who dared beard his den. When nothing came out, Jasper called, "I brought her, master."

"Send her in." Rand's voice sounded rough, as if he'd been crying.

But when Sylvan stepped through the door, she knew he had not. He probably hadn't cried since he was a child, and he needed to. As Betty said, men were fools all.

He sat propped up in his bed, frowning at his palm. He wore more than he had that afternoon—a white bed gown covered his shoulders, arms, and chest. "Did Jasper tell you?"

"That you have a splinter?" she asked calmly. "He did."

"I didn't think you'd really come."

"Of course. I'm your nurse. When you call, I come running."

His blue eyes glowed in the light of the candles, his ebony hair stood on end, and she saw the flash of his white teeth when he grinned. "I doubt that."

"Within reason," she temporized. Holding out her hand, she said, "Let me see."

He gave her his hand and she cradled it between her palms. The fingers were long and thick, with calluses on every pad. Lines crisscrossed his skin—some natural, some the result of wounds. Flecks of red covered the places where the other splinters had been removed, and she saw the reason for this visit at once. Large, black, and deep, the splinter had worked its way beneath the pad below his index finger. It had to be painful, and if not extracted, it would lead to infection.

Rand could reasonably have called for his nurse to remove it.

She didn't believe that was why he'd called her.

"Do you have tweezers, needle, and basilicum?" she asked.

"Aye, miss." Jasper showed her the instruments and the dark stoppered bottle.

She needed to hold the hand still, yet at the same time have both her hands free. If she rested his hand on the mattress, it sank among the feathers and out of the light. Yet . . .

"Sit on the bed," Rand instructed, "and hold it in your lap."

Betty gasped. "Lord Rand!"

"Betty, get out of here," Rand commanded.

"I will not, sir." Betty placed her fists on her hips. "'Tisn't decent, Miss Sylvan being here in the night, and she needs a chaperone."

"Jasper's here."

Betty was unconvinced.

"And Sylvan's not afraid. Are you, Sylvan?"

Sylvan stared at Rand and saw challenge personified. "No. I'm not afraid of you."

"Go on, Betty. Run away and play." Rand pointed toward the door, but Betty just stood there, stubborn and unyielding, and to Sylvan's surprise, he gave in. "Oh, for God's sake, just go and get me some sliced cold meats and some biscuits. I didn't eat dinner, and I'm hungry."

Betty relaxed her stance and considered.

"Really, Betty, you can go," Sylvan said. "If he tries any mischief, I'll bash him."

Rand looked Sylvan over from top to toe. It didn't take long. "Ooh, I'm frightened."

"You'd best be, Lord Rand, because if you give me reason for grief, I'll see that you're sorry." With that startling pronouncement, Betty said to Jasper, "You watch them," and left.

Rand looked after her. "I suppose I'd better do my mischief early so she doesn't catch me." Switching his concentration to Sylvan, he commanded softly, "Now get on the bed and remove this thing."

Betty's lack of respect left Sylvan feeling smug and a little superior. After all, if the housekeeper could speak to Rand that way and get away with it, what harm could it do to sit on his bed? The man was paralyzed, and she was his nurse. Calmly, she climbed onto the mattress.

"Miss Sylvan!"

Jasper sounded even more scandalized than Betty, but neither of the bed's occupants paid attention. Sylvan sat on her feet, facing the headboard, and tucked her skirt around her so that no bit of flesh might tempt Rand—although why she should worry about such a thing, she didn't know.

His hand rested on the sheets where she had put it, as limp as if it, too, were paralyzed. But when she picked it up to place it on her knee, vitality leaped from the flesh. Never had she touched a person so alive, so vibrant. It was as if life channeled itself through Rand to the rest of the world—and if Rand died, the world would end.

An odd notion, and one Sylvan dismissed as part of her weariness.

She pressed the flesh about the splinter, then picked up the needle. "This will hurt."

"I know."

The gravelly sound in his voice startled her; he seemed almost to relish the pain. Using the needle, she had to dig, and dig deep, but Rand bore it stoically, even when she spread basilicum over the laceration to prevent infection.

Had he found that pain proved superior to no sensation at all?

"There you are." Wiping her hand on a towel, she asked, "Is there anything else?"

"No." She started to slide off the bed, and he caught her arm with his undamaged hand. "Yes."

She looked at him inquiringly.

"I want to apologize."

"Sir?"

"For my brother."

Amazement buffeted her, then fury, and she shook off his grip. "You're apologizing for your brother? After all *you've* done today?"

He opened his mouth, shut it, then ran his hand over his face. "I never thought of it that way. But yes, I apologize for my brother."

"You ought to be . . ."

He lifted one eyebrow and smiled. "Spanked?"

"Ashamed of yourself."

"No. I've been insufferable, but I wasn't the one who lured you here."

"How did you—"

"Know?" He grinned. "I'm familiar with Garth's methods, and I can imagine the tale he wove for you. 'Poor Rand, confined to his bed and a wheelchair and languishing. He's lost his will to live.'"

Since that was almost exactly what Garth had insinuated, Sylvan blushed furiously, and Rand laughed. "Garth's a good man, but my father raised him to be the duke, and my father believed that the duke of Clairmont stood just below the apostles in importance and should always get his own way, regardless of the means."

"And you do not?"

"My father raised me to believe the entire Malkin family could stop the tide with a word."

"Then why don't you?" she asked nastily.

His blue eyes glinted with mischief. "It is not my desire."

She slid one leg off the bed. "I'm not interested in your desire."

"Aren't you?" His tone arrested her, and she froze completely when he said, "I liked the look of you in Brussels."

"Sh." She glanced at Jasper.

"Go on, Jasper." Rand waved an impatient hand. "I don't need you."

"But, master—"

"Go on, go on." Rand scowled impatiently. "Miss Sylvan can get me everything I want."

With a look of wounded resentment, Jasper shambled to the door.

"Shut it behind you," Rand called.

"No!" Sylvan said.

Jasper shut the door with just a touch of force, and Sylvan tried to slide off the bed, but Rand's injured hand, which had been lying so limp against her, suddenly turned and grasped her knee. "I like the look of you now."

Irritated, Sylvan snapped, "Your eyes still work, then."

"It makes me wonder why I notice. What good does it do a crippled man"—his fingers worked their way up her thigh—"to like the look of a woman?"

She slapped his wrist.

He rubbed her through her skirt. "And what good does it do a woman to kiss a man?"

"Kiss?" He wanted to kiss her?

In Brussels, he had attracted her. In spite of her good sense, her caution, she'd wanted him for his strength, the way he moved, the way he looked. It had been a merely physical attraction. Hadn't it?

"Especially one as harmless as I am," he added.

"Harmless?" He was as harmless as a sleek and hungry tiger.

"Come close," he whispered.

And she was stupid enough to want to pet the tiger and feel it purr.

"Consider it one of your nursing duties." The tiger's paw prowled up her leg, touching so lightly she scarcely believed it moved. "Like taking the sliver out of my hand. It keeps me awake nights, wondering if I'm still a man."

Living with her father had bred cynicism into her bones, and her own sense of self-preservation returned a measure of good sense. "You've probably kissed every maidservant working at Clairmont Court to find out if you're still a man."

"Have I?" He watched his hand as it slipped up to the bow on her bodice and untied it. "Then perhaps you should kiss me for another reason."

She looked into his eyes. "What is that?"

"You're wondering if you're still a woman."

He must be right, damn him, Sylvan thought, because she allowed him to slide his hands around her waist. He pulled her toward him, and she let him, holding herself carefully so her body didn't quite touch his body. He acknowledged her caution with amusement, and kissed her.

One closemouthed, off-center kiss, with her gaze fixed on the stubble of his cheek.

Disappointing.

Deep in his chest, he growled. "Let's try again."

Manhandling her—tiger-handling her—he settled her across his chest and tucked her head into the crook of his arm.

And she let him do it.

With two fingers he closed her eyes and brushed her hair off her forehead, then leaned over her and kissed her. Little tiny bites on her lips, really, and when she opened them, soothing little touches with his tongue. He'd been drinking brandy, she discovered, and he liked the texture of her inside lower lip, for his tongue kept sliding across it in repeated expeditions.

For such an obnoxious man, he had a delicate touch.

When she took her lip between his teeth, she almost stopped breathing. He didn't hurt her, but the threat was there. Instead, he sucked at her lip as if it were an expensive sweetmeat that melted in his mouth.

She melted in his arms, and waited, breathless, for his next move.

His hand cupped her breast, weighed it, and he muttered, "Perfect," against her lips. His thumb brushed her nipple, back and forth, rubbing the texture of lace across her skin, and she shuddered with pleasure.

Carefully, he parted her lips and touched his tongue to her teeth. She jumped and tensed, wondering at his boldness, wondering if she liked it. He paused as if surprised, then cuddled her closer and did it again. He seemed to be searching with his tongue, looking for something, although she didn't know what. She only knew this was intimate and intrusive, and it made her feel closer to him than she'd ever felt to any other person.

She didn't know him that well. She didn't even like him that well. But this was the thing she'd sensed when they danced in Brussels.

They would be good together.

"Making me do all the work, eh?" His day-old whiskers scratched her when he spoke. "I never would have suspected."

Her eyes flew open and he winked. Her mouth dropped open and he kissed. Really kissed. The taste, the texture, the insistence made this nothing like his previous tentative forays. This was open mouths, straining toward a liaison with nothing concealed. He chased her tongue until he found it, then sucked on it until she obeyed his directive and penetrated his mouth. Until everything was Rand, filling her every sense and blotting out past and future.

"Lord Rand. Miss Sylvan. That is enough!"

Someone shook Sylvan's shoulder, and Betty's stern voice commanded, "Lord Rand, let her go. Let her go *now*. Jasper, make him let her go!"

Sylvan opened her eyes and looked up at Rand.

His blue eyes seemed unfocused, but at the sight of her, they sharpened. "By Jove," he said, "I think we found something. Betty, you came back too soon, but you can stop nagging, I'm through." He brushed his thumb one last time across her nipple. "For the moment."

Sitting up, Sylvan glanced at the scandalized Betty and the wooden-faced Jasper. Then she tied her bodice bow. She looked at Rand again, and with shaking fingers, tied a double knot.

"You can't erase what we did."

Rand's dark voice caressed her, and she put another knot in the tie.

"I think it proved something to both of us."

Her gaze dropped to his lap, then she pressed her hands to her hot cheeks. She'd never been so close to a man in his condition, but he didn't appear to be suffering.

He murmured, "Yes, it certainly proved you heal the sick."

His air of possession infuriated her, and without thought she snapped, "Heal the sick, not raise the dead."

Rand threw back his head and roared with laughter, but Betty sounded shocked. "Miss Sylvan, that was cruel."

"She's not cruel, Betty." Rand leaned forward and incited Sylvan. "She's frightened."

"You don't frighten me."

"I ought to."

The query hovered on the tip of her tongue. Why? Why should he frighten her? But she knew she wouldn't like the answer, and whirled to escape.

He let her get to the door. He let her have that first

taste of escape, then, as if she'd asked, he called, "Because you excite me, and I excite you."

Sylvan wanted to curse him with the language she'd heard on the battlefield. She wanted to damn him to hell and back, but her early training prevented her, and she said only, "You are an odious creature!"

Long after her footfalls had faded, he stared at the doorway where she had stood.

"Lord Rand?" Wearing a sly grin, Jasper waited to prepare him for bed. "She's just like everyone said, isn't she?"

Reluctantly, Rand transferred his regard to Jasper. "How's that?"

"She's an easy rider."

Still groggy with desire, Rand repeated, "Easy?"

Jasper came a little closer and companionably nudged Rand in the ribs. "She climbed right on that bed without a complaint and made herself at home."

Comprehension flashed through Rand, and he grabbed Jasper by the shirt close to the throat and dragged him until they were face-to-face. "Don't you ever say that again. Don't you ever tell anybody what happened here. Unless you want to go back to your father's farm, you'll forget what you saw and treat Miss Sylvan with respect. Understand?"

Eyes bulging from lack of air, Jasper nodded, and Rand knocked him aside. Jasper stumbled backward and landed on his rump. But Rand couldn't stay angry, not with the triumph of his discovery, and he said, "The rumors about Hibbert were true."

4

The dead were calling.

"Please, Sylvan, help me, Sylvan."

The odor of rot clogged her nostrils as first one corpse, then another grabbed at her. Their fingers, dank and pale, curled onto her skirt, her arm, her neck. She could hear their nails scratching, dry as gorse in winter.

"Help me. I'm too young."

They dragged her down, beseeching her aid. The edge of the grave crumbled beneath her feet as she fought for purchase. Mold stained her skin. Dirt rained down.

"Not yet. I can't be dead yet."

One by one their specters sucked the air from her lungs.

"Help me."

She struggled, tasting the too-familiar fear.

"Sing to me."

She tried to scream, but dust clogged her throat.

"Hold my hand."

She wanted to strike out, but she couldn't.

"Help me."

"I can't!" Heaving herself out of the high bed, Sylvan landed on her knees. She welcomed the pain of impact, the irritation of the carpet's nap. She looked wildly around, unfamiliar with the surroundings, then sank down until her cheek rested on the rough wool. "I can't help you. I killed you."

The ghouls still danced in her mind, but gradually they retreated, trailing their winding clothes, their hollow cheeks and amputated limbs. They retreated, but they would be back.

She wiped her eyes, but they were dry, then deliberately she pushed herself upright and leaned against the bed. The polished wood cut into her back, bringing reality into focus, returning Sylvan from the edge of sanity.

Now she remembered. Rand Malkin. Clairmont Court. The ghost that walked at midnight?

No wonder she had dreamed.

Groaning, she sank down and cradled her head in her arms. Would the dead never leave her alone? Would she never sleep peacefully again?

Scratch. Shuffle.

She lifted her head and stared at the door.

What was that?

She strained to hear but caught no further sound.

It must be nothing but the shattered remnants of her nightmare.

Staggering to her feet, she looked around. Moonlight burned a cold streak across the floor, and she crept to the window, parted the heavy curtains, and peered out.

Her room overlooked the back of the manor where the ruins of the old castle had been blended with a charming garden. Lumps of ancient stone supported creeping vines, and walls that long ago listened to old sorrows now heard nothing but the sigh of the wind. Stark in the moonlight, it seemed as eerie as anything in her imagination.

Yet nothing moved out there. Everyone, everything, was asleep.

Loneliness struck at her, scratching the thin coating of control that kept her sane. Was there no one in the world who kept vigil in this night?

As if in answer, something smacked her door.

She found herself behind the curtains, shivering, heart thumping, eyes so wide they hurt from the strain. *Please, God*, she thought. *Please, God*. But what could she promise Him that she hadn't promised on all the other lonely nights?

No other sound followed the first, and she peeked out. Nothing stirred within the room. It was as still as a graveyard.

La! What had made her draw that comparison?

Perhaps the echo of Jasper's shaken voice. Perhaps the memory of Betty's demeanor when she admitted that she, too, believed that the ghost of the first duke walked the halls this night.

Gathering courage in hand, Sylvan tiptoed into the room. A candle burned by the bed, but that wasn't enough. Taking it in her shaking fingers, she began to light every candle in the room, and the Malkin household placed their candles with a generous hand. One by one, the wicks caught flame, chasing the shadows back to the grave from whence they came.

The room blazed like a ballroom when she finished, and the odor of melting wax smelled like safety. She sank onto one of the chairs and pulled her knees up to her chest.

One never knew when a phantom might grab at her toes.

One never knew when a phantom might walk through the wall.

One never knew if the phantom stood outside, staring through the massive, heavily carved wood door and right at her, huddled in a chair.

Ugh! Why did she think of things like that? Why now, in a strange place with nowhere to go and no one to run to?

She didn't believe in ghosts, she'd told Betty.

Well, she didn't. Why should she fear a long-dead someone, when she knew, from cruel experience, it was the men she'd tried to help who so deliberately haunted her?

Nevertheless, Betty said it best. At night when the wind howls and the moon drifts in and out of the fog, it was easy to forget.

Only tonight, the wind wasn't howling. Silence pressed down on Sylvan as if she were a rat trapped in a glass dome. Her breath made too much noise. She could hear the great clock ticking all the way down the hall, and the smaller clock ticking within her room. Then with one dramatic note, the minute hand reached the hour hand, and, in unison, the clocks began to strike midnight. Each chime reverberated through her head. Now time would stop, and that specter in the hall would step through the wall and—

With a tremulous laugh, she leaped to her feet. Stupid, she scolded. Scaring herself into next week.

She was Sylvan Miles, bold and dashing adventuress. By heavens, she'd prove herself to her father, fulfill the duke of Clairmont's every expectation, and in the process, lay her own ghosts to rest. Taking a quivering breath, she nodded. A long dead duke couldn't walk, and by God she'd prove it.

The last notes of the clocks struck as she picked up the candelabra, went to the door, and swung it wide.

She froze in shock and horror.

The white-cloaked figure of a man walked away from her down the hall.

When she got her breath and gasped, he seemed to hear it. He half turned and looked, and she realized she had been wrong. He didn't stare at her from cavernous holes where his eyes had been. He stared with the menacing glint of long dead eyes.

"He looks just like me, doesn't he?"

Sylvan gripped the handles of the wheelchair so tightly Rand could feel her tremble. "He does," she admitted.

"Radolf was a mean old bastard, they say." The trembling increased. What was wrong with the woman this morning? "Bred children all over the estate, but he cared for nothing but Clairmont Court and establishing a dynasty. He married heiress after heiress, but none of them lasted long."

"One of them must have lasted long enough to produce an heir," she said. "*You're* here."

He straightened the ruffles on his white shirt and smoothed his trousers. He'd gotten dressed for her this morning, and she hadn't noticed. "Yes, he got his heir at last. They say the wife that gave him his son led him a merry dance, and when she died he refused to marry again."

"Why should he? He got what he wanted." If bitterness could be distilled, she'd have produced a pint. "A son."

"One son?" Rand swiveled around and looked at her. "Even today, a son is easily lost. No, the duke should have remarried and produced more, but he didn't."

"Maybe she turned the tables on him and made him miserable. Maybe he discovered how dreadful it is to live, day by day, in a bad marriage."

"The story is, he swore never to leave Clairmont Court from the day of his wife's death. They say he never would leave in life, and that's why he's still here."

She jerked the wheelchair as if her knees had given out, and Rand gestured to the window stools that lined the long gallery. "Sit down before you fall down. You're trembling like a leaf. Don't you know I'm the only invalid allowed in this house?"

He sounded grimly amused, but he watched her with concern as she sank onto a seat. What was wrong with the woman? After that kiss last night, he'd expected her to be shy this morning. To blush and bridle when he teased her.

Instead, she'd shown up looking as if she'd been dragged through a knothole by a team of farm horses.

"Didn't you sleep last night?" he demanded.

She tore her gaze away from the portrait of Duke Radolf and stared at Rand as though she didn't know him. "What? Oh, yes, I slept."

"How much?"

"You know how it is. One doesn't sleep deeply the first night in a strange place."

"Perhaps you should go to your room and try again."

"What?"

She was staring at the duke again, and that irked Rand. True, his ancestor was an impressive figure, painted in full armor. His cape flowed around his shoulders and his dogs leaped around his feet. But his face had a wooden appearance and his sternness looked more like a snarl. The first duke had been known for his parsimony. Obviously, he had scrimped on his own portrait artist, although his eyes followed wherever one moved in the gallery.

He repeated, "Perhaps you should go to your room."

"No." She jumped to her feet and gave a poor imitation of a smile. "Just because it's raining doesn't mean you shouldn't have your constitutional. You can show me more of the manor now."

"Damn rude of the rain to interrupt your plans for me, isn't it?" He thought bleakly of how he had failed himself and his brave ancestors on the previous day, and wondered if his aborted plan would have been more palpable today.

He doubted it. Not with the memory of that kiss burning in his heart—and places lower. It would have to be done, of course, but he blessed the rain for removing that burden for one more day.

"I'll take you to the library," he decided, wheeling himself toward the end of the gallery. "Maybe you can find a volume there which will bore you sufficiently to put you to sleep."

She smiled and relaxed as she walked beside him. "Yes, I'd like that. I left most of my books at home."

He admired the way her dimples pressed the cream of her cheeks inward when she smiled. He liked the shape of her just as much as he had yesterday, and just as much as he had in Brussels. Indeed, something about Sylvan made him the man he had been before the battle. He thought again about the man-elf who had put her together, and wondered if that creature had been drunk after all.

The sound of running feet distracted him, and before

he could take evasive action, a slight figure burst through the door of the gallery.

"Uncle Rand!"

The child flung herself at him, and he wrapped her in his arms. "Gail!"

She hugged him as if she might never see him again. "Uncle Rand, I missed you. When are you going to invite me down to tea again?"

"I had you to tea only three days ago," he said.

"Three whole days." Gail sat in his lap and leaned her head back against his shoulder. "It's a wonder I haven't starved."

Sylvan stared in horror at the mock-pathetic waif.

Uncle Rand, indeed.

The Malkin blood must run strong, for this child showed her kinship to Rand with more than her familiarity. She had his blue eyes, his dark hair, and his handsome features, softened by youth and gender. By her height, she looked to be twelve, but her figure showed none of the dawning of womanhood, and Sylvan guessed her to be more like ten—and quite illegitimate, for she'd never heard a whisper of her existence before.

Rand's child.

Then Sylvan shook herself. Not necessarily Rand's child. The girl looked like Garth, too, and James, and like the first duke. But the first duke was dead and she couldn't imagine Garth indulging in a casual romp with a parlor maid, so it had to be James . . . James? Elegant, fashionable James? Sylvan couldn't imagine it.

"Stand straight, miss." Betty spoke from the door, and her sharp voice brought Gail out of the chair. "Curtsy to Miss Miles and show the manners that I taught you."

Gail blushed and bobbed a curtsy in Sylvan's direction, but Rand caught her hand and squeezed it. "Miss

Robards, allow me to introduce you to my nurse, Miss Miles. Miss Miles, Miss Robards."

Gail shot a grin at him and a shy one at Sylvan. "I'm pleased to meet you, Miss Miles."

"And I you, Miss Robards." No, Gail had to be Rand's child. The hell-raiser of yesterday had disappeared and a civil human being had taken his place. Only the power of parenthood could bring about such a change.

And who was the mother? Sylvan blinked and made an extra effort to smile at Gail. "Are you taking time from your studies to see your . . . Lord Rand?"

"My governess said I must have sat on an anthill this morning, I'm so squirmy, so I'm to run it off in the gallery." Gail studied Sylvan, and her sharp intelligence showed in her eyes. "Is that what you're doing here?"

"Yes. Lord Rand was squirmy this morning, so he's showing me around the house."

Gail giggled and glanced back at Betty. "Can I come?"

"You're too bold," Betty said.

"Ah, let her come," Rand begged. "That old witch you call a governess won't care. You know she lives only to conjugate Latin verbs."

While Gail giggled more, Sylvan changed her mind once again. That was not a fatherly statement, designed to uphold discipline and promote education. Maybe James was the father. Maybe Garth. Maybe some unknown cousin?

Betty rebuked Rand. "You know Gail repeats everything you say. How am I going to explain that?"

Taking Gail's hand, Rand patted it and said to her, "Don't tell the old witch what I said. She's a nice lady. She can't help it if she can't keep up with us."

"I won't tell her." Gail sounded stuffy and adult. "I like Miss Wainwright, and that would hurt her feelings." She dropped her voice to a whisper, the kind of whisper that echoed through the gallery. "She's in love with you, you know."

"Is she?" Rand whispered right back. "I won't tease her about it."

Gail thought about it, then said, "Neither will I."

"I hate rainy days," Betty muttered, her gaze on Gail.

Sylvan sidled over to her. "Do you do everything around here? Housekeeper, personal maid, and nursemaid of the, um, child? Whose daughter . . ." Betty looked at Sylvan with such an appalled expression, Sylvan blushed for her own boldness. "I beg your pardon. I really don't even want to know."

"Miss, I don't think . . ." Betty faltered.

"I vow, I don't want to know."

"Sylvan!" Rand called. "Come with us." He and Gail had raced clear across the gallery and were waiting at the opposite door. "We're going to raid the dining room."

With what sounded like relief, Betty said, "You go on, miss. You need another meal. You didn't eat a thing this morning."

Sylvan went, but only because she wanted to observe Rand with this child. He seemed to like Gail immensely, treating her like a small adult and delighting her with his attention. She talked all the time, and Rand called her "Windy Gail," making her giggle and roll her eyes at Sylvan. The other servants treated Gail well, too, not like an outcast bastard, but like the child they'd all helped to raise. She'd spoken of her governess, so obviously Rand, or Garth, or James, had acknowledged her as his own and gave her the advantages of wealth. If only

Sylvan didn't so urgently hope the father were someone other than Rand, for what did that say about her?

"Lord Rand!" The minister hailed them from the doorway of the study as they were about to enter the dining room. "How good to see you're feeling better today."

Sylvan almost laughed at the vicar's euphemistic phrasing. Feeling better? She supposed Rand was feeling better than yesterday, when he knocked out the windows and rampaged through the house.

From the expression on Rand's face, he thought much the same. "Ah, Reverend." Rand nudged Gail along. "Thank you for your good wishes. I hadn't expected to see you out on such a miserable day."

Gail got a look at the good reverend and bolted toward the dining room, but the Reverend Donald caught her arm in a lightning move that startled Sylvan. He stood taller than the middle shelf on the china cabinet, but his face had the soft look of a man who spent more time reading than working. Still, his knee-length black frock coat must conceal a muscled body. His mouth smiled, but his eyes were stern as he said, "Gail Emmaline, why have I not seen you in church these many weeks? It's a sad thing when a young lady is allowed to dismiss her communion with God as unimportant."

"I don't do that!" Gail blurted. "I do my Bible lessons every day, but my mama says—"

"You should go and find your mama," Rand interrupted, catching the vicar's wrist and shaking his grip loose. "Mr. Donald wants to speak to me in private, I'm sure."

Her mama? Then Gail's mama was still alive, and Sylvan desperately wanted to know the identity of the woman, to question her about the child's paternity. But Sylvan recognized this as more than the usual stick-her-nose-in kind of curiosity that had previously got her into trouble. This was personal, vulgar, and Sylvan resolved to fight it.

Gail darted away, and the vicar inclined his head. "You're right, of course, Lord Rand. I'll speak to the child of sin at some other time."

Sylvan didn't like that, and from Rand's savage grin it appeared he didn't either, but he proceeded with his self-sacrifice. "If you'll come into the study, I'll call for refreshments."

The vicar bowed his head. "Thank you, Lord Rand. I'd enjoy that."

Rand waited until the vicar had entered the study, then he bellowed at the footman who stood not ten feet away, "Hey! We want some food and tea in here."

It was a travesty, a return to the tyranny of the previous day, but it expressed his opinion of the Reverend Donald in an explicit way, and when he saw Sylvan staring at him, he murmured, "Best run off as Gail did. It's not a pretty sight when Donald starts hacking at my sins."

Cowardly as always, Sylvan wanted to do as he said, and for that reason, if no other, she said, "I'll come in. I might want to hack at you myself."

With a seated bow, Rand answered, "As you wish, but you lack the necessary aptitude to hack with our dear minister."

His tone gave her pause, but his unpleasant smirk challenged her, and she swept into the study.

The clergyman stood by the mantel in front of the flames. It was right he should do so; his damp clothes steamed where the heat touched them. At the same time, she believed his position to be a bid for power. She couldn't remain erect; women didn't. Rand couldn't stand to challenge the vicar's supremacy; Rand couldn't. So the Reverend Donald held the floor.

Sylvan seated herself with a demure smile, and the vicar smiled back with equal restraint. A pleasant-looking man, his blond hair, blue eyes, and tanned skin showed no sign of harshness, and she couldn't in reality find fault in his calling Gail a "child of sin." She didn't know a minister who wouldn't do the same. None of them, in her opinion, were as good as they should be, but her opinion was biased.

Most of her life, she had received nothing but grief from the clergy, and that would continue until she bowed to her father's wishes.

Rand wheeled himself into the room, bumping the end table and setting the candelabra to rattling. "I miss your pleasant wife."

"The rain would settle into Mrs. Donald's lungs," the Reverend Donald answered. To Sylvan, he said, "Clover isn't strong, and I look out for her. But Lord Rand, this young woman and I haven't officially met."

"Yes, we must keep up the courtesies." Rand backed into the sofa where Sylvan sat, and the impact rocked her. "Sylvan, this is the Reverend Bradley Donald. His family has lived here on the estate since time immemorial. He showed special gifts, so my father sent him away to be taught. He went to divinity school, returned as our parish minister, and has been here ever since. It's been about five years, isn't that correct, Donald?"

"That's correct, Lord Rand." The Reverend Donald sounded mild and earnest. "And you're Miss Miles, of whom I've heard so much."

"Don't believe everything you hear," Rand advised. "She's not as righteous as she looks."

Sylvan didn't know how to take that; she only knew she didn't like it. Putting her foot on the back of the chair, she pushed Rand away.

"Women are never as righteous as they look, and it's a wise man who keeps that in mind." The Reverend Donald gestured to the footman who hovered outside the door. "Do bring in the tea."

His presumption irritated Rand, Sylvan could see, and his comment about women irritated her, so she said, "Yes, bring it here. I will pour."

Assuming the role of hostess removed the Reverend Donald from the center of attention and thrust her into the limelight, but her governess had trained her well. The next moments were taken up with inquiries about milk and sugar, and the beneficial effects of a good cup of tea in a chilled body.

Too soon the Reverend Donald put his cup aside and loomed earnestly over Rand. "So, my son, have you decided to put your bitterness aside?"

"May I have some more of that jolly cream cake, Miss Sylvan?" Rand asked in the supercilious voice of a London dandy. "It's delicious."

"As soon as you have submitted to God's dictates, you'll once more be at ease."

"Here's your cake." Sylvan passed a plate to Rand and played her role in his social parody. "Your confectioner is extraordinarily talented."

Ever tenacious, the vicar said, "Outbursts such as yesterday's would cease, and you could do good works, with me to guide you."

"You!" The Reverend Donald had broken Rand's sham tranquillity at last. "What can *you* teach *me*?"

"While it's true I am younger, I feel I'm older in wisdom. My education and experience has helped me grow far beyond my years." He leaned over Rand. "And I know what troubles you."

Rand shoved the cream cake into the vicar's chest with such force it sent him toppling over an ottoman. "Nobody knows what troubles me."

Sylvan could scarcely believe Rand's actions, but the vicar stood and with a napkin wiped himself off as if such violence occurred every day. In forbearing tones, he said, "The Lord has seen fit to show me the reason for your fear and desperation. If you would work with me to save the souls of this parish, I would dispense with your uncertainty."

"Goddamn you."

Rand was working himself into a frenzy, and the situation had escalated beyond anything Sylvan could imagine. She hated seeing Rand with two red spots on his cheekbones and his hands shaking. The Reverend Donald had the knack of being unerringly irritating, but Rand didn't have to respond. He'd been doing so well today; he didn't have to retreat to the chaos of yesterday.

But it was too late. Rand shouted at the Reverend Donald, "You're nothing but a pile of manure with two dispensers."

"Lord Rand!" Both the vicar and Sylvan spoke at once, both offended, both embarrassed.

"Lord Rand, there's no excuse for your lack of control," Sylvan said.

"Lord Rand, you shouldn't speak so in front of a lady!" the Reverend Donald said.

Rand looked wildly around him. "She's no lady. She's a camp follower."

"Lord Rand, although that's true in a sense, we must forgive her sins, for her intentions were pure."

Sylvan found herself on her feet, staring at the

Reverend Donald and considering him as a specimen for medical dissection.

The vicar seemed not to notice, however, and laid a gentle hand on her head. "A woman's place is in the home, and those lambs who stray outside their bounds swiftly find themselves delivered unto the wolves. But a wise shepherd does what must be done to herd the lamb back into the fold, and welcomes her back when the proper penance has been made."

"You are an idiot."

Rand's flat pronouncement echoed Sylvan's sentiments. The sentiments she would have expressed if she could have spoken. And why was Rand defending her, anyway? He'd just finished tossing her out to be savaged.

Folding his hands before him, the vicar bowed his head. "I am an idiot in the eyes of God, but I know the word of the Lord. I had already heard of Miss Miles's transgressions, and while we must not cast stones, your condemnation of her showed your own good judgment has not completely deserted you." Earnestly, he reached out to Rand, but Rand scooted away. "That's why I know you are the one who can help me convince Lord Clairmont to cease building his cotton mill and dismantle his stable of wantons."

Stunned, confused, Sylvan said, "Wantons?"

Tears sprang to the Reverend Donald's eyes. His voice sounded choked, his grief too real. "Good women who used to tend their homes and families, and now go out every day to toil while their husbands cook and care for the wee ones."

"Ah, so they're not really wanton, they're just not bound by tradition." Sylvan felt an empathy for the women who so labored.

"My dear daughter, I can see how misguided you are,

and I welcome this challenge to put your feet on the right path."

Her feet were about to make a path up his back when the thump of running boots sounded in the hallway and James spun into the room. He stared at Rand, red-faced with fury, at Sylvan, standing with fists clenched, and at the Reverend Donald, patient and serene. "Heard you were here, Reverend." James's voice was too loud and his manner too hearty, and for the first time, Sylvan saw him with a lock of hair disturbed. "I had wanted to speak to you about . . . something . . . which disturbs me very much."

"Of course, my son." The vicar seemed untouched by the suspicion that James might be acting as a shield for Rand.

He waited graciously for James to continue, but James said, "In private, Reverend."

"If you'll excuse me." The vicar tried to shake Rand's hand, but Rand refused him. Sylvan was not so brave, and she let him take her hand in his cold fingers as he said, "By the way, a woman from Malkinhampsted was attacked last night, and badly beaten."

"Beaten?" Rand said.

"Beaten?" James sounded bored. "Oh, by her husband, I suppose. Another provincial tempest in a teapot."

"Not at all." The Reverend Donald drew himself up. "She was walking home from the mill."

"Who is she?" Rand asked.

"Pert Seward. You know her, don't you?"

Rand nodded, a nasty taste in his mouth. "I know them all."

"The thug knocked her nearly unconscious with a rock first, and she says he wore a scarf over his face."

"Impossible." James glared fiercely at the vicar. "Women always walk home together. Husband probably beat her, and this Pert person doesn't want to admit it."

"She didn't walk home with the other women. It was late evening. For some reason, Lord Clairmont had kept her behind when the other women left, but in his defense, he had no reason to suspect a problem such as this, and he gave her a lamp to light her way home."

Sylvan feared to know, and feared not to know, but she had to ask. "Was she . . . otherwise forced by her attacker?"

The Reverend Donald took a horrified breath, and Rand and James both cleared their throats in acute masculine discomfort. "Certainly not," the Reverend Donald said.

"Why 'certainly not'?" Sylvan demanded. "A man who will attack and beat a defenseless woman undoubtedly wouldn't balk at further degradations."

"There were no further degradations." The clergyman's eyes glowed red with embarrassment and fury. "It is an insult to the woman to so claim."

Sylvan spoke half to herself. "I wonder if she would tell another woman what she won't tell you."

"She'll tell *you* nothing," the vicar said. "You're a stranger with a bad reputation. Her husband would bar you from the house." Sylvan jerked her hand free from his grasp, and he insisted, "She told me all, including a description."

James's boots gleamed as he shifted his feet back and forth, back and forth. "What kind of description?"

The Reverend Donald gathered attention to himself with a combination of showmanship and dignity, and Sylvan realized how mesmerizing he must be at the pulpit. In a deep, dramatic tone, he proclaimed, "Her attacker was tall and strong, with eyes that glittered in the dark. She seemed afraid when I spoke to her, but after much urging, she said"—he laughed a little—"it was the ghost of the first duke."

"Oh, nonsense!" James sounded annoyed—and frightened.

"Nonsense?" the Reverend Donald said. "I wonder. If you will recall, some of the women assert they have heard the sounds of someone following them when they walk home at night. And Charlotte claimed she was knocked down one evening by a stranger who appeared from nowhere, then disappeared again, and that was on a night the ghost appeared."

James sniffed in disdain. "Next you'll be pointing your finger at Garth or me because we look like the old duke."

Sylvan stared at James, his declaration sinking into her mind. Of course! How foolish she had been. That wasn't a ghost she'd seen, but a human being. Yet she'd immediately recognized the portrait of the duke this morning. So had her ghost been James . . . or Garth?

"Didn't do it," James said quickly.

Sylvan realized they were all staring at him.

Turning to Rand, James extended his hand appealingly. "Wouldn't go outside in the dark to tramp around after a smelly village woman who'd been working at that blasted mill all day. You know."

"No." Rand laughed a little, suspicion clearing from his face. "You wouldn't. The only thing you ever go out for is a London party or a tumble with your ladybird."

The vicar had a thoughtful cast to his face. "I should question everyone in the manor. Perhaps someone saw the ghost—or whoever is imitating the ghost—walk last night." He met Sylvan's appalled gaze, and held it. He seemed to be speaking to her alone when he said, "I hope to continue our discussion later."

"Much later," she said under her breath as he exited the room with James stalking after him. She didn't want him interrogating her—she had no intention of telling anyone about that ghost. She didn't want them thinking her crazy before she'd helped Rand . . . Rand. She glared at him as she remembered his earlier insults.

"He's a jackass," Rand declared, but his voice shook.

"So are you," she snapped, preparing to walk out.

He grabbed her hand. "What's wrong?"

"A camp follower?" she shouted. She shouldn't shout; a lady never raised her voice. But this place, this post, this *man* made her lose all her manners and most of her good sense. "You called me a camp follower!"

"I was angry." He excused himself as if she should understand.

"You were angry?" She gestured so hard, he ducked. "You were angry? And when you're angry, you can say anything you wish and everyone has to forgive you? Because you're crippled?" She backed away from him as if he were unclean. "There's nothing wrong with you except that your legs don't work."

"There's more to it than that!"

"What?"

But he couldn't tell her. He wanted to, so badly. In one day, she'd managed to gain his trust, make him feel as if he were in command again. But he wasn't. He didn't know if what the vicar said was true, but Rand knew he had no right to drag Sylvan into his private nightmare.

She saw he wouldn't speak, but clearly she didn't think it a noble act. She thought he had nothing to say, and she tried to regain self-control. He saw her fight for breath, then the question burst out of her. "Where did he hear the rumors about me?"

"The vicar hears everything. Every bit of gossip. He doesn't sleep, I don't think. Always visiting his sinners, and with the uncanny knack of coming at the worst times. Consequently, he's the best informed man in the parish."

"He wouldn't know about the . . . kissing?"

"Not that," he quickly assured her. "Only Jasper and Betty saw, and they're totally reliable."

"Yes." She put her hand to her heart, and when she looked at him, he had the feeling he'd shrunk in her eyes. Softly, as if she were speaking to herself, she said, "There are veterans of Waterloo who are begging on the streets of London. I give them coins. Sometimes they recognize me. Sometimes they thank me for saving their lives. Most times they curse me. And you're sitting here warm and fed, with a comfortable wheelchair under you and a loving family around you, and you feel sorry for yourself." Whirling, she ran to the door, then turned. "I feel sorry for you, too. Your family wants you to get better, but even if you walked, you wouldn't be better. You'd still be a craven coward, afraid to face all the nasty little incidents of living."

She raced out and left him there, hand extended, explanation on his tongue. But his hand fell into his lap, and he looked at it as if he'd never seen it before. In the last eleven months, it had grown stronger than before. Veins rose beneath skin; each tendon and bone had broadened with exercise. His arms, chest, and stomach, too, showed the results of constant use. And his legs . . . he rubbed his hands up and down his thighs. His legs hadn't shown much deterioration yet. Of course, Jasper exercised them, one at a time, morning and night. But after the months of inactivity, one would think they'd be as spindly as a poorhouse boy's.

It hadn't happened yet. Nothing had happened as it should. He still dreamed of walking, working, tumbling a woman. . . . Last night it had been Sylvan, and this morning he'd sworn to entice her into his bed so he could find out what was dream and what was reality.

Instead, he'd insulted her. He couldn't die until he'd satisfied his curiosity about her. In spite of his taunts, he knew he had to earn her respect before she'd allow him to touch her once more.

The Reverend Donald was wrong all the time, but now he was right about one thing. Rand hadn't grown resigned to his fate. He had to take this one last chance.

5

Seated in his wheelchair beside Sylvan as she lay in the grass, Rand saw the moment she slipped into slumber. Her clenched fists relaxed, the toes that were curled in her thin leather slippers straightened, and her knees fell apart just a little. The frown that had pressed a crease between her brows smoothed, and she released a ladylike snore from between her slightly open lips.

Not for the first time, he wondered why she needed to be in full sunshine, in the open air, before she could sleep. Every day for the last three weeks she had dragged him outside. She'd pushed his wheelchair up and down the hills, taking him to the wild places that, she said, would heal his soul. If anything, she seemed to need their solitude more than he.

Three weeks in her company, and he still didn't know her at all—and he spent all his time thinking about her.

She directed Jasper in the manipulations of Rand's legs. She watched what he ate and gave him vile tonics to drink. She discussed sending him to a therapeutic hot springs, and when Rand furiously disputed her plan, she just smiled. She'd get her way eventually, because she'd conquered his family.

Worse, she'd conquered him. As though his body were a compass, she was magnetic north and his arrow always pointed in her direction. He'd been scheming to touch her again, and she treated him as if he were some kind of . . . cripple. Not as if his legs were crippled. As if his mind were diseased. Perhaps he shouldn't have called her a camp follower and subjected her to scorn, but he'd thought she would forgive him. Everyone else forgave him every other despicable thing he did.

Her cottage straw bonnet remained where she had cast it. From frequent exposure to the Somerset sun, wisps of her brown hair had bleached to blond, and they framed her face in bits of curl. The breeze from the sea fluttered her skirt, and the sun warmed her skin to the gold of fine-grained oak. For her, he wanted to be the breeze and the sun, and pass along her skin with gentle fingers and slide under her skirt. Instead he pretended he stood guard over her like an ancient warrior over a sleeping princess, and scanned the countryside for menace.

Nothing moved among the windswept ridges except bracken, heather, and spring's green grass, pressed down and released in rhythmic waves. He couldn't see the surf, but he could hear it, and he could see the deep blue of the ocean and the haze that always obscured the line between water and sky.

Together Rand and Sylvan had explored the most remote spots on the estate, and Beechwood Hollow was now their favorite. It was not too far from the house, and it was easy to get to, but its seclusion drew them. The beeches grew, protected from the wind by stony boulders. Pinks bloomed in fragrant clumps, and a rivulet trickled down the draw. The brook plunged off the cliff farther on, a silver arc that splattered on the rocks below and became one with the sea. It had made her happy to dangle off the rocks and see the waterfall.

It frightened him to death. He knew what he should do, if he weren't such a coward. If he weren't such a coward, he would start at the top of the smooth headland above him, set his wheelchair in motion, and career down the hillside until he followed the brook in its plunge.

But not yet. First he wanted to—

Sylvan woke with a jerk. Her eyes, so similar in color to the grass beneath her head, stared in panic at some unseen peril. The muscles that he'd seen lax now tensed once more, and her legs twitched as if she longed to run.

No, he couldn't kill himself just yet. Not until he'd unraveled the tangled threads of Sylvan's terror.

Leaning over, he lifted her foot. She tried to jerk it away, but his grip tightened on her ankle. "Keep still," he said. "I only want to massage you."

She brushed at her face as if it were sheathed in cobwebs. "No."

"You'll like it." Stripping off her shoe, he placed her foot on his knee.

"No." She sounded fretful, and she must have realized it, for she tried now for cordiality. "I mean, yes, I'm sure I would, but I'm ticklish."

Firmly, he began to rub her toes through her white silk stockings. "A friend of mine taught me the essentials."

"You mean one of your mistresses!" she snapped.

"A dancer," he admitted. "But it feels good, does it not?"

She struggled for another reason for him to desist, and at last wailed, "You'll see my underthings."

"Believe me, I'm not in the least interested in looking at your underthings." He couldn't have been more sincere, and she must have sensed it, for after one last futile tug, she shut her eyes and let him have his way.

He hadn't lied. He didn't care about her underthings.

He only cared for what was inside them. "Why aren't you sleeping at night?" he asked.

She answered too quickly. "I don't need much sleep."

"I thought maybe the ghost was disturbing you." Her foot twitched in his hand, and he crowed, "Ah-ha! You have seen the ghost."

"Only once."

She sounded as grumpy as a fretful child, and he picked up her other foot, too.

She tried to wrestle it away, saying, "Quit!"

"It doesn't tickle, does it?"

"No," she said sulkily.

"That's because I'm an expert. If you like, I can massage your shoulders and your back." *And your front and your legs.* But he didn't say that.

"I really don't think so, Lord Rand."

She sounded insufferably prim, but her skirt slipped up to expose her leg and he looked hungrily at the flesh between her garter and her pantalettes. For one awful moment, he couldn't move, and she stirred as if she would open her eyes. Hastily, he began his massage again. "When did you see the ghost?"

"Um." She seemed to struggle before deciding to answer. "The first night I came."

"The night Pert was attacked."

"Yes, but that was nonsense, wasn't it? Ghosts don't hit people with rocks."

"Then perhaps your ghost was a person." He leaned over her. "Listen to me, Sylvan. Bar and lock your door tonight and sleep. There's no ghost, and a man can't break through that barrier."

She murmured, "It's not the ghost of Clairmont Court that keeps me awake."

So something did keep her awake. Was it desire for him? He wanted to ask, but she appeared to be so relaxed. Her chest barely rose and fell with her breaths, and she seemed unaware when her skirt fluttered higher. And higher.

He shouldn't look. It would only make him want more what he couldn't have. But he could no more have turned away from the view than he could have turned away from the gate of heaven.

For him, Sylvan was the gate of heaven.

What torture! He loved giving her the gift of repose, and wanted to take it from her at the same time. She moaned when he pressed his thumb into the arch of her foot, and it sounded like ecstasy.

He wanted her so badly he could almost taste her. He wanted to taste her so badly, he suffered starvation.

Briefly, he rubbed her ankle, then pressed the long muscles of her calf. Wetting his lips, he asked, "Do you stay awake thinking of me?"

Her eyes opened, not in panic, as they had before, but in a kind of sleepy curiosity.

He touched her like a healer, but his gaze was that of a lover. She froze, and he glanced at the place he longed to kiss. The slumber in her gaze cleared away like clouds before a noontime sun, and she jerked her foot out of his grasp and rolled away. Sitting up, she grasped the hem of her skirt and held it down as if he could lift it with his thoughts. Then with one-handed haste, she crammed her bonnet back on her head. "You are a wicked man."

"I am a hungry man," he corrected. "Is that why you can't sleep?"

"No! No." She turned her face away, giving herself

privacy in the depths of her hat. "May I please have my shoe?"

He prepared to hand it to her, but she stuck out her hand so stiffly and kept her head turned away so resolutely, he hesitated. After all, she already considered him wicked. Why not add to his sins? Placing it back in his lap, he said, "Come and get it."

He cured her embarrassment with one swift stroke. Coming to her feet, she stalked over and towered above him. He grinned up at her and when she grabbed for her shoes, he snatched her by her wrists and tumbled her into his lap. She tumbled right out again, but he kept hold of her wrists, and as she wrestled with him, she railed, "You are a blackguard, sir, a criminal of the first water and I shall—"

"Kiss me?"

"Why? As a reward for deplorable behavior?"

"No, as payment for your shoe."

Jerking her hands free, she reached for the slipper once more and he let her grab it before trapping her hand. Color flooded her cheeks once more when she realized his condition. "Your juvenile actions, sir, do not impress me."

"Your touch impresses me." He leaned toward her. "One kiss."

"No." She tried to twist away.

He held her. "Two kisses, then."

He should have seen it coming, but he didn't. She smacked him so hard with her free hand that his ears rang. Wrapping his arm around the back of her head in a wrestler's hold, he brought her face close to his and laughed into her eyes. "You've got a punishing right, my lady, and you owe me three kisses for the gratification you got in using it."

She squirmed through the first kiss and stayed rigid during the second. But the third . . . ah, it hadn't been the darkness and proximity of the bed that had freed her inhibitions last time. He proved it when he wrung a response from her here, in the sunshine and the wind. When he finally drew away, he caressed her cheek and whispered, "You've got to come to me some night, and let me show you what pleasure can be."

Her lids fluttered down and her dark lashes cast shadows on her cheeks. She whispered, "Can *you* find pleasure?"

"I don't know, but if I can't, I can still promise it to you."

He didn't know if he'd embarrassed her again, or if she didn't understand, but before he could ask he heard, "Uncle Rand, what are you doing?"

Sylvan and Rand's heads swiveled, and he saw Gail standing off to the side, head tilted, observing them with furrowed brow. Sylvan gasped, and this time when she grabbed for her slipper, he let her take it.

"Wretched child," Rand said. "How long have you been there?"

Primming her mouth in a masterly imitation of Aunt Adela, Gail replied, "Since you started wrestling."

"Why didn't you say something?" Sylvan sounded quite fierce as she hopped up and down, trying to pull the limp leather over her foot.

"I did, but you didn't hear me."

Sylvan glanced at Rand, then looked up at the sky as if solutions could be found within the wispy clouds. "I was probably yelling too loudly, huh?"

"Uncle Rand was laughing, too, and then he kissed you, but I don't understand why."

Rand thought of and discarded several replies before saying, "I was showing Miss Sylvan how much I like her."

"What were you doing it like *that* for?"

Rand recognized distaste when he saw it, and he even remembered feeling the same way at her age. But it would take a stronger man than he to explain the attraction between man and woman to a ten-year-old. "What are you doing here, Windy Gail?" he asked.

"I wanted to go to the mill, and I'm not allowed to go alone." Gail's blue eyes, so like his own, widened in patent appeal.

Rand grinned. She reminded him so much of himself, with her quick mind and cunning tricks. He hoped life treated her well. He wished he could live long enough to see her grown. He prayed for a shield to protect her from the arrows of cruelty the world cast at a bastard. "So you want us to take you?"

"Oh, would you?" She gave a little hop. "What a wonderful idea."

"I agree," Sylvan said dryly. "What a wonderful idea."

"Although I hate to leave our solitude." Rand glanced slyly at Sylvan and ducked when she glared. "But I suppose we should leave before Miss Sylvan is once more overcome with desire."

"The desire to slap your face," Sylvan snapped.

"Again." He rubbed his still-stinging face. "We'll go."

They turned away from their regular route to the manor and moved instead toward the path along the cliffs toward the mill. Sylvan pushed and he strained to keep the wheelchair moving through the clumps of grass. One steep rise offered them a challenge, but with Gail's help they topped the hill and saw below them the mill.

The sea washed into a small harbor below it, and the hills ringed it, but the mill dominated its surroundings. A massive building of native stone with a slate roof, it rumbled with noise and belched black smoke from its coal-powered steam engine. A villager stood atop a ladder, whitewashing the walls, but he fought a losing battle. Cinders filled the air and covered the grass around the building, although they seemed of no concern to the women taking their dinner outside.

Rand fought his instinct to cower. These were the women Lord Rand Malkin had greeted at church, the women he'd provided for in rough winters, the women he'd teased as he made the traditional visit to their homes at Christmastide. He'd been the beneficent lord, and now he was confined to a wheelchair.

He didn't want to see their pity or know that they whispered behind his back.

Gail ran on ahead, shouting their names, but Sylvan touched his shoulder, giving him reassurance when there was no way she should know that he needed it.

When the women caught sight of him, they rose en masse and stared, and he closed his eyes for a moment, looking for courage inside himself. When he opened them, he saw a dozen beaming faces.

"Lord Rand, how good to see ye out." Loretta rushed forward. Big-boned, big-bellied, she was the spokeswoman for the village and knew Rand well. "We've had you in our prayers this last year."

While Loretta kissed his hand in hearty goodwill, Nanna from the farthest farm stood off to the side. Roz and Charity held Gail's hands as she jumped up and down and babbled, and Rebecca, Shirley, Susan, and all the other women he'd known and cared for crowded around him. They smiled shyly or openly, depending on their natures, and tried to kiss his hands or touch his shoulder. He blushed beneath the sincerity of their welcome, and wondered why he'd avoided them.

"We missed ye this last Christmas, Lord Rand,"

Shirley said. "We got our part of the ale and meat, but we had no one to flirt with us."

"Aye, made our husbands right uppity," Roz added.

"But ye brought yer husband back down, didn't ye, Roz?" Loretta stood with her hands on her hips, and Rand laughed when Roz blushed.

"Yes, she's a randy character," he agreed.

"'Tis a shame about yer legs, m'lord." Loretta broached the subject with no discomfiture. "But His Grace says yer nurse is the best to be had, and she'll take proper care of ye." Loretta took Sylvan's hand and kissed it, too. "And I'm sure ye will, miss. Ye have a kind face, as well as a beautiful one, and we know we can depend on ye to help our dear Lord Rand."

Now Sylvan blushed, and Rand liked that. Let her be embarrassed, too.

"I don't see Pert," he said.

"I'm here, sir." The tiny woman stepped forward.

The bruises around her eyes had faded to green and yellow, and she had a cut beside her mouth that looked sore. She'd lost two teeth since last he saw her, but she might have lost teeth from natural causes. She smiled timidly when he reached for her hand. "This ghost sports quite a wallop for a vaporous spirit."

Pert's eyes filled with tears, and she glanced over her shoulder as if she feared whoever stood behind her. "It wasn't even fully dark, but he was dressed all in black. It was my fault, I suppose, for being out so late, but His Grace paid me to stay and help, and I never thought someone would . . . would . . ."

Loretta wrapped her arm around Pert's heaving shoulders. "It's not your fault some misbegotten coward hit ye. Don't ye ever say so again."

Nowhere in Malkinhampsted could one find as timid

and self-effacing a woman as Pert, and someone had done this to her, Rand thought.

Some person. Some man. Some maniac.

"Lord Rand," Pert cried. "Ye're hurting me!"

Hastily, he released her hand and watched with horror as she rubbed the red marks he'd left with his too-tight grip. "I am sorry," he said. "My mind was wandering."

Pert tried to smile. "No harm done."

"No harm," he muttered.

"Ye're not to worry," Loretta said in her bossiest tone, still cuddling Pert. "We're not stupid, no matter what ye men think. We're not going out alone at night."

"That does relieve my mind," he answered. He couldn't see the mill, the women pressed in so closely, but he heard the door open.

Garth called, "Have you finished your dinners yet? We're behind, you know."

The women glanced at each other, then parted to let Garth see the objects of their attention. Garth smiled in delight and surprise, and striding forward, he called, "Rand! Thank God, you've come. I need you to help with these hussies." He frowned at them in mock displeasure. "They'll work for you when they won't for me."

"'Tis not our fault we're behind, Yer Grace," Loretta protested. "The machines still aren't running right. They're still breaking the threads all the time, and when we reach in to tie them, we're lucky if that instrument of the devil doesn't buck."

"I know it, Loretta." Garth gingerly patted her shoulder. "I'd swear there were gremlins in the cotton. Go in now, and we'll see if we can't make up time."

"Will we work late, Yer Grace?" Shirley asked.

"At least until the machines are working smooth." Grimacing in disgust, Garth offered, "I'll pay extra."

The women smiled and headed for the mill with hearty goodwill.

"Miss Sylvan." Garth wiped his hand on a greasy rag, then took her arm. "And Gail." He offered his other arm to the child, and she took it with a glowing smile. "How good to see you." Leading them toward the door, he said, "Allow me to show you my pride and joy."

"Hey!" Rand called from his wheelchair in the yard. "What about me?"

"Well, come on," Garth ordered. "Don't lag behind."

Sylvan broke away from Garth and, going back to Rand, gave him a shove to start him on his way. Pushing his way toward the door, Rand entered the mill without flinching.

Sylvan could not. Her father held a part interest in several clothing mills. She'd visited them before, and she hated the noise, heat, and odor. Women stood at their stations, placing the cotton on the machines, taking off the thread when it was ready, binding it together when it broke. It required little strength or intelligence, but the women of Malkinhampsted performed their work willingly, alternating tasks as another group stopped to eat their suppers.

Gail hung on Garth's arm, chatting with fiery excitement, and Garth watched her with such affection Sylvan's heart was touched. Maybe Garth was her father. The more Sylvan came to know Garth, the more she accepted the possibility that he might have indulged in a moment of frivolous passion in his youth and then gravely taken responsibility. He certainly enjoyed Gail and treated her as a father should, but was he doing so because James would not or Rand could not? Every time Sylvan thought she had settled the matter, something occurred to change her mind.

When Sylvan and Rand came up, Garth shushed Gail gently. "Let's show Miss Sylvan our mill."

"Oh, yes," Gail said enthusiastically. "It's a great plant. It's not in full operation yet. We can only spin the thread, but when we get the weaving machines set up, we'll make the finest cloth in the country and we'll help support the families of Malkinhampsted. A family like ours has a responsibility to its people, and this is the best way to fulfill it."

She recited the phrases as if she'd heard them many times, and Garth smoothed the hair out of her eyes. "I'm prejudiced, of course, but she's unusually clever, don't you think?"

"Very clever," Sylvan agreed, and thought surely Garth must be Gail's father.

Rand watched them with poignant melancholy. "You spoil the child."

"Who better?" Taking Sylvan's arm, Garth explained the process by which cotton was turned into thread and thread became cloth. As he spoke, Sylvan marveled at this duke who cared for that which he might easily leave for an overseer.

With tact and a stifled curiosity, she'd also sought Gail's mother, but without success. Yet that lack seemed unimportant. This family, these Malkins, showed more compassion for their people and their children than any noble family in England.

Gail broke in. "It's the Malkin family salvation. With this mill, we'll make enough money to support Clairmont Court forever. At the same time, it'll keep our people home and away from the cities."

Garth's face lit with enthusiasm. "Yes, the men can work the fields, and the women—"

A shriek pierced his complacency, and Garth shoved Gail against the wall. Sylvan looked wildly around. Rand yelled at the machine operators, and in the center of the

plant, a cluster of women raced to one of their own.
Loretta ripped at the spinning threads around Roz, whose
eyes bulged as she screamed. A patch of red appeared at
her feet, splattering her shoes, the floor, the threads.

Sylvan froze.

Not now. Please not now. No more blood. No more
pain. No more useless death and helpless terror. Please
not—

Sylvan jerked herself free of the horror and ran to
Roz.

Her hand had tangled in the spinning threads and the
flesh had been sliced to the bone. Blood spurted, and
Sylvan grabbed Roz's arm, applied pressure, and
wrapped the hand in her skirt. "Get me some place to sit
her down," Sylvan shouted.

Garth gently lifted Roz into his arms, and with Sylvan
still holding her arm, he started toward the corner of the
plant. They entered a small room with a desk spread with
papers, and he lowered Roz into a massive leather chair.

"Water," Sylvan said tersely, unwrapping the cut.
"And needle and thread." It looked bad, with shreds of
muscle and tendon showing.

"Will I lose my thumb?" Roz shook in massive
tremors. Her lips were blue and her skin turned chill and
moist.

"Your Grace, have you got a blanket and a place this
lady can rest while I fix her thumb?" Sylvan smiled at
Roz. "This looks like the hundreds of saber cuts I treated
after Waterloo."

"Ye can fix it?" Roz shivered as Garth threw a blanket over her shoulders.

"I'll do my best."

Garth swept the paperwork off his desk and helped
Roz onto it, and Sylvan went to work.

*   *   *

"Miss Sylvan!" Gail ran from Rand to Sylvan's side when Sylvan stepped out of Garth's office. "Will she be all right?"

Sylvan had never been around children much. She didn't know how to respond to them, but right now, the sight of Gail's fresh, bright face fed a need in her. Gail was whole, untouched, as far from the reek of death as it was possible to be. Reaching out with one trembling hand, she smoothed Gail's cheek. "She'll be fine."

"Is her hand going to work again? 'Cause she has eight children and her husband fell ill six months ago, and he wasn't ever worth much anyway. If Roz can't work here, I don't know what she'll do." Gail peered up at Sylvan. "But you fixed her, didn't you?"

The noise of the machines assaulted Sylvan. The air stifled her. Fragments of cotton floated like a blizzard of unwoven cloth. Windows on high illuminated the threads spinning in a constant, dizzying motion. "I did what I could. The rest is in God's hands." Looking at her own hands, her incompetent hands, she saw blood under the fingernails. It sickened her.

"But think of her children," Gail said. "You had to have made her better. You just had—"

"Gail." Garth stood beside Sylvan. "Don't nag."

Rand said, "I've arranged transport for Roz, and Loretta will ride with her and care for her tonight."

Garth nodded. "Good. I'll pay them both, of course."

"It's not your fault."

Rand spoke so gently, Sylvan thought he was speaking to her. But before she could reply, Garth said, "I know, but it seems this endeavor is plagued with accidents. Are we cursed by heaven?"

"More likely, we're cursed by inexperience," Rand said.

"I hired the best set-up men in England." Garth rubbed his eyes with his hands and left two oily rings.

"We'll get better," Rand assured him. "We're just too new to all of this, as are all our workers, and when we've been at it longer—"

"We." Garth stared at his brother. "Does that mean you're coming back to help?"

Rand looked around at the anxious women, the concerned machinists, and at his brother, worn with worry and struggle. He didn't say no, and he didn't commit either. Instead he promised, "I'll help while I can."

"Miss Sylvan." Gail pointed to Sylvan where she leaned against the wall. "You have blood all over your skirt."

Sylvan picked it up and stared at the fine lawn fabric. Crimson smeared the material with the weight and wet of the blood, and for some reason, that seemed more than she could bear. She glanced wildly at Garth and Gail and Rand, seeing them through a shifting red mist. She saw Rand's lips move, but heard only a buzzing.

Then the floor came up to meet her.

6

Leaning forward, Rand tucked the carriage blanket tighter around Sylvan's waist, then pushed Gail closer. "Cuddle up," he instructed. "Keep Miss Sylvan warm."

It wasn't really cold, only the chill of a spring evening by the ocean, but Sylvan cherished the heat of the child and the blanket, and it was only pride that made her object. "There's nothing wrong with me. It was just a reaction to the excitement. I've certainly seen worse wounds than that."

Rand ignored her, as he had each time she protested. Jasper had arrived with the closed traveling carriage that had been especially outfitted for Rand. The door had been widened, and the backward facing seat had been removed. Straps held Rand's wheelchair securely, and he seemed quite comfortable as he said, "We're almost back at Clairmont Court."

Sylvan glared at his shadowy figure in resentment. She hated to have anyone see her in distress, and she had been in distress back at the mill. That whole plant was an accident waiting to happen. In reality, it hadn't been the noise or the moving parts that made her ill, but the potential for injury that she saw existed at all times.

Since Waterloo, she had seen danger everywhere. She was like a mother whose child had just learned to walk, imagining the worst possible mishap in every instance—and she seemed to be mother to all the world. It made her sick to think of all the blood spilled without reason, because of war or carelessness.

But Rand offered solace. "Garth took Roz and Loretta home in one of the other carriages, and he'll stay until they're comfortable. The cook's sending a basket of food. Mother's sending blankets, and Loretta promised to do just what you said to treat Roz." She saw the flash of his teeth in the dark. "Loretta thinks you can work miracles, so she told me. Do as I'm told, she said, and you'll cure me, too."

Sylvan gave a laugh that sounded remarkably like a sob. She hadn't ever cured anyone. She'd just bandaged them and prayed, and usually they died anyway.

"So you can eat and go to bed. Everything's taken care of. No arguments, and no brooding over ghosts."

"Ghosts?" Her mind flew to the corpses she'd seen at Waterloo, to the once vibrant men who walked in her dreams. "How did you know about my ghosts?"

He hesitated, then said gently, "I wasn't talking about your ghosts, but about the ghost of Clairmont Court."

"Oh." She laughed shortly. "*That* ghost. No, it's not your ghost who frightens me. It's the madman who masquerades as the ghost and attacks the women." She broke off when Gail wiggled. "But I have great faith that he'll be caught soon." Infusing her voice with false cheer, she added, "Really."

"Are you afraid of the ghost, Miss Sylvan?"

"No!" Sylvan could have kicked Rand for opening the subject, and kicked herself for speaking on it. She wasn't used to having to watch her words, but Rand was. Didn't he worry about scaring the child? "Big girls aren't afraid of ghosts."

"There's a reasonable explanation for this nonsense about the ghost." Gail's voice took on strength and depth as if she quoted one of the adults. "We'll catch the ghost and we'll see an end to it."

The carriage jolted to a halt, and Sylvan almost didn't hear Rand murmur, "That's the truth. That'll be the end."

Jasper jumped down from his perch and flung the door back so vigorously, it shook the carriage. Sticking his ugly, worried face inside, he asked, "Mr. Rand, are ye still well?"

Servants stood up and down the terrace stairs with lanterns, which they protected against the ever-present breeze. "I'm fine," he said. "Help the ladies out."

"But, sir . . . Aye, sir."

He offered his hand to Gail, but she leaped out without help. When he grasped Sylvan, the tremor in his fingers shocked her.

"We heard all kinds of rumors about the accident and who was hurt." Jasper squeezed her hand a little too hard. "I couldn't stand it if anything happened to Mr. Rand while I wasn't hard by."

He reached in to help Rand free the chair from the restraining straps, leaving a shaken Sylvan standing on the steps.

Jasper was jealous.

She knew he didn't like her taking Rand out every

day, for every day he had given his help more grudgingly. But the sensation of menace he emanated startled her and left her staring at the servant's broad shoulders. Could he have been the ghost in the hallway?

No, surely not. Why would Jasper want to frighten her? What reason would he have for perpetrating this kind of hoax? Besides—she relaxed—he didn't look like Radolf. Once again, she was seeing danger where none existed.

A cry from the top of the stairs had her whirling, her heart in her throat.

"My son!" Lady Emmie rushed down, her hands outstretched. "Are you well?"

Sylvan closed her eyes and took a deep breath. Yes, she'd better calm herself before she surrendered to screaming hysterics.

"I'm fine." Rand suffered her hug. "Mother, I'm fine."

"Your mother was worried about you." Aunt Adela descended the stairs in a dignified manner, leaning on James's arm. "Convinced that you were hurt in the mill, she was. I told her that Malkins were tough and strong, but would she listen?" Rand passed her on the stairs, carried in the arms of Jasper and the footmen and accompanied by a softly babbling Lady Emmie. Aunt Adela began to ascend again. "No. She invariably frets about that mill. It's a constant worry to all of us, and a shame that you and your brother insist on continuing construction of a project which can mean only our ruin."

Sounding desperate, Rand interrupted. "Mother, it's Sylvan who's not well."

Lady Emmie stood at the top of the stairs and looked back. "Sylvan, dear, what's wrong?"

She started down, and Sylvan held up her hand. "A footman can help me up."

"Gail can help her up, too." Betty stood at the top of

the stairs, her hands wrapped in an apron so wrinkled she must have been wringing it. "You do it, Miss Gail."

Gail snapped to attention. "Yes, ma'am." She took one of Sylvan's arms and a footman took another, but Lady Emmie still bore down on her with Aunt Adela and James in her wake.

"You poor dear." Lady Emmie got a good look at Sylvan, and her eyes widened. "You've got blood on your dress. Were you hurt?"

"No, Lady Emmie." Sylvan negotiated the first few steps. "I only cared for the woman who *was* hurt."

"Thank heavens! I would hate to have to explain to your father you'd been injured in our service. You got a letter from him today, and so did I. Here, Gail dear, let me do it, you'll hurt your beautiful straight back helping Miss Sylvan." Lady Emmie nudged Gail out of the way and took Sylvan's arm.

"I got a letter from my father?" Sylvan could have groaned. "And he wrote you, too. Was he obnoxious?"

"He cares about your reputation a great deal. It's obvious from his missive."

That was no answer, and Sylvan knew it. She cringed at the demands her pushy father must have made on this lady.

"You got a letter from a doctor, too."

"Dr. Moreland?"

"I believe that was his name," Lady Emmie conceded. "I only glanced at the post. So rude to read other's letters."

"And one of my father's favorite pastimes."

Lady Emmie excused him as she helped Sylvan up the stairs. "Every parent has his own methods. Tell me if you feel faint, so I can catch you."

Sylvan looked down on the diminutive figure.

"I'm behind you, Miss Sylvan," Gail piped.

"I feel quite secure now," Sylvan answered.

"So dreadful that your illness occurred while you are our guest." Lady Emmie kept her arm wrapped around Sylvan's waist in what felt like a gesture of affection. "Of course, you're the nurse and you were probably right in the middle of this tragedy."

Aunt Adela did an abrupt about-face when they passed her, and she proclaimed, "I always said women weren't strong enough to handle the sight of blood and whatnot, but young persons nowadays don't listen."

"Adela, dear, that's not strictly true." Lady Emmie steered Sylvan to the top of the stairs and past Rand in his wheelchair. "Think of all the years when women were midwives and healers. You must admit women are stronger than men give us credit for."

Betty caught Gail to her in a powerful hug, then said, "If you don't have further need of me, Your Grace, I'll put Miss Gail to bed."

"Excellent." Lady Emmie broke away from Sylvan and planted a swift kiss on Gail's cheek. "Sleep well, child. You've been a brave girl today."

"Women nurses are scandalous! They are required to look upon"—Aunt Adela swooped in to take Lady Emmie's place at Sylvan's side, and lowered her voice— "men's parts. You know you agree with me."

"Mother!" James stopped beside Rand and glared, embarrassed by the direction of the conversation.

"Oh, I might have once, but that was before I met Miss Sylvan." Lady Emmie rushed up, ordered the footman away, and took Sylvan's now free arm. "She's such a lovely woman, so charming, with such exceptional manners. And so brave!"

"But there's something wrong with her now," Aunt Adela said triumphantly. Together, the women urged

Sylvan through the door and into the study. "So she must not be equal to the tasks."

"I'm fine." Sylvan felt like a hank of bone between two small, feisty dogs as they tugged her cloak off. "And I assure you, Lady Adela, that while I have seen men's parts, one doesn't notice them when blood is spurting."

"No," Aunt Adela said, "I suppose not."

"There you have it, Adela." Lady Emmie brought Sylvan a sherry. "Although I do think you're making light of your illness, Sylvan, or Rand wouldn't have brought it to our attention."

"Rand just likes having everyone concerned about someone else for a change." Sylvan sipped the sherry and sighed. The Malkins served very good sherry, and she treasured its restorative properties right now.

"Our Miss Sylvan seems fine." Aunt Adela poured two more sherries, handed one to Lady Emmie, and they both studied Sylvan. "When one thinks of the difficulties and . . . er . . . body effluents associated with childbirth, I think it's surprising that so many persons consider women unfit for nursing."

"We are the weaker sex," Lady Emmie said.

"But you can't leave these matters in a man's hands." Aunt Adela frowned at Rand and James as they entered the room, treating them as if they were personally responsible for the vagaries of the male gender. "Why, my dear husband, the late duke's brother, quailed when James scraped his knee, and I know your husband, the dear late duke, did the same."

"That's true, but Roger was happiest when he fought and drew blood. No, dear, I'm afraid women aren't fit to be nurses."

"Dear, they are."

Sylvan's head spun in confusion, and from the

expressions Rand and James wore, she thought they were experiencing the same sensation. But they, obviously, were used to it, for Rand diverted the ladies with one simple statement. "Miss Sylvan swooned."

The ladies paused in midquarrel.

"Garth caught her," Rand continued. "But I think she should be put to bed at once."

"When I'm ready," she snapped. He smirked, and she realized he really did like transferring the attention to someone else. It was a sign that he was healing, and she relaxed another degree.

"Dinner has been waiting," Lady Emmie said. "Miss Sylvan, would you prefer a light meal in your room, or would you join us as our guest of honor?"

With an invitation like that, Sylvan couldn't refuse, and a pleasant hour laden with food and wine passed before the family returned to the study to finish their gossip. Sylvan lagged behind, her gaze on the letters tossed on the table in the entry. She shouldn't read them now, she knew, but she worried what her father had said, so she slipped them into her pocket and carried them into the study where already a quarrel had developed.

Standing in front of the fireplace, Aunt Adela folded her hands across her stomach. "This is what comes of owning the mill."

Seating herself, Sylvan accepted a sherry and sneaked the letters out.

Rand sighed loudly. "Oh, Aunt Adela, we're not going to go through that again."

Sylvan first sighed as she juggled the missive from her father, then smiled as she clasped the missive from her mentor. Bad medicine first, she decided. With a guilty glance at her hosts, she broke the seal on her father's letter.

With lofty indignation, Aunt Adela said, "Why not? It's the truth, isn't it? I admit, I had my doubts about this young woman before she arrived, but she has proved to be a well-spoken, genteel lady. And what have we turned her into? A drudge who treats the village women with their ailments."

"It wasn't an ailment, it was an accident!" Rand protested.

Garth sneaked toward the doorway.

"There wouldn't have been an accident if there weren't a mill," Aunt Adela answered.

Garth backed out of the room.

"Come back here, young man." Aunt Adela chased into the hall after Garth.

Skimming the sprawling epistle, Sylvan wondered if her father simply recopied one letter, over and over.

She was a disappointment. He'd worked hard to make money so she could have everything she ever wanted. He'd bought a barony for himself to help her get into the ton with the expectation she would find a nobleman to wed. But no. She'd obstinately refused all offers. She'd ruined her best chance when Hibbert died, but living at Clairmont Court, she could get herself a duke. Stop dithering and nab him.

"We've discussed this before, and nothing has changed." Garth appeared with Aunt Adela dragging him by the arm. His rough appearance contrasted with the spotless room and its fashionable occupants. "Use all the excuses you like, but we all know you care only for the spoiled reputation of the duke of Clairmont."

Sylvan crumpled the letter in her hand, walked to the fire, and threw it in.

"Well, somebody has to," Aunt Adela said. "Obviously it's of no concern to you."

Sylvan wished she could toss her anger aside as easily. Slipping Dr. Moreland's letter in her pocket, she decided to save it for the morrow. It would be discourteous to read it amid the discussion swirling around her, and after her father's letter—she sipped her sherry—she had a bad taste in her mouth.

Going to the rack of bottles, Garth poured himself a brandy. "My reputation is my own."

"But it's not! Your reputation will taint us all. Trade!" Jumping into the fray, James said the word as if it were dirty. "The dukes of Clairmont have lived right here in this spot for five hundred years—"

"Four hundred," Rand interrupted.

"—And not one of them ever dirtied his hands with trade."

"I'd say it's about time someone did some work, then." Rand accepted a brandy from his brother, and their cut-glass goblets clinked as they touched.

"Oh, yes, you two will stick together. Always do." James's bitterness was palpable. "Don't appreciate that it's damned embarrassing when a fellow makes the rounds in London and some upstart merchant asks me how our enterprise is proceeding." His lip curled in disgust. "A merchant, daring to speak to me as if I were an equal."

"When of course you're not," Garth said.

That sounded like sarcasm to Sylvan, and apparently it sounded like sarcasm to Aunt Adela, too, for she swelled with indignation. "James is the most dutiful of cousins. Although he is in direct line for the dukedom, he begrudges you boys nothing. He wants only his position and his dignity."

"I have stripped him of neither," Garth said.

"For God's sake, you don't take me seriously," James

burst out. "No one ever takes me seriously, but I know my politics, and I have no patron. Just sponsor me—"

"Send you to Parliament so you can work against everything I believe in?" Garth laughed, short and ugly. "I think not."

Amazed, Sylvan stared at the duke she'd thought mild-mannered and tranquil. His serenity masked a powerful will, it seemed, and a determination to proceed on his own course whether or not it met with approval. What other secrets did his composure hide?

"Privileges of the aristocrats are daily being eroded by the middle class, and if something is not done, we'll all be serving tea to our butlers," James argued.

The spectators looked from one to the other with more than speculation. Sylvan thought these must be old quarrels, old wounds.

"So we should legislate our privileges rather than adjust to the times and earn them? It's a losing battle, James." It sounded as if Rand had mediated this conflict before. "Can't you see that?"

"Better to fight a losing battle than surrender without a shot."

"Oh, I'm not surrendering," Garth said. "I'm joining the enemy."

James flipped open his snuff box and took a healthy pinch. "You should be ashamed."

A paroxysm of sneezing muffled any further protest, but Aunt Adela took up the banner. "There's no use talking to him, James." She swallowed her sherry in one large, unladylike gulp. "His Grace revels in his disgrace."

Garth put his hand on one hip in exaggerated gentility. "Does this mean you'll be unsupportive when I start my drapery factory?"

"Tell me you're jesting," Aunt Adela said.

"Garth never jests, Mother." James took his mother's arm and led her toward the door. "We'll just go to our rooms now and practice threading a needle."

"My heart." Aunt Adela pressed one hand to her chest and let James lead her out. "My heart can't bear such demands."

Garth watched them with a crooked smile, then said, "I'm sorry you had to listen to that, Miss Sylvan."

Looking down at the residue of sherry in her glass, Sylvan was sorry, too. She hadn't realized the discontent that bubbled beneath the surface of this seemingly temperate family.

Garth continued, "But we fight about it every few months, and that will continue until they realize I'm not going to back down."

"Or until you sponsor James in Parliament," Rand said.

"I'll not pay to have my own cousin work against me," Garth roared.

"Then you're a damned fool," Rand roared back. "At least we'd have peace at Clairmont Court, and what could he do? One man could no more stop this revolution than he could halt the tides."

"James would work specifically against me."

"He wouldn't." The long-quiet Lady Emmie spoke up. "James is a nice boy with a good sense of family."

"He might be a nice boy, but he's a frustrated boy, too." Picking up the decanter, Garth poured himself a brandy, then took it to Rand and filled his glass. Sylvan held out her sherry glass, and after a sharp glance at her features, Garth poured it full, also. Holding it up, he asked, "Mother?"

Lady Emmie made a face, then reconsidered. "Maybe a little. There's no malice in James."

"He doesn't pull the wings off of flies, if that's what you mean," Garth said. "But he hates my mill, and he'd do anything—"

"Not anything," Lady Emmie insisted.

"*Anything* to destroy it." Garth laughed a little. "He actually worries about other people's opinions."

"One does that, Garth, if one is not the duke," Rand said with fine irony.

"You never did," Garth said.

"Of course I did. Why do you think I wouldn't go outside before Miss Sylvan forced me?"

"I never thought," Garth said.

"I wish you would, dear," Lady Emmie said. "I doubt even Sylvan could persuade Rand to return to London, and until James has a patron he'll not return. A frustrated man in the house is very difficult to live with."

"I'll consider it." Garth glanced at the doorway and said to someone out there, "Are you ready?" Apparently someone nodded, for he said, "Well, I'm off. Good night, all. Let's sleep on this and see what the morrow brings."

Lady Emmie stared after Garth, and Rand commanded, "Don't fret, Mother. You know there's no use worrying about Garth. He's strong-minded, and he'll do as he thinks best."

"I know." Lady Emmie hoisted herself to her feet as if she were exhausted. "I just wish I agreed with his assessment. Good night, dear." She kissed Rand's cheek. "Good night, Sylvan." She kissed Sylvan, too, and drifted out of the room.

Rand was amused to see Sylvan touch her cheek and look at her fingers as if she expected to see some residue of the kiss. "She's a lovely lady, isn't she?" he asked.

"You have a lovely family." Standing, she located the decanter and poured herself another brandy.

"After witnessing an outburst like that, you say I have a lovely family?"

She looked at him, and the expression in her eyes seemed as ancient as the hills. "My family fights, too." Taking a drink, she shook her head as if to clear it. "Our fights consisted of my father saying unspeakable things in a controlled voice, and my mother murmuring reassurances, giving up everything to make him happy." She chuckled bitterly. "And not succeeding."

"What about you?"

"Me? Oh, I'm stubborn and silent and disobedient as always."

"Funny." He rolled closer to the fire and she followed. "You've never mentioned your mother. I thought she was dead."

"She is. She's still breathing, but she doesn't dare talk, and she's never allowed to think."

"Sit down." He pointed to the chair opposite his, and she obediently slid into it. "Is that why you haven't married?"

Tipping the glass up, she took a drink. "The husband has all the power, the wife has none, and I'll never submit to that kind of tyranny."

"It's not all tyranny. My parents adored each other until the day Da died, and though you'd never suspect, Aunt Adela adored Uncle Thom, and he her."

She bit her lip and rolled the glass between her palms while watching the swells form on the brandy. "No marriage for me."

"Did Hibbert ask you to wed him?"

She smiled poignantly. "Hibbert was my dearest friend."

"So you said. But did he want you to marry him?"

"Yes." She looked at him, her eyes heavy lidded.

"And if I didn't marry that sweet man, you can wager no one else will persuade me to the altar."

Funny, Rand experienced intense gratification at having his curiosity allayed. Hibbert had been the best of men, the kind of fellow one liked in spite of his predilections, but Rand didn't want to think of Sylvan living with him—not in sin, and not in innocence.

"So you sacrificed your reputation for Hibbert."

Sylvan laughed, a tipsy laugh that ended in a hiccup. "Not really. I lost my reputation the moment I stepped into a hospital in Brussels."

Rand remembered the filthy sheets, the stench of blood, the unmoved corpses. It made him shudder even now to think he'd been there for a short time. "Then why did you do it?"

"I was searching for him."

"Hibbert?" Rand wrinkled his brow. He'd been unconscious or in a frenzy after the battle, trying to deal with his condition. Hibbert had died, he knew, but he remembered no other details. "Did you find him?"

"On the battlefield." She rubbed the glass on her forehead and shut her eyes against the tears that leaked out. "Quite dead. He'd been stripped of every valuable, including his teeth, which they tell me are selling as transplants for those fortunate to be alive yet unfortunate enough to be toothless."

"Sylvan." He stretched out his hand, but she ignored it.

"There were other women who searched the battlefield, too, but they searched for husbands or brothers, and they didn't succumb to the urge to help those still living."

His hand dropped back to his side. She didn't want his comfort right now. A combination of rage and sorrow squeezed the words from her, and she continued,

"The thing that I didn't understand—the thing I'll never understand—is how the noble ladies can hate me so much."

The candles guttered out, and Rand allowed his gaze to drift toward Sylvan's face. The firelight glimmered on her lips, moist with brandy, and she slurred her words. But she knew exactly what she was saying.

"Before I went to Brussels, the ladies gossiped about me. They put their fans before their faces and gossiped, then they came to me and made snide comments, and all the while I knew they envied me my freedom.

"Then I went to Brussels to dance and drink and create more scandal, and instead I became a nurse."

Her breath rasped into the glass as she lifted it to her mouth. "I found out what prejudice really was. I would speak to a lady whose son was alive because of me, and she'd give me the cut-direct. I'd try to tell her how to care for him, explain how to irrigate his wounds, and she'd turn her back on me. I saved her son. I saved his life, and that's what ruined my reputation. When all I did was dance and drink and act like a fool, I was exciting, fascinating, wicked! When I did something worthwhile, when I got blood on my hands and saved good English lads, I became a pariah. Where's the justice in that? I gave up my peace, and for what? God."

The glass fell from her hand and rolled across the stone hearth. She rested her head against the back of the chair. He saw her swallow, and his tenderness all but choked him. How had this beautiful woman come to such a pass? What could he do to help her?

"I have no friends, no family who cares about me."

"How can you say that? We care about you."

She continued on as if she hadn't heard. "I can't even sleep, and all for men who treat me like a tramp and for their mothers who don't trust me at all." She stumbled to her feet.

"Don't go away." Rand caught her hand before she could flee. "My mother thinks the sun rises in your smile, and the only other people she thinks that about are her children. James teases, and Gail worships you."

"Gail's a child." She peered at him searchingly. "What does she know?"

"Gail sees more than most adults," he answered gently. "Anyway, even Aunt Adela approves of you, and if Aunt Adela approves . . ." Carefully, he chose his next words. "You've won me over, too. Let me show you."

"How?"

"Come to bed with me."

She didn't stop to think. "No."

"We'd be good together," he urged.

"No."

"It's not because I'm crippled." It was a statement, not a question.

"Not that."

"Then what? I'd take care of you." He wanted to take care of her. "I'd make you happy."

"You don't understand, do you?" She jerked her hand free and glared at him as if she hated him. "I don't want to be your experiment. I don't want to be the woman you use to find out whether you still have your masculinity."

"That's not—"

"Oh, isn't it?" She stripped his pretensions from him with one scathing look. "Isn't it?"

She ran from the room and he cursed his own stupidity. Yes, he'd wanted to find out if he were still functioning properly, but there were any number of women around the estate who would be glad to help him establish that fact. In truth, he hadn't been interested until Sylvan

Miles came into his life, and if she were to leave, he'd be uninterested again.

But he knew better than to proposition a lady so bluntly. Women liked to be courted, flirted with, not offered a toss between the sheets as an anecdote to melancholy. In the morning, he'd—

The great outer door creaked open, then slammed.

That wasn't Sylvan, was it? She wasn't going outside, was she?

Wheeling himself to the window, he cursed as he saw her race down the steps. "Jasper!" he yelled. "Jasper, come here." When no one arrived, he picked up a gold candlestick and beat it against a table. God, had he chased Sylvan into danger with his eagerness?

He could barely see her now; she danced like a silvery shadow across the lawn. "Damn it, Jasper!" Rolling back, he grabbed an upholstered stool and threw it through the window.

It shattered in a glorious dissonance. The breeze blew into the room and he shouted, "Sylvan!"

A footman ran into the room, then another, and another, and the disheveled butler followed them all. "Lord Rand," Peterson said, gasping. "How can I serve you?"

"She's getting away!" Rand gestured to the window. He couldn't see her anymore. "Can't any of you dolts stop her?"

The footmen milled about like sheep, confused and bleating. Rand cursed them, then a half-dressed Garth ran into the room. "What's the matter, Rand?" Feeling the wind on his face, seeing the shattered glass, Garth roared, "I was in bed! I'm not in the mood for a scene."

"Sylvan's outside," Rand said. "You've got to go after her."

"Couldn't you have told us in some less dramatic way?" Garth demanded. "These broken windows are—"

Betty stepped into the room and took in the situation in one glance. Calm as always, she said, "Garth, this is important. There's a madman loose, and we don't want Miss Sylvan hurt."

"There's probably no danger." Rand failed to reassure even himself, and he said hoarsely, "Organize a search party. Bring her back."

Lady Emmie and Aunt Adela arrived in a flurry of Belgian lace and feather-light cotton, elbowing each other for first place through the door. Their outcry only added to the babble of voices as Garth organized the men and sent them out to comb the estate. Rand struggled to still his panic, but the men's drawn faces told him how seriously they took the rumors of ghost and attacker.

"I don't want to hear about the ghost frightening you," Garth told them severely. "You're grown men, and you know better than to believe that a ghost could attack a woman."

"Nay, Yer Grace," one of the men said, "we don't think the ghost attacked the women. We believe the ghost is warning us about a killer who stalks the night."

"He hasn't killed anybody yet," Garth said, "and you'd be wise to fear me more than some unknown assailant. I'm sending you out in groups of two. You'll be safe."

The wind howled through the shattered window as if to contradict him, and the men fell silent. Rand thought for a moment they would defy Garth, but then Peterson shrugged himself into his coat and said, "We've got to go after her. Can't have Miss Sylvan out in the dark all alone. She might hurt herself."

With little murmurs of agreement, the men drifted out to do their search.

"They like her," Rand said in amazement.

"They get tired of sweeping up window glass." Garth kicked at the glittering shards. "That's the first one you've broken since she came. Where's James?"

"Here." James strolled out of the shadows, still dressed in an appropriately frayed coat and hat, and wearing scuffed boots.

"You'll go with me," Garth commanded.

"I think not," James answered, plain and flat.

Garth collared him. "Dammit, James!"

"I'm the one who fought at Waterloo while you waited in safety at home," James said fiercely. "When it comes to battle experience, I'm miles ahead of you, Your Grace, so I suggest you unhand me."

"James." Aunt Adela sounded frightened.

"Garth, please." Lady Emmie had tears in her eyes.

Garth and James glared, eye to eye, until Rand drove his wheelchair into Garth's legs. "By Jove!" Garth released James with a jerk. "What do you think you are doing, Rand?"

"If you want to fight James, then do it. But do it after Sylvan's been found." Rand stared at Garth until Garth glanced away, then he turned to James and said, "Locate her for me. I depend on you. Bring her back."

James smiled, swift and angry. "I will, Rand. I will." He left without another glance at anyone.

Betty brought Garth his greatcoat and helped him into it. He looked embarrassed, sheepish. He shouldn't have alienated James, and he knew it. But his drawn face testified to his weariness, and Rand said, "We'll talk about it tomorrow."

Garth nodded, then he said to Betty, "You'll organize the men as they come back?"

She nodded, white-lipped. "I'll get them tea and

biscuits, but I won't let them stay until Miss Sylvan's found."

Coming to Rand, Garth put his hand on his shoulder. "Go to bed. We'll find her."

Rand's weariness struck at him bone deep.

"Go to bed," Garth repeated. "You really don't need to worry. Sylvan's a nurse. I'll wager she's stronger than any of us."

Rand thought about the things Sylvan had told him—her pain and anguish. He remembered the sadness that had been haunting her during her stay.

Then he thought about her search of the battlefield, her service in the hospitals, her strength in the face of social stigma. She was strong. No one knew how strong. She was the only woman he could depend on, the only woman who neither feared him nor feared for him. She'd left him on the cliff as a token of her confidence in his abilities.

Shouldn't he show the same confidence in her?

"Betty will help me to the sofa, but you must promise—"

Garth lifted his hand. "I swear Betty will come to you when Sylvan is found." He walked toward the door, then turned. "But what I want to know is—what madness made Miss Sylvan flee the house?"

"Not madness," Rand said. "Stupidity. *My* stupidity, and I'll never forgive myself if—"

"If she's the madman's next target?"

Rand rubbed his hands up and down his thighs. "She's got to be safe. She's got to be."

7

What stupidity had chased her from the warmth and light of Clairmont Court? The wind in Beechwood Hollow whipped Sylvan's skirt and raised goose bumps along her skin, but it offered no answer.

At least no answer that she wanted to hear. Perhaps she could blame the drink, or her fainting fit, or her frustration with Rand, but the truth was that her own stupidity had chased her out the door. She had no reason to resurrect the memories of Brussels, and she never should have told Rand. Most assuredly she shouldn't have been tempted by Rand's offer of solace in the comfort of his bed.

Sylvan stopped walking, took off her slipper, and shook a pebble free.

And what did she think a jaunt outdoors would solve? True, she loved the fresh air, the sound of the sea, and the sense of freedom. But she discovered that none of the three could light the darkness, and in the country, darkness reigned supreme.

Sylvan had, for the most part, grown up in London. Light glowed from windows, from carriages, even from gaslights on a few stretches of street. But out here, Sylvan could stand on the side of the hill, sweep the area with her gaze, and see nothing. Nothing except . . . what was that?

She tensed and stared at a light that bobbed along, then vanished. What *was* that? Did the ghost need a light for his jaunts around the country? Worse, did the light of spectral death shine from within him?

Or did the person who attacked Pert seek a new victim?

Ghosts frightened her, but even with the sighting on her first night, she didn't really believe in them.

She *did* believe in murderers.

With little, embarrassing whimpers, she started to run, fell over a stump, and skidded into a boulder. Head spinning, she slowly eased herself erect and searched herself for injury. She found it, too, when she poked her finger through the rip in her dress and touched her knee. Wincing, she explored the oozing patch of skin and wished this didn't remind her so much of her youthful exploits. After all, she was no longer a young hoyden trying to escape her father's domination, and she needed to stop acting like one.

Painfully, she stood erect and started limping in what she hoped was the direction of Clairmont Court.

It would have been better if she hadn't gotten lost. Conceited as she was, she thought she could find the paths she'd explored in the daytime. But it was so dark out here—wait! There was another light. She crouched as if that would shield her from the distant glow, but it vanished just as the previous one had. Vanished, she supposed, around some rock or over some hill.

Standing, she redoubled her efforts to get back to Clairmont Court, hoping that the downward grade was nothing more than a dip in the moist soil.

At Clairmont Court, the servants kept the fires stoked night and day, and a warmth permeated everywhere. When she got back, she'd call for warm water and ask Betty to help her get into bed. If only it weren't so dark out here.

The wind whispered fear into her ear. Or was it the wind? Did she hear a voice? "Good evening," she called, and her voice quavered. "Who's there?"

Only a rattle answered as gravel tumbled down a stony lip.

Small animals, she thought. Little, skittering beasts with sharp teeth and big eyes who peered at her but were totally harmless.

But if they were harmless, why did they need those sharp teeth?

The stony lip became such a sheer rise she walked while touching it with her hand, and the slope declined rapidly beneath her feet. She didn't ever remember coming this way, but Clairmont Court was this direction. Soon she'd be seeing lights, wouldn't she?

House lights, not those damned walking flames that she glimpsed again out of the corner of her eye.

The rocks that rattled off the cliff above her this time were bigger, and she jerked her guiding hand away from the smooth stone.

Small animals couldn't have caused this slide, and wolves had not roamed England for hundreds of years— so she'd been told.

She smeared her hands across her face. She couldn't lie to herself. It wasn't wolves or small animals or even an assailant she heard. Fear stalked her, not some lurking menace. Tonight, she was her own worst enemy, not knowing which direction to turn, and she wanted to go home. Groaning, she reached for the stone cliff again—and heard an answering groan of piteous distress.

Leaping back, she looked high where she thought the top of the cliff might be, and saw nothing. But she heard it. A muttering. A scuffle. An intimidating, wordless whisper.

The scrape of rock against rock.

She ran backward just as a boulder plummeted off the cliff right to the place where she had stood. She kept running when she heard the roar of rage—then she stepped off firm ground into midair.

Rand woke in his bed, totally bewildered. A candle burned on the stand. Wind howled around the windows. Night still pressed against the glass, yet he felt as if hours had passed since he lay on the sofa.

Sofa? He passed his hands over his eyes. When had he gone to bed? Who had put him to bed? Why was he still in his clothes from the previous day? And why was the outcry of men growing in intensity?

Sylvan, he thought, and yelled, "Sylvan!"

No one answered. Probably no one heard him. The tumult grew with every moment. "Jasper," he shouted, but Jasper didn't answer.

But Jasper had to be there, else how would Rand have gone from the sofa to the bed without waking?

A chill crawled down his spine, and he fought off that sense of anguish with a roar of fury. His door burst open at the sound, and James stood in the doorway with Sylvan in his arms.

She was covered in dirt like a confection rolled in

chocolate powder. Wrapped in James's cloak, she shivered pitiably, and Rand feared he saw bruises on the caked forehead.

"I'm not hurt." Her teeth chattered as she spoke. "I was very lucky."

James's expression belied her attempted cheerfulness. "She fell off the middle ledge near Beechwood Hollow."

"God!" Rand stretched out his arms and James brought her to him, presenting her as if she were Rand's possession. Cold seeped from her through Rand's shirt, and he wrapped her in a warming hug. "What's broken?"

"Nothing," she said quickly.

She didn't try to get away from him, Rand noted. Whatever had happened during her nocturnal wanderings had frightened her enough that she huddled close, tucking her head against his chest.

"Nothing that I could find," James answered. "But she was unconscious when I found her, although she revived almost immediately. She said she'd heard noises on the cliff above her and jumped back to avoid a rockfall."

Rand brushed at Sylvan's face, and as dirt and bits of grass fell away, he confirmed a bump on her forehead and a bruise on her cheek. He glared at James, furious at the desecration of her elfin beauty.

James patted his pockets until he found his snuff box. "Don't glare at me, Rand! I'm not the one who imagined a voice on the cliff." Flipping it open with his mutilated hand, he lifted a pinch to his nose and sneezed violently. Then, turning his head toward the hall, he announced with a distinct lack of pleasure, "His Grace has returned."

Garth had indeed returned. He charged into the room like a bull on the rampage, and with one look, took in the situation. "Miss Sylvan, you're safe." He heaved a sigh of relief. "Because of Loretta, I feared . . . well, let's save that for the morning."

Rand and James exchanged glances, and Sylvan stirred in Rand's arms.

"You're nothing but a big lug!" Betty spoke with open aspersion from the doorway. "You could have waited to say something as leading as that. Miss Sylvan, what are you doing in bed with Lord Rand?"

"I'm cold," Sylvan said.

Betty stared, her eyes narrowed in disapproval, until Rand said, "Oh, leave her. It's innocent enough. Half the family and all the staff are in here, and I'm surprised Mother and Aunt Adela haven't appeared."

Betty gestured toward two serving maids weighed down with trays, and directed them to place their burdens on the table. When they left, she took the flickering candle and lit more until the room glowed. "Your mother and aunt were asleep in the ladies' wing when I went to check on them. You behave yourself, Lord Rand, and I'll not get the urge to go wake them."

"I'll behave myself." Rand's promise was fervent and heartfelt. To Garth, he said, "Tell me what happened."

"We might not have found Sylvan, but we found Loretta."

"Loretta? Wasn't she staying with Nanna?" Sylvan struggled to sit up, and Rand held her tighter. Glaring at him, she whispered, "Unhand me."

"Later," he whispered back.

Garth reached for the first cup of tea Betty poured, but Betty sailed past him and gave it to Sylvan. This time Rand let Sylvan sit up—well, she couldn't drink that tea in a half-reclining position—but he didn't let her out of his lap. He wasn't likely to, either. "So, tell us about Loretta, Garth," Rand commanded.

"Are you sure?" Garth looked significantly at Sylvan. Betty said, "Tell them."

With an injured look at the housekeeper, Garth said, "Loretta stayed at Nanna's until Nanna was resting quietly and Nanna's older girl said she could handle things, then Loretta left to go home and check on her own family. Her husband doesn't like it when she's gone, you realize. We found her—"

Horror began its slow, familiar build inside of Rand. "Found?"

Disgruntled, Garth admitted, "Jasper found her crawling in the dirt, trying to get home. She has a broken arm and probably a broken hand from trying to protect her head."

Betty put the pot down with a rattle. James cursed, and Rand caught Sylvan's cup before tea slopped over the edge.

He couldn't believe he was hearing this. Not again. Not now.

"Blackguard hit her with some kind of rod. Marked her up horribly. Her face . . ." Garth pulled out a soiled handkerchief and wiped the sweat that started from his forehead. Then, with resolution, he said, "But Loretta's a tough old bird and she's already swearing she's not going to die from this."

"No." Rand took a shallow breath. "No deaths."

"I'll send a package over from the duchess," Betty said, half to herself, then lifted the teapot in her shaking hands.

"Mr. Donald was arriving just as I left, and Jasper guarded Loretta's bedside so closely I wondered . . . well." Garth kept his eye on the hot brown stream as Betty poured again. "Her husband ranted a bit until I spoke to him." Again he reached for the cup, but she stirred in sugar and presented it to James.

"By Jove," Garth protested, "ladies first, and all that, but I'm the duke."

Wrapping his fingers around the fine china cup to warm them, James smiled smugly. "*I* found Sylvan."

Sylvan. Rand looked at her, close in his arms, and found her looking back at him. Maybe he didn't deserve someone like Sylvan. Maybe he'd sinned too often and too well. But he wanted her in his life, and he'd take her now and make himself worthy of her later . . . if there was a later.

"Yes, well." Garth squirmed and glanced around. "You tracked dirt all the way from the front door."

He couldn't have been more ungracious, and Betty punched Garth in the arm. "That's a fine praise to give your cousin for tramping all over Clairmont Estate in the middle of the night. You're just jealous because you didn't find her with your well-made plans and your men and their lanterns." She poured tea. "Besides, you're none too clean yourself. There's dirt tracked from the front door more often than not, and everyone pretends ignorance when I complain."

She presented the cup to Rand with a flourish. Now he had to let go of Sylvan, but he did it unwillingly. This might be the last time he would touch her. The last time . . .

Sylvan settled on the pillow next to him and asked, "Who did it?"

Guilt brought Rand's mind back to Betty's complaint. "Who tracked dirt?"

Heads swiveled in his direction, and James had recovered enough of his good humor to say, "Don't be daft, man. She wants to know who attacked Loretta."

"You would not relish the knowledge." Garth took the last cup of tea in his rough hands.

Garth was right. Rand wouldn't relish the knowledge, but he feared he already knew. "The ghost?"

"Tall man, dark hair, but she couldn't see his face. Loretta didn't say it was the ghost. In fact, she even scoffed when one of the neighbors made mention of it." Staring into the cup, Garth seemed to have forgotten to drink. "The fact remains, everyone in the village thinks it's the ghost, come to avenge himself on me for operating the mill."

"The ghost," Rand repeated dully.

"Then he should attack you," Sylvan said to Garth.

"No." James finished his tea and returned the cup to Betty. "Whoever it is—assuming it's *not* a ghost—knows that the best way to attack Garth is to attack his people." At Sylvan's murmur of surprise, he shrugged. "We have our disagreements, Garth and I, but I'm not blind to his good points. He's just blind to mine."

"I know your good points," Garth said with irritation. "I just wish you'd apply them to doing your duty to me."

"Rather than to my country?" James shot back.

"You're not doing your country any favors by agitating for a return to the Dark Ages."

Before the timeworn quarrel could erupt again, Betty took Garth by the sleeve. "Your Grace undoubtedly wishes to freshen yourself."

"Dammit, woman!" Garth jerked himself loose. "You—" he paused and observed the expression on Betty's face, "are undoubtedly correct. I do want to . . . um . . ."

He started for the door, and Rand freed himself from his living nightmare: he had to know the location of everyone, especially—"Where's Jasper?"

"He's still at Loretta's." Garth started back in. "Do you need help?"

"God, no!" Rand couldn't have been more horrified.

And Garth couldn't have been more mortified. "I'm sorry. I thought you'd let me . . . ah . . . assist you."

Garth's distress shook Rand. He hadn't meant to hurt his brother. He hadn't meant to hurt anyone. "I don't want to rise right now. If I do, James will help me."

At the look on Garth's face, Rand cursed himself. He hadn't helped with his unthinking comment.

"James helped you after the battle, didn't he? Yes, I suppose he's better at it than . . ." Garth shuffled his feet. "By the way, James, excellent work finding Sylvan. Excellent."

If anything, James looked as embarrassed as Garth. "It was nothing. A mere bit of luck."

"Yes, well." Garth backed out of the room. "Congratulations."

The silence that followed his departure swallowed all words. Betty looked from the place where he had been standing to Sylvan seated on the bed, then picked up her tray. "Some men," she said to Sylvan, "don't understand that there's more to heroism than fighting a war or finding a lost soul." She bobbed a curtsy. "But thank you for finding Sylvan, Sir James."

She left, and James asked thoughtfully, "He really didn't like being left behind, did he?"

"Garth does his duty," Rand said. "And if that includes tending Clairmont Court while the rest of us go to war, he does it."

"He hasn't married," Sylvan said. "Isn't that a duke's duty? To produce heirs?"

"Oh, well." James thrust his hands into his pockets. "It never mattered—"

He paused, aghast, and Rand finished the sentence for him. "When I could walk. It was understood I would provide the heirs for the dukedom. Now Garth says he'll do his duty, but not until the mill is running. It *is* distasteful for him."

"Yes, a quandary," James agreed uncomfortably.

Shivering, Sylvan began to wiggle her feet under the covers.

In a flurry, Rand grabbed for her ankles. Catching them before they'd gone more than an inch, he pushed them away. "It isn't proper," he said, trying to wipe the startled expression from her face, but his remark obviously startled her more.

He was going to lose her. Already, he feared, she could see the insanity in him, but he wanted to divert her. Taking the comforter, he wrapped her feet in it. "Is that better?"

"Much better."

She still stared, trying to fathom his uneasiness, and he quickly turned the subject. "James, tell me how you found her." He knew James would be more than willing to tell his tale, and he knew Sylvan's attention would be caught.

"I was looking for Miss Sylvan," James said eagerly. "I'd watched you two as you wandered about, and thought Miss Sylvan might have gone to Beechwood Hollow and gotten lost on her return. So I walked down toward the Terraces, and I heard a rock tumble and a woman scream. I ran toward the ledges, calling, and another stone tumbled down."

"Didn't you hear him groan?" Sylvan demanded.

James shook his head. "I didn't hear anything but the ocean, the wind, and some animal mating in the dark."

Rand didn't believe James. He'd seen that look before when James knew something he didn't like and didn't want to admit.

But James's scorn infuriated Sylvan, and she said, "It wasn't an animal, mating or otherwise. It was a man, I tell you!"

"Anything's possible," James answered. "All I know is that I found you without interference from either the animal in ecstasy or the man in pain."

Rand laid a hand over Sylvan's when she would have snapped at him again, and she looked at him with open rebellion. But he nodded and smiled, letting her know that he believed her, and she tucked her mouth tight and scooted off the bed.

Did she suspect? Probably not. James and his doubts would have clouded her mind, and Rand was glad of that, at least.

"There's an answer to this puzzle, I have no doubt, but I can't decipher it until I have a clear mind. I'm going to sleep for what remains of the night. I'd suggest the same for both of you." She staggered a little as she walked toward James. Her voice sounded cold, but she took his hand politely. "Thank you for coming to my rescue. If not for you—"

"If not for me," James interrupted, "you wouldn't be here. You owe me your life."

"No modesty, James," Rand muttered.

Sylvan's smile wobbled as the memory of her alarm suddenly possessed her. "I fear that might be true."

Clucking her under the chin as if she were a child, James commanded, "Go to bed and dream sweet dreams. No one tried to kill you tonight. You were just foolish and female, and those two things march hand in hand always."

Stiffening again, she said, "I can't think where you got your reputation as a flatterer." She marched out without a backward glance.

James watched her with a droop to his fine mouth, and his fingers twitched.

"What did you really hear?" Rand asked.

James turned back. "I told you. The ocean, the wind, and an animal in heat. Nothing more."

"You wouldn't lie to a cripple, would you?"

"You wouldn't try to make me feel guilty, would you?" James countered.

Rand couldn't restrain his bitter amusement, and he laughed. James nodded, yawned, and said abruptly, "Need anything before I retire, coz? One hates to lose one's beauty sleep."

"Nothing," Rand said hoarsely. "Just go."

James stared at Rand's abrupt command, then shrugged. "G'night, then."

Rand waited until the ring of James's boots had faded, until he was sure everyone had left him completely alone. Then, moving with the slow anguish of an amputee about to view his mangled limbs for the first time, Rand pushed the covers away. Slowly, he leaned back and stared.

It would do him no good to curse the light that showed him the truth, nor cry to God for understanding. He'd tried it before.

He already knew nothing could erase the stain of mud from the white linen sheets, nor clean the dirt from between his toes, nor wipe the sin from his soul. The proof was there.

He'd been walking again.

8

But he wouldn't have tried to hurt Sylvan. He loved her.

Dammit. Rand buried his head in his hands. He loved her, and he'd tried to kill her. If that wasn't mad, he didn't know what was.

He'd come home from Waterloo furious, indignant at being bound to a wheelchair, and livid that he was even alive. One brief moment on the battlefield had saved his life and branded his soul, and he didn't know if he could ever forgive himself.

But he'd ignored his guilt. Put it aside and resolved to live a useful life as compensation for the deaths.

Then he'd woken one morning with dirt on his feet, a trail from the front door to his bed, and the rumors of a ghostly visitor floating the halls of Clairmont Court.

He hadn't believed it. It wasn't possible that he had walked at night when he couldn't during the day. He'd even tried to walk to prove it to himself, and he'd fallen on his face like the poor pitiful creature he was. So someone must have come at night and rubbed dirt on his feet and created a false trail. That was the only truth he would accept.

But he had a soldier's ability to sleep lightly. One developed that talent when one worked for Wellington, and he hadn't lost it in six short months. When no one arrived to disturb his constant nocturnal vigil, he became convinced he had been drugged. He ordered Jasper to taste all his food and drink before him, and slept only sparingly. He would catch the culprit by hook or by crook.

He hadn't. He'd just had another one of those dreams of walking, and woke once more to dirty sheets. He wanted it to be a nasty trick, a perverted joke, but he couldn't cozen himself again. His muscles ached from unaccustomed use. The soles of his feet had been cut by rocks. Worst of all, the ghost of the first duke had been sighted again, and by Betty, the woman he would trust with his life. When she'd told him about seeing the ghostly duke looking in her window, Rand had screamed at her in front of everyone—his mother, Aunt Adela, James, the Reverend Donald, timid little Clover Donald, and Garth, who'd been first amazed, then furious.

After that, his nocturnal wanderings became an irregular ritual that occurred without warning or reason. He came to think of his other self as the ghost, a wily creature who untied self-inflicted knots, avoided Garth's traps—and attacked women.

How could no one suspect? Dirty sheets, dirty feet, a trail of dirt, and his own increasing lack of control seemed to him to be unassailable signals to anyone who had eyes to see. He watched servants and family members alike for guilt or awareness or any betraying emotion, but while everyone wanted to lift his pain and share his grief, it became obvious nobody comprehended anything of his guilt.

The sort of guilt no decent man could live with.

Well. He knew what he had to do.

Her toes bumping the risers with every step, Sylvan walked up the stairs. She'd roused Bernadette, the sleepy-eyed maid, to ask her help in removing her clothing, but Sylvan fought a pounding headache and the sick feeling she should be doing something for someone. Her feet dragged across the polished wood floor. It was a familiar feeling, one she'd experienced frequently since Waterloo, but tonight all her instincts directed her back down the stairs.

Rand needed her.

But he didn't. He didn't need anyone right now. The predawn hour was meant for slumber, and like everyone else in the manor, he was going to go to sleep. As was she.

"Miss?" Bernadette held her sitting door open.

Determined, Sylvan walked in and watched as the maid laid out her nightgown.

Rand hadn't looked like a man who would calmly lie down and go to sleep. He'd worn the same expression the soldiers wore when they'd been mortally wounded and knew not how to die.

Or did he? Bernadette worked free the copper hooks of her gown while Sylvan covered her eyes with her hand and sighed. Was her imagination acting up again? Had the events of the day accelerated her predilection to see disaster at every corner? Had the lump on her head and the alcohol she'd consumed ruined her judgment?

Yes. She caught her gown as it slipped free of her shoulders and stared at the gilt curlicue molding on the picture frame.

There was nothing wrong with Rand, and even if there was, what could he do? The man was confined to his bed or his wheelchair. He couldn't just get up and walk away.

Walk away . . .

She jerked free of Bernadette's hands.

"Miss, you ripped your gown!"

Sylvan never noticed as she strode into the hallway. That was it. She'd seen something, heard something, that niggled at her. She didn't know what, or why, but she knew she had to find Rand before he . . . She broke into a run, fastening the top hook of her dress as she sped down the stairs. She might be too sensitive, but she was right to be concerned.

She reached Rand's room as the first rays of dawn lightened the sky, but Rand wasn't in residence. Instead, she saw a trail of dirt—surely not surprising, with Garth and James tramping in and out. But the trail led right to Rand's bed, and bits of grass hung from the hem on the sheets. Carefully, she folded the blankets back and stared.

There it was. The muddy stain.

She stared at it as a ripple of anguish grew into a whirlpool. All this time, she'd been infatuated with Rand: with his magnificent body, his incisive mind, his sharp tongue. Yet at the same time, a tiny part of her despised him. Why hadn't he mastered his emotions? Why hadn't he conquered his natural woe at being confined to a wheelchair, and why hadn't he comforted his mother and aunt, assisted his brother with the mill, and helped his cousin achieve his dreams?

Before her lay the reason.

Sometimes, he walked. Sometimes, he wandered the halls of Clairmont Court, scaring the housemaids and foolish new nurses. Sometimes, he wandered outside and tracked mud onto Betty's floors.

And sometimes, women were attacked when he walked.

Sleepwalking. What a dreadful, wonderful way for Rand's mind to rehabilitate his body. What an absolutely revolting hoax was being perpetrated with his unknowing assistance.

No wonder Rand threw chairs and tantrums.

No wonder her infatuation had blossomed into something resembling love.

No! She jumped back from the bed as if it threatened her. It wasn't love, only a great lump of contrition and desire that clogged her throat and brought tears to her eyes.

She didn't love. She wouldn't love.

Carefully she covered the evidence with the blankets and rushed into the dim hallway. "Rand," she called. "Rand!"

No one answered. Where had he gone? *How* had he gone? "Rand!"

In the brightly lit dining room, she found Cole, the very young footman, struggling to pull on his formal coat. "Miss? Might I assist you?"

"Where's Lord Rand?" She grabbed him before he had thrust both his arms into the sleeves. "Have you seen him?" The gangly youth flushed red. She'd seen the reaction before; a person made so uncomfortable by another's handicap that he could scarcely speak. But she had no time to soothe his sensibilities. "Did you hurt him?"

"Hurt him?" He looked down at her hands. They clasped the ends of his cravat and threatened to pull the knot so tight it would cut off his breath. "I had to help him."

She managed to whisper, "Explain yourself."

"He was crawling."

"Crawling?"

He couldn't look her in the eye, and his prominent Adam's apple rolled as he swallowed. "More like dragging himself down the hall from his bedroom."

"Not walking?" she insisted, wanting to be perfectly clear.

"He can't walk, miss." Young Cole looked indignant. "Did ye think he was bluffing us?"

"No." No, she thought he was walking in his sleep. "Where was his chair?"

"In the study." He pointed as if she might not know where the study was located. "So I brought the . . . er . . . the . . ."

"Wheelchair," she snapped. "It's called a wheelchair."

"Aye, ma'am." Bobbing his head, he seemed intent on assuring her he knew the name. "A wheelchair. His wheelchair. I brought it to him and I had to . . . ah . . . pick him . . . ah . . . he couldn't . . ." He caught sight of her impending eruption and finished hastily. "I picked him up and put him in the chair and got the other fellows out of bed to help me carry him down the stairs. We're not supposed to be awake at this hour, but— "

She choked. "What stairs?"

"Out . . . er . . . out . . . er . . ."

"Outside?" She couldn't wait long enough to hear his answer. Running to the outside door, she struggled to open it, but the young footman understood his physical duties better than his vocal ones. He nudged her aside and unbolted the locks.

"Why did you let Rand out?" she asked, appalled.

"He wanted to go out."

"And you let him? No"—she held out one hand—"never mind. Of course you let him. But why lock the door behind him?"

"He couldn't come back up the stairs without help, and there's the ghost to worry about," Cole explained as if she were the dense one.

She wanted to ask what protection a lock would be against a ghost, but he got the door unlocked before she could vent her exasperation, and she dashed onto the terrace. The east was rapidly brightening. The nocturnal animals had ended their forays and the morning animals had not yet begun their activities. Nothing moved. Nothing made a sound. Rand was nowhere in sight, but she couldn't see far. "Where would he go?" she muttered.

"Miss?" Cole sounded uncertain.

She scanned the area one more time.

"Miss!" Cole said urgently. "I have to tell ye, I've seen Lord Rand knock out windows and scream like a babe, but I've never seen him so . . . ah . . ."

"Tell me!"

"Grim. Resolved." He squirmed. "He asked my *forgiveness*."

"Your forgiveness?" A shudder ran through her. "Oh, Rand, what do you propose to do?" Running down the stairs, she hurried along the rutted path to the place on the cliff where they had gone the first day.

She remembered Garth's assurances to her. Garth thought that Rand wouldn't hurt himself, that Rand was too brave, too strong, too honorable. But Garth hadn't realized the depth of Rand's despair and self-loathing.

Rand believed he suffered fits during which he rose to stalk and ambush the village women.

The very attributes that made Garth certain his

brother would never take the coward's way out made it imperative Rand do so, and those attributes made Sylvan sure he was not guilty.

Reaching the top of the cliff, she saw no sign of Rand. The waves tumbled below and her heart sank. "Rand," she whispered. "Please, wait for me. Don't . . ." Headed toward the edge, she skidded down the first rise and stopped. Had he been here and propelled himself off the cliff? A swift examination of the ground and the memory of his terror that first day decided her. This wasn't the place.

The breeze off the sea stirred her mind, but she didn't know whether to believe what it whispered. Would he have gone to Beechwood Hollow? It was farther away, more difficult to reach, but perhaps the fondness he felt for the place would ease the bitterness of what he saw as his obligation—the termination of his life.

Swiftly she retraced her steps to the place where the path forked toward Beechwood Hollow. Her sides ached. She gasped for breath. The sun began to do its duty. Every moment brought more light to her surroundings. Puffing up the last gentle rise to the hollow, she espied them—wheel tracks in the damp grass.

He *had* come this way. But how long ago?

Redoubling her efforts, she topped the hill. There he was. His wheelchair perched on the highest point above the draw that led to the ocean. Turned sideways from her, he looked out at the horizon as if he could see eternity there.

She feared he could.

She shouted, but the same breeze that blew his hair away from his face blew her voice into nothingness. He put his hands on the wheels. She screamed and waved her arms. He gave himself a push. She sprinted down the hill.

His chair careened forward. Leaning into it, he concentrated, controlling his downhill ride as if it were a sport and he the master. Panting, Sylvan dashed to intercept him. Clumps of grass flew back under the force of his wheels as he neared the drop-off. He shouted his determination, and the sound moved her to a greater effort. She sprang at him just as he realized she was there. He jerked himself sideways; she hit the chair with all the force of her body. He flew out of his seat, and they hit the ground hard.

Everything stopped.

All sound—the creak of the wheelchair, the pounding of her feet, his laughter, her panting, the whistle of the wind—stopped. His reckless plummet, her mad dash, ended with the taste of grass and the slap of dirt. Opening her eyes, she saw a blur of green and brown under her cheek. Beneath her, she felt the rise of Rand's chest beneath his white shirt as he tried to get air. Was he hurt? Had she injured him in her rush to save him?

She pushed herself up by her hands, but something slammed her back onto his body.

His arm. It cut across her back like a steel blade. "Damn you, Sylvan Miles." His voice rasped with agony and fury. "Do you know what you've done?"

"Yes." She tried to crawl forward, but he wouldn't let her. Then she tried to crawl backward, and that he permitted. She moved until they were face-to-face. Fury narrowed his eyes, and he pressed his lips into a thin line as she reiterated, "Yes. I know what I've done. I've saved a good man's life."

"Not a good man's life. *My* life."

She hated it, that he should so doubt his own value, and she blurted, "You're not doing it."

His chest began to rise and fall with large breaths beneath her. "Doing what?"

"Assaulting those women."

The pupils of his eyes widened, swallowing the blue of his iris. His hand slid around to her throat and he circled it with his fingers. "How could I assault any woman from a wheelchair?"

She swallowed and felt the pressure of his grip, but it was too late to back down now. "You're walking in your sleep."

Anguish, horror, and fury followed in quick succession on his face. "Who told you that?"

"No one. I realized it by myself."

"Did you see me?"

"No, but I saw the dirt in your bed."

The hand at her throat shook. "And how many people did you tell?"

She almost answered, then rage gusted through her. "What kind of woman do you think I am?"

"Just like every other woman in the world." He caught her jaw in his grip. "Loose-lipped and fast-tongued."

Pointing toward the edge of the cliff, she said, "I just saved your miserable life."

"For what?" He pulled his hand away as if he couldn't stand to touch her. "To have me committed to Bedlam?"

"No! Because you're not crazy, just . . ." She didn't know just what he was. She didn't understand what was happening to him, but she'd never met anyone so sane. She thought that somehow, his nocturnal wanderings were part of his healing, but how could she say so with any assurance? She, who was so ignorant that men had died under her care.

Rapidly, she said, "I don't know why or how you're walking at night, but I know you didn't attack those women."

"Why do you know that?" he asked scornfully.

"Because I want to do this." Driven to desperation, she mashed her mouth on his briefly, then lifted her head. "Would I kiss you if I feared you would hurt me? Would I make myself vulnerable to you?"

Impatiently, he caught the back of her neck. "Perhaps you're as crazy as I am."

"Perhaps I am, but it was midnight when I saw the ghost walk."

"What?" His fingers spasmed.

She winced and he let her go as if she burned him. "On the first night I was here, I saw the ghost. Remember? But it wasn't a ghost, it was you, I know that now. You were in the halls, and I saw you. God, I'll never forget." Closing her eyes, she raised the vision in her mind. "You wore a white gown—your nightgown. The man who attacked Pert was dressed in black."

"How do you know that?" he demanded.

Her eyes popped open. "She told us that day at the mill."

He hesitated as if tempted to believe, then shook his head. "That scarcely proves my innocence."

"Did you wake with dirt on your feet the next morning?"

"No, but my legs ached as they always do when I walk." He shifted again as if he were uncomfortable, but when she tried to remove herself from on top of him, he stopped her.

So he wanted to keep her perched over him. Loosening his grip on life had not been easy for Rand Malkin, and she vowed to place it in his grasp once more. "You walked, but you never left the house."

"How do you know that?" He sneered, but clearly, hope began to stir in him.

"Because Pert said it wasn't yet fully dark when she

was attacked." He would have objected, but she leaned forward and pressed her finger to his lips. "And that evening, you will recall, you summoned me to remove a splinter from your hand. It was almost eleven o'clock before I left you that night, and I saw you walking in the hall as the clock struck twelve." He frowned, thinking, calculating, and she insisted, "I was with you until the darkness was full, and when I saw you again, you had had no time to go out, assault a woman, and return."

Beneath her, he began to tremble. He didn't yet believe it, but she could see he wanted to. Clearly, she said, "Someone had seen you, realized your vulnerability, and for some reason sought to convince you you're both insane and brutal. But it's not you who's insane and brutal. It was never you." Clasping her hand to his shoulders, she pleaded with him. "Oh, please, can't you believe? For if you were to throw yourself off a cliff—"

"If I were to throw myself off a cliff, I would never be able to give you the reward you so richly deserve."

She leaned back with a sigh. "You do believe."

His grin was barbaric. "I do." If he could, she knew, he would run and jump and shout his jubilation. Instead he was earthbound, and restlessly he sought another way to celebrate. His hands roamed her arms, her back, then cupped her face. Firmly he brought her back to him and kissed her, first on each cheek, then on the nose, then on the lips. "You've saved my life," he whispered. "Now I'm yours forever."

She chuckled, weak and too relieved for words, and he took advantage of her frailty. With murmurs and urgings, he coaxed her to open her lips to him, and when she did his tongue created sensations made of texture and taste. Outside her, the ocean swept the world with its currents. Inside her, Rand swept her responses with his expertise. She breathed with him, moaned with him, ached with him. How could he do so much with a touch? How could she feel so much and want more?

Perhaps she shouldn't want, but a tide of thankfulness rose inexorably in her. He was safe. She had done that. She *had* saved a life—his life. She had proved herself worthy of love, and she wanted to share her exultation with someone. With Rand.

Then something slithered around her neck. Cool morning air slipped in close, and when she sat up, she realized why. The neck of her dress gaped and one shoulder peeked out. He'd unhooked her while he kissed, and she grabbed at the material.

He watched her with eyes that shone with admiration. "Just let me see."

Nervously, she licked her lips.

"If you're really not afraid of me, let me see."

She recognized his stratagem. He was using her compassion to manipulate her, to whip up the fire within him. But his self-destructive flame had been swallowed by passion's conflagration, and passion was for those who survived.

She had dreamed of this. Perhaps she would never have allowed herself the pleasure if not for the circumstances, but now, one by one, with fingers that fumbled, she slid her sleeves over her arms.

His gaze lingered on her breasts, still hidden by a sheer cotton chemise. Slowly, very slowly, he reached out with his fingers. She had the chance to retreat. Indeed, a lingering sense of modesty urged her to. But some of his misery had been replaced with anticipation, so she let him pet the highest point. "Immodest women wear no chemise," he said.

"I shall make a note of that." She watched as he

traced the dark circle of her aureole. Immodest surely must describe her, for as the sun came up, she sat in the middle of a glen and let a man touch her, and she enjoyed it. He urged her back down on top of him and she resisted—not because she feared him, but because she wanted him to stroke her some more. Then he lifted his head and caught her still-covered nipple into his mouth. He sucked, drawing all the stiffness, all the restraint, all the propriety from her and leaving only a wild tumble of sensation. Pleasure sped from that one tiny point to her curling toes, to the tips of her fingers, to a place deep inside her.

She collapsed on top of him, sure that *this* assuredly must promote her from immodest to wanton.

"Let me see," he urged again.

She complied quickly, lowering her chemise to her waist. She didn't want him to change his mind, but from the glow on his face, she suspected he had no such intention.

Hoarsely, he said, "I wondered what they would look like. I've peeked from the top and maneuvered you so the sun shone on those fine thin dresses you wear and the wind pressed the cloth against every ripple, but nothing could prepare me for this." Cupping them, he murmured, "Beautiful." Pulling her back to his mouth, he suckled on one, and sensation washed over her. Little moans escaped her, when she shivered, and he chuckled. "And tasty."

She suffered a pang of chagrin.

"What?" he asked.

"Are you laughing at me?"

"Am *I* laughing at *you*?" He chuckled again but with less humor this time. "I'm flat on my back, clad in yesterday's garb, incapable of moving, relying on an exquisite girl to ravish me, for I can't seduce her. I can't hold her, sweep her along with my passion, give her the benefit of my years of practice—practice for just this moment, may I add. Am I laughing at you?" He shook his head. "No, I'm waiting for you to dance away, sniggering at the man who dared dream of loving you."

Tears sprang to her eyes at his vulnerability. "We're a pair, aren't we?"

The rage of their passion faded, replaced by tenderness. The caress of his arms across her bare back made her twist and sigh.

"Even if you dance away," he whispered, "I will still be grateful. You've given me hope and a chance to start anew." The caress of his hands strengthened, and he shifted her until she matched him chest and hip. "But if you stay, little elf, I'll show you magic of my own."

The sun cast his face in rugged peaks and valleys, and she daringly touched the hollow of his cheek with one finger. "If you want me, I'll stay."

He rewarded her with a smile of considerable charm. "A touch from your finger means more to me than all the rapture the world has to offer."

"Then why are your hands sliding under my skirt?"

"I want to give you just as much rapture."

She recognized balderdash when she heard it. "Someone warned me about men like you."

"Your mother?"

"No." She moved under his urging until her knees wrapped around his hips. "Hibbert."

He chuckled. Then she adjusted herself, and he groaned. "God rest Hibbert, he kept you safe for me." He rubbed her back until the position seemed less awkward and she relaxed.

Then he tried to push her to sit up, and she buried her head in his shoulder. "It's not very elegant, is it?"

Beneath her, she felt him struggle against his laughter, and she turned her head and stared indignantly.

"*It*? Are we going to call it, 'it'?"

"What else would you suggest?"

"How about—" She covered his mouth with her hand, but he bit her palm lightly. "That's not what I was going to say," he reproved. "If you know that word, you've associated with too many soldiers. I was going to call it 'a delight fit for the gods.' Or perhaps, 'the most magnificent experience of my life.'"

She couldn't help but ask suspiciously, "When did you learn to be charming?"

"Long before I learned to be surly." He traced the curve of her lips with his fingertip. "As for elegance—*it's* not. *It's* sweaty and noisy and I'll make *it* so good for you, you won't care. Sit up, darling, and feel me against you."

Walking her hands down his chest toward his stomach, she did as he instructed. He was there, full, hard, extended, under her pelvis. She pressed herself to him, and he closed his eyes as if he were in pain. "Am I hurting you?" She tried to lift off.

Grabbing her, he held her in place. "Exquisite agony." The dark ruffles of his eyelashes rested against his cheeks, incongruously feminine on the starkly masculine face.

Sylvan wanted him always to look this way—wanting yet satisfied, desperate yet contented. Nature herself incited Sylvan to bravery. Seabirds rose from their nests and called encouragement, demonstrating promiscuity in their freewheeling flight. The scent of damp grass and fertile earth rose, a gift to the sun as it touched them.

She touched Rand all along his length, warming him as if she were the sun. His eyes sprang open and he stared at her, then he said, "You puzzle me. You're all bold, then all shy. But here." He shifted her up. "Let me solve the puzzle."

His fingers found the slit in her drawers and he touched her until she squealed and jumped back.

He caught her swiftly. "Don't you know how this works?" he asked.

"Yes." She did. She just hadn't expected it to be so . . . intimate. She knew where to find paradise, but it was discerning to realize he knew, also. And so expeditiously. Were all women built in a similar manner?

He answered the question before she could ask it. "Not all women are so sensitive—or so bashful." His forehead wrinkled as he thought. "Perhaps it would be better if I just looked first."

"No!" Looked? "Never."

He meditated more. "Would you be more comfortable if I tasted you first?"

"No!"

"I tasted your breasts, and you liked it."

"It's not the same." She struggled to explain, but his slight smile blocked her. "You're teasing me."

"Try me and see."

He'd do it, too. He might find her discomfiture amusing, but she didn't have a doubt that this wicked man would love to look, taste, and touch in any manner and for as long as he could. And she'd enjoy it, too, because he promised she would.

He pouted, trying to look like an injured boy while his body proclaimed him the rogue stallion. "Let me touch you," he coaxed.

When presented with the alternatives, she nodded.

She'd given permission, and his impertinent fingers took full advantage. "I like this," he said. "We'll have to come here often and—"

"No, we won't."

"I'll convince you."

He sounded very sure of himself, and she supposed he was correct. Right now, he could convince her of anything, and without saying a word. He dabbed at her delicately. Smidgens of enchantment, strokes of genius. Everything throbbed with the rhythm of her heart, and what had started as too much soon became not enough.

She must appear positively lustful, with her chemise and bodice bunched at her waist and her skirt pulled up to meet them, and her drawers pulled open while she straddled a man. A man with one arm bent under his head. A man who looked young, delighted, relaxed.

That was worth the sacrifice . . . if she could call it a sacrifice.

His fingers searched and pressed, and a moan whispered out of her.

He chuckled. "That sound means I'm doing *it* right. That means you like this. You *do* like this. Don't you?"

If what he said was true, he already knew the answer, but he asked again.

"Don't you?"

What difference would the word make?

"Don't you?"

His hand dropped away, and she said, "Yes!"

"I wouldn't want it said I forced you."

The movements of his fingers ravished her beyond caring. Her nipples tightened, her fingers and toes clenched, she tossed her head back and looked at the sky. She'd never come so close to flying.

"A little more, dear. A little higher." His every guidance had steered her along the path to paradise.

"Relax. Give yourself up to it."

The wind blew across her skin, the sun caressed her

with its brightest morning rays, and she concentrated on getting higher, relaxing, giving herself up to it—whatever *it* was.

Then it caught her in a spasm, lifted her, proved Rand's skill while pushing her to new limits. She hung onto him as if he could keep her on the ground when in fact he pushed her ever upward.

She loved it. She reveled in it. She wanted more and more, seeking it with greed and appetite, and he used his skill to give her all she demanded, and more.

Then it faded. Slowly, the pulsation eased, and she again became aware of the sun, the sea, the air. . . .

Taking a breath—surely her first breath since Rand had kissed her breasts—she tried to remember her customary demeanor. For some reason, she longed to look normal, as if she found ecstasy every day.

Rand wanted none of that. He reached for her, murmuring, "Come here." Catching her arms, he brought her back down to him, pressing her head onto his chest. She could hear his heart thundering, although she couldn't comprehend why. He hadn't experienced what she had. Yet he smirked and she wanted to ask him, as soon as she got her voice back, why he acted so satisfied.

But the screech of a raucous bird interrupted her before she could speak, and Rand said, "Damn!" He roughly tumbled her off of him on the far side, and when she tried to crane her neck to see around him he said, "Get down!"

Down? She was down, ripped from the cushion of pleasure and tossed into a sea of humiliation. "Rand?"

"Get dressed," he ordered tersely, looking away from her.

She struggled against tears even as she struggled to pull her chemise over her shoulders and her skirt over her legs. Hearing the raucous screech again, she stopped and listened. That bird had words mixed with its fury. It sounded like outrage.

Then she realized how Rand scooted, trying to shield her. Someone had caught them. Someone . . . no, faces loomed over them. Garth, duke of Clairmont. Jasper. And the Reverend Donald.

9

"In the fields?" Garth stood on the hearth in the sitting room and waved his walking cane as if he were conducting an orchestra. "You mated in the fields? Rand, have you gone mad?"

Rand winced at Garth's apt accusation. He *had* gone mad. Mad for Sylvan. What had started out as a suicide dash into the ocean became instead an exquisite experiment in love. The vicar's silent stalking fury, Garth's loud exasperation, Jasper's embarrassed assistance, scarcely existed when compared to his own disgruntled disappointment. Leaning close to Sylvan, he muttered, "One more hour. What I could have done with one more hour."

"An hour?" He'd wrapped her in his white shirt to cover her, and she hadn't been willing to give it up, even when they brought him a new shirt and tried to clothe her in a more feminine garb. Now she gave up trying to roll the cuffs, and stared at him incredulously. "An hour?"

He considered. "Maybe more. I've always like to linger over *it*, but *it* might take more time now."

"Sh!" She lowered her head beneath the vicar's glower. "They'll hear you."

Garth couldn't have determined their words, but his glare made it clear he didn't appreciate Rand's sly amusement. He raised his voice and pointed at Jasper, who lingered in the hallway. "Jasper was frantic with worry when he arrived home and you weren't in your bed. He roused me yet *again*—"

"That's why Garth's so grumpy." Rand jockeyed his slightly battered wheelchair closer to the stool where Sylvan sat. She looked as woebegone as a waif, and he wanted—needed—to shield her from the concentrated disapproval of his family. "He needs his sleep."

"—and we went careening across the countryside searching for you."

Lady Emmie and Aunt Adela had been pacing the terrace when they came into view. Clover Donald had been lurking in the shadows. The Reverend Donald had quickly apprised the women of the situation. His mother had been shocked and indignant. His aunt had been shocked and righteous. Clover Donald had whimpered. And poor Sylvan had been at the center of their disapproval.

Garth said, "If I hadn't remembered that James said you liked to visit Beechwood Hollow, we'd be out searching still!"

"At least you wouldn't have interrupted us."

Rand hadn't spoken loudly, but Garth must have read his lips, for he exploded in a frenzy. "You're not taking this seriously. We found you and Miss Sylvan—"

"In flagrante delicto?" James strolled into the room in his dressing gown.

Seeing Sylvan flinch, Rand began, "We weren't exactly—"

"A man can't sleep in this house without missing the most entertaining predicaments," James said.

"Shut up, James." Garth's voice gained volume. "Rand, she's covered with bruises."

"I fell off a cliff," Sylvan said.

Garth didn't listen, didn't care, or just didn't have faith in her rationalization. "How could you force yourself on a woman like that?"

Sylvan whispered, "He didn't exactly—"

"Of course he didn't." Aunt Adela clutched a handful of cloth over her bosom as she paced from the fireplace to the door. "This is all your fault, Garth, and I hope in the future you will listen to me when I clarify the proprieties. Miss Sylvan enticed the poor boy. *This* is the reward we get for embracing a viper."

Rand snapped, "She's not—"

"She's not a viper." Sitting on the sofa, Lady Emmie wrung her lace handkerchief. "She's a misguided girl and Rand has taken advantage of her."

"Then why does *he* have bruises?" Aunt Adela demanded.

Sylvan and Rand exchanged embarrassed glances, and Sylvan had no explanation to offer this time. Bruises covered them both, the result of Sylvan's flying tackle at Rand's wheelchair.

"If she only knew," Rand said sotto voce.

"And how could he take advantage of her?" Aunt Adela continued triumphantly. "He's in a wheelchair."

"He's in a wheelchair, not dead," his loving, yet honest mother answered. "Rand has charmed more worldly women than Miss Sylvan."

Aunt Adela turned to her son, elegant even in a

chintz dressing gown and Turkish slippers. "James, defend your cousin."

James said petulantly, "Can't do it. Women fall all over themselves for a smile, silly twits."

Aunt Adela's voice swelled with indignation. "Miss Sylvan was Hibbert's mistress!"

Aunt Adela was hurting Sylvan with her slander, James with his amusement, Lady Emmie with her disappointment, and the Reverend Donald appeared about to preach. It was clearly time for Rand to step in. "Don't be a gudgeon, Aunt Adela. Sylvan's as pure as the new-fallen snow." That stopped the conversation, he was pleased to note. Every head turned in his direction. Every eye fixed itself on him, then wandered to a red-faced Sylvan.

"How do you know that?" Aunt Adela asked, then held up her hand. "Never mind. Don't tell me."

Sylvan bristled with fury. "I am not a cow whose previous breeding record is of public record. I would appreciate, Rand, if you would refrain from—" She stopped, abruptly stifled by the fascination with which the family hung on her every word.

"I never thought of you as a cow," Rand said gently, and she pulled his shirt up just enough to cover her face.

"But if you know that, she can't still be so pure," James pointed out.

"Don't be an ass, James. They didn't finish the act," Garth said. Then he half smiled. "Although you could have, eh, Rand?"

Rand realized Sylvan was nodding behind her cotton shield. Brave girl. She was willing to blemish further her good standing for his, and he stroked the place between her shoulder blades comfortingly. "Everyone's interested in my private life."

"It's not private"—Garth lost his smile and his voice rose again—"if you conduct it in a field."

"So the rumors about Hibbert were true," Lady Emmie said thoughtfully, and the gentlemen turned to her in shock.

"Mother!" Garth said. "When did you hear the rumors?"

She smiled enigmatically. "Men aren't the only ones who gossip."

For the first time since they'd entered the sitting room, Aunt Adela subsided onto the settee and leaned close to Lady Emmie. "Hibbert must have been using Miss Sylvan as a disguise." She glared at her own son. "What typically thoughtless male behavior."

"That's fustian!" James said.

Lowering the shirt, Sylvan showed her reddened face. "Hibbert wasn't thoughtless. He wanted to marry me and I wouldn't do it."

"But my dear, why not?" Lady Emmie asked. "You'd have been the wife of a peer, and Hibbert was wholly wealthy. Think of the advantages."

"I didn't want to be a wife," she said with finality.

"I don't see that you have a choice," Garth answered.

Lady Emmie's hands fluttered to her throat. "Are you suggesting what I think you're suggesting?"

"Nonsense, Garth," Lady Adela said vigorously. "The Malkin family has no need to mend a reputation ruined long ago."

Garth answered, "Her reputation might be marred, but we know that she's untouched. We know she's a woman of impeccable character, and she fits well into our family."

"Her reputation is a blot!" Lady Adela exclaimed.

"She's a maiden," Garth answered. "A fitting wife for the heir of Clairmont."

Apparently, Aunt Adela could scarcely comprehend Garth's determination. "She must be dismissed."

"What do you suggest I do?" Garth's voice rose again. "Send her home with a note pinned to her bodice? *Dear Mr. Miles, let me assure you that your daughter whom I promised would come to no harm has been intimately examined by my brother and has proved to be untouched?*"

Sylvan pulled the shirt up again.

"Don't be crude, dear," Lady Emmie murmured.

"He's going to have to marry her," Garth said.

"Untouched." Lady Adela viewed Sylvan with a new vision. "It's true one wonders about these modern girls who make their bows before the prince in their white dresses after visiting the gardens and what-not with their suitors."

"Oh, for God's sake." James snorted.

"Wait," Rand objected. "Let's be fair to Sylvan. She doesn't want to be a nurse to a cripple for the rest of her life."

Peeking over the top of the shirt, Sylvan glared fiercely. "Stop calling yourself that."

"She doesn't seem repulsed by your condition. Quite the opposite." Garth stroked his long forehead from eyebrows to hairline. "Nothing restores a lost reputation like marriage to the heir to a dukedom, especially a dukedom whose wealth is increasing with the production of a successful cotton mill." He challenged James and Aunt Adela with his glance, but before they could object, he added, "And she'll fulfill her father's ambition."

The shirt covered her head again, and she mumbled, "There's an argument sure to convince me."

Garth squatted down in front of her. "You'll never have to live in your father's house again."

Total silence answered him. He'd struck a telling blow.

"I *am* going to have to marry her, aren't I?" Rand hadn't really considered it before. Sylvan would be wedding a madman . . . but he wasn't a madman. She'd just gone to great lengths to prove her faith in him. Such faith in him. Faith that spilled from her and engulfed him.

He examined his hands, front and back, and laughed softly. For the first time in months, he was free of the shadow of Bedlam. He no longer had to imagine how he stood on his own two feet and beat screaming women while they begged for mercy. He no longer had to seek his death for the well-being of womankind.

His heart raced, and he rubbed his chest and laughed a little louder. Then he glanced up. He didn't believe in his own madness anymore, but from the expressions on their faces, his family wasn't too sure.

Looking at the quivering lump of shirt and skirt that was Sylvan, Rand returned her faith with a love that more than equaled it. Nothing could halt their marriage now.

There would be a disadvantage to Sylvan. In the sunlight, at least, he was still a cripple without dominion over his limbs. But the day would come when he'd start walking, and then he'd be in command of their lives. He'd wrap her in the finest garments, take her to the finest plays, and travel with her. He'd force those contemptuous society matrons to accept her into their homes, and never would she worry about anything, ever again.

What had started out as the day he would die now looked like the day he would wed. Slowly, he said the words aloud. "It would be an honor to marry Sylvan."

She popped out of hiding, the beaten expression in

her eyes gone beneath the onslaught of fury. "Hibbert was kind and generous and the best friend I ever had. He never threw a chair out the window, so why would I marry you if I wouldn't marry Hibbert?"

Rand grinned with insolent delight. "Because I can give you the one thing Hibbert couldn't."

"I don't want—"

"Careful." He held up one finger, and she stared at it in uneasy fascination. "Liars go to hell."

"So do fornicators," the clergyman intoned, his blond hair glinting like a halo. "I have done my best to keep my counsel and let this family come to the correct decision, and I think it has. But you, Miss Sylvan, must be made to realize how grievous a sin you have committed. You have enticed a man to sample your goods and found pleasure in his arms."

Clover Donald giggled, a high-pitched shriek of embarrassment.

Her husband continued, "Is there any greater sin?"

For a moment, Rand forgot he couldn't stand. He wanted to beat that sanctimonious bastard with his fists, and he tried to shove himself out of his chair. Sylvan grabbed him and pulled him back, and Garth leaped into the fray. "You'll issue a license then, Reverend, and we'll dismiss the calling of the banns."

The vicar sniffed. "Although banns are the proper method, I will issue the license and perform the ceremony."

"In the morning, then?" Garth insisted.

"Wait!" Lady Emmie said. "We have no marriage contract."

She wasn't alone in her consternation, but Garth overruled them all. "Miss Sylvan will trust us to care for her, and I'll draft a contract. I only wish we could marry them this evening."

"Damn stupid law, requiring weddings be in the morning," Rand complained. "We could be wed this afternoon."

"No." Sylvan shook her head. "No."

"She's tired." Rand had her now, and he wasn't going to let her get away. "She'll be better by tomorrow."

"I won't."

Her lip quivered, and Rand's heart clutched in sympathy. His bold, valiant nurse could face his wrath and derail his suicide, but the thought of marriage sent her into a quivering wreck. "Come, Sylvan." He took her hand and tugged her to her feet. "Come and talk to me."

The relatives kept quiet until they left the room, then conversation exploded behind them.

In the hallway, Jasper had remained by the door, Betty stood guard to ward off any curious servants, and their knowing expressions made explanations unnecessary.

Betty curtsied, then took Sylvan's hand and kissed it fervently. "Congratulations, my lady."

"I'm not going to marry him," Sylvan insisted.

Betty humored her. "Of course you're not, miss, but I'll still serve you to my dying day."

She tried to take Rand's hand, too, but he waved her away. "Save your applause for the consummation, Betty. That will be the true test."

"I have faith in you, Lord Rand. If there's anything I can do . . ."

He grinned at her. "I think that's something Sylvan and I will have to handle ourselves."

"No marriage," Sylvan mumbled.

Betty ignored her and bobbed Rand a curtsy. "Yes, sir. Of course, sir."

"Miss Sylvan needs to be put to bed," he said. "Sleep might soften her abhorrence for the wedded state."

"I can't sleep that long," Sylvan said ominously.

Rand, too, ignored her. "Will you see to her personally?"

"That I will." Betty took in Sylvan's bedraggled state and asked, "How long has it been now since you've slept, miss?"

Rubbing her head, Sylvan admitted, "I don't know."

"Bernadette will sit with you after we have you in bed."

"Wonderful," Sylvan drawled. "After last night, she thinks I'm mad."

"What she thinks of Lord Rand's wife is no concern of yours." Betty chided and smiled. "I know you don't like having anyone in your room, but you might wake and want something, and I'll not have you coming all the way down in your battered condition. We've not heard the real story on that, have we?"

"Not likely to, either," Rand assured her.

"Come, then."

Betty tried to put her arm around Sylvan, but Rand stopped her. "I want to speak to Miss Sylvan before she goes upstairs."

"Of course." Betty blessed him with another one of her radiant smiles. "I'll just go and fetch Bernadette. Jasper, come and help me."

"Don't want to," Jasper said in a surly voice.

"But you will." Grabbing his arm, Betty jerked him off his feet. "We need to give these two a moment alone."

With one desperate backward glance, Jasper allowed himself to be dragged away.

"Jasper doesn't like the thought of you marrying me," Sylvan said. "You should listen to Jasper."

Rand dismissed him. "He's a good man, but he's not my conscience."

"Oh, don't wed me for your conscience' sake!"

"You know why I'm wedding you."

With a sarcastic flourish, she said, "For my reputation."

"Aye, for your reputation." He took her hand between his two palms and rubbed it. "Your reputation as a loving woman."

"Amusing."

"Sit down," he ordered. When she looked around, he pointed. "Just there, on the stairs." She perched on the second step, propped her chin in her hand, and stared at him defiantly. Rolling himself close, so his knees kissed hers, he declared, "If you don't want to wed me, all you have to say are the magic words."

"And what words are those, pray tell?" she asked suspiciously.

"There are several. You could tell me you're repulsed by me and my condition."

She snorted in a most unladylike manner.

"Yes, I'm afraid you ruined any chance to make that believable." He heaved a phony sigh of commiseration. "Or you can say you fear me."

"Why would I say that?"

"Someone *is* attacking women," he pointed out.

"I thought we settled that this morning." She kept her voice low, but emphatic. "You're walking in your sleep, and someone is taking advantage of that fact. Someone here—probably in the house—is watching you."

He'd thought of that before, when he realized that the attacks occurred only at the times the ghost appeared, but he'd dismissed his suspicion as his own desperate desire to place blame elsewhere. Now he could only ask, "Who?"

"Jasper?"

She might have flicked him with a sharp-edged sword. "Don't be a fool."

"Why not Jasper?" she insisted. "He's a big man, capable of hurting a woman, and I find it hard to believe that your own body servant doesn't know that you walk."

"Why would he?"

"Doesn't he sleep in the room with you? Doesn't he change your sheets? Those muddy sheets were the final betrayal for me."

Rand had worried about that, the first time Jasper changed the sheets, but Jasper had seemed oblivious. *Was* oblivious, dammit. "Jasper fought beside me at Waterloo." Rand struck the arm of his chair. "It's not Jasper."

"Very well, then." She abandoned that supposition easily enough, and he relaxed. Then she asked, "How about your brother?"

"Garth?"

"Who has this madman attacked? Women who work at the mill. Women who your brother has kept after hours."

The muscles of his shoulders bunched as tension seized him. "They're the easiest women to attack. Women alone are vulnerable to anyone."

"But His Grace has a temper. I've seen it more than once." She waited until he nodded in admission, then she added quickly, "And perhaps not much liking for the female gender."

"Garth?" Reaching out, he felt her forehead. No fever. It must be the exhaustion that made her speak so recklessly. "What are you talking about? Garth loves women!"

"He isn't married."

His eyes opened wide, then he threw back his head

and roared with laughter. "That's a stupid way to decide a man's propensities."

Her complexion turned bright red, and she snapped, "That's how Hibbert was judged. I met a few of Hibbert's . . . friends, and some of them were lovely gentlemen, but some of them truly disliked women. All women. Don't you think—"

"No." He laughed again. "Not Garth. There are things you don't know about Garth. And even if what you imagined were true—he's the duke. If he wanted to hurt women, he could do it without going to the bother of building a mill."

Her color subsided, but she wasn't done. "James."

"Oh, now you sound like Garth."

"James is a frustrated, angry young man with a grudge against the mill."

"He was with me at Waterloo."

"He's third in line for the dukedom."

"I saved his life."

She checked. "At Waterloo?"

"I was with my regiment, and I saw him. He'd got separated and was engulfed by Frenchmen and . . . Well, I was just at the right place at the right time."

"And you imagined *you* might be assaulting women?" Dimples blinked as she tried to subdue her smile, and he could have warmed himself by the fire of her admiration. "You, who would have destroyed yourself in battle to protect James? Who would have flung yourself off a cliff to protect the women of Malkinhampsted?"

He didn't know what to say. He only knew he liked having Sylvan act as if he were a hero. Fumbling for a subject, he said, "So we can discount James."

Her dimples slid away. "Sometimes putting people in your debt destroys the balance between you."

"Rubbish!" Then, sarcastically, he joined in her slander. "And if not James, perhaps the Reverend Donald?"

"Why not?" She agreed. "He's out day and night visiting parishioners."

Rand couldn't believe she would entertain such a thought for a minute. "You've met him!" He pointed toward the sitting room. "He's a sanctimonious bastard, but he's totally dedicated to keeping the word of the Lord."

"I'm trying to tell you anyone could be perpetrating these crimes and for any reason. Even your Aunt Adela—"

"Now there's a thought." He pretended to consider it. "Or my mother?"

"She's too short."

"Ah." Trying to shame her, he said, "On that basis, I'll have to mark you from my list of suspects, too."

"Generous of you, but you should mark me from your list for another reason. I wasn't here when the attacks began."

"Maybe you were lurking at the inn in Malkinhampsted, waiting for the chance to—"

"Oh, Rand, I know you don't want it to be anyone you know." She pressed her knees to his, leaned forward, and revealed a most glorious vista when her bodice gaped. "But it has to be somebody with a grudge against you."

He scarcely refrained from licking his lips. "We employ about fifty indoor servants here. Do you realize what a basket of snakes you're whistling up with these accusations?"

She smiled at him in an almost-normal manner. "It would be easier to declare you're guilty, I suppose, but I don't believe in convicting a man out of convenience."

The time had come, he decided, to redirect their conversation. "Nor do you believe in marrying a man out of convenience, it seems."

She jumped back, and something in his expression must have given him away, for she pulled the shirt over her bosom.

"I'll treat you well," he promised.

"As long as I behave myself?"

She snapped at him so nastily he wished he could speak to her father. "You'll be a Malkin, and in all likelihood, you will someday be a duchess. You don't have to behave yourself. You will set the standard."

"How very conceited."

"I just want you to realize there are some advantages to this match. And about this morning." He waited while she looked away, shuffled uncomfortably, then looked back. "I'm sorry for exposing you to such a scene. I should have protected you better. It seems I can't do anything right."

Her legs jiggled up and down as she recalled the way she'd greeted the dawn. "Oh, you did *something* right."

"Is that a compliment? Sylvan." Tilting her chin up with his hand, he leaned forward and kissed her until she clung to his shoulders with trembling hands. "We're going to wed in the morning. No more arguing about it." He looked down at her flushed face with its closed eyes and rapturous expression. "Right?"

"I'll do it."

Not the rapturous words he'd imagined from his espoused wife, but he received them with as much pleasure. "You promise?"

Her lids fluttered up. "I won't change my mind."

"Give me that hour tomorrow night," he whispered, "and you'll see you made the right decision."

"You're dreadfully arrogant. Were you this bad before Waterloo?"

"Much, much worse."

She stood up and shook out her skirts.

"And likely to be insufferable by day after tomorrow."

Before she could answer, Betty and Bernadette dashed out of the dining room where they'd been waiting. They took Sylvan, each by an arm, and marched her up the stairs while Rand looked after them.

"Sir?" Jasper stood by his chair. "Do ye want to rest, too?"

"I couldn't." When Sylvan disappeared from view, Rand turned to Jasper. "I'm too excited. Congratulate me. She's consented to be my wife."

With his head down and a solemn expression on his plain face, Jasper mumbled, "Congratulations."

"What's the matter, man?" Rand joked. "Are you afraid you're losing me?"

"It's my fault, sir." A tear dripped off the end of Jasper's nose, and he twisted his shoulders and wagged his head as if he were in agony. "I'm the reason ye have to wed. I wasn't here to care for ye."

Why was Jasper acting this way? Suspicion, ugly and unwanted, sprang up in Rand's mind, and he cursed Sylvan for placing it there. Where had Jasper been last night? "I heard that you found Loretta yourself," Rand said.

Jasper's fair skin reddened. "Aye, sir."

Even as Rand damned his own conjecture, he asked, "What were you doing out so late?"

"I—I just worried about the women . . . ah, the woman who'd been hurt at the accident in the mill. I went to her cottage, and when I left to come back, I found Loretta in the dirt." His big fists clenched.

"Loretta's house isn't in this direction. Perhaps," Rand suggested, "you went looking for her."

"I—I heard her yell. Aye, that was it. I heard her."

Rand pushed himself around Jasper to avoid watching the man bumble his way through these lies—surely the first lies he'd ever told. Was Sylvan right? Had Jasper been chasing after women to harm them? Did he know that Rand could walk? Rand shook himself. Sylvan had ruined his complacency even as she mended his self-respect. Whatever Jasper had been doing, there was no doubt an explanation. Probably he had a girl in the village. Knowing Jasper, he would eventually confide in Rand. Trying to comfort his man, Rand said, "Leaving me last night was a brilliant stroke on your part. You see, I *want* to wed Sylvan."

"But, sir—"

"Just promise you will serve Miss Sylvan as you would serve me."

"I owe ye my first loyalty," Jasper said, fierce and determined.

"So you do. And my wife is part of me."

Jasper's whisper sent a chill through Rand. "She's not yet yer wife."

10

Someone was calling her name. Sylvan woke slowly, responding to the call with the anticipation of a lover. Easing her eyes open, she looked around, seeking the man who had entered her bedroom.

Seeking Rand.

He wasn't there. It must have been another dream, but a curiously pictureless dream. Tonight, no suffering specters begged her to give them aid, and she sighed in relief and eased herself erect.

Bernadette snored in a steady rhythm on a cot by the fireplace. One branch of candles had burned down to the stubs and smoked, smelling of burnt wick and wax. Another's flames flickered close to the ends of the wicks. The clock ticked loudly, and Sylvan wondered how long she'd been asleep. All day and half the night, she guessed. It must be the deepest part of the dark, and she was wide awake.

She wanted a drink. She wanted some company.

Glancing at Bernadette, she saw that her maid still slept deeply.

She'd have to settle for a drink.

She slipped out of bed, her bare toes curling when they touched the cold floorboards. Scampering to the china pitcher, she poured a glass of water. Spooky, this big old house. She almost expected to hear—

Thump!

She stared, transfixed, at the door.

Thump!

Taking care not to make a clink, she put down the glass and glanced at Bernadette. The maid hadn't moved. She still snored, oblivious to the racket.

Thump!

Rand. Sylvan pressed her hand to her heart. He must be walking. Again. She had to stop him before someone caught him. They teetered on the edge of disaster now; if the servants discovered he could walk, he would surely be blamed for the attacks. Fitting the stub of a candle into a single holder, she slipped to the door and eased it open.

No one stood there.

She looked up and down the hall, and caught just a glimpse of a figure turning the corner at the far end. "Heaven help us," she whispered, and started after him. She turned the corner and saw him again. His chest glinted as she approached; he wore a silver shirt and she squinted, trying to discern its make. "Rand," she whispered, "wait for me." He did, watching from eye sockets that appeared eerily empty.

When she neared, he slipped away without a sound, leaving her alone. She stared at the place where he had been, then hurried around the corner.

There he was, at the end of the passageway that narrowed alarmingly. Here the night candles were tallow, not wax—they had entered the older part of the manor. She'd never been here before, but she knew the servants resided somewhere close. No doubt many of the doors opened into storage rooms. And if she didn't catch Rand before someone saw him . . .

He put his finger to his lips as if he were aware of her and not asleep at all. He wore an odd kind of cap that made him look as if his hair swept his shoulders, and the toes of his shoes looked as if they extended into a point. Where was he leading her? And why? Anxious, she trailed behind him, amazed to be in hallways she'd never visited and afraid she'd never find her way back. But she did. Tracking Rand as closely as she could—but never closely enough—she soon found herself back at the far end of the corridor by her room. The figure in the glittering shirt stood by her open doorway. "Rand," she whispered, "let me put you to bed." He stood still as she hurried toward him. As she reached out to touch him, he faded into nothingness.

Goose bumps rose on her skin, and when the scream erupted, she almost thought it had come from her throat.

But instead it came from her room, a full-bodied shriek loud enough to wake the dead. Sylvan ran, stumbling, sure Bernadette had seen what she had, but before she reached the door, someone raced out.

A man. Dark-haired, in a long white gown. He fled down the hall. Sylvan started after him, but as she ran past the door Bernadette cried, "No!" Sylvan hesitated, and Bernadette shrieked, "No, please, miss."

"Are you hurt?" Sylvan demanded.

Bernadette paid no attention. "Don't go. 'Twas the ghost of Clairmont Court, and he tried to kill me. Don't go after him."

"What did he do?" Sylvan supported Bernadette as she wobbled back into the bedroom and onto a chair.

"When I screamed, he hit me with a stick." Bernadette gasped as if she'd been running a race. "I put up my arm."

Running her hands along Bernadette's forearm, Sylvan asked, "Did he hurt you?"

"Yes!"

"Really hurt you?"

Bernadette wavered, then muttered, "No. I think I'm just bruised. But, miss, it was you he sought." Tears sprang to her eyes and dribbled down her cheeks. "He struck the bed first, and when he realized you weren't there, he went into a rage. He ripped the sheets off and—"

"No." Sylvan ran to the bed, but his attack had scattered her white linens like ghostly souvenirs. Rand would never do this, but someone had and only that beckoning apparition had saved her.

How many ghosts did this house harbor?

"Ghosts don't hit people." Sylvan paced over to Bernadette. "They frighten them or chase them or wail or . . ." Her imagination failed her. "But they don't pick up a stick and hit people."

"Then who . . ." Bernadette's eyes grew big, and she asked indignantly, "Are ye saying some *person* walloped on me fer fun?" Her eyes narrowed once more. "Ye mean, some person from this estate wanted to hurt *ye*?"

"I suppose you could—"

"After all ye've done fer Lord Rand and poor Roz?" Bernadette rose to her feet and towered over Sylvan. "Why, that's scabby. "

"What's the matter?" Lady Emmie stood in the doorway, her hair loose and her white nightgown flapping around her ankles.

"Did I hear a scream?" Aunt Adela shouldered her way in.

"Don't tell them." Gripping Bernadette's shoulder tightly, Sylvan begged in a low tone. "Promise me you won't tell them."

"But, miss—"

"Tell them you saw the ghost." Sylvan shivered. "They'll think you're a fool, but I want to see who wears the guilty face tomorrow."

Bernadette folded her arms across her chest. "But, miss, he wanted to hurt ye, and I cannot allow—"

She wouldn't budge, and Sylvan hurriedly promised, "I'll tell Rand what occurred this night."

Sylvan saw now why Betty had assigned Bernadette as her personal maid. Bernadette's expression sharpened into shrewd interest, then when Lady Emmie came closer it wilted into hysteria. "Oh, Yer Grace, 'twas the ghost," she wailed.

"What nonsense!" Lady Adela boomed.

"Not nonsense," Lady Emmie answered. "We do have a ghost."

The quarrel was well begun. Sylvan raced down the hallway and the stairs and headed straight for Rand's room. The door was closed, but she burst in unannounced and for one awful second, her heart dropped to her toes. Rand wasn't in his bed.

"Sylvan?"

His surprised drawl brought her whirling around. He sat, fully clothed, by a small table.

Betty sat beside him, her mouth and eyes wide. "Miss Sylvan?"

"What are you doing?" Sylvan asked, but she didn't wait for an answer. Going to him, Sylvan patted his white cotton shirt, seeking a long white nightgown—or a silver shirt.

He wore the white shirt and a light blue waistcoat, and his eyes danced when he caught her hands. "What are *you* doing?" He looked her over with thorough interest. "Running the halls in your nightgown?"

"Put this on, Miss Sylvan." Betty held Rand's black silk dressing gown. "Even in summer, it's always drafty in this great house."

"And you're chilly," Rand added.

Sylvan didn't ask how he knew, she just slipped her hands into the sleeves.

"Now." Rand pointed to the chair Betty had vacated and glanced at the clock on his mantel. "What are you doing here at two o'clock in the morning?"

"What are you doing up at this hour?" Sylvan seated herself.

"Preparing for our wedding." Rand waved a hand at the papers scattered on the table and the unstoppered inkwell with the quill nearby.

"Our wedding?"

"You agreed to marry me yesterday. Do you remember?"

Wedding. Sylvan pressed her hands to the sides of her head. Did she remember? Her first instinct was to deny it. Pretend she didn't remember sitting on the steps and talking to Rand, discussing the various suspects to this on-going crime, and agreeing, for some ridiculous reason, to a wedding. "When are we supposed to marry?"

"Today." He enunciated the word with exaggerated lip movement, as if she needed to connect the sound of his voice and the sight of his speech. "You agreed to marry me today."

"Why?"

"Because we were caught in a compromising position

in a wide open field, and you are either to be thrown out as a hussy or wed to a cripple. Not a pretty choice."

"That wasn't the real reason why I agreed to wed you."

"I know." He smiled with beguiling temptation. "It was because I promised to make you happy."

"No."

His smile disappeared, and he said in disgust, "Then I suppose it's because Garth promised you'd never have to go back to your father's house."

"No." Why had she agreed to marry him? There had been a reason, a very compelling reason. . . .

"Sylvan, this is an interesting subject and one I intend to explore further, but of more moment—why are you here now?"

Rand sounded patient, but his brow knit, and with a jolt, Sylvan recalled her mission. "Why are you up so late?" she demanded again.

Exchanging an irritable glance with Betty, he said, "Betty needed help organizing two separate feasts in such a short time. Every noble neighbor within driving distance is invited to our wedding, and we have to fete them properly. In addition, it's traditional for the Malkins to host a feast for the villagers and the poor as part of a wedding celebration. In addition to that, you need a tentative marriage contract drawn up, and I couldn't sleep anyway."

"Why not?"

Leaning forward, he examined her intently. "Sylvan?"

"Has Betty been with you the whole time?"

"Yes." He clipped the word.

She looked at Betty for confirmation, and Betty said, "Yes, miss. Been here ever since I finished speaking to the tradesmen about the food. The meals are going to be an embarrassment, I say, but they'll be the best I can manage on such short notice." Sylvan made a soft, impatient sound, and Betty said rapidly, "I've been here since about nine o'clock, I suppose."

Baring his teeth, Rand demanded, "Now *what's* the matter?"

"Where's Jasper?" Sylvan asked.

"He's running my errands," Betty answered.

Disbelief sustained Sylvan. "At two in the morning?"

Betty's soft voice strengthened. "Miss, we're out of time! It's all very well for His Grace to command the wedding be in the morning and know that all will be taken care of, but he's the duke and worse, a man, and hasn't the slightest notion of the work involved."

Wit now freed itself from the soft confines of sleep, and Sylvan blushed to realize the labor her misconduct had produced. Yet at the same time, she didn't know Jasper's location, nor Garth's, nor James's. She only knew Rand's, and that news could wait no longer. "I beg your pardon, Betty."

She drooped like a flower deprived of water, and Betty hurried to her side. "I beg yours, miss. I had no right to scold you so. Is there anything I could do for you?"

"Well . . ." Sylvan thought feverishly, then suggested, "I'm thirsty and hungry. Could I trouble you for a light repast?"

"Of course," Betty said heartily, and started for the door. Then she stopped and glanced between them. "I don't like to leave you alone at this time of night. You've proved your need for a chaperone."

"That's true," Rand agreed. "But Sylvan will swear not to attack me this time. Won't you, Sylvan?"

"I didn't—" Sylvan began. But she had. Yesterday

morning, it was her kiss that had precipitated the whole messy, magnificent lovemaking. If only Rand didn't wear his smug amusement with such pride. "I won't touch him. And that's a promise I will keep."

Betty hovered, torn in her duty, but at last she bobbed a curtsy and whisked from the room.

"She'll return as quickly as she can," Rand warned, clearly not duped by Sylvan's pretense. "Now why are you here?"

Leaning forward, she touched his knee and in a low voice, said, "The ghost paid me a visit."

Rand said, "The ghost—"

"Paid me a visit," she repeated. That wasn't the strict truth. Two ghosts had paid her a visit, but she found herself unable to speak of the silver-clad ghost, the one that had vanished before her eyes.

Snatching her hands, he brought her to her feet and looked her over. "You weren't hurt?"

She brushed his query aside. "The ghost paid me a visit. That's the final confirmation. It's not you!"

"I understand, but I knew I wasn't the culprit this morning when you told me I was not and demonstrated your faith in me so touchingly."

What did he mean? Did he have so much faith in her opinion?

No. She reseated herself to avoid his gaze. He couldn't have, for if he did, it meant he had that much faith in *her*.

Rand examined her hands, then folded them inside his. "Now that that's out of the way, tell me—were you hurt?"

Did he feel the tremor that shook her? "When?"

"When the ghost paid you a visit." He sounded insistent, as if he could ask forever.

"Oh, that." She looked away from him. "No."

Rand insisted, "He didn't attack you?"

"No!" He had attacked Bernadette. That was a lie of omission, but faith such as his would be a burden, and she couldn't carry it. Too many men had entrusted their lives to her, and she'd failed them.

"What did he do?"

"He tried to frighten me!"

Gazing into her eyes, he articulated clearly. "Where was he?"

"I saw him in the hall outside my room." That was the truth, anyway. He had been in the hall when he ran out of her room. And Rand was frightening her with his interrogation, as if he had the right to ask these questions. As if he owned her, body and soul.

Her fingers clutched, and her nails bit his flesh.

"I'll send the footmen after him."

"He's gone."

"And I'll post a guard at your door."

Jerking her hand free, she snapped, "With orders to shoot if I show myself at an inappropriate moment?"

"The guard is to protect you, not imprison you." He sounded so sincere, she was ashamed, but she didn't like it when he took her hands again. "I worry about you, Sylvan. I'll be happier when we're wed."

She shuddered, and he gripped her tighter. "You are going to marry me in the morning." It sounded as if he were making a statement, not asking for reassurance.

Quickly, impatiently, she answered. "I said I would." But she hadn't meant it. She wanted to be here to care for Rand. She wanted to be here to see him walk in the daylight. She wanted to sleep in his arms.

But she didn't want to pay the price of remaining and never the price of passion.

"Why are there so many rules, and why are they so

easy to break, and why do I have to be the one who gets caught breaking them?"

"The rules were made by men like me who want to hold on to women like you." He unfurled her clenched hand and kissed the palm. "Besides, someone has to rescue your virtue."

"I had no trouble hanging on to my virtue until you happened along," she said. Then, "Uh-oh." That hadn't been the thing to tell him. He had more conceit than any ten men, and she'd just admitted that he, and only he, had been capable of moving her to a response. His grin filled her with disgust. "Oh, stop beaming. All of the ton believes me to be a wanton, and you know they have the only opinion that matters."

He laughed aloud. "You don't understand men at all, do you?"

"I understand more than I like."

"If I—and everyone in the ton—thought you were chaste, and I married you, and it was revealed that you had had experience, then I would feel deceived, and our marriage would possibly flounder. If I—and everyone in the ton—believed you had had worldly experience, and I married you knowing about that experience, I would have no cause for complaint and I would, in fact, be looking forward to a long and glorious wedding night. But in your case, the ton thinks you're wanton, and I have discovered you are unjustly accused. On my part, the wedding night will be"—he took a breath—"restrained. Yet at the same time, I am delighted to know that what you experience with me is unique."

"Yes," she muttered, trying to rise. "Well, if that's all . . ."

He still held her hand, the palm of which had grown sweaty, and he didn't let her go. Earnestly, he said, "We will have a good marriage, I promise, but I'll need your cooperation."

She couldn't help her wary response. "My cooperation?"

"You do realize I'll need your cooperation to perform my conjugal duties?"

"Have I given you any reason to think I might not cooperate?" she demanded impatiently, then jerked her hand back when he chuckled.

"Not at all, but I understand there's more to deflowering a virgin than simple pleasure."

She jumped to her feet and walked toward the door. "I don't want to talk about this."

"I can't *make* you stay and talk about it."

His words stopped her in her tracks.

"If you choose to walk away from me, I'm helpless to stop you."

She chewed on her lip. He was right, and her sense of fair play would hardly let her take advantage of his paralysis. He was going to be her husband, and he was just talking to her. He was probably like her, and concerned about *all* aspects of their life after the wedding. Communication between them would ease their later differences, and she shouldn't run away from communication just because it was about . . . *it*. She could handle this. Briskly, she returned and seated herself. "As you say. What do you want me to do?"

"I don't want you to *do* anything. I just want you to promise you'll trust to my experience in the performance of our connubial duties."

Duties? That sounded funny coming from him. Somehow, she hadn't imagined he thought of them as duties.

"I'm just afraid that I won't be able to do the things normal men do to ease your fears."

"Like what?"

"My father and mother used to gambol together like two lambs in the spring." An affectionate smile lit his face. "They'd chase and tickle and giggle, until they disappeared into their bedchamber, or . . . well, they were once caught in our town house in London in a state of complete undress by the lord mayor. " He laughed out loud.

"You're bamming me." Her parents had never behaved in such a manner. Not in front of her nor, she was sure, when they were alone. For them, marriage was serious business.

"Later, of course, there'll be the times we quarrel, and you'll be able to stomp off in a huff and sleep elsewhere for as long as you like. I'm at your mercy."

"You'll have to trust to my mercy, then, won't you?"

"Your mercy I trust, but I've had a taste of your temper, and you'll have to admit you can be unreasonable when you're angry."

Bending her head, she pleated the robe into elusive folds that slipped between her fingers. "I don't have to admit anything."

"My parents spent every night of their marriage in the same bed, and sometimes half the day."

He was coaxing now, and the more she heard about his parents, the more she thought she'd like to have such a union. "As you say."

It was a grudging agreement, but he jumped on it. "So you promise to acquiesce to all my conjugal demands?"

"Ye . . . es."

"And we'll sleep in the same bed every night for all the time of our marriage?"

"As long as we're in the same town."

Relaxing into his seat, he lounged, his arm crooked over the back, and looked her over. "I think when we are married, I would very much like you to wear my robe to bed."

His eyes glowed like blue-hot coals, and she shifted in her seat, suddenly self-conscious within the confines of the clinging black robe. "Why?"

"When I think about rubbing that silk across your—" He checked himself.

She pulled her hands away from his, and he let them go. She rose, and he watched. She backed away, sure that somehow, he'd grab for her, but he made no move. He just watched and waited. Waited for tomorrow night.

11

The heavy signet ring Rand placed on her finger almost crushed it. Sylvan could feel the band shrinking as her skin warmed it; any tighter and it would cut off her circulation completely.

In a deep, expressive voice, Rand repeated the words honoring her as his wife and the ring as the symbol of their union, and he cupped her hand between his two palms.

He sounded sincere, and Sylvan supposed he was. She supposed that few men married with the intention of crushing their wives' spirits and turning them into creatures without will or fire. But it happened.

Lifting her drooping head, Sylvan looked around the terrace. The Reverend Donald had expected to perform the ceremony in the confines of the church, but Rand insisted on the open air. He'd insisted on providing a feast for all who attended, for he wanted everyone in the manor and beyond to witness their marriage.

Sylvan thought he had his wish. The vicar stood with his back to the door, prayer book in hand. She and Rand were in front of him, and the Malkin family stood in a semicircle around them. Gail and her governess were off to the side. Neighbors, the nobility who kept country manors in the area, formed a tight knot behind the family, and craned their necks in ignoble curiosity as they tried to get a view of Rand's bride. The house servants, Jasper and Betty at the front, formed a looser assembly that covered the terrace, and down the stairs and beyond were villagers from Malkinhampsted.

Too many people. Too firm a bond.

Someone thrust an equally ponderous ring into Sylvan's hand. She was to place it on Rand's finger. That would be the final part of the ceremony, the moment at which Sylvan Miles ceased to exist as a person and became an extension of Rand Malkin.

She didn't want to do it. Her mother had done it, and ever since Sylvan could remember, her mother had been a pale, sighing soul who lived to try and placate her husband.

Clover Donald had done it, and in the time since Sylvan's arrival, she hadn't heard Clover do more than echo her husband's sentiments.

"Sylvan." Lady Emmie nudged her in the back. "You need to place the ring on Rand's finger."

Sylvan looked dumbly at the ring.

"If you don't, he'll probably do it himself."

Sylvan looked at Rand. He probably would. For the first time since she'd arrived at Clairmont Court, his hair was combed, his face was washed, his boots shone, his coat was brushed and buttoned, and his cravat was tied impeccably. He was the epitome of a wealthy English nobleman in appearance, and in manner. He tried to appear comforting, but he didn't fool her. The bright sunlight sculpted his face and showed his determination. Nothing would stand in his way today. Certainly not her puny and incomprehensible desire to remain a spinster.

"Put it on my finger, Sylvan." He captured her gaze and kept it prisoner. "Then it'll be over, and all will be well. You'll see. Put it on my finger."

Reluctantly, she lifted the sculpted gold and matched it to his outstretched hand. The Reverend Donald intoned words that made no sense; she repeated words that made too much sense. She committed herself to Rand in the greatest gamble of her life. She became his wife.

A great collective sigh swept the assembly.

She leaned down to give Rand the kiss of peace, and he waited until she was off-balance and tipped her into his lap. The sigh of relief became a laugh, then a cheer as Rand leaned her back and kissed her. It was a very pleasant kiss, a kind of meat-and-potatoes kiss meant to sustain her through the rest of the day.

It would probably succeed. During her sojourn at Clairmont Court, she had been Rand's nurse, supporter, and advocate. Somehow, for today at least, it seemed the roles had been reversed. She didn't like it—she didn't ever want to depend on anyone so wholly—but she derived strength from the touch of his lips, his firm hug, and the buttress of his shoulder.

Why had she married him?

Now she remembered. Because she recognized the fury that drove him to do what was right, regardless of the cost to himself. It was the same fury that had driven her in Brussels.

And, worst of all, because she loved him.

Rand pressed little kisses on her neck and murmured, "You're the bravest woman I know."

"Don't be foolish." She pushed him away and stood up, straightening with elaborate motions her magnificent lace-encrusted skirt.

The family rushed forward. Garth embraced her first, the duke of Clairmont providing his official approval of his brother's wife. "I prayed for this from the first," he said. "You've brought him back to life."

It wasn't she who had brought him back to life, Sylvan wanted to say, but the knowledge of his own innocence. Before she could speak, Lady Emmie elbowed her son out of her way and clasped Sylvan to her capacious bosom. "My dear, I always wanted a daughter."

Sylvan nodded, dumb before such enthusiasm.

Aunt Adela hugged her more gingerly, but agreed. "She did. I always told her it was foolish to fancy a girl who'll marry away from the family, but she wanted one anyway."

"They don't marry away from the family," Lady Emmie said.

"Sylvan's mother isn't here," Aunt Adela retorted.

"We've already invited Lord and Lady Miles to come and visit. They'll be welcome at all times."

Sylvan moaned slightly, but Garth reassured her. "We'll send you and Rand on an extended honeymoon should your father overstay his welcome."

After he had slipped his prayer book into the pocket of his black coat, the Reverend Donald took Sylvan's hand and shook it. "I cannot imagine Lady Sylvan being anything but pleased at Lord Miles's visit."

"You haven't met—" Garth cut himself off sharply and folded his lips tight.

Sylvan sympathized with the duke. Her father had been at his most obsequious when Garth arrived at their home, then at his most obnoxious when he realized Garth wished only to persuade Sylvan to nurse Rand. Her mother, of course, had been pathetically eager to please, then pathetically agitated by her husband's outrage. The memory of a farce could only underscore Sylvan's fears, and she turned from the vicar's scrutiny.

Obviously, not soon enough, for he pressed the hand he still held. "My father, also, was a difficult man who failed to realize that my higher destiny lay with the clergy, but I look back on my early ordeals as the furnace that hardened the steel of my character." He waved his free hand across the vista of people, trees, and ocean. "The sun shines on this day of holy rites. Lift your heart and be glad."

Startled, Sylvan stared in fascination at the minister. So that was how he herded his flock along the right path. She'd seen only his austerity, but his gladness in the performance of his duty startled, then pleased her. "Yes," she said. "Thank you."

He must have gestured his wife forward, for Clover Donald appeared beside him, a tremulous smile on her lips and eyes reddened from the tears that spilled during the ceremony. "May I offer my congratulations, Lady Sylvan, on your marriage?"

"Of course," Sylvan murmured, feeling foolish at having to give permission and wondering if this noble union had completely cut her off from communion with those of less breeding. Always before she'd straddled that chasm, one foot placed with the wealthy aristocrats, one foot with the common folk.

She was, she supposed, lucky to have wed into a family so noble they felt no urge to prove it with sham snobbery.

Clover's smile wavered, and Sylvan said hastily, "Won't you join us for our personal celebration?"

"We would be honored," the Reverend Donald answered, and steered his wife toward Rand to congratulate him with equal fervor.

A long queue of neighbors formed to offer Sylvan their good wishes, and Lady Emmie and Aunt Adela stationed themselves on either side to perform the introductions. Whenever the guests expressed, through word or intonation, their vulgar interest, Lady Emmie or Aunt Adela stepped in. Sylvan, they made clear, was a Malkin now, and therefore beyond reproach. It was no small thing, Sylvan realized, to be a dowager or other relative of the duke of Clairmont. These women elicited respect by their station alone, and when that failed to quell the nosiest of the guests, their patrician demeanor squashed pretension.

One by one, the neighbors moved from the terrace into the house where they would be presented with a fine repast and a chance to watch the newlyweds.

Feeling a sharp elbow to the hip, Sylvan watched Gail struggle her way to Rand. "Uncle Rand, will I still be your girl?"

"My first girl." Rand enclosed her in a big hug. "And my best girl named Gail."

Gail giggled, and Betty called, "Miss Gail, you make your curtsy to Miss Sylvan."

"Lady Sylvan," Rand corrected.

Betty sniffled with joy as she looked from Rand to Sylvan, from one ring to the other. "Of course, Lord Rand."

As instructed, Gail curtsied, but Sylvan saw the wariness in the child's gaze and experienced a kinship. How could Gail not be wary, with this hurried wedding forced by extraordinary circumstances? Circumstances that must have caused gossip to run rampant through the servants' quarters and come finally to the child's ears. Regardless of her paternity, it must be confusing. Taking Gail's hand, Sylvan leaned over and whispered, "You'll always be his best girl, but he's afraid to say so for fear of hurting my feelings."

Startled, Gail withdrew her hand, and Sylvan blushed. Foolish to be so incompetent when dealing with a child.

Then Gail stood on tiptoe and whispered loud enough for everyone to hear, "Don't worry. Uncle Rand told me before he would've married you if you were ugly as a wart-causing toad."

The crowd roared with laughter, startling both Gail and Sylvan, and Rand took each of them by the hand.

"Garth!" Aunt Adela's voice boomed a little too loudly for discretion. "It's time you followed your brother's suit and took a bride."

Garth stiffened, then laughed with counterfeit jocularity. "I don't need to marry yet. I can still hold in my stomach."

There was a light spatter of chuckles, but no one seemed really amused, and Rand said, "Sylvan and I have no objection to providing the heir to the Clairmont dukedom. Do we, Sylvan?"

What was she supposed to say? All the platitudes about blushing brides came to her as she struggled to reply with a trifle of dignity.

James rescued her with a swift peck on the cheek and a cheery, "Let's go inside so the peasants can quaff their beer and swallow their meal without trying to display manners they don't possess."

"They have manners," Garth rebuked. "They're just not our manners."

"Amen to that." James pushed his way to the edge of

the stairs and shouted, "We'll just throw the raw meat down to you, and you can fight it out." A ragged cheer answered him, and he turned back to the family with a smirk. "See? They love me."

"They think you're naught but a fop," Garth answered sharply.

James put one hand on his hip in exaggerated astonishment. "I wonder who told them that."

"No one had to tell them," Garth said. "When a man hangs about doing nothing, the peasants, as you call them, recognize his worth."

"Gentlemen." Something about the tone of Rand's voice jerked Garth and James to attention. "This is my wedding day, and you'll do me the courtesy of calling a truce."

James flushed, but Garth rubbed his eyes tiredly. "I'll do better than that. I'll go to the mill. It's been one thing after another these days."

"You can't go, dear!" Lady Emmie hurried forward and took his arm. "It's Rand and Sylvan's wedding luncheon."

Garth smiled and patted her hand. "Rand won't mind, and Sylvan doesn't yet know what hit her." He lowered his voice, but Sylvan heard him. "Besides, you know how I am about weddings."

Below them, the villagers began their exodus to the back of Clairmont Court, where the food would be distributed and barrels of beer tapped. It would be a pleasant respite from the continual labor of summer in both the fields and the mill, and when they finished they would return refreshed and ready to work.

"Rand," Lady Emmie wailed, "talk to your brother."

"I will," Rand said. "Go and entertain our guests." He nodded at Aunt Adela. "Please, Aunt, take her inside."

"Garth needs to remain," Aunt Adela said stiffly.

Rand cut her off with a motion, and James laughed dryly. "Rand's back, Mother, can't you see? We'll all do as we're told." He presented an arm to each lady. "You know you can squelch the gossip with one look from your fine eyes." He led them toward the house, then paused. "Do you want me to take your leg shackle, too?"

It was meant to be amusing, but Rand wondered if James knew how close he came to disaster. "Go, James."

James went. Sylvan sat on the flat surface of the marble railing, her hands folded in her lap, and stared out at the rapidly emptying grounds. The tumult that went before only accentuated the growing quiet, and Garth burst out, "By Jove! Mother's right. I must stay here to lend my support to you and Sylvan. I try to forget, sometimes, that I'm the duke."

"I don't think that's true," Rand said. "I think you just weigh your primary duty and proceed with it, regardless of the consequences. Now, what's wrong at the mill?"

"Someone's . . . doing things."

"Things?"

"Breaking things. Hiding things. Making it as difficult as possible for the mill to operate."

Rand pursed his lips in a low whistle. "What are you doing about it?"

"I haven't done anything yet. I didn't even realize, the first few days, what was occurring." Garth thrust his hands into the top of his best waistcoat. "I'm a stupid fool."

"Not stupid," Rand denied. "Trusting."

"I'm going to organize a patrol of men at the mill. Men who'll watch for any unusual activity. But dammit!" Garth glanced guiltily at Sylvan. "Beg pardon,

Sylvan. By Jove, what will I tell them? How will I explain this sudden display of malice?"

"They're no dunces, Garth." Rand watched his brother with concern, noting the thinning of the broad cheeks, the way he held his hand over his stomach as if it ached. "They'll just be glad to know their wives have added protection when they work."

"Yes." Garth pushed his hand through his carefully combed hair. "I suppose you're right."

Rand wanted to hug his brother as he had done when they were boys, when Garth's idealism had clashed with reality and Garth had been wounded. But Garth wouldn't welcome it. Not right now when he'd just seen Rand wed the woman of his choice. Later, when the wound had healed a little . . . "Go on to the mill," Rand said. "I'll make your excuses, and when you come back, we'll talk."

"Something's wrong." Rand stared out the carriage window at the mill. He couldn't put his finger on it, but somehow, something was different and he couldn't help but remember Garth's anxiety.

"The machinery's not running," Sylvan said. "There's no noise."

Rand snapped his fingers. "That's it!" Foolish, he told himself. So foolish he didn't observe the obvious.

The square white building looked the same. The shingles toasted in the summer sun. The shorn grass around the foundation wavered in the wind. Charity, Beverly, Nanna, and Shirley straggled toward the sprawling structure, smiling and chatting about the wedding feast, so it would seem all the celebrations were winding down.

A good thing, too, for as they pulled to a stop, they

could hear shouting from inside the mill. It was Garth, and he sounded furious.

The women groaned, and Rand called from inside the carriage, "I'll go in, ladies, and divert his wrath."

"Blessings on ye, sir," Nanna called back.

"Congratulations to ye both," Charity said, and in a lower voice she wondered aloud, "But what are newlyweds doing *here*?"

Rand didn't take the time to answer. He waited impatiently as Jasper handed Sylvan down, then helped unbuckle the straps that held his chair in place. The women came to lend a hand with unloading him, then Sylvan gave him a push to start him through the grass into the mill. He let her go in first, of course, but just inside the door, she stopped and looked around with troubled eyes.

The stillness and silence reminded Rand of the hopeful time before the steam engine had been installed and started for the first time. Garth had been ecstatic, sure that the mill would immediately prove itself to all skeptics. Instead it had been a project that swallowed hours of Garth's time and much of his idealism. If only there were some other way to keep families on the estate, but there didn't appear to be.

"Damn stupid machine!" Garth's voice snarled from the center of the mill. "Stupid damn thing won't run!"

A loud, metallic pounding accompanied his invective, and Rand glanced at Sylvan apologetically. "We've found him."

Amusement brought some color back into her cheeks, and she said, "So we have."

About a dozen women sat in a circle on the floor, and they stood as Rand and Sylvan approached, clearing a path and bobbing curtsies while offering felicitations.

The commotion attracted Garth's attention, and he called, "Rand! Sylvan! What are you doing here?" He looked down at them from atop a ladder that leaned on the steam engine. "Did you enjoy as much of the company as you could stand?"

"Yes, thank you indeed." Rand glared at his brother.

Garth tried to be normal and make conversation, when clearly the steam engine held his attention. "I can scarcely believe you walked out of your own party because you found the neighbors shallow."

"You should believe it," Rand answered.

Garth's lip curled in disgust. "Was someone rude?"

"Yes." Sylvan chuckled. "Rand."

"Were you?" Garth took a moment to examine his brother. "Such a surprise."

"I wasn't the only rude one." Rand glared meaningfully at Sylvan. "But you're the duke. You should have had to suffer, too."

"Ignorant batch of beggars, aren't they?" Garth's blue eyes twinkled in puckish merriment, but he dripped sweat from the heat of the furnace.

"Not all of them." Rand took Sylvan's hand and patted it. "Just Lady St. Clare. She tried to question Sylvan about her ancestry."

Sylvan hung her head. "You were angry because I asked about her ancestry, too."

"No, I was not." Rand looked up at Garth. "Sylvan asked Lady St. Clare if her parents were married."

Garth released a bark of astonished laughter.

"She made me angry," Sylvan confessed to Rand. "She stared at you as if you were some kind of lesser creature. Whenever you spoke, she acted amazed."

Rand hid his hurt behind a jaunty smile. "The organ-grinder's monkey performed on cue."

"Believe me, I'm sorry." The engine clanged, and Garth clanged it back with a wrench. "I thought that our neighbors would be sophisticated enough to treat you with respect, as the son and brother of a duke and as a war hero should be treated."

He looked so guilty that Sylvan hastened to say, "Most of them were lovely."

"Most of them were civil," Rand corrected. "A few were lovely. I could comfort myself that they're cretins, but some of them I formerly called my friends. So who's the cretin?"

"You don't expect me to defend them, surely." Turning back to the engine, Garth tapped a pressure gauge. "I have no reason to love them."

Rand didn't like his brother's appearance. Garth still wore formal clothing, but his cravat had been torn off and black streaks marred the pristine white of his shirt. Placing a steadying hand on the ladder, Rand asked, "What's wrong with the damn stupid machine?"

"Did I call it that?" Garth tried to look innocent. "It won't start. It keeps hiccuping like it wants to, but it just doesn't catch."

Glancing at Sylvan, Rand experienced her anxiety almost as if she spoke aloud. Something gnawed at her, but when he took her hand and asked, "What is it?" she just shook her head.

"I don't know. I just don't like this place." She tried to smile. "I've seen my father's mills, and I don't like them, even when they're quiet."

"I shouldn't have brought you," Rand said.

"You would have left me at the party?" Sylvan asked.

He laughed at the exaggerated hurt in her voice. "No. I guess even a mill is better than a roomful of nosy aristocrats."

Around on the other side, Stanwood, the master mechanic, thrust his head out. "I just cleaned out the stuffing box, Yer Grace. Want to try it again?"

"Do it." Garth climbed down the ladder. "These delays are irksome."

"Perhaps Jasper could assist," Rand offered. "He's got a way with carriages. Maybe he can fix any moving parts."

Jasper didn't move out of the shadows. "Carriages aren't steam engines. These contraptions are inventions of the devil."

Garth laughed. "You don't believe that superstitious claptrap, do you?"

"This place makes me squeamish."

Sylvan looked as if she wanted to agree.

"But I wager you could fix this. Won't you try?" Rand coaxed.

With a sigh that rattled the piston rods, Jasper came forward and accepted the wrench Garth offered.

The big engine before them shuddered, and Stanwood called, "Stoke that fire. We've got it now."

Garth opened the door to the boiler and a blast of heat roiled past. Grabbing a shovel, he ladled coal inside onto the glowing fire until one of the women nudged him and took the shovel.

"Pressure's going up," Stanwood called, and Garth ran around to check the pressure gauge.

"Look at that," Jasper crowed. He circled the engine as the main piston began shoving the flywheel. "That rod thing is moving."

"We've got it now." Garth wiped a drip of sweat off the end of his nose. "We can start up again. Come on." He offered his arm to Sylvan. "Let's go to my office and have a congratulatory drink."

The noise level began to accelerate, the floor to vibrate. The women raised their voices above the rhythmic roar of the engine as they walked to their stations. Threads began to twitch, then roll, and Sylvan flinched as the mill developed its customary roar and cadence.

Rand held her hand tighter and said to Garth, "She'll come with me."

Garth's lips twitched as he subdued a smile, but he said nothing as he led the way.

Following close behind, Rand asked, "Do you think these problems are the work of the mischief-maker?"

Lines of care etched themselves around Garth's mouth and eyes. "He wouldn't dare mess with the engine. The danger's too great. If the pressure's wrong in that thing, if a valve sticks, it could blow this—"

Sylvan made a sound of distress, and Garth must have heard it, for he quickly added, "Of course, that won't happen." He held the door to his office as they entered, then followed them in. He pressed Sylvan down in a chair and brought a bottle of wine from his cabinet. Waving the dusty bottle, he said, "This is the last of the smuggled stuff. French wine is authorized for import now that Napoleon's been safely shunted off to his island, but I think the illegality gives this quite a tang." He poured three glasses and distributed them, then raised his in a toast. "May you find the kind of happiness I have found."

"God grant," Rand agreed, and tapped Sylvan's glass with his.

"Drink up, Sylvan," Garth urged. "It'll bring the roses back into your cheeks." He waited until Sylvan had complied, then asked, "Now, what really brings you here?"

"It occurred to me you might be interested." Rand placed his glass on the desk. "Sylvan had a ghostly experience last night."

Garth looked from one to the other. "A ghostly . . . ?" Comprehension swept his face, and he focused on Sylvan intently. "Were you hurt?"

She shook her head.

"I beg pardon." Garth looked furious and embarrassed. "I never would have pressured you into coming to Clairmont Court had I realized you would be subjected to danger. I suppose that since our ghost disapproves of everything I do, he also disapproves of you." Garth grinned savagely. "But I think he'll soon see the error of his ways."

Rand leaned forward. "What do you mean?"

"I've spoken to him." Garth perched one hip on his desk. "He's coming here. We're going to have a talk, and there's going to be an understanding reached."

Incredulous, Rand demanded, "You know who it is?"

"I'm a bit of a fool," Garth admitted. "But yes, I know who it is. The evidence has always been there, but I didn't want to think that it could be one of my own."

"Who is it?" Sylvan demanded.

"I don't think I should say until I've—"

Sylvan reached for her throat. "You sent for him? Now?"

"He'll be along directly, I imagine, and—"

"Don't you understand how dangerous he is?"

Sylvan didn't scream, but she came close, and Rand jumped. "Sylvan?" he questioned. "Is there something you should tell me?"

"Dangerous?" Garth visibly struggled with his disbelief. "He's misguided, certainly, but—"

"Misguided? You call a man who stalks women in the dark misguided?"

"He hasn't—"

"Killed anyone?" Rising to her feet, Sylvan slapped

her palms on the desk and leaned toward Garth. "Is that what it takes?"

"Sylvan, I'm going to punish him as he deserves, but—"

"How can you be so blind? He's taken Rand's recuperation and used it to try and drive Rand crazy. He came to my room and—"

"Recuperation?" Garth seized on that one word to the exclusion of everything else. "Rand's better, yes, but isn't recovery too strong a term?"

Sylvan looked guiltily at Rand, and he shook his head. In her excitement, she'd said more than she should, but he couldn't work up a fury. He and Garth were close, closer than most brothers, and ever since Sylvan had convinced him of his innocence, he'd wanted to share his delight.

"Rand?" Garth stood and came around the desk. "A recovery?"

Rand heard the lilt in Garth's voice and rejoiced. "I've been walking in my sleep." To temper Garth's dawning rapture, Rand warned, "But only in my sleep."

"Walking in your sleep?" Leaning down, Garth grabbed his brother in a bear hug that lifted him out of the chair, then dropped him back. "How long have you known?"

"For months," Rand admitted. "I thought that I—"

"Was the ghost?" Garth followed his thought with a sure instinct. "And that bastard let you think so?" He looked at Sylvan, at the fists she clenched in her lap and the earnest fright in her expression. "You think I'm a fool, don't you?"

"I think you're a man," she corrected. "Always thinking you're too big and strong to be hurt, always thinking you can protect everyone else from injury. But this scoundrel doesn't fight like a man; he lurks in the shadows and attacks when you're weak, and if you don't take him seriously—"

"Yes." Garth bowed his head. "You're right. I'll send some of the men to escort him here, and we'll confront him together." Looking at Rand, some of his serious mien disappeared. "But you're walking at night, and someday soon . . . I would give anything to have you walk again." Lifting his head alertly, he held up one hand for silence. "What's that?"

Outside in the mill, the sound of the machinery had changed. It seemed to stagger from start to stop and back again, and as Garth came to his feet in a rush, the door slammed back against the wall. Rand stared at the wild-eyed mechanic as he yelled, "'Tis making a chugging noise, Yer Grace, like it's trying to go somewhere, and the piston's freezing."

"Have you tried the bleed valve?"

"Nothing came out."

Garth pushed Stanwood aside and leaped out the door, and Rand snagged the mechanic when he would have followed. "What does this mean?"

"Means trouble," Stanwood said, and tore himself away.

"Dear God." Sylvan lunged at Rand as he pushed himself toward the door. "Don't go! Can't you feel that?"

He could indeed. Beneath them, the floor trembled. In the mill, the women shrieked, and he feared—

Boom! The blast hit them, hot and harsh. It rattled the hinges and threw her against the wall. It blew papers in a whirlwind.

It knocked Rand's chair over and sent him sprawling. "Garth!" Shoving the chair aside, he leaped up and ran toward the door. "Garth."

12

Sylvan grabbed for Rand and missed. He ran out into the mill, and she darted after him.

And staggered back. Beyond the office door, hell reigned. A new hell, one of twisted lumber and curling steam. The far wall had blown out. Sunshine beamed in inappropriate gaiety. Tiles of the slate roof fell in masses, like playing cards from a careless hand. Machinery rested on its side. Dust mixed with the wind, and Sylvan tasted it—the dust of defeat.

In an instant, the mill had changed from manufacturer's dream to worker's nightmare.

Sylvan coughed and squinted, trying to see through the floating grime. Rand struggled through the wreckage, and for the first time, Sylvan realized—he was walking. Without a thought to himself, he was walking. It was a miracle—the miracle they'd been seeking. He leaped overturned machinery, cleared a path through the devastation, and called his brother in a desperate tone.

Another beam crashed to the ground, and she jumped. God, a miracle, but at what cost?

Other voices joined Rand's, quietly at first, then louder. Women moaned, cried, called out names. One slowly built to a scream that hit a high note and stayed.

This looked like a battlefield. This looked worse than a battlefield.

Sylvan cringed. They wanted her. They needed her. She had to help them.

She couldn't. She couldn't help them. She already knew that. She'd already proved that.

Below the constant shriek caused by someone's pain, she could hear a low, steady weeping that begged for attention.

Across the room, someone staggered to her feet. A bedraggled, filthy Nanna swung her head back and forth like a pendulum, seeing the destruction through shocked eyes. Leaning over, she picked up a long fragment of wood and tossed it aside. Then another, then another. She collapsed onto one knee, then walking her hands up a crooked timber, she dragged herself erect again.

She needed help.

Sylvan took her first step out. Everyone needed help.

"Lady Sylvan." A feeble voice called her. "I think my ribs are broken, but if ye'll help me, I'll stand and give a hand."

Beverly. Sour-faced Beverly struggled to tear strips off her skirt so she could wrap herself and help the others. Sour-faced Beverly. *Brave* Beverly, who knew what was required and did it without question. Without whimpering.

Sylvan whimpered and clambered through the chaos to her side. "Let me." With her teeth, Sylvan ripped strips off her own linen petticoat. After all, she did know how to do that. She'd done it often enough. Assisting Beverly as she sat up, Sylvan bundled the strips around Beverly's chest and tied them. "Is that better?" she asked.

"Much." Beverly's white cheeks told of the lie. "Thank you, Lady Sylvan."

"I found her," Nanna called. "I found the screamer. Shirley's caught. Lady Sylvan—"

"I can't. Oh, God, please, I can't."

"Could you go find somebody to dig her out?" Nanna finished.

Jolted, Sylvan stared at Nanna, then at Beverly, and slowly she realized they didn't expect her to bandage them, cure them, help them. They didn't expect anything from her, now that she was a noblewoman, and that was fine with Sylvan. "I can't help."

She whispered, but Beverly heard her, for she patted Sylvan's hand as if she were the one in need of succor. "Lady Sylvan, if you would just prop me on my feet—"

The building released another shower of tiles, stone, and rafters, then, with a groan and a mighty bang, an oak cross beam hit the floor. Sylvan ducked, cowering, almost wishing something would strike her and put her out of her misery. Pain had to be better than this constant uncertainty, this debilitating cowardice.

But the dust settled once more, Sylvan was uninjured, and she raised her head.

Nanna had disappeared. The screaming had stopped. It was silent. Dead silent.

"No," Sylvan whispered. Staggering to her feet, she strained her eyes as if Nanna would rise from the rubble. "No, please." She started across the room. Each step seemed weighted, too slow to help yet so heavy it would produce another rupture in the mill's framework. Above where Nanna had stood the sky gleamed. Rafters hung askew. Heavy slate shingles slapped the floor as they slithered off the roof. Not a glimpse of Nanna remained.

Sylvan took a breath, then another; faster and faster until her head buzzed and she realized she didn't need air. She just needed courage.

Scorning breath, she started carefully moving sticks and plaster. A splinter jabbed her palm; she impatiently jerked it out. As she shifted down through the debris, she saw an apron and underneath that, the shape of a leg, trapped beneath beams and boards that crisscrossed like a child's game of pick-up sticks. Pull the wrong board, and the whole structure would fall on her head.

Cautiously, she moved a board. Nothing happened. She moved another. And another. Parts of two bodies appeared, then Nanna's face. At first Sylvan thought she, too, was unconscious, but her eyes flickered open as Sylvan uncovered her face. Her mouth was one thin line, held tight with pain, and when Sylvan uncovered her leg, she saw why.

The massive beam had landed right on her ankle and crushed it into the floor. There was no way to move it, no way to move her. If anyone had the right to scream, it was Nanna, but she clung to silence. Sylvan stared into her eyes, knowing what would have to be done and sick with the knowledge.

Nanna mined the bedrock of her courage—where was Sylvan's bedrock?

"I can help." One of the other women stood beside Sylvan. "I'm just a little scalded."

Scalded, indeed. The steam from the explosion had blistered one side of her neck and her cheek. More courage.

"Shirley's under there," Sylvan said. "Let's see if we can find her."

They carefully cleared debris. Others joined them. Pert, Tilda, Ernestine. All were injured, but they reported on the others. Ada had a broken arm. Charity was awake but seeing double. Jeremia had lost teeth and had both eyes swollen shut. Beverly was trying to herd them all outside.

The talk kept their minds off their increasing worry as no sound issued from beneath the rubble. Then—

"I've got her, Lady Sylvan." Ernestine dug eagerly for a moment, then sat back on her haunches. "She's here."

Sylvan didn't need to look beyond the expression on Ernestine's face to know Shirley's fate, but somehow she'd taken the lead in this small, besieged group. Solemnly, she leaned forward and pulled the last board away to uncover Shirley's torso—a torso robbed of breath and heartbeat by massive injuries.

She'd seen death before. Why did it always tear her heart out? Why did it always place another weight on the guilt in her soul?

A sob shook Ernestine, and Pert put her arm around the larger woman. "She was Shirley's sister," she explained.

"Of course." Sylvan looked into the sky. Shirley had been alive after the blast. Danger still hovered over their heads, and they never knew when another part of the mill would give way.

"Salvage something to build a shed over Nanna," she commanded.

"Should we send someone to the village and Clairmont Court to tell them?" Tilda asked.

"They know," Sylvan assured them. "I imagine they heard that blast for miles."

"Felt it, too," Tilda said.

"Yes."

"What are we going to do about Nanna?"

Sylvan looked at Nanna's agonized expression. "I'll take care of her." But she didn't move, still staring at the crushed foot that held Nanna in place. Visions of saws that separated flesh from flesh and bone from bone ripped at her until a man's voice brought her head up.

"Dear God." The vicar stood not five feet away, taking in the scene with horror, then comprehension. Swiftly, he came to Nanna's side and dropped to his knees beside her. With a gentle hand, he smoothed her face, then picked up her hand. "God has chosen you for a special mission, Nanna." His voice sounded deep, strengthening, and he rubbed her wrist slowly as if to massage the significance of his words into her flesh. "You're still alive, and God placed Lady Sylvan here at this time to save you. Do you hear me?"

Nanna's gaze clung to his, and she nodded.

"Do you believe me?"

She nodded again.

"Good." He beckoned Tilda and had her take his place at Nanna's side, then rose and took Sylvan's arm. "Lady Sylvan, you have already done much good in this place. It's time to do more."

Ashamed, she whispered, "I'm afraid."

"I'm here to help you. We're all here to help you. See?"

He pointed, and for the first time, Sylvan saw the others. Lady Emmie and Aunt Adela stood before the carriage that had brought them, taking in the scene with a shock that equaled Sylvan's own. Through the open wall, she could see James running down the hill toward them, his elegance in disarray. Then she looked up into the Reverend Donald's eyes. Tears leaked from the corners, and a great compassion gleamed from the depths of his soul. As Nanna had before her, Sylvan gained strength from his boundless sympathy. Somehow, without words, he conveyed his faith in her, and she straightened.

"Oh, I'll do it. I'm just afraid."

"You have every right to be afraid, but God will guide your hand." He patted that hand, and said, "Now, tell me what you need and we'll find it somehow."

Somehow she managed to tick off the required supplies, and he replied, "It shall be as you require."

He released her and gathered the other women around him, and Sylvan once again had a demonstration of his power. Was it just this morning that he'd performed her wedding with such majesty? Then he had been an apt representative of the church. Now he was more the able servant of God. She might not like him or his unbending attitude, but he had a deft, sure touch in steering panicked people in the right direction.

Using the strength he had lent her, Sylvan knelt beside Nanna's head. "I will take care of you," she promised.

"Aye, Lady Sylvan," Nanna agreed, but she didn't really seem to hear. Her gaze never left the Reverend Donald, and she took a sustaining breath. "At bottom, he's a good man."

"Lady Sylvan."

The shout jolted Sylvan, and she swiveled to stare at Jasper. He stood outside the mill's former wall, waving his arms.

"Lady Sylvan, ye've got to come!"

"Rand," Sylvan whispered. Amazingly, she'd forgotten about Rand, but then, she knew Rand could take care of himself.

Or could he?

With an anxious glance, she located Lady Emmie and Aunt Adela. James had them both by the arm, holding them still and speaking rapidly. Although Sylvan couldn't hear them, it was clear by their gestures that they argued in return, and she seized the moment to escape the confines of the mill. She didn't want to talk to them now. Not before she discovered the extent of the tragedy.

"Look." Jasper pointed before she had even cleared the mill's foundation. "Look."

Rand sat among the remains of a wall, holding his brother's body, his head held to Garth's chest as if listening for a heartbeat.

It was useless. Even from a distance, Sylvan could see it was useless. Garth's limbs flopped and twisted, and his head kept slithering off the support of Rand's knee. He was dead.

Sylvan turned away.

Jasper grabbed her. "Where are ye going?"

"Back inside to get Lady Emmie. There's nothing I can do here."

"Lord Rand is yer husband," Jasper snapped. "Help him."

Sylvan hesitated. Her first instinct was to leave Rand to his grief, but was Jasper right? Was it her function as Rand's wife to comfort him? Gingerly, she approached him and laid her hand on his shoulder. "Rand?"

He tilted his head and looked at her. "What?"

His intense frown reminded her of Gail when she sought to understand something beyond her comprehension. "Can I help you?" she asked, then immediately cursed herself. Stupid question, for all the world like a hat shop girl with a customer. But she didn't know what to say. What did one say in the face of death? "I'm sorry."

"Why?"

Oh, God, this was worse than she thought.

With exquisite care, Rand laid Garth on the ground and arranged him so his body looked as if it were in repose. He tucked the singed, torn clothing into a semblance of normal form. He frowned at the face; nothing could return it to its original shape. "Do you think it hurt him?"

Hurt him? To be blasted through a wall, to have every bone in his body broken?

"He was gone when I found him, and I was angry at first, because I didn't get to say what I wanted." His eyes shone glassy with the fever of trauma. "But then I thought how much he would have suffered, and I wondered if you thought he might have died instantly."

"Of course he died instantly. I've seen a lot of death, and I know." Know? Sylvan wanted to laugh at her own idiocy. She was telling a falsehood, but it was surely a good falsehood. Rand seemed to believe it, and it seemed to comfort him. Maybe her lie would cushion the blow until he was ready to face the truth. Maybe he would never face the truth. Maybe—she touched Garth's cold hand—maybe the truth didn't matter.

"I'm always the lucky one," Rand said. "Always the one left behind while the others go on to glory."

She hadn't known Garth long, but she'd liked him, respected him.

"I'm the only one left alive out of my regiment, did you know that?"

Garth had been a good duke: too arrogant for his own good, of course, but he took responsibility for his people and his lands in a manner almost lost in modern England.

"I'd been fighting for hours with no surcease, and my

regiment had been commanded to charge the French. The French were winning." He laughed harshly. "We would have done anything for Wellington."

Rand's narrative and Garth's dead body before her sucked her back into the past. She remembered holding her parasol over her head and observing the battle from a distance. The distance had provided a buffer between her and the suffering.

"But my horse had been shot out from beneath me, so I found another—there were riderless horses all over the field, adding to the madness—and mounted, and a boy ran up with water. I took the cup. I lingered to refresh myself, and when I tried to catch my regiment, I couldn't. The French line surrounded them, swallowed them, and I never saw another person alive."

The buffer hadn't survived her first hour with the wounded.

"Now it's happened again. I'm alive, and my brother's dead, and just because I was a moment too late."

She looked at his guilt-stricken face, and realized she still didn't know the words to comfort him. Feebly, she said, "This isn't your fault."

"Easy to say."

"And you can't blame yourself for drinking water."

"It torments me to think that if I'd been a minute faster—"

"You'd be dead, too." This wasn't right. Sylvan jerked with the realization. Why was she here, offering comfort where there was no comfort to be had, rather than inside, helping the living? She was such a coward, using Rand's grief as an excuse to avoid her duty.

And what was Rand doing, assuming he had the power of life and death? His brother's body lay on the ground, and he was mourning his own existence.

"If I'd got out to the steam engine—"

"You'd be dead, too."

Her voice was stronger now, more belligerent, and it penetrated his haze. "Sylvan?" He groped for her hand.

She slapped it away. "You're alive."

He covered his face and groaned. "I disgust you."

"Yes . . . you . . . do."

Her bluntness, her outrage brought his head up. "What?"

"You're a milksop."

He looked so shocked, she would have laughed, but she seemed to have forgotten how.

"You're alive, and you're cowering. You took a drink, you were lucky, and you're blubbering about it."

"I beg your pardon!"

"I should hope so." Her own words pumped strength through her veins, and she dropped to her knees in the rubble and shook her finger in his face. "You're alive because it wasn't time for you to die. Because there's work to be done on this earth, and God has decided you're the one to do it. I wonder how many times he's going to have to cuff you before you pay attention."

He gestured to the mill. "You call this a cuff?"

"I call this work to be done. Your brother would want his people cared for, and you had best stay on your feet and care for them." Standing, she cast him a scornful glance. "Afterward, you can mourn."

"What about you?" He stopped her with one question. "What will you do afterward?"

She stood with one foot lifted, frozen by his derision, and wished she could answer that she never mourned. But that would be a lie. No matter how she struggled, no matter how she worked in her mind, she couldn't face her fate with courage, nor her past with resignation.

She heard Rand groan, and she wanted to echo his pain, but he said, "Dear God, it's Mama."

Lady Emmie stood by the side of the mill, Aunt Adela and James on her heels. As she took in the scene before her, her kind face struggled with recognition and shock. She swayed, her tiny frame crushed beneath the weight of this new horror, and behind her Aunt Adela commanded, "Hold her, James."

James caught Lady Emmie, and Aunt Adela wrapped them both in an embrace, but Lady Emmie shook them both off with surprising vigor and ran forward. Rand sprang to meet her, clasping her in his embrace for one moment before she broke free once more and fled to Garth's side. Her hands fluttered over Garth's frame before one came to rest on his chest above his heart. With the other, she reached for Rand, and he took it and held it. "My baby," she said, looking at Garth. Then she turned to Rand. "Did he give you back your legs?"

Slowly, Rand nodded. "Yes, I suppose he did."

Aunt Adela passed Sylvan, rushing to succor Lady Emmie, and James dropped to his knees where he stood. They were a family, mourning one of their own, and they didn't need Sylvan now.

She strode toward the mill, planning Nanna's amputation and ignoring the voice that whimpered inside.

13

Dr. Moreland held the pink, sore-looking stub of Nanna's leg in his hand. Lightly, he touched the seam where Sylvan had lapped the skin over the bone and muscle to form a natural bandage, and smiled at Nanna. "I wager you were thankful Lady Sylvan was near at hand when the explosion occurred."

Nanna cast a grateful glance at Sylvan, who waited nervously for his verdict. "That I was, sir. If it had been left to the stupid ol' horse doctor we used to call for emergencies, I'd be dying in pain and agony. Not that there's anything wrong with Mr. Roberts, but I'm not a horse."

"You certainly are not. Well, I couldn't have done a better amputation myself." He carefully placed the limb on the pillow where it rested in the makeshift hospital in the halls of Clairmont Court. "I would that all young surgeons learned as well as you did, Your Grace."

Sylvan stared at Dr. Moreland without understanding. "Your Grace," he called her, and that was right, but she wasn't used to it.

Garth lay in state in the grand salon. His brother— her husband—was now the duke. It was a progression unbroken through four hundred years, so why had it taken her by surprise? Why had it never occurred to her that, in the case of Garth's death, Rand would become a duke?

And she would be a duchess. *Was* a duchess. The daughter of a merchant would be the duchess of Clairmont. Somehow, that seemed the ultimate, most horrible irony.

"You couldn't have had a better nurse here for this crisis," Dr. Moreland said to the mill women who stood in a circle around him.

They murmured their agreement, shifting their crutches and adjusting their slings.

"We never expected such kindness and care from a duchess," Dorothy said, then glanced at Lady Emmie in discomfiture. "I mean . . ."

"I know what you mean." Dressed in the black of deep mourning and looking suddenly frail and old, Lady Emmie sat on a stool and attempted to smile at Dorothy. "Sylvan has an experience I cannot hope to match."

In similar garb, Aunt Adela stood behind Lady Emmie. "I think everyone would agree that our dowager duchess and our new duchess have brought distinction to the Clairmont title, especially in regard to my nephew."

Lady Emmie's smile became genuine as she looked on her only remaining son. "I can't believe it, even seeing him with my own eyes. He's walking. Walking!"

Rand nodded at his mother and Aunt Adela, then glanced around at the women of Malkinhampsted. Universally, they watched him with tender approval, and Charity lifted her bandaged head off the pillow. "It's been a dread and ghastly year since ye returned from the war all crippled. That ye're walking is a sign that the bad times are turning."

Leaning on her elbow, Nanna said, "It's put the heart back into us all, Your Grace, when this blast might have torn us apart."

Moving with the care of one who had only recently relearned the skill of walking, Rand wrapped his arm around Sylvan's shoulders. "If not for Sylvan, I'd not have lived long enough for this miracle to happen. It's Sylvan we all should thank."

All gazes swiveled to fix on Sylvan, and Sylvan wanted to fend them off physically. Nothing she had done had cured Rand, and the gratitude weighed on her. If only she could say so, but when she looked at him, saw him on his feet, observed his occasional wobbles, she wanted to cry for joy. One thing—one thing only—had gone right in these last wretched days, and it was so right she forgot the pain and remembered only the rapture.

She didn't realize it, but her eyes shone as they looked on Rand, and his shone with equal delight as he examined her. Then he frowned, and said, "But she's tired. She's worked unceasingly for the last two days. It's been all I could do to make her snatch some rest in a chair."

"Yes." Dr. Moreland examined her with his sharp gaze. "On the battlefield and in the hospital afterward, she was relentless in her devotion to the men. She seemed to think she could personally keep death at bay." He patted her head as if she were a puppy. "That's why gentlewomen could never assist with wounded on a regular basis, I suppose. Their delicate sensibilities are strained by the horrors."

Resentful at being patronized, yet afraid he might divulge her secrets, Sylvan stirred within Rand's embrace. "Do you mean I wasn't effective in the hospital?"

"No, I mean you almost drove yourself mad caring for the lads."

Sylvan flinched when Dr. Moreland looked at her meaningfully.

Satisfied he'd made his point, he patted her head again. "Of what use is an exhausted nurse? Your devoted husband sent for me, and I came at once. You can go to bed and sleep, and leave the nursing to me."

"Adela and I will help, too, dear," Lady Emmie said. "We've discussed this, and we'll personally supervise the care of our patients so you can sleep. Except for this afternoon, of course, when we . . ."

Her voice wobbled, and Aunt Adela took up where Lady Emmie left off. "You haven't slept since your wedding day, young lady, and I doubt that you slept the night before that, either." Aunt Adela glared, her imperious manner belying the red glaze of her eyes. "We can't have the new duchess fall into a decline."

Rand wrapped his arm around Sylvan more tightly. "I won't let that happen."

Sylvan looked at him helplessly. All unknown to her, he had sent for Dr. Moreland. That proved his doubts in her ability, but she couldn't blame him for that. He'd been at her side when she amputated Nanna's foot. He'd heard the rasp of the saw and Nanna's screams. He'd seen the other women cower and turn away, and he'd held her head when she vomited afterward.

Men studied at French universities to become physicians, and even surgeons now had some respectability. Sylvan had practiced medicine with no knowledge except practical experience, and she knew that regardless of Dr. Moreland's kind words, she was guilty of gross incompetence. Worse, she hid the paralyzing fear that by trying to help, she'd committed murder.

Certainly, no one was suggesting that Rand had overexerted himself, although he had dark circles under his eyes.

As if Dr. Moreland read Sylvan's thoughts, he asked, "Your Grace, if I may be so bold as to inquire, how are those legs?"

Rand seemed to have accepted his rise to the dukedom with a good deal more grace than Sylvan. He didn't jump guiltily or look behind him, but answered simply, "The muscles cramp when I stand too long or walk too much, but every day seems easier."

Tugging at his beard, Dr. Moreland nodded. "It's these types of miracles which make my task worthwhile. Remember that, young lady." He waggled his finger at Sylvan. "You might have had to cut off a foot, but you cured your husband, and both actions were in the best interests of the patients."

"I didn't cure him," she denied.

"He thinks you did, Your Grace."

Your Grace—again. What a jest! What other duchess in England had had to amputate a woman's foot? What other duchess had set bones and stitched wounds, applied poultices to burned and scalded skin and mixed herbs to relieve infections? What other duchess . . . She clenched her fists and tried once more to realize—she was a duchess.

"She's going to swoon," Lady Emmie said.

Rand swung her off her feet, then braced himself as if he thought he might stumble. He did not, and he looked both pleased and surprised. "You're a tiny thing," he said to Sylvan. "Tinier than I'd realized."

He started toward the stairs, but she shook her head. "I can't sleep yet."

He didn't slow.

"Not until I've paid my respects to Garth. Not until . . . you're burying him this afternoon, aren't you?"

Rand hesitated. "Yes."

"I should be there."

He looked down at her, and she realized his equanimity had failed him. With tears in his eyes, he said, "We've discussed this, and even"—he struggled to keep his breathing steady—"Aunt Adela says that you should rest rather than attend the services. No one will mutter about your absence if Aunt Adela says it's permissible." He pressed a kiss to her forehead, then rubbed her with his chin as if he were a cat gaining comfort from her touch. "Garth would understand."

Yes, Garth *would* understand. Sylvan believed that. Of all the Malkins, she comprehended Garth's mind more than that of any of the others. He cared for his family, his patrimony, and his people, and he would bless her for her feeble attempts to help his people. "I want to see him," she insisted.

Rand carried her to the grand salon and set her on her feet. The odor of camphor permeated the air. The coffin stood in the center of the large room, drawing one's eye with the magnificence of the carvings and the sheen of the dark wood. It was decorated with wildflowers, some set in a magnificent arrangement, others woven into small, wobbly looking wreaths.

The lid was not open.

Rand watched the coffin with dry eyes and a brooding anger. "We have to bury him this afternoon. We can't wait any longer, and the body . . . the body was so injured . . ."

She interrupted him, trying to divert him from his grief. "I'd like to sit."

Chairs stood around the coffin for the mourners who wished to pay their respects, and Rand took the one nearest the door.

Sylvan didn't want to face the reality. As with all the deaths she'd seen, there existed in her no resignation. When she thought of Garth, she thought of a man who'd worked for the good of his people. To think that one of those people had killed him was beyond Sylvan's comprehension. She wanted to shout, "No!" and to demand that Garth rise and take his proper place once more.

As she moved forward to touch the coffin, she almost tripped on a woman's figure, dressed in widow's weeds, prostrate on the floor in front of the coffin. Had the Malkins hired a professional mourner to take the place of Garth's wife? But no, real sobs shook the woman, and Sylvan knelt on the floor beside her and touched her shoulder. Betty turned to face her.

Sylvan froze in shock.

Coming to her knees, Betty took Sylvan's unresisting hand and pressed a kiss on it. In a voice made hoarse by unceasing tears, she said, "Thank you for coming to pay your respects." She took a quivering breath. "It gives me comfort to know you are here."

A widow's speech, Sylvan realized, from the woman who considered herself Garth's widow. No wonder Garth Malkin, duke of Clairmont, had never married. He had loved his housekeeper.

Betty chuckled with soggy amusement. "You look so confused, miss."

"I don't think I'm confused," Sylvan answered. "I think I see things clearly for the first time."

"Likely that's so." Sobering, Betty touched the coffin with a trembling hand. Her voice broke repeatedly as she said, "He would have cast . . . propriety to the wind, would His Grace, but I refused to marry him." Her fingers clutched the curve of wood so tightly her knuckles turned white. "One of us had to do what was proper."

A waste, Sylvan thought. Such a waste. "It was proper to live with him, but not be his wife?"

"Now don't you start, miss." Betty pushed the black veil off her face. Her shiny pink skin looked blotchy, her dull eyes drooped. "He wasn't a big one for society, but if he'd married me, I'd have been as out of place as a fish trying to fly. The ton would have cut me, and he'd have had to defend me." She took a quivering breath. "It would have been just awful. *You* know, miss. Just like those so-called gentlemen and ladies tried to do with you on your wedding day, but you know how to act the lady and confound them, and I do not."

It was true. Betty comprehended her situation and understood her limitations. "But it's such a shame!" Sylvan cried, rebelling at the injustice.

"I had many good years with him. He's been my love since I was a lass, and I'm glad for the time we had." She stroked the coffin. "Well, he's dead now. Appearances no longer matter, and I can mourn him openly. If the ton gossips, it'll hurt no one now. Not even Gail. She's so sure of herself, she's a lady already."

"Gail." So Gail *was* Garth's daughter. Not James's, and certainly not Rand's. She turned and looked at him, and found him gazing straight at her. She had wanted to think Gail was Rand's daughter because it had been her way to prick at the growing balloon of her attraction to him, and it had amused him to watch her flounder toward the truth. Then the object of her thoughts stumbled into the room; a small, thin, painfully dejected girl who had just lost her father, and Rand took her in his arms and comforted her.

Gail *was* his daughter now.

*   *   *

Although tiredness weighed on her, Sylvan couldn't sleep. Too many worries preyed on her peace. Through the bright afternoon, the death knell rang out and she counted each dull clang. When the bell stopped, she lay back on her pillow, stared at the fire Bernadette had built, and thought about Gail. The child had been happy and carefree, the daughter of love if not matrimony, and her sense of security had exploded with the mill. She still had Betty, she still had Rand, she still had Lady Emmie and Aunt Adela, but she would never again bask in the arrogant carelessness of childhood.

Could she help Gail? Sylvan thought she could, for even with all her legitimacy, she had never had her father's love or approval. The quake that had just destroyed Gail's world had shaken Sylvan throughout her life; perhaps she could guide Gail around the looming obstacles.

A board outside the door creaked, and she shivered with a chill that came from deep inside.

If the ghost only walked when there was trouble afoot, he'd done so with good reason this time. Danger had lurked in the halls and on the estate of Clairmont Court. Danger still lurked, as far as she knew, for no culprit had been seized in connection with the explosion of the mill. She didn't really know *what* Rand had discovered these last few days—not much, she supposed, when he had spent so much time assisting her. But would Rand have considered confiding in her if he had discovered something? She wasn't part of the family, not really, and she was a woman. Men frequently thought women should be shielded from the reality of life— which was another way of saying they thought them too stupid to withstand life's harshness.

Again she heard a noise outside the door. A jingling

or ringing, like sleigh bells. She looked at the bright sunlight that warmed a long rectangle on the floor and thought, *How foolish to be afraid of a ghost in the afternoon.*

Stupid to be afraid of a ghost who had done her such a favor, too. If he hadn't lured her from her room on the night before her wedding, she'd have been hurt, perhaps badly, by a sham ghost. By the person who even now lurked outside her bedchamber?

Silently she slipped from the bed, and shivering, she crept to the door. Opening it just a crack, she looked out into the hall.

A new table stood against the opposite wall, draped in a tablecloth that hung almost to the floor on the sides, and beneath it sat Jasper. He held a ring of keys and sorted through them one by one. Occasionally one clinked against the other, and he jumped. Then the keys made the jingling sound she'd heard, and he moved the edge of the tablecloth to peek guiltily down the hall.

Carefully shutting the door, Sylvan leaned on it. What was Jasper doing? She'd never seen anyone behave as oddly as Rand's coachman and body servant, and she hoped he hadn't gone quite mad. In fact—she gulped—she hoped that guilt hadn't driven him insane. She had suggested him as the sham ghost once before, but she hadn't really believed it. Jasper had seemed so normal, but when she thought about it, he had had the opportunity to attack those women, and her, too. He'd been assisting the mechanic when the steam engine exploded, and although Stanwood had died, Jasper had not sustained a single scratch. Was he lurking outside her door waiting for the proper moment to murder her? Or was he part of a team who planned to . . . to what? Sylvan still didn't understand what the madman hoped to accomplish with his vicious attacks on the women and his destruction of the mill.

Hearing voices in the hall, she leaned her ear to the door. She could hear the rumble of men's voices, then the doorknob twisted and the door began to move. She braced herself against it, and she heard a grunt from the other side, but the pressure didn't ease. Her feet slid inexorably on the smooth floor until the door opened completely and Rand poked his head around. "Sylvan! What are you doing?"

The voices in the hall took on new meaning, as did Jasper's unusual behavior. Had Rand asked him to guard her? Seeing Rand's puzzlement, it seemed a logical conclusion. Smiling with false good cheer, she stepped away from the door. "Sleepwalking."

Rand moved into the room. His eyes were red-rimmed, and he still wore the formal knee breeches, white stockings, and black pumps that a funeral required. However, he'd removed his black coat and waistcoat, and his cravat hung loosely around his neck. The starch in his white shirt had failed, and his informal appearance was explained when he let someone—Jasper, she supposed—toss in a pile of bags. To her, he said, "You should be in bed. You're obviously overtired." Her white nightgown might be modest in its sweep from neck to toes, but Rand's worried frown lightened at the sight. "No, Jasper." He held up his hand to his manservant who still stood in the hall. "I'll unpack."

She sprang toward the bed and scampered beneath the blankets as he shut the door. "What are you doing here?" she asked brightly.

"Moving in."

The pile of bags gained new significance, and she eyed them with foreboding as she tucked the sheets tight under her armpits. "Already?"

If anything, he looked taken aback. "Already?"

"Well, it's just so soon after . . ."

To her surprise, he gave her a wobbly grin. "After Garth's funeral? I assure you, Sylvan, Garth had an earthy nature. In fact, I wouldn't doubt that my crafty brother . . . had marriage in mind the first time he met you." His voice sounded thick with tears; obviously, he wasn't as composed as he appeared. "Let me assure you, if he were here, he would have carried the bags in for me, regardless of the grievous circumstances." He hesitated, then said delicately, "I looked for you first in the duke's chambers."

Her toes curled as she pulled her knees closer to her chest and tucked the skirt of her nightgown around her toes. "I like this room better."

"It's very nice," he said politely, and did not point out that it scarcely compared to the grandeur of the duke's apartment. "However, if you are avoiding me, let me relieve your mind." Opening one carpetbag, he began to unload bottles onto her table with false briskness. "You don't need to feel you must perform your conjugal duties now. I would prefer to have a bride who doesn't doze off during the initiation."

"It's not that," she protested, knowing it to be the truth. "I'll have to move there someday, but not today."

He looked at her inquiringly.

Stumbling, she tried to explain. "Not when it seems the bed still bears the warmth of Garth's body, and the scent of Betty's love still lingers among the linens."

Rand stared at her for one more moment, then tears sprang to his eyes and he returned to his work with the feverish intensity of one driven. "I hadn't thought of that. You're right, of course." He wiped his cheek across his shoulder. "At the funeral, Betty bore herself with all the dignity of the finest lady, and James . . . poor James." Rand sighed. "I'm afraid his guilt has placed him beyond consoling."

"Guilt?"

"At the many fights he and Garth indulged in."

She didn't answer, but wondered if James . . .

Rand reached the bed before she realized and lifted her chin. His blaze of indignation had dried his eyes, and he said, "I know what you're thinking, and I want you to stop. James didn't sabotage the mill. He's our *cousin*, for God's sake."

"But the guilt—"

"If you're going to use guilt as a gauge, the culprit is standing before you. I'm guiltier than anyone. I didn't help Garth with the mill, and if I'd just seen beyond my own problems, perhaps I could have discovered whether the source of my problems and the source of Garth's was the same. I think he must be, so don't judge me or my people."

A scathing rejection, and one she supposed she deserved. She wasn't one of his people, and she leaned back with a sigh and closed her eyes.

He noted the weariness that tugged at her sweet mouth and the lines where dimples had once resided. He had done this to her; he and the riddles at Clairmont Court and his own volatile reactions. He tried to relieve the burden of responsibility from her. He wanted her to stop worrying, yet here she was, awake and restless, observing him as he wrestled with his sorrow and, no doubt, wrestled with her own. "Have you slept at all?"

"No."

"Why not?"

She tugged the blankets closer around her chin. "I'm cold and I'm . . . well, it just seems I can't shut off my mind. Every time I close my eyes, I see the women, suffering, and I just can't"—her eyes popped open—"sleep."

He knew of a cure for insomnia, and a salve for their grief. It was an attestation to the spirit, a consummation of their marriage, and, in a sense, a toast to Garth and the pleasure he seized in life. Rand trembled with the need to lift the blankets and slip between Sylvan's legs. Her delicate appearance restrained him, and he wondered if he would be the worst sort of cad to help her in that manner. Then, drawn by an irresistible force, his hand reached out and he smoothed the hair off her forehead and away from her ears. She turned her head toward his touch. His hand slipped behind her neck, and when his fingers massaged a strained spot, she moaned. "You want to sleep?"

She nodded.

"I can help you." He withdrew his hands and walked to the table. He searched among the scattered bottles until he found the one he wanted. Going to the fire, he set it where it would acquire the warmth, and laid enough wood on the grate to last for hours. Then, taking the warmed bottle, he returned to the bed to find her watching him warily. She was no fool, his Sylvan, and her suspicion seemed appropriate, considering her virgin state and his intentions. He asked, "Do you believe in me?"

She hesitated.

"When I could only walk in my sleep and women were hurt on those nights, you believed in me so much you forced me to believe in myself. Has that changed?"

"No. No, I believe in you."

Her gaze clung to his with the sorrow of a pet caught in a poacher's trap. She needed him to rescue her and heal her wounds, and he needed her just as badly. Stripping the blankets away, he sat by her feet, and she bounded up. He pressed her down to the pillows with his hand on her shoulders. "You have to relax."

"I am."

He grinned and wished he could strip away the night-gown that covered so well and tantalized so much. He poured a bit of oil into his palm. The citrus scent incited him, and he waved the bottle in her direction. "This one smells good, but I've got some rose oil over there. Would you rather have that?"

"No. This is fine."

"You didn't even smell it."

"I'm sure it's fine."

Rubbing his hands together, he picked up her foot. She jerked away reflexively. "You're not relaxing," he rebuked.

"I'll try harder," she promised, and stretched her arms out stiffly and clenched her hands into fists by her side.

She was as tight as the cotton thread the women had spun on the machines and just as likely to snap.

This was going to be harder than he thought.

In a soothing tone, he said, "You liked this last time. Remember?" Starting with her toes, he rubbed with a firm touch and slowly, gradually, she relaxed. He extended his range, rubbing the arch of her foot, the point of her heel.

Each time he changed position, she tensed, and at last she said, "I don't think I can bear this."

He touched the callus on every toe and the pad of skin that cushioned her heel, and said, "Any woman who has earned calluses like this can bear anything." He started again, manipulating the tiny bones of her toes and the rough texture of her sole, and this time she relaxed completely.

That was it; the most important part. He had touched

her, stroked her, accustomed her to his hands on her, and now he could move on. Move up. Again he wet his hands with the oil, then laid his hands on her ankles. She didn't jump quite so completely this time. Her gaze didn't cling to him quite so anxiously, and as he worked the joints, her breathing began to deepen. Casually he worked up her calves, pushing the prim nightgown ahead of him. She watched him from beneath heavy lids, and he couldn't decide if she was suspicious or tired, so he rolled her onto her stomach.

She tried to sit up, but he placed his hand on her back and pushed her down onto the mattress. "Relax," he said. "Believe."

She took a big breath when he slid her nightgown up, then a bigger one when he slid it all the way up to her shoulders. "Take it off," he whispered, easing it over her head. She let him strip her, although she trembled.

"You are so lovely." From the dimples at the base of her spine to the coil of hair at her neck, he worshiped her. He wanted her.

Damn! He wished that he'd undressed before he started, but how did a man casually remove his clothes with a terrified woman watching him? Now that she was no longer terrified, he had to try to slip out of his garments without breaking the spell.

He ripped the fasteners off his breeches, dropped his shoes off the edge of the bed, and skimmed out of everything that covered him below the waist.

The shirt could wait.

Climbing onto the bed, he trickled oil in a thin stream down her spine, then straddled her, taking care not to touch her with his body.

Not yet.

He smoothed the oil across her skin, rubbing the

tightness from her neck. Lubricated by the fragrant oil, his hands slipped across her shoulder blades, then his fingers kneaded each sinew and muscle in her back and arms. Anxiety that had held her tight when he started now eased, and he asked, "What do you think?"

In a halting voice, she said, "Troubles are dripping from my fingertips."

He laughed softly. She had a funny way of saying it, but he knew it was true. Troubles were dripping from her fingertips, and relaxation had drifted in to replace it.

So drowned in tranquillity was she that when Rand twisted her onto her back, she made no move to cover herself. Exposed to his gaze in the bright daylight, she lay as he placed her: arms swung out from her side and legs slightly parted. Beauty was there, and something he had scarcely hoped to win: trust was there, too.

Staring at her, Rand shook with suppressed passion. His woman was prone before him, plucked of all her feathers like a bird at a feast. All except the fanciest ones, and they waved with silken splendor. His eyes burned and possessive fervor knotted his stomach, but the dependence implicit in her supine form kept him from taking her as she drifted.

He ripped off his shirt and rubbed it over his chest. He'd broken a sweat, not from the exertion of massage, but from looking, wanting, and restraining himself. Tossing the shirt aside, he proceeded with the tortuous ascent of her body. He manipulated her calves, her sweet and sensitive thighs. He massaged the firm wall of her stomach, her ribs. With both expert hands, he pulled and stretched her arms, rubbed the hollows around her collarbone, rotated her neck. His fingertips prowled her face until her tense jaw loosened and the worry wrinkles were obliterated.

Sylvan was only aware of her own body, not of the male body holding her down. Her soul hovered outside her body, floating freely above the scene on the bed. With no real care, she wondered how she would reenter the flesh. She experienced no desire to return to that earthly vessel, nor could she discern a thread connecting that soul with that body lying lax in a trance.

Then she perceived the lightest touch on her nipple and heat bloomed in the pit of her stomach. Warm oil lubricated her bosom, dispersed by Rand's slick palms. Just grazing the tips with his callused thumbs, Rand forced her to inhale deeply and bring air into her lungs. Resurrected by the life-giving breath, Sylvan endured a tingle of perception along her atrophied nerves. The slow excitement built as he stroked over and over her sensitive breasts, stroked up to her throat and across her belly to her inner thigh, brushing aside her crumbled defenses, ending her innocent isolation.

In one glorious revelation, Sylvan traced the thread that hooked her soul into her flesh. It was her senses; her skin alive to every vibration, her nose quivering with the scent of male sweat and citrus, her ears attuned to the rasp of his breath and the crinkle of the pillow beneath her head.

"Sylvan." Rand called her, and she opened her eyes to look on the stern face above hers; to see his miraculously nude body, all muscle and drawn sinew; to see his tanned hands as they caressed her white skin, bringing it to a fine-tuned anticipation. His knees were between her knees and he sat back on his heels to view her. "You are so beautiful."

She wasn't, she knew, but when he said it, why shouldn't she believe?

When he met her gaze once more, his eyes were fierce

blue slits. She hadn't realized how thoroughly passion would heat him or how strong his will must be to restrain himself, but she realized now what would happen when he let it go. And he would let it go.

She tried to cover herself with her hands, but he soothed her distress with a whispered reassurance, then bent and put his mouth there. Nothing prepared her for the sweet shock. It was like flowers and candy, a flickering courtship; wet and slow and riveting. Centering her whole concentration on one tiny nub, his tongue wrung smothered cries from her chest as she arched up to meet him, then writhed away. She didn't know what she wanted, but she called, "Please, please," and Rand knew.

He knew. Sliding up, he rubbed her all over with his body. The oil lubricated them so each motion was redolent with pleasure. The heat built quickly. She heard herself making different noises now, like a kitten when it is hungry, and she couldn't stop. He kissed her mouth. Her hands twitched, then rose to dab at his neck. He stretched. She grazed his shoulders. He sighed. She stroked his chest, then slowly, daringly, she lurched along his breastbone to his stomach.

Was she doing it right? She must be, because he said things that should have shocked her. Then he thrust himself into her hand, and that *did* shock her.

She tried to let go, but he liked it so much. She might not know much, but she knew that. He was slick, all over, and she was slick, too, and Rand said, "This is perfect. Put me where you want me."

It was all so new, but she couldn't pretend she didn't know what he meant. Trying to be bold, she placed him and glanced up into his face. He was smiling at her, and he promised, "It'll be easy."

He nudged himself forward, entering her just a little,

and her muscles tried to clamp down, but he uncorked the bottle of oil and poured it into his hands. She thought he would use it to ease his way, but instead he leaned back and rubbed it on her breasts.

Funny, to have him handle her with such care, as if she were precious. Funny, to have his touch on her nipples transmuted to a chill along her spine and a warmth deep inside. He rocked his hips to some yet unknown rhythm, entering her while his palms slid to her stomach and smoothed the skin. Entering her while too many sensations buffeted her and she didn't know which to heed. "Talk to me," he coaxed. "Tell me if you like this."

Another distraction. He wanted her to talk. "I like it."

"Which?"

She gasped at the pressure inside—the pressure he created, the pressure her own body manufactured.

"Do you like it when I do this?" He circled her hip bones. "Or this?" Taking her nipples, he pinched them hard between his thumb and forefinger.

At the same time, he plunged forward. She came off the bed with a squeal, not sure where she suffered the most and not sure if she'd been tricked or given a treat. "That hurt!"

He was trembling all over, and his forehead glistened with a fine sheen of perspiration. "Do you want to stop?"

She gaped at him, then considered. Her insides felt as if they'd been pinched, her nipples knew they'd been pinched, but the sensation was fading. Not as fast as she would like, but fading.

And *he* was suffering. He hadn't taken a breath since he asked the question he now clearly regretted. Moving carefully, she edged herself back onto the pillows. "No."

His chest rose and fell as he sucked in air. "Good. I'm glad we agree on such an important issue."

14

He'd spent the hours worrying about an act he'd finished too quickly. At least, *he'd* thought it was quickly. For Sylvan, it had lasted long enough to erase the sting of deflowering, and she'd fallen asleep with her hand over his heart and her head on his shoulder. He'd been rubbing her back and wishing she had had all the experience the ton had gossiped about, because once hadn't been enough and probably never would be enough with Sylvan.

So in lieu of *making* love, he pulled on his rumpled clothes and waited for her to wake up so they could *talk* about making love. He'd tell her how well she'd done for a rank beginner. He closed his eyes. She *had* done very well for a rank beginner. In all his imaginings—and there had been quite a few—he'd never dared hope she would respond with such enthusiasm.

After he'd praised her, she'd tell him how magnificent he'd been . . . he hoped.

Of course he'd been magnificent. Hadn't she spasmed and whimpered and moaned and—he twisted around, trying to see his own shoulders—scratched?

He looked toward the bed where she slept heavily, and grinned. God, married life was good.

A timid tap alerted him to the sound of voices in the hall, and he opened the door. Jasper leaned against the wall, glaring mightily at Betty, who held Sylvan's maid by the arm.

"Sh. She's asleep," Rand warned them. Then, taking a look at the mutinous expression on Bernadette's face, he said, "Thank you, but I don't think Her Grace needs an abigail's services right now."

"That's not why we're here. We're here to tell you something you should have been told when it happened." Betty shook Bernadette. "Tell His Grace."

Bernadette ducked her head. "Miss Sylvan—Her Grace—promised to tell him the night before the wedding. She even went to his room. Why do ye think she didn't?"

"Because I saw His Grace after she left his room that night, and they hadn't been discussing anything grim. Quite the opposite, if you ask me." When Bernadette would have interrupted, Betty added, "*And* His Grace would have had her swaddled in cotton and wrapped in a ribbon these three days if he'd known."

Rand had stiffened. "I know about the ghost. She did tell me he was in the hall outside her room."

"And?" Bernadette stared and waited for more.

But what more? Rand realized now he'd been distracted that night and hadn't asked all the questions he should. Now his servants were acting as if something had happened to Sylvan, something dreadful, and he did not know about it. Leaning forward, he urged, "Tell me, Bernadette."

"I promised Her Grace I wouldn't tell Lady Emmie and Lady Adela." Bernadette bit her lip. "Betty, ye always told me I shouldn't betray my lady's confidence, no matter what the reason."

Jasper interrupted. "I'll tell him."

Everyone turned to Jasper in surprise.

Jasper was morose with regret. "I was chasing after Her Grace, or I would have never missed him."

"Missed who?" Rand stepped into the hall and shut the door behind him. "Chasing Her Grace where?"

"'Twas the night before yer wedding, and I was watching Miss Sylvan's door."

Rand began, "I thought you were with—"

"No!" Jasper put up his hand. "I wasn't. I was watching Miss Sylvan's door." Bernadette was obviously salivating to know who Jasper might have been with, but Jasper paid her no attention.

"Why were you watching Miss Sylvan's door?" Rand demanded.

"I feared for her."

Jasper studiously avoided meeting Rand's gaze, and Rand remembered his misgivings regarding Jasper. Misgivings without foundation, he assured himself, but misgivings nonetheless.

Jasper plodded along, his speech slow and deliberate. "It just seemed, after that attack on Loretta and Miss Sylvan, that there was reason for alarm. Someone doesn't like Her Grace."

"I know that." Rand did know that, but the solemn expressions these servants wore warned him that knowing was not enough.

"I was watching Miss Sylvan's door, and I admit, I was dozing a little. 'Twas the middle of the night, and I'd had little rest. But I swear to you, Miss Sylvan suddenly opens her door and starts down the hall toward the servants' quarters, calling yer name, Yer Grace, and talking as if ye were right in front of her. Well, she was sleepwalking, of course, but I followed nonetheless."

"I never heard her leave." Bernadette excused herself to a frowning Betty.

"She led me on a merry chase," Jasper continued. "Around the halls, all the while talking to ye, Lord Rand—I mean, Lord Clairmont—I mean, Yer Grace—"

"Lord Rand will do nicely," Rand said, almost dancing with impatience.

"Aye, my lord." Jasper was thoroughly tangled in the courtesies, but he took a look at Rand's grimace and plunged ahead. "Miss Sylvan was trying to convince ye to go back to yer room."

"Why didn't you stop her?" Betty asked.

Jasper's eyes shifted away, looking everywhere but at Rand. "I've some dealings with sleepwalkers, and I know ye're not supposed to wake them as long as they're not a danger to themselves."

Slowly, Rand nodded, all the while thinking, *Jasper had known about his walking.* Jasper had kept his own counsel, but had he been trekking along after Rand the same way he'd followed Sylvan? Did he seek Garth's death in a twisted desire to elevate Rand? Did this man who had been Rand's faithful servant hide a vicious streak?

"Anyway, Miss Sylvan led us right back to her own hallway, and all of a sudden there's a shriek and a dark-haired man dressed in sheets runs from her room. I chased after him, fast as I could, and followed him into the old part of the castle, and there I lost him."

"How?" Rand shot the question at him, sure for just a moment that Jasper's tale was nothing but a sham to hide his own involvement.

"There are rooms and rooms in there, as ye know, and the ghost knew better where to hide than I knew how to find him." Jasper spread his hands in regret. "I'm sorry, Yer Grace."

"So am I." Sorry to hear the story, because Rand worried that Jasper had implicated himself. Turning away from him, Rand demanded, "What damage did he do?"

"He had a stick and beat on her bed," Bernadette answered.

"He was looking for her, then?"

"I told her he was. She said she was going to tell ye."

Bernadette obviously wanted no fault to rest on her shoulders, and Rand was not inclined to place it there. It was Sylvan who should have told him that she was in danger.

"Your Grace," Betty said softly. "The ghost—"

Bernadette snorted. "'Twasn't a ghost. 'Twas a man, Miss Sylvan said, and Miss Sylvan was right."

"Of course it was a man, just as it was a man who vandalized the steam engine and killed my Garth." Betty's eyes shone brightly with tears, but her resolution could not be swayed. "But he's not really a man, he's a coward who does his work in the dark and preys on the helpless, and we're going to get him."

Putting his arm around her, Rand hugged her. "Betty, you're an inspiration."

"But I don't want Miss Sylvan caught in the middle, and for some reason, this coward seems to hate her as much as he hated my . . . as much as he hated the late duke. She has to live, and Your Grace, this ghost-man was ready to do harm, for he beat on Bernadette."

"Beat on her?"

"Show him, Bernie."

Bernadette bared her arms, and there they were.

Fading strips of yellow and green, mute testimony to inexplicable violence.

Betty said, "I fear Miss Sylvan is in danger."

Rand wanted to shout in frustration, to fling himself at the people before him and command that they go back in time and do what should have been done. "But why? Why is this lunatic hunting Sylvan?"

"He didn't go after her until after you'd decided she would marry you," Betty said. "I think it's all part and parcel of my Garth's . . . death." She had to stop and collect herself, and the others waited respectfully. "I think this killer wants to destroy the whole Malkin family."

"Well, he'll not have Sylvan."

Rand must have been glowing with anger, for Jasper said feebly, "I've been watching."

Oh, there's comfort. "That's not enough." Restlessly, Rand paced the hall. For the first time in hours, he was aware of the pain in his legs and an ache in his back. The servants watched him and waited, like soldiers, for their orders. "Betty's right. Sylvan has to be protected. She has to be safe, and I don't know how to accomplish that here." If anything, his fury rose higher. "I'm going to have to send her away."

"You're fooling yourself if you think she'll go, Your Grace." Betty smiled scornfully at Rand and his imaginary supremacy over his new wife. "Miss Sylvan's not one to turn tail and run. If she were, she would have told you the story of the ghost before the wedding. Seems like it could have successfully delayed that wedding, and she was none too keen on marrying you."

Did Betty have to rub his face in it? He tried to think how to remove Sylvan without a fight. "I'll talk to her. She's a reasonable woman. She'll see my point."

Jasper laughed once, sharply. "If she's reasonable, she's the first woman to so be."

Bernadette whacked him on the arm. "Hey! There's no need to be rude about Her Grace."

With a sniff, Jasper said, "So ye think Her Grace will go at her husband's bidding?"

A sinking feeling enveloped Rand as Betty and Bernadette exchanged glances. The jeopardy of this situation could not be dismissed because of Sylvan's stubbornness. She had to go, or he would be shielding her when he should be searching for his brother's killer. Firmly, he said, "Bernadette, pack Miss Sylvan's things."

"'Tis a good decision." Jasper praised him.

Rand's lips twisted at the irony of having his unmarried body servant approve his decision, and what did Jasper's praise mean when weighed against Rand's suspicions? But he said only, "She's going to London to stay at her father's house."

"For how long, Your Grace?" Betty asked.

"For as long as it takes," he answered. "We'll trap our man before I allow her to return."

"Your Grace, it's time to rise and get ready to go."

Gradually, Sylvan opened her eyes and looked into Betty's face. Go? She had to go? She jerked herself erect. "The patients!"

Betty laid a hand on Sylvan's shoulder. "No, Your Grace, the patients are all doing well. Your doctor's here taking care of them, and a right good job he's doing, too."

"Oh." Sylvan laid her hand on her pounding heart and subsided onto the pillows. "I remember." Yes, Dr. Moreland had arrived on Rand's request, and this morning, Sylvan was glad. She could rest, loll in bed, then rise and assist the doctor as he needed.

But why was Betty here? Sylvan said, "You shouldn't be resuming your duties so soon after the . . . after the death of . . ."

"I know what you're trying to say, Your Grace, but I cannot bear to sit and think." Betty stared into space, then shook herself and bustled over to the porcelain pitcher. "I've got to work."

"Surely you could spare yourself everything but the truly important duties," Sylvan protested.

"There's nothing more important than the health of the new duchess. 'Tis ten in the morning, and the carriage will be waiting for you in an hour." Pouring a basin full of water, she handed it to Bernadette with a cloth and a towel. "Here's your water. Best wash those cobwebs out of your eyes. You've slept more than the clock around!"

Sylvan held the sheet around her chest while Bernadette handed her a clean shift, then she dove under the covers and pulled them over her head. Surfacing, she asked, "Are we going away?"

"You are," Betty agreed.

A smile tugged at Sylvan's lips while she tried to imagine Rand's plans. Were they taking a ride in the country? Were they going to visit London? Or were they—she scarcely dared to think it—were they going abroad, where they could spend time reveling in each other's company, visiting ancient ruins, quoting poetry beneath a full moon . . .

She caught sight of Betty, saw the way the housekeeper wrung her hands inside her apron and how her eyes were rimmed in red, and realized how inappropriate her day-dreams were. Rand's brother had just died, a murderer was on the rampage, and they were all in danger.

But she and Rand were married, and they could cure the cancer that threatened to kill them all. She knew it. Together, they were invincible. "Where's Rand?"

Betty and Bernadette exchanged glances, and Bernadette muttered something that sounded like, "Hiding."

Betty coughed and said, "His Grace discovered he had business elsewhere."

That single phrase jerked Sylvan to attention. *Business elsewhere.* Her father had frequently had "business elsewhere," especially when she'd displeased him.

But there was no way Rand could know the significance that phrase had for her, and anyway, she hadn't displeased him. Had she?

Elaborately casual, she accepted the damp cloth from Bernadette and washed her face. "Where are we going so early in the morning?"

Betty folded her hands and smiled placidly. "His Grace thought you'd be pleased to visit your parents and inform them of your marriage in person."

Sylvan jumped up so fast the basin went flying and Bernadette had an unexpected baptism. "What?"

"Visit your parents and . . ." Betty's placid demeanor failed. "Miss Sylvan? Are you feeling well?"

Standing on the mattress, Sylvan shouted, "Alone?"

"That was his—"

"*Where's Rand?*"

"I . . . he . . ."

Sylvan had seen guilt on a servant's face before, and she recognized it on Betty's now. Stalking across the bed, her feet sinking deep with each step, she articulated, "Where . . . is . . . His Grace? Where . . . is . . . my husband?"

Betty surrendered without a protest. "He's at the mill, looking over the remains of the blast."

"Get me dressed." Sylvan jumped off the bed and landed so hard both her ankles tingled with the impact. "I'm going out there."

Three walls of the mill remained largely intact. Some of the machinery had withstood the blast; some had withstood the collapse of the roof. If the explosion hadn't torn the bearing wall out from under the roof beams, the damage would have been substantially less.

But what could he salvage from such a wreck? Rand stood in the middle of the floor and looked up into the sky. Garth would have known the answer. Rand did not. He didn't know enough about manufacturing to make the right decisions, he didn't know who had caused the explosion, and he didn't know how to cure the ills of the estate.

His brother was dead, and all his dreams and plans had died with him. Rand was the duke now. He was responsible for the people on the estate, for the family fortune, and, most precariously, for the safety of his wife.

Picking his way through the rubble, he stepped outside into the sunshine and groaned.

The carriage was coming toward him full tilt, and he knew what it meant. Betty and Bernadette had agreed to try and send Sylvan away without seeing him—they seemed to lack faith in his ability to enforce his will with his new bride—and without offending her. Obviously, they'd failed, and she'd bullied Jasper into bringing her out here.

Now he wished he had done as he originally planned, and talked to her reasonably. Surely she would understand.

He groaned again when the carriage door opened and

Sylvan tumbled out, holding her parasol before her as if it were a sword.

His heart almost failed him when she started toward him. Her blond hair stood up and danced with the wind. Her big eyes narrowed and sliced him to snippets. Crimson blotched her normally pale complexion over her cheekbones and at the end of her nose, and it crept up from the bodice of her frock.

This threatened to be a brawl, not a dignified confrontation between a man and his wife. He looked at her again. Between a man and his livid wife.

He had to take control at once, or he would have control over neither her, for she was plainly ready to destroy him, nor over himself, for he saw her passion and wanted to keep it close. When she was near enough to hear him, yet he was still out of range of the parasol, he said, "Sylvan, have you come to view the destruction?"

"I certainly have." She stalked toward him, her gaze fixed on the vulnerable area of his body.

He walked away. "I haven't been to the mill since the day of the explosion, and I had hoped my imagination created a chaos greater than the reality." He gestured at the building. "Obviously, that is not the case."

Sylvan glanced at the ruin, then slowed and stared with appalled fascination. "It is awful, isn't it?"

Giving her a wide berth, Rand circled her. "I wonder at the lengths the killer is willing to go to destroy the Malkin family."

She jerked her attention back to him. "You don't know the motive for this."

"No, I don't," he admitted. "It may be that he seeks the extermination of the Malkin family, or it might be the Malkin prosperity that he seeks to obliterate. In either case, God help any who get in his way."

"That's nonsense," she said stoutly. "What reason would someone have for such malice?"

"Well, there's James. He's a frustrated, angry young man with a grudge against the mill, and he's now second in line for the dukedom. There's Aunt Adela, an ambitious woman who might do anything to advance her son."

Her face flushed to a deeper crimson when she realized that he was throwing her list of suspects back in her face.

"There's Vicar Donald, who is so dedicated to the word of the Lord, but not, I think, to the significance. And there's Jasper, who—"

"Oh, shut up."

Taking a chance, he got close enough to touch her. When she took no aggressive action, he grasped her shoulders and turned her to face him. "Sylvan, I don't know why someone is after us. Maybe, sometime, one of us created a personal enemy. Maybe someone envies us our wealth or our influence. Maybe . . . maybe, I don't know. But surely you can see you'd be safer—"

"Safer?" She watched him with narrowed eyes.

"Safer in your father's house."

She knocked his hands away. "I don't care about my safety!" Stomping closer to the mill, she kicked one of the squared blocks that had formed the wall. He saw her miss a step as she experienced the pain. Then she tried to pretend it hadn't happened, and raged, "I'm an independent woman. I've been taking care of myself for years. To have you try to protect me is an insult."

"An insult." Someone had been insulted by that statement, and he thought it was he.

"How can you even consider sending me away?" She strode back and forth in front of the mill; the destruction forming a backdrop for her beauty. "*You* have no reason to think anyone would harm me."

"No." Anger began to burn in him, slow and steady, but he held it off, and probed, "Is there any reason to think someone would harm you?"

She missed her step again, but not because she'd kicked anything. She missed it because of guilt. "No. No reason at all," she said.

She refused to look at him, and his rage burst its bounds. She was *lying* to him. He'd planned on talking to her about the ghost-man who'd tried to attack her, but he had never imagined she would deliberately try to mislead him. And if she were telling him a falsehood now, what might she do in case of future attacks? Might she even now be hiding the truth about other assaults? "Damn you," he burst out. "I can't trust you at all."

She turned with a flutter of skirts. "What are you saying?"

She had the audacity to look indignant, and he was glad. He knew why she was doing this. She wanted to stay, but her deception made the performance of his duty easier. "Blood will tell. Only a merchant's daughter would make a scene about this."

She froze. In a tiny voice, she asked, "About what?"

"Isn't it obvious?"

She actually staggered back. He hadn't said anything. He'd asked a simple question in the surliest voice possible, and she'd placed her own interpretation on it.

"You're sending me away"—the parasol fell in the dust—"because you're ashamed of me?"

She might stoutly deny it, she might defy society's precepts to hide it, but she was sensitive about being a merchant's daughter—and he was sensitive about her getting killed. "Tell me something," he said, "do you think my aunt Adela would have blessed my marriage to such a notorious woman if she had known I would recover?"

All the color fled her face, leaving her pasty with agony.

Rand took a step toward her before he remembered his mission, and stopped. He knew well how to act the part of a haughty duke, and he pressed his point. "Do you think Aunt Adela would have blessed my marriage to a merchant's daughter if Aunt Adela had known I was destined to be the duke of Clairmont?"

It was a stupid question. No other person in the world thought as highly of the duke of Clairmont's pres- tige; no doubt Aunt Adela had weighed the effect Sylvan's entry would have on the family's status and judged the ill effects negligible.

"Aunt Adela doesn't want me?" She clenched her hands close against her waist. "Lady Emmie and James despise me?"

"What do you think?"

The wind blew, the morning lark sang, but through it all Rand could hear the harsh rasp of Sylvan's breathing. Softly, he said, "There has never been an annulment in the Malkin family before."

"No!" Sylvan screamed as if she had been stabbed. "You . . . by-blow. You . . ." Her hands bunched into fists, and she quivered like a cannon about to discharge. "If you despised me so much, why did you have to make me happy? Why did you have to encourage me, make me think you admired me, act like you liked me? You could have sent me away before you made me what the world thinks me—a stupid, wanton, stupid, incompe- tent, stupid . . . woman." Picking up a dirt clod, she flung it at him, and it exploded on his chest. "You didn't have to make me like you. You didn't have to—"

To his horror, tears streaked her face. She wiped them, defiantly, leaving a muddy streak, then stooped and jerked clumps of grass and soil out of the earth. In a continuous battery, she flung them at him and they hit him, striking his face, his hair, his stomach. He made no attempt to defend himself. How could he? If this release made her feel better, he wanted it for her. She sobbed out loud as she hurled each clod, ugly sounds that must have torn at her throat and ripped at her guts.

They were ripping at his.

Just when he could stand it no longer, just when he was about to go to her and take her in his arms and assure her she meant the world to him, she stopped and stared.

She was no gift of the man-elf now, but a human woman wounded beyond recovery.

"Sylvan." Rand held out his open hands.

"Get your annulment then. Last night didn't mean anything to you. It didn't mean anything to me, either. Just never, never come near me again." She spit at his feet and ran to the carriage, and Jasper drove her out of Rand's life.

15

Rand stared at Sir Ogden Miles, Sylvan's father and his host. This was worse than James had suggested. "Sylvan won't speak of our marriage?"

Sir Miles pressed his shoulders against the tall flat back of his chair and rubbed his palms over the knobs on the bare wooden arms. "Worse. When I questioned her, she denied all."

"She denied our marriage?" Rand felt the clutch of his heart. "And you believed her?"

"Not at all." The man looked nothing like his daughter. Tall and thin, with clear brown eyes and a thick head of white hair, he bore himself with a dignity that completely hid his shrewdness. "But my daughter is ever defiant, and I have not been able to enforce my paternal will since she was nine."

"She didn't tell of the events which took place at Clairmont Court two months ago?"

"She refused."

"Why?" Rand shot at her father.

"I was about to ask the same thing of you," Sir Miles returned. He had welcomed Rand into his lavish home with every expression of gentility. He had taken him into a sitting room decorated in the latest style, and his servants had appeared with a generous tea aimed at refreshing the weary traveler. Sir Miles had expressed his sympathy at the loss of Rand's brother, yet didn't dwell on the still-sore subject, and he waited until Rand had dusted the crumbs off his lap before pressing him for an explanation of the marriage and its aftermath.

Sir Miles knew of the wedding because the Malkin family had notified him, but he knew nothing else. Apparently, Sylvan's wariness prohibited any disclosures on her part, although why this man inspired such prudence in his daughter, Rand could not comprehend. Now he rubbed his eyes wearily. "I don't understand her at all."

"That is in bearing with the confusion I have experienced since the day she was born."

"She is truly a woman." Rand chuckled and expected to share a moment of communion with Sylvan's father.

Instead Sir Miles seemed stiffly unamused. "May her father inquire what caused this breach?"

Sinking against the back of the chair, Rand studied the toes of his shiny black boots. "I sent her away."

"Why?"

"It was, I assure you, for her own safety." Sir Miles expressed his dubiousness with a mere twitch of his brow, and Rand wondered if the man was always so skeptical or if Sylvan alone affected him in that manner. Rand asked, "Where is Sylvan?"

"I believe she has gone to spend a few days with one of her friends." Sir Miles observed the effect of his pronouncement on Rand, then clarified unnecessarily, "One of her female friends. Lady Katherine Renfrew invited her to her country house for a week of frivolity."

"Lady Kathy the Madcap?"

"Ah, you know her."

Indeed Rand did, and thoroughly disapproved of Sylvan associating with such a woman. This, too, fitted in with the warning James had sent. James had gone to London after Garth's death, not to spy on Sylvan, but to do what he wished—to talk politics, to go to Parliament, to practice being the important man he longed to be. James had done all that, but he'd heard rumors about Sylvan, too, and passed them on to Rand. Although Rand hadn't believed them, he had seized the chance to come to London and to Sylvan.

Sir Miles seemed to discern more than Rand cared to say. "I spoke to Sylvan when she left, expressing my displeasure at her antics, but she has been in a state of manic activity since her return from Clairmont Court." He templed his fingers and looked at them intently. "I did not understand why before."

"Do you mean you understand why now?" Rand demanded.

Sir Miles inclined his head. "Not at all. My daughter and I have never reached accord except in one matter."

"And what was that?"

"I make money. She spends it." Reaching out, he rang the bell at his elbow. "I think perhaps we might wish to question my wife. Sylvan may have confided in her, although I find it hard to believe Lady Miles would be so unwise as to keep the truth from me." A footman came in, Sir Miles directed him to summon Lady Miles, and Sir Miles turned back to Rand. "Allow me to offer my congratulations on your recovery from your unfortunate paralysis. Is there . . . any chance it will return?"

His delicate pause made Rand realize that Sir Miles might demand more from his son-in-law than a title and a fortune. Somehow Rand felt inadequate, a failure for allowing himself the weakness of paralysis. Yet he narrowed his eyes, swept his gaze down the spare figure of the merchant, and said coldly, "I don't believe so."

Sir Miles nodded and imitated the way Rand looked at him. Rand recognized the fact that Sir Miles was no stranger to intimidation or to the inflicting of it. Sir Miles must have sat opposite many a fine lord and listened while that lord begged for money or for an extension on a loan already given.

Sir Miles had become wealthy because of his recognition of opportunities, and a baron because of his discreet touch with usury.

Perhaps Rand could discern a reason for Sylvan's rebellion against her father. But why was she rebelling against *him*, against Rand? Surely she could be brought to comprehend his reasons for sending her away so abruptly. Any woman as brave and clever as Sylvan would understand once her initial anguish had begun to fade.

The door behind him opened, and Sir Miles spoke. "Come in, Lady Miles, and meet Randolf Malkin, duke of Clairmont."

Good manners brought Rand to his feet. Facing Lady Miles, he bowed and discovered that the same man-elf who had assembled Sylvan had also assembled her mother. Lady Miles was, perhaps, the original and was also, perhaps, the lovelier of the two. But her pale skin had probably not seen the sun in thirty years, and her fine green eyes appeared frightened. It gave him an uneasy feeling to see this older version of Sylvan shrink from him as if he were a beast. "Rand Malkin. At your service." Rand tried one of his guaranteed engaging smiles and noted that it didn't work. All of Lady Miles's attention remained fixed on her husband.

"It would seem Sylvan has not told us the truth about her marriage. It would seem she has fulfilled my every desire and captured a fine old title," Sir Miles said.

"Captured a fine old title?" Lady Miles frowned apologetically, as if she didn't understand. "What do you mean?"

Rand took her hand and led her to the sofa. "He means that I have the honor of being your new son-in-law."

Lady Miles stared at him in puzzlement. "But that is impossible. To be my son-in-law, you would have had to—"

"Marry our daughter," Sir Miles intoned.

Lady Miles abruptly sat down, and she whispered, "Oh, no."

What *had* Sylvan said to her mother? Rand wondered.

Sir Miles said, "I wonder why she denied it."

Twisting the fringe on the shawl that ringed her shoulders, Lady Miles said, "I can't begin to imagine."

"Or did she just deny *me* the truth?"

Lady Miles cocked her head and stared at her husband for long minutes, then a trembling rose from her toes to the top of her carefully arranged topknot. "She didn't tell me."

"No?"

"She didn't tell me." The topknot quivered, loosening little wisps. "She really didn't. I didn't know."

Rand could stand it no longer, and interrupted to reassure her and distract Sir Miles. "I think we can safely assume you didn't know. However, I brought the marriage contracts for you to examine, Sir Miles. We drew them up swiftly, but I hope they find favor in your eyes."

Drawing the contracts from his traveling bag, he presented them to Sir Miles. Sir Miles looked at them for a moment, then accepted them in his long, tapered fingers. "You drew them up in a hurry, you say?" His brown eyes bored into Rand. "Why was that, pray tell?"

Rand could have groaned. Of course, Sir Miles would seek the reasons behind such a hasty marriage. Seen through the eyes of the Malkin family, their ardor in the meadow had been embarrassing, but not ugly or lewd. Seen through Sir Miles's eyes . . .

Staring directly at Sir Miles, Rand said, "When I at last convinced Sylvan to wed me, sir, I would allow no formality to impede our nuptials."

Sir Miles placed the contracts on the table beside him. "I don't need to look at these. I'm sure they're more than adequate, considering the condition of the goods you bought. I'm only grateful you were willing to pay the price."

Rand came to his feet, fists clenched. "You cold, despicable—"

A soft noise of anguish beside him brought him to a halt. Lady Miles was wringing her hands, her gaze sick with despair.

So Rand had a choice. If he followed his impulse to smash his fist into Sir Miles's thin face until he obscured its lack of emotion, he would be gratified, but Lady Miles would suffer. It was a choice Sylvan must have faced many times in her life, and it had marked Sylvan.

And Sir Miles? He sat calmly, observing Rand as if he were a butterfly under glass. He had prodded Rand into action and now watched, interested in the results.

Carefully, Rand unbunched his fists. "I used to wonder how a young, unmarried woman came to Brussels as a guest of Hibbert's. I begin to understand at last."

Sir Miles's gaze frosted over, and he might have been carved from ice. "As I said, Sylvan has not responded correctly to my guidance for years."

"You held the purse strings and the moral responsibility for her reputation."

"When I tightened the purse strings, she fled to her friend Hibbert, and as for responsibility—well, I gave her the best education, the best clothing, the best—" He seemed to realize that he was excusing himself, and he snapped, "You're an impertinent young pup."

"Oh, I think I'm old enough for you to accuse me of being a dog." Rand mocked, but inside he fumed. In the Malkin clan, when one of the women strayed, every member of the family shouted and cursed, but they still cared, and the man culpable assumed his responsibilities.

Sir Miles cared nothing for Sylvan. She was nothing more than a china figure he'd bought to place on a shelf, and as each hairline crack developed in her perfect exterior, her value plunged.

No wonder Sylvan kept flinging herself off the shelf.

For the sake of Lady Miles, Rand felt he ought to stay and smooth the relationship with his new in-laws. But he doubted his own ability to maintain his temper, so he bowed and smiled at Lady Miles, trying to appear a model husband for her wayward daughter. "I'll seek my wife at Lady Katherine Renfrew's country home, then. I thank you for your assistance."

He found himself on the top step of the mansion, clutching his hat and gloves and shaking with frustration—the same frustration that had walked with him every day since he'd sent Sylvan away.

Two months. No, more than two months, and not a single event had occurred on Clairmont Estate. Oh, there had been a few births, a few marriages, even one death, but nothing out of the ordinary.

Everyone in Malkinhampsted and at Clairmont Court had waited, breathless, for the next ghostly visitation, and nothing untoward had materialized. The ghost had disappeared.

Rand waited for it, wanted it to appear. He tried to imagine every possible motivation for the beatings of the women, for the attack on Sylvan, for the explosion of the mill. He refused to suspect the culprits Sylvan had suggested, yet at the same time, he kept his own counsel and did not consult James or Jasper. He made sure his womenfolk were guarded at all times, and he frequently slipped from the house at night to exercise his legs to restore them to full use. He reasoned he might as well stand guard. He couldn't sleep without Sylvan in his bed, anyway.

Yet all his preparations were for naught. The ghost had disappeared.

Of course, the village women didn't go out walking alone at night. With the mill gone, they stayed home, preparing meals, caring for the children—and worrying about the crops their husbands tended.

It hadn't been a good time for him, and it hadn't been a good time for his people.

At last, the inactivity had convinced him to come to London and bring his bride home again. He knew Sylvan would resist him. He kept his shirt unwashed—the one she'd thrown dirt at. It reminded him not to expect too much from her in the way of civilized behavior. Yet his whole being sizzled when he remembered the night they'd spent together, and he knew that the feeling between them was anything but civilized. Tonight he planned to prove his dedication to her and to their marriage.

"Yer Grace?" His carriage stood before him, and the footman held the door. "Where shall I direct the driver?"

"Home, first. The town house." Rand swung himself into the cramped quarters of the carriage. "Then we'll be going to visit Lady Katherine Renfrew's country house outside of London."

The footman looked confused. "But Yer Grace—Lady Katherine Renfrew?"

"Absolutely. Lady Katherine may be vulgar, but at least I know she will welcome a visit from the duke of Clairmont, and she won't object when I abduct one of her guests." Rand waved an imperious hand. "Drive on."

"You are the most vulgar woman in the country." Sylvan was furious, staring at the spectacle Lady Katherine Renfrew had made of herself with her frizzed hair, her clownish makeup, and a gown so low-cut her nipples flashed when she bent over—and Lady Katherine found many occasions at her own ball to bend over. She would have served the wine if she thought it would give her a better chance to display her wares.

"I may be the most vulgar woman in the country," Lady Katherine answered with a flush of fury, "but at least I'm not mincing around like some choir nun who's never had a man."

Sylvan opened her mouth, then shut it and blushed.

After all, she had had a man, and she'd been so defective he'd sent her away the very next day.

"Well might you blush." Without pause, Lady Katherine smiled over Sylvan's shoulder and wiggled her fingers at one of her guests. "With your reputation, darling, you ought to be grateful to have men like Lord Hawthorne and Sir Sagan after you."

"They're not after me. They're pleasant young men."

Lady Katherine ignored Sylvan's protestation. "Not to mention Lord Holyfeld."

Sylvan shuddered. "He's a slug."

"He's an earl."

"Then *you* take him."

"He doesn't want me, darling. He wants you, and I'm afraid I have to insist that you be polite to him." Lady Katherine trailed her long nails down her neckline. "After all, you are my guest."

As Lady Katherine sauntered away, Sylvan drew the curtains over the alcove where she hid and muttered, "Not for long." When Lady Katherine had invited her to this house party, Sylvan accepted without interest. She didn't care where she went or what she did. For two months, she'd been intent on proving her reputation was just as awful as gossip had made it. She waltzed when she shouldn't, laughed too loudly, offended the matrons, and flirted with the men. After all, why not? She'd proved to the one man who mattered she wasn't a whore, and he treated her like one anyway.

But Rand wasn't the one man who mattered, she reminded herself. Rand was nothing to her. She just didn't like having men leer at her, nor did she like having her hostess urge her to encourage Lord Holyfeld. It had been a very unpleasant scene when Sylvan discovered he couldn't keep his hands to himself.

She was taking her servants and leaving this place. She didn't want to go back to her father's house; one of the reasons she'd cleaved to Lady Katherine was because Lady Katherine fit the criteria for Sir Miles's disapproval. If Sylvan returned in the middle of the night, his unspoken "I told you so" would echo through the chilly halls. Nevertheless, it seemed safer to face the highwaymen who populated the road to London than to stay in this place where the second-rate nobility danced and drank and crept into each other's bedchambers.

With her resolution firmly in mind, she stepped into the ballroom. Scornfully, she swept the company with her gaze. They appeared to be no different than the best of the ton during the height of the London season—except when she looked closely. Then she saw the silly affectations of the men, their bright-colored coats and the too-high shirt collars. Then she saw the ladies' ankles as they kicked them up during a stately dance. Then she saw Rand, standing at the entrance to the room and speaking to Lady Katherine.

Rand. That scurrilous bounder.

She whisked back into the alcove, pressed herself against the wall, and held her hand to her throat. What was he doing here? Had he decided to lower himself to visit Lady Katherine's in hopes of finding a lady friend?

Thoughtfully, she considered ripping his heart out.

Did he have business with one of the gentlemen?

She wasn't her father's daughter for nothing. She could undermine him somehow.

Had he come to find her?

The blood in her veins surged with the force of a storm on the sea.

Stupid of her to think Rand would follow her here. He'd certainly been able to avoid finding her when she stayed at her father's house. Stupid of her to hide from him, too. She tossed her head although no one could see her. If he had come here for her, he'd come for one reason and one reason only—to cajole her into the annulment he desired.

An annulment. She shut her eyes against the pain. An annulment. He wanted to pretend that night had never happened. He wanted to pretend he hadn't taken her maidenhead or given her such piercing-sweet pleasure that she still dreamed of it. When he'd said that word on that day he sent her away, she'd been ready to kill him, to rip out his eyes and pluck out every hair on his head. She'd spit at him. *Spit* at him, and she wished she'd done worse.

No, she really didn't want to see Rand again. Let their solicitors handle the legal details. Cautiously, she lifted the curtain to escape, and came face-to-face with Lady Katherine.

Lady Katherine purred like a lioness about to shred her prey. "There she is, Your Grace. I told you I could find her."

"And you did."

Rand stepped up and Lady Katherine moved a few feet away in one smooth, rapid transition—so rapid, in fact, that Sylvan wondered if Rand hadn't pushed Lady Katherine out of the way.

Did discarded wives have to be courteous to their worthless husbands? Sylvan took note of Lady Katherine's avid interest and supposed that they did. Better to be polite to Rand and escape this situation quickly than create gossip where she wanted none at all.

"What are *you* doing here?" Oh, that was polite.

"I've come for you."

He smiled at her as if he thought she would jump into his arms.

If only he knew how desperately she had to fight her impulses—both her murderous impulses and her lustful impulses.

Lady Katherine peered around a big potted plant, watching them with ill-concealed interest, and Sylvan knew it was up to her to quash all rumors of enmity. "What's the matter, Rand? Can't you find another woman to spit on you?" That wouldn't quash the rumors, but words kept leaping from her mouth like frogs from a lily pad.

He didn't seem offended. "None that I'm interested in."

He looked good. A little thinner, perhaps, with a watchful cast to his eyes, but she understood that. He'd been trying to catch his brother's killer, so of course he'd be ever vigilant.

His voice sounded good, too, like the voice she always heard in her new dreams. The dreams that had replaced her nightmares and come on a regular basis to relieve her frustration. The dreams that ended with . . . well, she'd better not think about that now. Rand might read her expression and realize . . . His arm snaked out around her waist, and he drew her close.

"I had resolved to court you in a seemly manner, but when you look at me like that, all I can remember is the night and the bed and the massage that led to—"

A choking noise interrupted him, and for a moment Sylvan thought it was her own choking. But no, it was Lady Katherine, still hovering, still listening, and now shocked and thrilled with her unforeseen knowledge.

"Why don't you take yourself off?" Rand asked, an edge in his tone.

Lady Katherine scuttled off, torn between exaltation at hearing some juicy gossip, and despair at being forced to leave.

"Now." Rand circled Sylvan closer to the heat of his body. "We were discussing our mutual desire."

"No, we weren't." She whirled out of his grasp and followed up with a swift jab to his stomach. While he clutched his midsection, she snapped, "We were discussing how repulsive you are to me."

He looked up at her with surprise and with an admiration that rattled her. It took him a few moments to regain his breath, but not his wit. "If I'm repulsive to you, come away with me and prove it."

"Oh, no." He was a slimy worm, but his misplaced confidence made her chortle. "Very clever, Your Grace, but you'll not trap me like that. I'm staying here."

Stroking his chin, he stared at her. "Something is different. Your hair is longer. I like it like this, but I liked those little wispy bits that play peek-a-boo with the nape of your neck, too."

She clapped her hand over her neck.

"It makes me want to kiss it." He rearranged the wisps of hair that framed her face and she knocked his hand away. "I would have thought this place was repugnant to you."

"Not at all. Lady Katherine Renfrew is my dearest friend, and I love all the people she invited to her home."

He seemed to doubt her sincerity, especially when she grinned with maniacal brightness.

"I especially like the gentlemen." His smile faded, and she could barely restrain a cheer.

"What gentlemen?"

"Lord Hawthorne and Sir Sagan are here."

"Hawthorne and Sagan?" Rand was soothed. "They're good men. Fought with them on the Continent. Haven't seen them since we sent Nappy running with his tail between his legs."

"They've been most attentive to me."

"Shows they're bright," Rand conceded.

She tried again. "They're courting me, so you don't need to worry. You can get your annulment and I'll be none the worse."

"Ah." Rand stirred uncomfortably, then gestured to the seat hidden deep in the alcove. "Perhaps we should talk."

"Talk?" She batted her eyelashes in exaggerated regard. "About what, Your Grace?"

"About my reasons for suggesting an annulment."

"I thought it was more in the line of a demand," she said heatedly, then took a breath. "It's not important."

"Perhaps not to you, but to me." Gently, he urged her to the seat, but she rejected him with her stance.

"You have your mother's beauty," he said.

"You've been there?"

"To your father's house?" His gaze sharpened. "Of course."

"You've been sneaking around behind my back?"

"I was looking for you. I wanted to explain why I really didn't want an annulment. Where else would I go?"

"You saw them." Her father, putrid with greed and manipulation, and her mother, ever wanting to conciliate. She had carefully concealed the scars of her upbringing, but if Rand had been their guest, then he knew too much about her.

She panicked. Rand had retracted his appeal for an annulment because he'd seen the impasse in her family, and he pitied her. Of all the things she wanted from him, pity was the last. "You really shouldn't worry about me." The sympathy in his gaze made her ill. "I have an earl who's courting me."

Rand's chin jutted at a dangerous angle. "And who's that?"

"Lord Holyfeld."

Fury gleamed from Rand's eyes, and he roared, "Holyfeld? I don't think so, *Your Grace*. Why don't you explain to your husband—"

"Beg pardon?" Lord Hawthorne stuck his head into the alcove and waved a dance card. "Miss Sylvan, I believe this is my dance."

"Of course it is." Sylvan evaded Rand and grabbed Hawthorne's arm. "We'll go now."

Rising to his feet, Rand started after them, but a steely arm barred his path, and Sir Sagan stepped in front of him. "Are you bothering our Sylvan, Your Grace? Because your recent rise in status doesn't matter. If Miss Sylvan doesn't like you, and you persist in annoying her, we'll be forced to twist your head off."

Rand started to knock Sagan aside until he realized the arm that barred his path was Sagan's only arm. The sleeve on his other side hung empty, its cuff neatly folded and pinned.

This man was picking a fight. For whatever reason, he felt strongly about Sylvan, and Rand stared at Sylvan's form as she moved through the figures of the quadrille and wondered what was happening. Why wasn't she throwing herself into his arms, forgiving him for his harsh words, and going with him to the nearest bed? Hadn't she learned anything in the months they'd been apart?

He glared at Sagan as if he were at fault. Sagan stared right back, challenging him.

Sylvan should be here, defusing this ridiculous situation, rather than prancing around with Hawthorne. She was acting the same way she'd acted when he accused her of being a camp follower. "Hm." He smoothed his chin. "She's acting as if I've said something unforgivable."

"Did you?" Sagan's one fist bunched.

"Well, I didn't mean it."

Sagan grabbed Rand by the cravat, and Rand said, "She knows I didn't mean it! She even knows why I said it."

"Women are such odd creatures." Sagan mocked him with his tone. "You insult them, and even if they know in their minds you were just being an unreasonable, bumptious, beastly, spoiled ass, they still need to believe with their hearts that they have your esteem."

"Sylvan has my esteem!"

"It would appear she doesn't believe it in her heart, old boy." Shaking Rand a little, Sagan commanded, "Don't interfere until she expresses her belief."

He stepped back, leaving Rand reflective and agitated. Was Sylvan still hurt by their quarrel on the day she left? He had assumed that the longer she was gone from Clairmont Court, the more she would perceive the intelligence of his actions. Instead she seemed to think him the unreasonable, bumptious, beastly, spoiled ass which Sagan called him.

He examined Sagan again while adjusting his spoiled cravat. This was Sylvan's companion, her champion as of old, and in the easy cant of a soldier, Rand said, "Hadn't heard about your arm, Sagan. Waterloo?"

Sagan examined Rand in return, and when he was satisfied Rand contemplated no action, he answered. "Bit of a cannonball." Shrugging, he made light of what surely was a harrowing experience.

"Tough luck." Sagan wouldn't have liked further commiseration, and Rand turned his gaze to the dance floor once more.

"Could have been worse." Cautiously, Sagan removed his blockade from Rand's path. When Rand didn't move, he sought the object of Rand's interest with his gaze.

"Hawthorne's not much of a dancer anymore," Rand observed.

"Can't bend his leg," Sagan said.

Rand began to discern a pattern. "Waterloo?"

"Lucky shot from a sniper."

"Did you meet Sylvan at Waterloo?" It wasn't a guess so much as a certainty.

"*Miss* Sylvan," Sagan corrected gently. "And yes, we met her there. She found me on the battlefield, chased away some French looters who were just about to put an end to me, and got the doctor to me. Held me when they cut off my arm, too." Sagan grinned. "Almost made it painless."

Rand contained a shudder as he remembered Sylvan's bravery during another amputation. It hadn't been painless. It could never be painless, and Sagan hid a world of agony behind his jaunty smile. "Sylvan help Hawthorne, too?"

"Fever almost did him in. Might have, too, but Miss Sylvan kept bathing him with cool water. Stayed up all night with him, he says. Remembers her beautiful face hovering over his, telling him he couldn't die. Says she's an angel."

"She was for me, too," Rand said.

Sagan examined him from top to toe but clearly found no defect. Incredulously, he asked, "Wounded at Waterloo?"

"Couldn't walk," Rand allowed. "Sylvan got me on my feet."

He again found Sagan's hand tangled in the starched folds of his cravat. "*Miss* Sylvan," Sagan insisted.

"Her Grace," Rand retorted.

Confusion loosened Sagan's grip. "Pardon?"

"Even before Sylvan got me on my feet, I married her." Rand grinned at Sagan's astonishment. "She's my duchess, old man, so do you think you could let me go?"

"My apologies." Sagan patted Rand's rumpled cravat. "Can't believe it. She never hinted . . ."

"She's angry at me, and with reason," Rand said. "But I've come to take her home, if she'll have me."

"We've been protecting her." Sagan was getting over

his amazement. "Didn't seem to give a damn about her reputation. Took up with bad company. Well, you see." Waving an encompassing hand, he glared reproachfully at Rand. "Where have you been?"

"Had a bit of a blow at Clairmont Court. Heard about it?"

"Your brother lost in a nasty accident, I believe. Dreadfully sorry."

Rand nodded. "Thanks. Tough on my mother. Tough on all of us. Worse part is . . ." He hesitated. He hated to tell anyone his business, but he needed Sagan's aid, and Sagan had a reputation for being closemouthed. "Keep a secret?"

"Of course."

"Brother's death wasn't an accident. Had a madman loose on the estate." The waltz was winding down, so Rand finished hastily. "After Sylvan, too, the bastard."

"The bastard," Sagan repeated in tones of wonderment. "Have you caught him?"

"Disappeared. No more problems. Want my wife home."

"Better get her, then." Sagan's mouth had a grim cast to it. "Holyfeld's giving her the easy eye, and he's in need of funds which he thinks a marriage with her would provide."

Sylvan was talking to Hawthorne, hanging on his sleeve, when Rand started toward her. "We'll just have to make it clear she's already claimed, then, won't we?"

Sagan kept pace, muttering, "Hawthorne'll need an explanation."

The closer Rand got to Sylvan, the louder was the buzz of gossip. Lady Katherine had done her job well, and Rand hoped Sagan would finish it. Rand had come prepared to coax, to apologize, to give explanations to Sylvan in the humblest of spirits, but he hadn't been prepared for her to play the "I've got another suitor" game. He could deal with Hawthorne and Sagan, especially now when he knew why they followed her like devoted dogs. Indeed, he probably owed them a debt of gratitude, for it sounded as if Sylvan had been playing a dangerous game. But the thought of handsome, decadent Holyfeld sniffing after Sylvan brought a chill that hardened Rand's resolution.

Sylvan would go with him tonight. When they reached Hawthorne and Sylvan, Hawthorne stepped in front of Sylvan, but Rand called, "How unlike you, Sylvan, to hide behind a man."

Sylvan made no attempt to step out. "Maybe I'm smarter than I used to be."

"But not braver," Rand answered.

"Now, look here, Clairmont," Hawthorne began, but Sagan stopped him with a simple phrase.

"Clairmont is her husband."

He hadn't said it loudly, but it seemed to resound through the ballroom. The orchestra, in the process of beginning another tune, stuttered to a dissonant halt. The women stopped laughing, the men stopped grumbling. The gamblers in the card room came to the door, cards still clutched in their hands.

The earl of Holyfeld shouted, "What?" The dancers still on the floor fell away as he charged through. "What?"

Rand tingled with satisfaction as he faced the imperious Holyfeld. "The former Miss Sylvan Miles is now the duchess of Clairmont."

His announcement brought Sylvan out from behind Hawthorne and face-to-face with Rand. "Not for long," she said.

"What do you mean, not for long?" Holyfeld demanded, just as if he had the right.

"His Grace has graciously agreed to allow me an annulment."

Sylvan's voice had started out strong, but it faded at the last word and Rand thought that the walls of the ballroom itself leaned inward to hear it.

"An annulment?" Holyfeld's glance flicked over Rand and he grinned viciously. "You didn't expect to get untouched goods, did you?"

Sagan, Hawthorne, and Rand all jumped on Holyfeld at once. Rand threw the first punch, catching Holyfeld on the jaw and snapping his head around. Sagan caught him in the gut, and Hawthorne finished him off with a fist to the eye.

Holyfeld was still falling in a circle when Rand seized Sylvan's fist and pried it open, then tangled his fingers with hers. Holding her hand aloft, he proclaimed, "Lady Sylvan was my virgin bride."

Sylvan moaned. "Rand . . ." but the crowd parted without a sound as he hustled her toward the door.

"G'night," Hawthorne called.

"G'luck," Sagan added, and he sounded as if he thought Rand would need it.

16

The Clairmont carriage boasted a matched pair of chestnuts, an armed footman to discourage highwaymen, and an accomplished coachman, a crest on the door and a duke who thrust Sylvan inside, then crowded her into the corner of the narrow seat and seemed to have no intention of allowing her any freedom.

His presumption infuriated her, and she struggled to free her hands and feet from the snare of her cloak. "I'm not going with you."

He tapped the roof of the carriage and the horses sprang forward. "Aren't you?"

He'd wrapped the cloak around her deliberately just to frustrate her. She was sure of it when she realized one side was wrapped over the other and the edge trapped beneath him. She jerked it loose and freed herself, but by then the horses were moving too swiftly. Inside the carriage the torches cast bright squares that grew long and thin, then faded altogether. She was trapped in the dark with a rogue husband.

Trapped, but not defeated. Gathering herself together, she shoved him with all her weight. "Sit on your own side," she commanded rudely.

He shifted slightly. "There's not much room."

"Then sit across from me."

"If I did that, I couldn't hold your hand."

"Good."

"But I'm afraid of the dark." His fingers groped for hers.

"Aren't we all?" she muttered, moving her hand out of his way. Then she jumped and shrieked, for he fastened on her knee.

"I missed," he said pitifully, but when she tried to pry his hand off, his fingers twisted and caught hers. He sighed. "Now I'm satisfied."

She sat stiffly and waited for his next move, but nothing happened. Relaxing, he settled beside her. He held her hand, she noted, without a tremor. He didn't speak, and after a moment, she considered her options. Their entwined fingers rested on the seat between them, wedged between their bodies and serving as a perfect divider. She could free her hand, but he'd no doubt find another part of her body to hold. She could remove his liver with a spoon, but she had no spoon. Or she could sit here, pretend she didn't care, and grind her teeth down to their roots.

The silence that settled was thick in its intensity. It seemed part of the darkness inside and out, twins with the night of her soul. Anger and hurt fought a battle within her, and together they combined to strip her of pride and leave only anguish. There was nothing that could make her forget the way he'd ripped her that day outside the mill. He'd insulted her background, made it clear his family didn't approve, and insinuated that one brief bedding was all the union he could bear.

And she sat here placidly holding his hand. It was a good thing her teeth were young and healthy, for her jaw was strong and the ride to London would take over an hour—if that was indeed where they were headed. She hated to be the first to break that silence, but she had to know. "Where are we going?"

"We're going to our town house."

"*Our* town house?"

"The town house of the duke and duchess of Clairmont." He squeezed her fingers. "You and I. I'm the duke and you're the duchess."

"Temporarily," she muttered, then said, "In London?"

"Yes, in London."

"Leave me on my father's doorstep, then."

He chuckled and said nothing, as if her demand wasn't consequential enough to require a reply.

"You can't take me to your town house. This merchant's daughter might dirty the atmosphere."

He released her hand, and she was grimly satisfied until his arm slid around her shoulders and brought her close against him. "You're not just a merchant's daughter. You're the savior of Waterloo and my wife."

His voice sounded soft in her ear. His breath ruffled the hair at the nape of her neck. His body warmed her whether she wished it or not, and she rejected everything, all of him, all his phony comfort and his seductive comprehension. With the sharp point of her elbow wedged in his ribs, she said, "I'm the daughter of a merchant who extracted a barony from the regent in a rather hideous case of blackmail."

"Did he?" Rand sounded entertained rather than shocked as he used his other hand to move her elbow to a place behind his back and trap it there. "Got his claws into Prinney, eh? What a scene that must have been."

Speaking with precision, she said, "So I am not only the daughter of a merchant, but the daughter of a merchant without ethics."

"I'll not hold you responsible for your father's methods of making money and gaining respectability."

"That's not what you said two months ago. Two months ago you said you were ashamed of me."

"No, you said that."

"Don't play games with me! You said—"

"*You* said, 'You're sending me away because you're ashamed of me?' and when I didn't answer you assumed the answer was yes."

Silently, she reviewed their quarrel in her mind. He was right, the rat. She had jumped to an unsupported conclusion.

"I hadn't previously realized what a fragile ego you have, darling. We'll have to work at that."

Was he sneering? Laughing at her? She wished she could see his face, the better to read his expression and perhaps to nail his ears to the wall. "I do know you said your Aunt Adela wouldn't have approved our marriage if she'd known you were going to recover and inherit the title."

"No person in the world comprehends the line of descent as well as Aunt Adela. She knew very well I was second in line to Garth, and she undoubtedly calculated the chances that you would be the duchess. If Aunt Adela had objected, believe me, she would have made it clear to you."

It was the voice of reason speaking from out of the darkness, calming the turmoil that rocked her. Yet that same voice had ignited the turmoil and she didn't understand what he wanted with her now. She'd spent two months telling herself she didn't care, she didn't want him, she could forget him, and now in the space of an hour he'd tempted her to wash away her fury in a flood of tears.

But the only place to cry was in his waistcoat, and Sylvan Miles didn't blubber all over a man who didn't want her.

"So." Something touched her ear softly—his finger, she guessed, tracing the whorls. "Have I answered your every objection?"

She swatted at his hand as if it were a bothersome fly. "For what reason does it matter?"

"For this reason."

His lips swooped, locating hers unerringly in the dark. It didn't seem to matter that she sat strictly unresponsive under his persuasive mouth, he still feasted on her as if she were sweet marzipan. Indignation bubbled beneath her calm exterior, but she tried to keep her temper. If she didn't, every word she longed to utter, every insult she longed to yell, would come frothing out in an incoherent mass. And she didn't want him to realize how thoroughly the venom of his rejection had corroded her spirit.

Still, he didn't stop. There wasn't room in this carriage for anything more than kissing and embracing, but he opened the frogs on her cloak and kissed her bare shoulders. He moved back, and she thought perhaps he'd comprehended at last—she wasn't interested. She didn't want him to touch her. Her skin heated and her breath caught not because she liked his tongue lapping the edges of her bodice, but because she was angry.

Then she heard the crinkle of material. Straining, she tried to see what he was doing. Starlight barely illuminated him, and he was moving, but what . . . ? Taking her hands, he put them around his neck and she discovered that he'd ripped off his cravat and removed his shirt.

"What are you doing?"

Laughter lit his voice. "I thought that was obvious."

"Not to me." She shoved at him, but he'd already proved himself an insensitive, uncaring brute, interested in nothing but his own pleasure. He didn't budge. "Not here. Not now."

Placing an arm on each side of her head, he asked, "When and where?"

"Not ever!" She tried to duck away from him, but his next words arrested her.

"I never thought of you as a perjurer," he said thoughtfully.

"Perjurer?"

"You gave me your promise."

Mystified and infuriated, she asked, "Do you mean our wedding vows?"

"There are those," he agreed. "But no, this was a personal vow which you made to me."

"A vow," she repeated, searching her mind. "What vow?"

"The night before the wedding. Remember?"

A vague uneasiness nudged at her mind.

"We were discussing my incapacity, and you promised to acquiesce to all my conjugal demands."

She remembered now. Of course, she remembered now. But—"You're not crippled anymore!"

"I don't remember that being an addendum to your vow." With each word, he moved closer until his breath fanned her face.

She tried to jerk back, but there was nowhere to go. "But I promised you against my better judgment."

"Circumstances have changed, haven't they?"

But her vow had not, she could almost hear him add.

He waited to see what else she would say, but she was speechless. "Sylvan, you're all I want." He kissed her, long and lingeringly. "I haven't slept, haven't eaten." Her ruffled cap sleeves slid down easily beneath his urging, and his palms skated along her skin in a slow, seductive slide. "Let me show you how much I need you."

"This is unfair." She tried to sound stern, but that was difficult when he cupped her breasts and his thumbs grazed her nipples.

"It's more than fair. It's magnificent."

She didn't want clever word games. She wanted to be left alone. She needed to be left alone—now, before she gave in and told him how she'd missed him. "I'm not going to mate with a man who wants an annulment."

He sat back on the seat, giving her breathing room and somehow disappointing her. "There's not going to be an annulment. There's never going to be an annulment. And next time I send you away for your own safety—"

Tugging at her neckline, she said, "Oh, now there's an excuse I hadn't imagined."

Her sarcasm should have made him defensive. Instead, it seemed to incense him, and for some reason, *she* felt defensive. Quietly, he asked, "Would you like to tell me about the ghost?"

Her mind skipped around, touching on her various thoughts and experiences with the ghost, and lighting, she feared, on the incident to which he referred. "The ghost?"

"Specifically, would you like to tell me about a visitation you received the night before our wedding?"

"When did you find out?" she asked, then cursed herself for sounding guilty.

"Not long after I helped you get to sleep on the day of Garth's funeral."

She winced.

Putting his hands on her waist, he drew her toward him until her face matched his and her chest rested against his. He said, "Perhaps you can explain how it came about that you neglected to tell me?"

"I meant to," she said feebly. She stared straight ahead, able to see only the dim outline of his features but sure that should she look down, it would be perceived as an apology. Maybe even a sign of weakness.

"You lied to me the day I sent you away. I was going to talk to you about that attack, and you told me you were an independent woman. That to have *me* try to protect *you* was an insult."

Had she wounded him with her easy dismissal of his protection? "I didn't mean that in a hurtful way."

"You said there was no reason to think anyone would harm you."

"I didn't want you to worry."

His chest rose and fell beneath hers, his diaphragm laboring like an overworked bellows. Somehow that told her what he thought of her excuses, but his voice was genial when he spoke. "So we both have reason for anger, and we both have words we must forgive. But there are more important things to discuss." He untied the bow at her back. "Like your promise to acquiesce to all my conjugal demands."

She couldn't think of a clever retort, although she desperately needed one to stop his onslaught. She blurted, "You never wrote or sent a message. You left me at my father's house."

Now his hand smoothed her gown down her spine. His palm came to rest on the cleft of her rump, and his fingers flexed like a cat's. "I apologize for that, but in all fairness, you never told me everything about your father."

"I don't know how I could have missed it. And I did so want to impress you." Sarcastically, she imitated her own confession. "'Lord Rand, my father is cold and manipulative and he has browbeaten my mother until she has not a spark of spirit. That's the reason that I . . ." She paused, breathless with a sudden stab of pain. "Well, never mind."

He didn't say a word. He just kissed her mouth and rubbed his cheek against hers. His silent comprehension humiliated her. Taking advantage of his lax hold, she leaped back and seated herself opposite. Struggling to right the disorder of her clothing, she banged her elbows against the sides of the carriage and tried to speak coherently at the same time. "You may not have said I was too lowly for you, or that you wanted an annulment, but you implied that was the truth, and you let me believe it for two months." Her voice gained strength.

"I didn't mean it," he said.

"I don't care what you meant."

"You are unreasonable."

"You are detestable."

"Sylvan." He didn't raise his voice, but she heard him too clearly. "I had to do it."

Each breath hurt her, and her chest ached with a sensation that might have been the need to cry.

"To keep you safe."

She released a quivering sigh.

His hands groped through the darkness and drew her back into his embrace. "I'm only a bumbling man. Please forgive me."

An apology. From Rand. He wanted her to forgive him, and he sounded sincere. Maybe he was sincere. She couldn't imagine that those three words—*please forgive me*—would ever pass his lips unless he was absolutely convinced that he was wrong.

But what if she was wrong? What if she forgave him and he once more trampled on her heart? For all his cajoling, he was still a nobleman and she was still a merchant's daughter, and merchants' daughters, and their hearts, had been fair game for centuries. She tested him. "Why? So you'll feel better?"

"That's what forgiveness is for. To make us both feel better."

If she forgave him and he destroyed her once again, she would never recover. It would be the last burden she would bear. She would give up, crawl into her father's house, and die.

The bleakness of that vision made her shudder, and he clasped her closer. "Sylvan, please. Don't go away from me like this. Please, I'll make you happy, I promise. Please, please forgive me."

It was the catch in his voice that decided her. She would do it. She'd forgive him now and try to protect herself later. Some people would say that wasn't forgiveness, but he'd never know what he lost. He'd never miss that part of herself she held in reserve.

He must have felt her body relax, for in adoring tones he murmured, "Sylvan." He kissed her warmly, seeking passion with his lips and tongue and finding a stray tear. It embarrassed her, and to distract him, she caught his mouth with hers. It felt good to have human contact. Probably if she kissed anyone right now, she would enjoy it. Probably this upswelling of pleasure had nothing to do with Rand and everything to do with her loneliness. Probably . . . his lips moved on hers. He tucked her head into the crook of his elbow and leaned her back and kissed her more.

Probably it was Rand she wanted, and only Rand. She luxuriated in the smooth skin of his arms pressing against her back and stomach, in the closeness of their bodies. These kisses required nothing else. Desire was there, close but not demanding. It would grow, she knew, but right now she was content. Good thing, too, because the road was rutted, the carriage bounced, it was dark as a pit, they'd be in London soon, and the interior was too small for further activity.

"I want you."

He said it firmly, and it stirred a bit of uneasiness in her. "Rand, you're not planning . . . ?" He lifted her and caught her nipple in his mouth, and cognition abandoned her.

She stiffened and moaned, and he whispered, "Do you want me, too?"

"Yes. Or rather . . . I can't."

"But you do."

Her gown slithered all the way down, and she realized that somehow he had lifted her, kissed her senseless, and finished loosening her clothing all at the same time. The strength of his upper body, his ability to maneuver, surpassed that of other men. He manipulated her skillfully, and it irritated and thrilled her at the same time. "Whether I want you or not means nothing."

"Perhaps it means nothing to you." His hand stroked her thigh, her calf, then he freed her feet from the tangle of her petticoats and gown. "But it means everything to me."

Then it occurred to her—except for her pantalettes and knee-high silk stockings, she was nude. She was traveling the London road in almost nothing, and all because she'd relaxed her guard around the man she'd married. She scrambled for a cover. His hands obstructed her. Without being deliberate, he kept her close and he kept her bare, and she finally cried, "What are you doing? We can't—"

"Sh," he warned. "The footmen might hear you."

She snapped her mouth shut, then realized how

ludicrous it was to wrestle in a carriage with her own husband. He was acting like a boy, too eager to wait and clever enough to get his own way. Once again, she recited the litany of reasons why they could not mate here. They were on the road, the interior was too small . . .

"Here," he murmured, drawing her onto his lap. "Sit here."

His trousers had disappeared! She gave a shriek of surprise, then clamped her mouth shut. "Rand! You can't imagine that we're going to . . . to . . ."

"Do *it*?" He chuckled warmly. "I've imagined nothing else." His voice dipped into a deep moan. "Darling. Put your leg here. Like you're riding a horse, and not sidesaddle."

"Sidesaddle is all I know."

"It's time you learned something new."

He pulled her knees close around his hips. She'd been warm before, but when his groin pressed against her, bare and intimate, the heat between them tripled. She could feel him, hot and long, thrusting, trying to find her center almost involuntarily while his hands roamed her body, reacquainting himself with each contour.

All the reasons that before seemed like impediments now incited her. The speed at which they hurdled through the night, the darkness which pressed around them, the servants close by—it all seemed wicked and wanton. It was like nothing she'd ever done before, combining the long-suppressed desire for Rand with a glorious sense of daring.

Should she give in? Should she give him what he wanted? If she did, he'd know for certain she couldn't resist him. *She'd* know for certain she couldn't resist him. She could conceive a child. He could have all he wished from her and reject her once more.

But, oh! His skillful fingers persuaded her well.

"Lift up," he whispered. "Sylvan, lift up. Let me touch you here."

Her fingers bit into his shoulders and she stifled a moan. He was good. He was very, very good. She already knew that, of course, but it seemed that familiarity did not breed contempt. It only bred more desire, more need.

In the dark, she could hide the love that shone from her when he stripped away her defenses. Yes, better here, in the dark, than in the town house in the light of the candles. Better here, knowing he would drop her off at her father's afterward without seeing the pain of her disappointment.

"Are you ready?" He adjusted her, adjusted himself, and she felt the first nudge as he began to enter her. "Sylvan, please, tell me what you like."

"This." She pushed against him and he filled her. "And this." She pushed up, then slid down again. He cupped her buttocks, helping her with the motion. She tried something new, moving with a swivel, and his groan joined hers as he reacted.

He bucked beneath her, thrusting deeper, touching something in the center of her being. The jostling of the carriage drove him deeper yet, and she desperately wanted to cry out. Instead she clamped her teeth over her lips and rose again and again. If the interior of the carriage was too small, she didn't notice now. She didn't notice the dark or the jolts or anything but Rand inside of her and the pleasure singing in her veins. She wanted it to go on forever. She wanted it to stop at once. It was too much and not enough, it was glorious and terrifying. All the emotions she had ever experienced roiled within her, coming close to an explosion.

He began a slow chant. "Sylvan. Give me more. Give me all." He strained beneath her, as reckless and excited as she. "Let me hear you. Darling girl." His movement became stronger. "Sylvan. Let me feel you."

He seemed to think he was fighting a battle, that she was holding back, that she relished her current power too much to surrender and release. And maybe it was true.

But his patience had run out. He spread his legs beneath her and brought his hand up between them. Still thrusting, he touched the place where they joined, then above and below, and her control snapped.

She paused, hovering on the edge of delirium, then powerful convulsions rattled her. Each spasm brought him closer inside, and each movement inside forced another spasm. Sounds escaped her, but she could still hear, and Rand willfully encouraged her.

"A little more, darling. Move again. Again. You're wonderful. You're draining me. You're"—his sensuality battered her as he strained toward his finish—"all I could ever want."

Little thrills still ran through her. His hands still petted her, worshiping her with a kind of desperation. They came to rest, two souls who had traveled far to reach this destination, and Sylvan had no thought beyond the heaven of his scent, the closeness of his embrace. Then a light flashed through the window, and she stiffened.

"London." He groaned. "Already?"

She sat up so fast he had to catch her before she tumbled backward. "Someone might see."

"Won't they be envious?"

His voice had a laugh in it, and she could have slapped him. "Your own servants are the most likely to discover us. Doesn't that bother you?"

"If my servants don't know what we were doing in here, they must have been deaf. Now sit still and let me find your gown."

"Deaf?" Remembering the little screams that had escaped her, she covered her eyes with her hands. Then she brought them down and glared at his face touched by an occasional illumination. "My gown? What good is my gown going to be? It's going to be wrinkled and—"

"And I'm afraid I've had my feet on it." He held the crumpled mass in his hands and searched for the neck and sleeves, then assisted her as she pulled it on. Carefully, he moved her across to the other seat. "If you'll allow me to dress myself, I'll wrap you in your cloak. That'll cover the worst of the damage and we can get you in the house without exposing you to any curious onlookers." The laughter came back into his tone. "We can't have the gossips chatting about how the new duke and duchess of Clairmont arrived at their London home."

"The servants will talk."

"Oh, probably." The lights of London were coming more frequently now. Wealthy homes shone brightly, and in their light, she could see that his trousers were now buttoned and he'd pulled his shirt over his shoulders. But his collar and cravat had disappeared, and his shirt studs decorated the floor rather than his chest. They were a disreputable pair, and she had no business allowing him to take her into his house as if she belonged there.

She began, "You could drop me at—"

The cloak descended over her head like a great dark bat, smothering her speech. When he freed her, he fastened the frogs at her throat and said, "You are the duchess of Clairmont. Gossip can't touch you. The

Clairmont duchy has been held by the Malkin family since its founding, and no one—not even boorish old Prinney—can claim such a lofty status. In fact, you'll undeniably find that we've set a fashion. I have no doubt that half of the London ton will perform coitus in their carriages tomorrow night." He wrapped the cloak so tightly her arms were trapped once more. "Or try."

His attitude annoyed her, and she snapped, "Is there anyone above me in the whole kingdom?"

"I hope to be." He laughed. "Just as soon as we get inside."

She blushed from the top of her knee-high stockings to the roots of her hair. "You can't be serious."

His hand touched her cheek as the carriage rattled to a halt. "Wait and see."

The footman rapped on the side of the carriage. "May I open the door, Your Grace?"

Rand mocked Sylvan with a knowing grin. "You may." London air rushed in and Rand leaped out at the same time, then he leaned back inside and gathered her in his arms.

She didn't dare move for fear of revealing her dishabille, but she glared at him balefully. "I won't do it."

"But darling." He ascended the stairs to the open front door and paused on the threshold, then swept inside. "Remember your vow."

17

Rand leaned over Sylvan as she stretched on the bed, and with a hand on each side of her head, he said, "Four more times."

"What?" She blew the wisps of hair out of her eyes.

"Last night in the carriage, I wondered how many times I would have to pleasure you before your reserve broke enough that you could let me hear your enjoyment again." She stared at him, wide-eyed with dismay, and he leaned forward to whisper in her ear. "Four more times."

"It . . . I . . ." She struggled for coherence while he waited gravely. "Was I too loud?"

"Not at all. I liked those little moans." He ran his finger over her slightly open lips. "I just wonder how many other barriers I have to break through before you'll trust me to love you as you are."

Her guilty gasp assured him he'd guessed right. When he started last night, he'd known there were depths and dark places that Sylvan did not want him to see, but he'd imagined his lovemaking would strip away her clothes and her inhibitions, and her mind would be revealed to him, too.

Wasn't that the way it was supposed to work? Weren't women supposed to be malleable in the hands of a gifted lover? Either he wasn't a gifted lover—and her sated expression told him differently—or Sylvan feared to confide in him.

He couldn't imagine why. She knew now why he'd sent her away so cruelly. True, the coldness of her father must have taught her caution in her dealings with others, but he didn't want to be lumped in with others. He wanted to be the one to whom she gave herself wholeheartedly.

He smiled, but his lips had a tightness to them. "A few more barriers, it would seem. Why not give them up now?" Deliberately, he challenged her. "It would save us trouble, for I'll win in the end."

"I don't know what you mean. I have no barriers erected." She mouthed words of innocence, but her gaze shifted away from his and she looked around the chamber. "Goodness. We've made a mess."

She must be desperate to distract him if she willingly mentioned their debaucheries of the night before. He had expected a little maidenly shyness. Instead she donned the disguise of a housewife. Leaning back from her, he adjusted his shirtsleeves and tucked the tails into his trousers while he reminded himself he could afford to wait for the barriers to tumble. Ramming them down didn't work—he'd proved that last night. "It's worse downstairs."

"Oh. Yes, I suppose . . ." Her eyes lost their focus as she remembered, then she pulled the covers closer around her bare shoulders as if that would wipe her passion from the slate of his memory. "You shouldn't have knocked that candelabra off the dining room table. It slid off and took the lace runner with everything on it."

"I didn't see it." At that point, he hadn't even seen the dining room table. "You had enchanted me."

"Don't blame me."

"You kept enticing me."

"I was *trying* to put on some clothes."

"That's what I mean. Enticing me." While she was sputtering, he said, "We leave for Clairmont Court today."

She stopped sputtering and lost color. "I don't want to go back to Clairmont Court."

Startled, he studied her. "Why not?"

"May I have a cup of tea?" she asked.

Nodding, he went to the door, called for the upstairs maid, and gave her order.

Distance, it seemed, gave Sylvan bravery, for she sat up and adjusted the sheet with becoming modesty. "You can go to Clairmont Court. That's fine, now that I know you're not going to annul our marriage. In fact, I appreciate your traveling to London to reassure me. But, la! I need to do some shopping, and have people to visit."

She chattered nervously, and he wondered what that meant. Did Clairmont Court intimidate her? Did his family? "Are you frightened?"

Her hands clenched the blankets and she brought her knees close to her chest. "Frightened?"

"That this villain who killed my brother and sneaked into your room will succeed in hurting you?"

"Don't be ridiculous. I'm not—Yes! I am frightened of the ghost."

She had interrupted herself. He was sure of it. So she wasn't afraid of the man who masqueraded as a ghost, but she was afraid of something. "Sylvan, what is it?"

"I don't want to be a victim of this madman. I do think I had best stay in London."

"For the rest of our lives?"

Taking a corner of the sheet, she rubbed it on her forehead. To blot the perspiration? To ease the headache? Or to cover her face from him? "That's not possible, is it? No, of course it's not. But a few more months, or at least until the next season is over."

"The next season won't officially start until May and won't be over until next summer. I had hoped to spend Christmas with my family."

"You could do so," she assured him. "I wouldn't object."

"We're married, and now that we have all our problems solved"—such a jest!—"we're going to stay together." He took care to give the appearance of yielding. "I'll stay in London with you. We can stay at your father's house. Your father and I can further our acquaintance."

"That would be—"

"And I'm sure you wish to help your mother."

Abruptly, she abandoned her pretense, and with sadness and resolution said, "There's no help for my mother. She won't change. I had to face that years ago. But you're right." She stared him straight in the eye. "There's nothing to be gained by avoiding Clairmont Court."

"Then we'll go home at once."

"Yes." She threw back the covers, giving him a brief glimpse of all that had captivated him the night before.

He gave her time to slip into a bed robe and the shield it afforded, and wrap it around herself before going to her.

She said, "I'm looking forward to seeing your family."

She sounded so normal he almost believed her, but when he turned her in his arms he saw how she protected herself, and he felt as if he were chipping at a great stone of resistance that blocked his way to her. So he would retreat now and fight the battle later, on his own turf and on his own terms. "It will be an interesting journey."

A homecoming.

"Stop!" Sylvan called. "Stop the gig right here."

As if he'd been expecting it, Jasper brought the horse to a stop and slewed around in the seat.

"Let me out," she commanded Rand, and he stepped out ahead of her and gave her his hand.

A homecoming.

She hadn't expected to feel that way when she again laid foot on Clairmont land, but she did. Rand had arranged to have Jasper pick them up in the Stanhope gig, and just as he had the first time, Jasper examined her critically, finding fault. Just as she had the first time, her breath caught when they topped the first hill and she caught sight of the untamed panorama before her.

As always, the wind blew off the ocean. Autumn had only sweetened the air, and Sylvan took deep, healing breaths. She hadn't wanted to come back. She hadn't wanted to be where Rand had so bluntly pointed out her deficiencies. And she was afraid to face the women from the mill, to ask about their injuries and hear how badly she had bungled when she tried to cure them. She was afraid that, while on Rand's estate, he would somehow discover the trail of blood that followed her all the way from Waterloo, and it would freshen his disgust for her. But right now none of it mattered, because she'd come home.

She didn't have the right to feel that way, she told herself, but when Rand wrapped his arms around her waist, she leaned back against his chest.

The sea still extended into an eternity of blue haze and lofty gray clouds. The hills still jutted and tumbled. But the foliage had begun to change from tired green to brilliant red and gold. The grass stood high where the sheep had not grazed and a yellowish tinge touched the tops. Far in the distance, she could see squares of mature wheat and barley basking, first in sun, then in shadow as the clouds ripened and grew tall.

"Looks like we've got a bit of a blow coming in," Jasper observed. "Ye'd best get in the gig, Lady Sylvan, or ye'll end up drenched afore we get to the Court."

Rand helped her up with an intimate hand on her hip, but he sounded distracted. "Is the corn in yet?"

"They've harvested on the sunnier slopes, and a few have started their regular fields, but most of the tenants say to give it a week. Waiting for the greatest weight in the heads, just like my da used to." Jasper jerked his head at the cloud that billowed and massed offshore. "Farmers are all damn fools."

"It's a gamble," Rand said. "It's always a gamble."

"Aye, and my da wondered why I'd rather serve ye than take over his land." Jasper urged the horse forward. "Said I wasn't free if I wasn't a yeoman, but I say I'm a damn sight freer than a man who waits on the weather."

A sudden cold puff of wind whipped Sylvan's hat from her head, but before she could call for Jasper to stop and get it, Jasper cursed and Rand ordered, "Drive faster."

"What's wrong?" Sylvan asked. The wind had disappeared as rapidly as it had come, and the afternoon was still.

"Hail," Jasper explained briefly. "There's hail in that cloud."

She looked again at the gray monster that was rapidly filling the horizon. "How do you know?"

Rude as ever, Jasper drove intently, ignoring her as he guided the horse at a trot along the winding road.

Rand answered her question. "That cold came off of ice. In the autumn here, there's always a chance for a freak storm. Really, it doesn't happen very often." Lightning snaked out of the cloud, and he waited, counting, until the boom sounded. "Sixty miles away, Jasper."

"Not far enough, Lord Rand. It's moving fast."

To Sylvan, Rand said, "They blow up quickly and leave just as quickly, but sometimes, if it's the wrong time of year, they can destroy the corn." He had a grim cast to his mouth as he watched the cloud move. "That's the cash crop for the people of Malkinhampsted."

"Will this destroy them?" Sylvan stared in horrified fascination as the lightning descended again, then again and again in rapid succession.

"It might go right over the top of us with a splash of rain." Rand's words spoke of hope, but his grieving tone told the true story.

The thunder sounded louder now, and the lightning now flashed continuously. The wind began to blow steadily, with gusts that brought drafts of freezing cold. Rand removed his wool greatcoat and pulled Sylvan close against him, then wrapped it around her as she huddled into a little ball. When she flinched against one particularly brilliant flash and boom, he pressed her head against his chest and tried to reassure her. "Maybe we can make it into Malkinhampsted before the storm hits."

Jasper leaned forward and spoke, and the gig jerked as the horse broke into a gallop.

Sylvan cast her gaze upward. They weren't going to make it, she realized. Nothing could outrun this cloud. A dark akin to the blackest night overtook them first, then the freezing rain hit them with a roar.

She cowered and Rand drew his greatcoat over her head just before the hail struck. The gig jerked to a stop; she peeked out and saw Jasper had disappeared, then a tiny ball of hail struck her forehead and she jerked the greatcoat over Rand's head, too. "Where's Jasper?" she yelled against the shriek of wind and the rattle of hailstones.

"Holding the horse so he won't bolt."

She couldn't see Rand, but his voice sounded comfortingly close, and his lips grazed her cheek. "Won't he be hurt?"

"He's got a hard head."

If she weren't there, Rand would be out with Jasper, she knew. He only huddled under his coat to take care of his silly little wife. He'd been most solicitous during their journey from London, and it bothered her to think he had seen what she sought to hide. But the knowledge she'd gained of men from her father told her that if she put on a good face, Rand would eventually be lulled into forgetting her past.

She could act like such a demure lady he would forget she'd been a merchant's daughter and a nurse. Men didn't care about another's misery; they only wanted everything to go their way.

The lightning flashed so brightly she saw it under the coat with her eyes closed, and the thunder obscured her cry of dismay. Right now she didn't care that Rand should be outside with his man and his horse. It was selfish, but she didn't want him out there being battered by hail, and she dug her fingers into the front of his shirt. She was afraid to reveal herself to him, yet at the same time he gave her more comfort than she'd ever received from another human being.

"This reminds me of Waterloo."

His reminiscence made her stiffen.

"The pounding, the noise, the anguish, the discomfort. Doesn't it bother you?"

Her denial was as automatic as a knee jerk. "I wasn't at the battle."

"But you were in Brussels. You heard the bombardment. Maybe you even watched the battle from afar."

It was stifling under the greatcoat.

"And you were on the battlefield afterward. Did it bother you to see the bodies, to hear the moans from the dying?"

Too hot, and she couldn't get a breath.

"I wonder sometimes if you don't suffer with your memories more than the soldiers suffer with—"

Gasping for breath, she clawed her way out into the fresh air and lifted her face to the sky. Hail mixed with rain splattered her face, but she didn't care.

"The worst of the weather's over." Rand lowered the greatcoat and glanced around as if he saw nothing unusual in her behavior.

Had he been prodding her? she wondered. Surely not. He didn't really suspect anything, did he? He was just a man, and not intuitive. He leaned out of the gig and called, "Do you think we can go on now, Jasper?" Then he met her eyes. "I'm worried about the villagers."

No, not intuitive at all.

The village, when they reached it, had a creek running down the main street. Beneath the dripping eaves, the women stood, arms crossed, looking out at the ruin. They didn't speak to Rand or seem to notice Sylvan, but just stood there in silence. Jasper brought the gig to a halt in the square, but when no one moved, he drove on.

Through the fields of flattened corn, past men who squatted as if the act of standing took too much energy.

On the ascent to Clairmont Court, the gig got stuck in

a mud hole and Rand and Jasper had to get out and push while Sylvan guided the horse, and when the wheels had jerked free of the morass and she stopped to let the men climb back in, the gig got stuck once more.

By the time they drove up to the house, even Sylvan's dark traveling costume sported smears of mud. Rand nursed a sprained finger, and Jasper released a stream of good Anglo-Saxon curse words.

Sylvan's homecoming had become a time of mourning. "At least there are no flying chairs," she murmured.

"No, but look, Your Grace." Jasper pointed. "The hail knocked the glass out of half the west-facing windows."

Rand put his arm around Sylvan's shoulders as if together they could minimize the bleakness, and he scanned the face of the manor. "Not half. Not more than a dozen. The glazier's been missing my business, anyway."

Shaking his head at such levity, Jasper said, "I'll get the horse taken care of, Your Grace, and then if you don't have need of me, I'll dry off and change."

Their voices attracted one small, shorn head that popped out of an empty window frame. "Uncle Rand!" Gail waved both arms. "Uncle Rand is home, and he's brought Aunt Sylvan."

A frozen piece of Sylvan warmed with the excitement of Gail's welcome. A larger piece warmed further when Gail pulled her head in and Lady Emmie poked her head out. "Sylvan! Sylvan, he's brought you at last."

She pulled her head in, too, and Sylvan heard Aunt Adela's measured tones. "It's about time she returned to fulfill her duties."

Rand grinned at Sylvan, and desolation retreated a bit further. As they climbed the steps to the terrace, Betty came out the door, a plump, dark-clad creature who opened her arms and beckoned like a beacon on the stormy shore. Sylvan didn't expect to find safety here at Clairmont Court, but she walked to Betty and laid her head on Betty's ample bosom.

A homecoming.

Raising her head, Sylvan looked into Betty's face. "How are you keeping?"

Tears sprang to Betty's eyes. "As well as can be expected, with a daughter who cries for her father and an empty bed for myself."

"You're never far from my heart," Sylvan said.

"I know." Blinking hard, Betty put Sylvan away from her. "But you need your tea, and I'm standing here blathering. Get you inside. Her Grace'll be frantic by now."

Frantic? What did that mean? Wariness touched Sylvan again, but Betty urged her over the threshold.

"I should have carried her," Sylvan heard Rand say. "She is my bride."

"You've left that late enough," Betty said tartly.

"Typical man." Lady Emmie posed in the doorway of the study, then flung herself into Sylvan's arms. "Rand would be just as bad as the rest of them if he weren't my son. I taught him any manners he knows. Heaven knows his father could be arrogant and primitive."

Remembering the night at the town house, Sylvan thought that *arrogant* and *primitive* described Rand very well.

Rand must have suspected the trend of Sylvan's thoughts, for he said, "Mother, I brought her home."

"Not as soon as Lady Emmie instructed, though." Aunt Adela waited inside the study, her hands folded across her stomach and her mouth curved just the proper amount for a smile of welcome.

Lady Emmie wrapped her arm around Sylvan's waist and ushered her into the study. The violent winds had died, the cold had vanished, and the broken window brought a Jezebel breeze to the room. "I didn't presume to tell him how to handle his marriage."

Aunt Adela moved aside. "You told him he'd made a mistake when he sent her away."

"Well, someone had to tell him!" Lady Emmie protested.

At her most obnoxious, Aunt Adela said, "Rand is not only the duke of Clairmont, but he's practical and disciplined. One must give him the benefit when one doubts the wisdom of his actions."

"I don't need you to tell me about my son, Adela."

"Mrs. Donald!" Rand moved smoothly to break up the impending quarrel. "How good to see you."

Timid little Clover Donald was tucked into a settle by the fire, trying to appear inconspicuous and doing a good job of it. Rand's attention made her shrink further into herself, and her gaze darted about the room as if she sought an escape. When she perceived there was none, she whispered, "And a pleasure to see you, Your Grace."

"How is the Reverend Donald?" Rand looked around him. "*Where* is the Reverend Donald? I don't think I've ever seen you without him."

Clover bent her head and hunched her shoulders, and Sylvan closed her eyes. Looking at Clover Donald was like looking at her mother; a waste of humanity, an embarrassment of diffidence, and all because of a husband who intimidated his wife.

She thought of Rand, and told herself he would never try to intimidate her in any fashion. He liked her as she was and would never seek to change her. He said so, and she believed him.

"I didn't come here by myself," Clover said in her miniature mouse voice. "I wouldn't put myself forward in such a manner. The vicar my husband says it's unattractive when a woman puts herself forward, and I try never to put myself forward."

"You succeed admirably," Rand assured her.

"The Reverend Donald will question me about my behavior while I was here alone, so I wish you'd tell him so." She pleated her skirt between shaking fingers. "If that's not too forward."

Gail rolled her eyes, and Betty took Gail's arm and gave her a shake.

"Not forward at all," Rand said. "Where did he go?"

Apparently, Clover had finished speaking, for she didn't seem to hear Rand's question, and he repeated it to his mother.

"He went out to visit the farmers and view the damage. Did you see our windows?"

"How could I not?" Pacing to one of them, he crunched across broken glass and stared out at the desolation. "This has not been a propitious year for Clairmont Court."

"The ghost walked for a reason, I expect," Betty observed.

Rand cast an ironic glance at Sylvan, and she looked quickly away. He treated her as if she were of delicate mind now; if he discovered she'd seen the real ghost, he'd have her committed to Bedlam.

Gail could no longer contain herself. "Sylvan, Sylvan, see me!" She fluffed her hair. "Do you like it? It's just like yours!"

Sylvan realized the child's dark hair had been cropped in a style like her own, and she found herself absurdly pleased.

"What did you do with her hair?" Rand demanded.

"Adela cut it." Lady Emmie poured a sherry for Sylvan and offered it. "Gail wanted to have hair like Sylvan's, and after we caught her trying to bleach streaks into it, we decided it would be better if we gave in."

"You decided, Your Grace." Betty helped Sylvan out of her traveling jacket. "I didn't see any reason to reward the child for defiance."

"I just like to indulge her a little now, Betty." Lady Emmie reached out a trembling hand and smoothed Gail's head. "She's all I have left of Garth."

"Tugging on my heart strings'll not make me agree we should spoil the child," Betty said austerely.

No real reproof tinged her tone, and Sylvan realized how difficult Betty's position must be now. No one knew better the anguish Gail had experienced with the loss of her father, and probably no one wanted to spoil her more. But Betty was a practical woman with a practical view of the future, and Gail's life as the illegitimate daughter of a duke would require strength of will and a hardiness of spirit.

Gail studied Rand, and her face dropped. "Uncle Rand doesn't like it."

"Of course he does." Sylvan dug her elbow into Rand's ribs. "Men just like to have a few days to get used to anything new."

Recovering, Rand said, "I don't need a few days. It's charming."

"Just be careful," Sylvan warned. "Now he can kiss your neck like he kisses mine."

"Not quite like I kiss yours," Rand murmured in her ear.

She dug her elbow into his ribs again, and he winced.

"Our travelers are hungry, I trow, and Lord Rand is

looking grieved. Come, Miss Gail, and help me prepare the tea." Betty held the door for her daughter.

"No, I don't want to. Uncle Rand just got home with Aunt Sylvan and I haven't got to hear about London." Something about her mother's stance and expression must have warned Gail, for she changed her defiance for wheedling. "Please, let me stay. Please."

"Please, Betty, can't she—" At a glance from Betty, Lady Emmie cut herself short.

"Now," Betty said to Gail.

Gail dragged her feet, casting tear-filled eyes toward Rand and Sylvan, but neither of them was foolish enough to challenge Betty. When the door had shut behind them, Lady Emmie sighed. "This is very difficult. I wish Betty had agreed to marry Garth. Even a secret marriage would have made matters easier."

"Gail would still have to obey her mother," Rand said.

Aunt Adela said, "The child is running wild half the time. Her governess doesn't know where she goes, and I say no young girl should have so much unseemly liberty, much less the child of a duke."

"She seems fine most of the time, then every once in a while, I see her staring at nothing, or crying. That's when she disappears, I think." Lady Emmie subsided in a chair. "When she misses her father."

"Sylvan and I are here now," Rand said. "We'll help. Sylvan knows all about grief and loss."

Sylvan stared at him, but he was accepting a brandy from Aunt Adela and he paid her no heed. What did he know?

Nudging him toward a chair, Aunt Adela asked, "Won't you have a seat, Your Grace?"

"No, please, Aunt." Rand rubbed on his rear. "I can't sit anymore. I've been sitting for three days."

With ill-concealed anticipation, she asked, "Did you see James in London?"

Guiltily, he sipped his brandy. "I had planned to, but I didn't take the time."

"Not take the time to see your cousin after his absence of over six weeks?"

Rand grinned at that. "I would imagine he has not yet stopped celebrating his escape from Clairmont Court."

Aunt Adela stiffened. "He was not so surly."

"Not surly, Aunt, but frustrated. It was not as if he wished to go to London to debauch, after all." Rand turned back to the window with a sigh. "Garth shouldn't have kept him here."

"I was glad that he did," Aunt Adela said in a low voice. "But I am a selfish old woman who wants to keep her son close."

"He's better in London," Rand said. "Happier. We'll hear from him soon, I'm sure."

A bustle in the entry interrupted them. The door opened, and the Reverend Donald walked in. He had shed his greatcoat and stood in his stocking feet, and he bowed to Rand and Sylvan. "Your Graces, how good to see you back! Perhaps you're the cure we need for this inauspicious day."

"I would that we could effect a change." Rand shook the vicar's hand. "However, I fear that is beyond my feeble powers."

Lady Emmie smiled. "Perhaps Sylvan brings us luck once more. After all, the last time she arrived she cured the lame."

"What an unfortunate choice of words, Lady Emmie!" The vicar stiffened in horror. "The Lord God cured His Grace."

"Of course." Aunt Adela tried to soothe his shock.

"What Lady Emmie means is that Sylvan was the instrument of God's remedy."

"An interesting theory, Lady Adela." The Reverend Donald smiled tightly at Sylvan.

"No theory," Rand said. "If not for Sylvan's faith in me, I would have been fish bait."

"You exaggerate," Aunt Adela said.

Coming to Sylvan's side, he picked up her hand and brought it to his mouth in elaborate homage. "Not at all."

"Newlyweds are given to open displays of affection, aren't they?" The clergyman averted his eyes. "Charming. Lady Emmie, I hope you'll forgive my lack of ceremony, but my shoes are covered with mud. I didn't want to track on the carpet, nor could I leave without greeting the duke and duchess, and I had my wife to collect."

"Nonsense, Reverend, no apologies are necessary," Lady Emmie said. "Come, sit and warm your feet by the fire. Tea will be here directly and you can give us the news of the estate. Are all the crops quite gone?"

The Reverend Donald sank onto the settle beside his wife.

"I haven't been too forward," Clover quavered.

She looked so guilty, Sylvan could have groaned, but the vicar patted her hand. "Good, good." Stretching his hands to the fire, he said, "God's scythe has cut a swathe through the heart of Malkinhampsted and its people. I hate to see so many disheartened men and women."

"I suppose more of them will migrate to the city." Aunt Adela poured herself a glass of sherry. "I long for the good old days when they starved without feeling they had to leave."

"That's nonsense, Adela, and you know it," Lady Emmie said.

Aunt Adela drank her sherry with one gulp. "I know it."

A moment of profound silence greeted this moment of historic importance—Aunt Adela agreeing with Lady Emmie. Lady Emmie looked as if she'd swallowed a marble, and Rand exchanged a conspiratorial grin with Sylvan.

"The poor have always been with us," the clergyman said. "They simply must resign themselves to their fate."

"Why should they resign themselves to their fate when, with a little ambition, they can raise themselves in the world?" Rand asked.

The vicar listened to the blasphemy with an expression of sorrow. "Your Grace, I know there are those who have such a view, but it's not attractive, nor is it the traditional judgment of the church."

"The world is changing, Reverend," Rand said.

"God's truth is eternal, Your Grace."

Sylvan hated it when men of God twisted God's word to suit their own beliefs, then used their respected position to give themselves authority. Hotly, she said, "If we are to depend solely on tradition, then my father could never have raised himself above his lowly beginnings to the position of a man of wealth."

Rand nodded. "Then you never would have been a part of the ton, gone to Waterloo, gained experience in nursing, come to Clairmont Court, and married me."

His smug grin brought her hackles up, and she said, "There's something to be said for the vicar's theory."

Her sarcasm didn't dim Rand's grin, and Lady Emmie said, "Dear, you and Rand sound just like my dear husband and me."

18

"Dear, you know I don't like to be an interfering mother."

Turning away from the sunny window in his former bedchamber on the main floor, Rand stared absently at Lady Emmie. She stood framed in the doorway, watching him with the anxious expression she had worn so often since he and Sylvan had returned less than a month ago. He hated seeing her fret, but how could he alleviate it? He worried, too.

"Dear?"

He started, then answered, "You never interfere."

She took a few hesitant steps forward. "But I am your mother, and I can't help but worry. Is there trouble between you and Sylvan?"

He blinked in surprise, then leaned against the sill and gestured to the single chair that remained in the remodeled room. "Why do you think that?"

Fidgeting with her fichu, Lady Emmie perched on the edge of the seat. "Sylvan's so subdued."

She wasn't telling him anything he didn't know, but he tried to pretend ignorance just as he'd been trying to pretend everything was fine between him and Sylvan. "What do you mean?"

"She spends much of her time with Adela and me, doing a good imitation of a lady with no interest except in needlework. The only time she's not sitting with us doing needlework is when she consults with Betty about meals, or sneaks off to be with Gail."

Rubbing his hands across his eyes, he said, "Subdued. Yes, that's the word for her, isn't it?"

"She looks tired."

"She has nightmares." Nightmares that she denied having when he questioned her.

"If I didn't occasionally hear her and Gail giggling, I'd think we somehow destroyed that madcap, loving personality who visited us first."

He clenched his teeth and stared at the blank wall in front of him. *We* didn't destroy Sylvan's madcap, loving personality, but sometimes he wondered if he had.

"The women from the mill have called on her. Pert, Loretta, and Charity have all been here. Even Nanna has ridden over on a pony cart to show how proficient she's become with her crutches. Sylvan has refused to see them."

"Refused?"

"Well, perhaps not refused, but she's not been available. The women are hurt. They want to thank her for healing them, and she wants no part of their gratitude. She doesn't understand, or doesn't want to understand, that it is a gesture of disrespect to so scorn their appreciation."

Rand didn't know what to say, and his gaze wandered over the bare room. The bed had been removed.

Every sign of his previous occupancy had been purged, leaving only a single chair. His belongings had been placed in the master chamber on the floor above, as had Sylvan's possessions. None of the furniture that had formerly made this room a study had been returned, yet Rand found himself spending time alone within the confines of his former chamber. "Why didn't you explain that to Sylvan? I'm sure she'd listen to you."

"I thought you might talk to Sylvan about it. Because, dear, I hesitate to say it"—Lady Emmie touched the hair at the base of her neck, then rubbed the muscles there as if they were tense—"but you seem quiet and, oh, thoughtful."

"Surely you don't object to thoughtfulness."

"Well." She smiled with a bit of sly humor. "I find myself missing the days when you knocked out the windows."

Startled, he studied her. She held out her arms and he went into them, kneeling beside her and laying his head on her shoulder. "Mama, she doesn't trust me."

Her muscles tensed beneath his cheek. "Do you blame her? After you sent her away?"

He leaned back and looked into her face. He knew his mother hadn't approved, but she'd said little except to urge him to bring Sylvan back. Apparently, she'd been waiting for this chance, for her brown eyes snapped with irritation. He tried to explain, to excuse his actions. "She wouldn't go by herself. I tried to convince her, to explain she had to go or she'd be in danger here, but she wouldn't leave."

"No. Of course, she wouldn't leave. You were in danger, too. What kind of woman would leave the man she loves to face evil alone?"

"A smart one."

"A cowardly one."

"I did it for her own good."

She slapped her hands on his shoulders and shoved him backward. He landed on his rear with a thump, and he stared at his usually gentle mother in astonishment.

"For her own good?" Her voice rose. "Is that what you think a wife is? A thing to be protected whether she wishes it or not?"

"I didn't think you—"

"You didn't think. Exactly. Just like every other man in the world." She shook her finger under his nose. "Haven't you wondered why Sylvan and Gail spend so much time together?"

He scooted away from that peremptory finger, but found he hadn't quite the nerve to stand and tower above his mother. "They do seem to have found a great deal in common."

"Of course. Gail couldn't have lost her father at a worse time."

Confused, he asked, "Why is this time worse than any other?"

"I had forgotten how obtuse men can be." Lady Emmie sighed in exasperation. "Because Gail is growing up. She's perched in that precarious place between child and woman. Haven't you noticed?"

He thought of the painfully thin, awkward girl who had grown so quickly in the last year. "She's only eight."

"She is ten," Lady Emmie corrected.

His protest was automatic and heartfelt. "She can't become a woman yet."

"With or without your permission, she is ripening."

"Is not."

But he had muttered under his breath, and she ignored him. "Maturation is a delicate process for girls— they want to develop confidence, but the least setback can be fatal. That's probably why she and Sylvan have discovered a kindred spirit."

"Why . . . oh." Lady Emmie watched him closely as he digested that. "Are you saying that, at a critical moment in Sylvan's development, I crushed her with cruelty?"

"Maybe you're not quite as imbecilic as I thought."

"But Sylvan's no adolescent who's lost her father in a dreadful accident," he objected.

"No, it's worse for Sylvan. Do you remember when I received a letter from Sir Miles?"

He shook his head.

"That was during your chair-throwing period." Picking her words with care, Lady Emmie said, "He seems to be a cold gentleman with little paternal pride in his daughter or her accomplishments."

"I think you can safely say that." Then it struck him with a frigid sensation in his gut, and he drew out his words as he thought about them. "She lacks confidence because she never had her father's support?"

"I think you can safely say that." She mocked him with his own words. "Her mother doesn't care for her, either, does she?"

"Not enough to protect her." He was still working this novel concept in his mind. "But you can't say Sylvan lacks confidence. Look at what she did before she came here. She kicked aside all reins on her respectability, acted the wanton, danced and laughed and was"—he took a breath when he remembered—"totally irresistible."

"Could she ever have won her father's approval?"

He ignored her question with single-minded intensity. "Then when they needed nurses and most Englishwomen refused to help more than their own sons or brothers, she boldly stepped into the breech." He faltered as she slowly shook her head. "You think we gave her confidence with our approval of her, don't you?"

"Yes, we gave her confidence, but it was mostly you, with your admiration, your confidence in her abilities, your delight in her very eccentricities."

The cold spread from inside him to the tips of his fingers, and he crossed his arms and tucked his hand tight against his body, battling to warm himself. "Then I stripped it from her in the cruelest manner possible."

"I don't think anyone who mattered to her has ever applauded her virtues, or even noticed them."

"Do you think I matter to her?"

"I don't know." She wouldn't give him anything, not even a smile to ease the sting of her denunciation. "I only know she's trying to make herself over in the image of the perfect lady, and I suspect she's doing it because she thinks it's your desire."

"She's becoming her mother, but I never wanted her to be anything but what she is."

His feeble protest made her lean toward him with more aggression than he'd ever seen from his gentle mother. "You insinuated she wasn't good enough for you."

"I didn't mean it."

"Did you tell her that?"

"I did better than that."

She snorted. "You mean you made love to her."

"Nicely!"

Using her hands for emphasis, she said, "Women need the words. How can she know what you're thinking if you don't tell her?"

"I thought she'd—" He shrugged, then shrugged again. "I thought she'd just know by the way I . . ."

"Son." Lady Emmie leaned back and crossed her

arms. "No woman with any kind of intelligence believes a man is devoted because he likes to tumble her."

"Mother!"

"There are all kinds of marriages. There are marriages based on passion alone, marriages made for money, and marriages where each spouse is happier apart. Those marriages are the most common." She touched the gold ring she still wore. "Then there are a few blessed unions where husband and wife talk and laugh and love as one, and nothing—not even death—ends that."

"Like you and Papa."

"He's still here with me." She pressed her hand over her heart. "You have to decide what you want from Sylvan. What do you want to have between the two of you?" Rising, she patted him on the head as if he were a dog. "You think about it."

What did he want from Sylvan? Just everything, and he'd proved he couldn't get it with sexual prowess alone. Perhaps his mother knew something he didn't. Perhaps she understood that Sylvan's hesitation to trust him stemmed from more than one incredibly stupid outburst on his part. Perhaps she'd told him how to regain his wife's trust.

Rand failed to notice that his mother watched him as he hurried down the hall and up the stairs. He was unaware of his aunt Adela when she stepped out from one of the other rooms, and he never saw their conspiratorial grin.

The door of the duke's bedchamber was closed, and he slowed as he approached. He'd been so sure he'd done everything right, yet he hadn't. How could he repair the damage, when he now questioned his every gesture? He placed his hand on the doorknob and took a sustaining breath, then opened it and walked in.

Sylvan sat staring out one of the newly repaired windows—or she would have been staring out, if the curtains had not been pulled tight against the morning sun.

Whatever he did, Rand realized, could scarcely make things worse.

"Greetings, Wife." In the dimness, he saw her turn her head, and he walked to the window and pulled the curtains. Sunlight flooded the room, and she lifted her hand against it. With false jollity, he said, "I'm going for a walk. Come with me."

"Not today." She lowered her hand, but didn't look at him. "Thank you."

"Are you ill?"

"That's it. I don't feel well."

"Are you bleeding?"

Her gaze flew to his, shocked and embarrassed. "No!"

"Hm." He lifted her chin with his hand and turned her face to the light. She stared at him defiantly for one moment, then she looked down, and he wondered if she denied the truth. Yet breeding or not, this melancholy could not be healthy. "Come out with me," he coaxed. "You've scarcely been out of the house since we arrived."

"That storm we encountered outside of Malkin-hampsted frightened me."

She sounded almost childlike, offering the excuse with no hope of being believed, and his faith in his mother and her theory increased. "Frightened you? Frightened the woman who faced me down when I was in a rage and ignored a ghost with a club?"

"You and the ghost were mere men, but if another storm blows up, I'll be at its mercy. That's not the same at all."

Rand stared at his wife's silhouette and wondered whether she realized how much the sunshine revealed of her expression. She was afraid, all right, but not of a storm. The woman who had taken such pleasure in wandering the estate now cowered inside Clairmont Court, and Rand didn't like it. He didn't like it at all. "It hasn't even rained since the storm, and by October you'll be regretting these days you've spent inside. Come, I'm going to go to our favorite place today, and perhaps we could make memories there."

Her lips parted, and she turned her head to look up at him with such naked longing that it tore at his heart. With all the conceit in the world, he couldn't think it was the prospect of lovemaking with him that excited her so. It was the idea of going to Beechwood Hollow.

He answered her as if she had spoken. "All right then. I'll have Betty pack us a basket."

"I really . . . I don't want . . ."

He backed toward the door. "Put on your walking clothes and I'll meet you in the entry in half an hour."

"I don't think—"

"Be there, or I'll come and get you." He shut the door on her protests and headed for the kitchen, a frown etched on his face. He had somehow broken more than her fragile trust in him with his cruelty, and it was up to him to heal her—or to show her how to heal herself. He could do it, couldn't he? Hadn't she already shown him the way?

As he descended the stairs, the front door opened with a bang and a brisk wind swept through the entryway. "Make way for the prodigal son," a laughing voice cried.

"James!" Rand leaped from the fifth step and landed on the hard floor.

"Rand!" James leaped through the door and slid on the slick wood.

Rand ignored the irritating tingle in his hip joints as

he and James laughed together. Rand said, "You don't look like a weary traveler."

"But I am." James laid the back of his hand against his forehead in excessive dramatics. "All the way from London in five days."

"I made it in three," Rand observed.

"Ah, but I hazard you didn't have to stop and spend time with a lonely dowager countess in need of personal attention." James had a wicked twinkle in his eye.

"No, I had Sylvan with me."

James's relief was not the product of dramatics. "You prevailed and brought her home, then?"

"How could she resist me?"

"How indeed." James glanced out the door, then yelled, "Hey! Don't drop those portmanteaus off the top of the coach. Hey!" He tromped out the door and hollered at the hired men, then spotted Jasper in the stable yard. James hollered, "Hey! Jasper, come and supervise these cabbage heads, will you?" He tromped back inside. "Damn fools. Don't have a care for anything."

Tongue in cheek, Rand said, "Maybe they fear their vails will be insufficient."

"Are you saying my pockets are to let?" James demanded.

"They've never been anything but," Rand answered. "What brings you home?"

"Vulgar curiosity." James snapped his fingers at the hovering butler and Peterson helped him remove his greatcoat and beaver hat. "I wondered why you hadn't come to visit when you were in London. Have I displeased you in some way?"

"Not at all," Rand said warmly. "I simply thought it best that Sylvan return to Clairmont Court."

"Why? Are you in a hurry to be a widower? Thank

you, Jasper." James smiled with satisfaction as Jasper and three of the stable hands each carried a portmanteau up the stairs and into the house. "Jasper, care for the trunks, if you would."

"What about the coachmen?" Jasper asked.

James feigned ignorance. "What about them?"

"Oh, for God's sake." Rand dug into his pocket and handed Jasper coins. "Give them their vails and send them on their way."

"You're a brick," James said warmly.

"And you're back because you've already run through the allowance I gave you."

"Rand, you have such a suspicious mind."

"Which is no answer." Rand clapped a hand on James's back and pushed him toward the study. "Your mother'll be glad to see you, anyway."

"A face only a mother could love," James replied, deriding himself.

"Come and have a drink and tell me your fortunes."

"Just a minute." Pointing to Peterson, James said, "You! See to getting those bags to my room, will you? And tell Betty I'm back and she needs to prepare a nice joint for dinner, with plum pudding and a blancmange to finish."

"You're so charming to those born to a lower station," Rand mocked.

"I was polite," James protested. To the butler, he said, "I was polite, wasn't I?"

Peterson bowed. "Indeed, Lord James, you were."

"There you have it." James waved an expansive hand. "I was polite."

"You don't even know his name."

"Why should I?"

"He's been here for twenty years."

"Well." James poured himself a whiskey and tossed it off. "He does his job well, then." Rand groaned and James laughed. "You're a stick, cousin. I heard rumor that some storms did damage here."

Rand lifted his brows and stared. "Where did you hear talk like that?"

"In London, if one keeps one's ears open, one hears many things. But this is more than a rumor—I saw that driving through the fields. Wiped the wretched buggers out, did it?"

"Pretty much."

"Going to reopen the mill to help them?"

Rand stared at James in amazement.

"I knew it, I knew it!" James exploded with frustration. "I can see it in your face. You're guilty as hell."

Rand found himself on the defensive. "The women have asked me, and I've been thinking about it."

"Thinking about it." James threw his glass into the fireplace and the crystal shattered. "Dammit, Rand, are you addled? Do you want to start the whole thing all over again?"

Honestly puzzled, Rand asked, "What do you mean?"

"I mean some thatch-gallow out there doesn't much like that mill."

"*You* don't much like that mill."

"I'm not snuffing people over it."

"Snuffing people over—"

"It was the mill, always the mill." James strode over and grabbed Rand by the lapels. "Can't you see? The women who worked at the mill, the mill itself, Miss Sylvan."

Rand jerked himself free and stumbled backward. "Sylvan had nothing to do with the mill."

"She helped one of the mill workers when she was

injured. If some crack-pate wished to shut the mill down, then Miss Sylvan was a villain greater than the others."

"The only one worse, in fact, was Garth." Much struck by James's good sense, Rand rubbed his chin. "Interesting theory, James. Makes sense out of nonsense."

James stood and stared intently at Rand, his chest heaving. "Then you're not going to do it."

"Opening the mill," Rand said softly, "will flush out the bastard who killed my brother, then, won't it?"

With a loud curse, James threw himself into a chair.

It rocked back on its rear legs, and Rand caught it before James toppled. "What difference does it make to you? You'll be in London. No taint of business will affix itself to you."

James fixed his gaze on Rand. "I'm not going back to London."

Ever cynical, Rand said, "Never fear, James, I'll fix you up with another allowance."

"Won't go back for anything."

Surprised, Rand studied James. His cousin looked as if he suffered from the ague. "Did you get yourself in some kind of trouble?"

"Yes, there's some kind of trouble, all right." James ran his fingers through his travel-tossed hair, and his disheveled appearance reminded Rand, just for a second, of his brother. "You don't understand trouble. Nor did Garth. Go blithely through life, never thinking about the consequences to those of us to whom the consequences have meaning."

"What?"

"Never mind." James hauled himself erect. "Just don't be surprised if you see me dogging your footsteps."

19

Lunch basket in hand, Rand returned to the entry to find Sylvan triumphantly heading for the study. Within, he could hear Aunt Adela greeting her son and his mother exclaiming about her nephew, but Rand caught Sylvan and swung her around. "No, you don't."

"But, James—"

"Can wait to see you. I have something I wish to discuss which concerns you."

She stopped tugging at him and stared suspiciously.

"Not that." He gave her a push toward the door and teased, "Although you're a wanton to think of it."

Sylvan glared at him, then plucked her shawl, gloves, and bonnet from the impassive butler's hand and said, "Thank you, Peterson."

Remembering his conversation with James, Rand chuckled as he wrapped the lacy white shawl around her shoulders. Peterson, too, remembered, for he nodded and smiled as he held the door for her.

Then they stepped onto the terrace, and she flinched from the light.

Rand was struck by a wave of déjà vu. Hadn't they played this scene once before? Hadn't he been the one who feared to be outside, and hadn't she forced him to go out into the sunshine where his healing would begin? He looked to see if she remembered, but the coburg bonnet, with its soft crown and floppy brim, hid her face as she tied the ribbons beneath her chin.

Remembering how aggressively she had stormed his reservations, he resolved to try like tactics. He waited only until they were out of earshot of the servants before saying, "I need your opinion about something."

"My opinion? Why?"

He gripped her arm as they started down the stairs. "Because I respect your opinion."

"Do you?"

She sounded distant and distracted, and he grappled for a way to prove himself as they strolled the same rutted path they'd taken in April. "It seems to be a common trait at Clairmont Court. Haven't you noticed? The village women respect you, too."

"I . . ." She twisted her arm until he would have been a brute if he'd held it, and when she was free, she said, "The mill women have called on me, but . . . I . . ."

"They probably arrived at a poor time for you to receive them." He excused her, then administered obligation. "Of course, they consider you an ally, and right now they need their allies."

Her face reddened, and she snapped, "I don't know why they would consider me an ally."

"Because they want to convince me to reopen the mill."

"The mill." She skidded to a halt. "How can you do that?"

"If I finance the mill, the men will have work with good wages. They'd be constructing the mill, and that'd get them through the winter." He took her arm again and gave a gentle tug, and she lurched after him. "The mill will be finished by next summer, and the women would have work then."

"But why would you do it?" She pushed at the bonnet's brim as if its properties of concealment irritated her now. "Devote a year of your life and a good part of the family fortune building and setting up a mill when your brother died violently in the last one?"

"You know why." They reached the ocean and he turned toward the mill. "Since the storm, the villagers have been asking—begging, really—that I rebuild. They don't want to leave Malkinhampsted. It's been their home for generations."

Loosening her bonnet, she let it dangle by the strings around her neck. "Yes, and Mr. Donald can say what he likes about resignation to God's will, but nobody in the village or on any of the outlying farms wants to watch their children starve."

"You know that without even talking to them, don't you?"

Her mouth drooped at his pointed comment, and with surly disdain she said, "It would take a lesser genius than mine to know that."

"You have a gift for empathizing with others."

"No, I don't."

"I think you do."

"No. I don't understand *you* at all."

"Hm." He pretended to think as they climbed the rise near the mill. "I suppose that might be a problem between us. After all, we're married and as close as two people can be. We share an intimate bond."

"Sh."

"We make love in every imaginable way, but I still don't know what you're thinking." Keeping one hand beneath her arm, he slid the other around her waist and turned her to face him.

Her chin firmed. "Why do you care?"

"Because you're my wife. I married you because—"

"Because the vicar and your brother caught us in an improper embrace."

"No! They caught us in an embrace because you appealed to me, body and soul."

She stepped out of his arms and walked rapidly away. "That's nice."

"I didn't have to marry you." He was talking to her back.

"Yes, you did." She pulled her hat up and tied the ribbons again with a savage gesture. "You said so."

He'd said it then, but he hadn't meant it. "I am— *was*—the brother of a duke. I didn't have to do anything I didn't want to."

Sylvan laughed with what sounded like genuine amusement. "Oh, Rand." Stopping, she cupped his face in her gloved hands. "Do you really believe that? Don't you know the only way you could have left me at the altar is if you were a different man with a different family? Only a boor would leave a woman in such a dilemma, and you're not a boor."

"You'll turn my head with compliments like that."

She ignored his pique. "Can you imagine what your mother would have said had you refused to wed me? Or your brother? Or even Aunt Adela?"

"Well, yes, they would have been upset." He understated the matter, and he feared she knew it. "But I really could have refused."

"Another man could have refused. Perhaps James could have refused. But not you, Rand." She patted his cheeks. "Not you. So." She walked on again. "Why are you telling me about the mill?"

This wasn't turning out as he had hoped. "I want to consult with someone about the mill. Unfortunately, the someone I want to consult with is protecting herself and excluding everyone—everyone!—from her thoughts."

"You don't know that!" But she refused to turn and look at him until she topped the rise above the mill. There she halted until Rand came up beside her.

Staring fixedly at her shoes, she clung to her protective shell, and he didn't know that he'd accomplished anything with his probings and fumblings. Awkwardly he waited for her to say something, anything that would set things right, and when she didn't, he reached out and untied her bonnet and slipped it off her head. He just wanted to look into her face, to see the messages there. With his hand he ruffled her hair, completing the disarray that the wind had initiated, and she looked so like the jaunty Sylvan he'd first met that he wished he could kiss her.

And he could, of course. She would respond promptly, and possibly pull him to the ground and make him forget his every scheme to uncloak the reason for her unhappiness. He hadn't realized it until this moment, but he'd been making love to her, thinking she'd have to reveal herself through the act; she'd been making love to him, using it to conceal herself.

Perhaps his mother was right. Perhaps Sylvan needed more than two bodies on a bed. Perhaps she needed words—real words, words that would convince her of his devotion.

If only he knew what they were.

Tears gleamed in her eyes as he gazed on her, but she

refused to let them fall. Her chin firmed, and she jerked her head toward the hollow below. "The mill is a wretched sight, isn't it?"

The same sunshine that shone kindly on the earth and sea bludgeoned the wreck below. It had been a scar on the land before; now it was a bleeding wound.

Sylvan walked forward, leaving him standing, her hat in his hand. "Could you really repair it?" she called.

The wind whipped off the ocean, as it always did, and he opened his hand and let the bonnet fly. It sailed inland a long way before it descended, then tumbled into a hiding place in the long grass.

He smiled with satisfaction, and hurried to catch her. "I think so. Most of the stone from the wall is still usable, and slate for the roof is plentiful around here." The mill loomed before him, and he sighed. Rebuilding had seemed a good idea when he thought about it; faced with the reality of the destruction, he thought himself mad. "But James is against it, of course. Aunt Adela has never approved, and if we rebuild, I fear it will resurrect my mother's grief and worry her beyond all telling."

"I hated the mill, too. I hated the noise and the smell and the constant danger." Removing her gloves, Sylvan ran her hand over one of the still-standing walls. Whitewash flaked off beneath her touch.

The joints in his legs ached from the long walk, and he sat on one of the squared boulders that the explosion had flung free. Stretching his legs out, he rubbed his hips with his hands. "So you think it foolish to rebuild?"

She buffed her fingers together as if to dispel the dry feeling, and shivered. "We have to rebuild."

Startled, he said, "But if you hate it . . ."

"I'd hate to see this perfect corner of England lose its people because it can't support them. We have to rebuild."

"And if the ghost comes out again to attack women and sabotage the mill?"

Frowning, she chewed on her lower lip. "The ghost may have been your brother's enemy, and everything he did was aimed at destroying Garth."

"It's possible," he acknowledged. "But James says it was the mill that caused the problems."

"James knows you're thinking of opening the mill?"

"James guessed," Rand corrected. "And very unhappy he was, too."

"I can imagine." She watched him as he gently worked his legs, but she offered no assistance. "Nevertheless, we can't let fear of a ghost control our decision. We know he's a man, and you're no longer an easy victim of his hoaxes."

The old worry for her safety swooped on him, and he said, "He only strikes at night, and I'll be with you, but we'll be extra careful."

She watched her hands as she carefully threaded her fingers together. "Do you want me to go?"

"Go?"

"Back to my father's house. Is that really why you brought me here? To tell me once more that I'm . . ."

"You're . . . ?"

"Inadequate." She looked right at him, and her grief broke his heart.

"It is I who am inadequate when I am without you." He shook his head. "I will never send you away again. I was a fool to do it the first time." She said not a word, and he asked, "Do you believe me?"

"I want to."

She did want to, he could tell, and he asked, "Do you remember that you promised to acquiesce to all my conjugal desires?"

"How could I not?" she asked with a flash of her old spirit. "You remind me at every opportunity."

He tried to coax her to cheer. "Let me command you once more, as your duke and as your husband—believe yourself my own beloved, and know that you'll never leave my side again. Can you do that?"

It wasn't a real smile that she gave him: more of a hopeful one, but her reply gratified him. "I'll try."

The silence around them deepened, and when she realized it, she blushed and said, "We'd best be careful with all of the women. Tell the mill workers to stay inside after dark, and keep vigil over Lady Emmie and Aunt Adela."

He hated to come back to reality, but he had to agree with her. "We'd best watch Betty, also."

"And Gail."

"Surely the ghost wouldn't hurt a child." The concept was so outside Rand's experience, he couldn't imagine it.

"No." But she looked troubled. "Surely not. If we could bring your brother's murderer to justice, that would be a bonus added to the good the mill will bring."

He had considered all angles and would do all that was necessary to protect those he loved. "So we'll do it." This woman was all he thought her, and more, and however long it took him to win her trust again, it would be time well spent. Holding up his hand, he said, "Help me up."

Grasping him, she tugged, but he tugged back and tumbled her into his lap.

She struggled halfheartedly as he turned and positioned her, but she quieted when he showered her face with light, loving kisses. When he rocked her, she laid her head on his shoulder and announced, "We shall put in an infirmary."

Wrested back from his pleasure in her, he stammered, "W-what?"

"We'll put in an infirmary, with bandages and herbs

and splints and a bone saw." She choked slightly in remembrance. "All the things we needed that day of the explosion."

He hugged her tighter. "Anything you wish, Your Grace."

He didn't sound sarcastic, but she thought he must be, to be so obedient, and she struggled out of his grasp. He let her go, but her mind lingered on him, his motivations and aims, as she walked beside the mill. What had brought this change? He'd been so convinced he was right to protect her, to treat her like a fragile flower and dismiss the knowledge that might have made her a useful partner to him. And she'd been willing to behave as she thought he desired—like a lady whose head was filled with nothing but the ringing of the servants' bell and the color of embroidery threads.

But now he was talking to her, saying that he valued her opinion and acting as if it were the truth. Somehow, in the confusion that her life had become, she'd lost sight of the truth. It taunted her in her nightmares and leaped at her at the most inappropriate times, but it came to her now and again that she didn't know who she was.

She was so deep in thought that when a man rose from the wreckage, she jumped and shrieked.

"Beg pardon. Didn't mean to scare ye . . . Yer Grace?"

Blushing at her foolishness, she nodded at the smiling, broad-shouldered youth. It wasn't that she expected to see Garth's ghost—or any other ghost, for that matter—but a pall hung over the place.

The man dropped an armful of wood and pulled his forelock with a gleam of curiosity in his eye. "Yer Grace, I'm Jeffrey the carpenter. I hope ye don't mind, but I've come to salvage what I can from the mill. It'll be a hard winter, and I can use the boards for repairs."

"I . . . well, I . . ." She glanced back at Rand, but he was standing and stretching as if some cramp had caught him unaware. "Recover what you can. I'm sure my husband won't mind."

One by one, Jeffrey picked up the boards he'd dropped. "Been hoping to get a glimpse of you. The village women talk about you all the time, and Nanna is me cousin, ye know." She flushed, imagining censure in his tone, but he continued cheerfully, " 'Course, everyone is my cousin. Most of the village and the farms is family."

That caught her attention, and she watched Jeffrey carefully for his reaction as she said, "You'd hate to see them move."

Jeffrey's grin slipped. "I would. I wish that—"

"That—?"

"Ah, I hate to nag, but I wish His Grace could see his way clear to rebuild the mill. Then there would be jobs for everyone. We'd all be rich." His ingratiating grin appeared, and again he bowed and pulled his forelock as Rand strolled up. "Yer Grace, we was just talking about ye, and how ye'd profit from opening the mill."

Rand took Sylvan's hand. "We're thinking about it."

After one gasp of joy, Jeffrey bowed, then bowed again. "Glad to hear it, Yer Grace. It'll mean so much to all of us." The boards slipped from his grasp once more, and he scrambled after them, still talking. "I'll be fer telling them in the village, shall I?"

Rand looked at Sylvan, and she understood the questioning lift of his brow. If they gave Jeffrey permission to announce their plans, the news would spread like wildfire and the whole chain of events would be set in motion once more. It frightened her, and thrilled her, too. She nodded at Rand, and he nodded at Jeffrey.

"Yes. Tell them."

Jeffrey's queries and babblings of joy kept Rand in place, but Sylvan slipped her hand free and wandered into the mill. She didn't plan to go anywhere specific; just to walk and see the condition it was in.

Opening the door to Garth's office, she glanced inside. No one had stripped anything from this room. The door was still closed firmly, and the contents were still intact. Much of the building around his office still stood with its roof and walls, and what remained of the machinery had been pushed under the shelter to protect it from the weather. In fact, only the mill's far wall had been completely removed, and the walls beside it tapered from nothingness to their full height. Some of the giant oak beams tilted from the roof to the floor where the roof had been destroyed, and she found herself glad she was a merchant's daughter, for she could estimate how much of the building they could restore.

She believed she wished only to estimate, but as she walked, she found herself at the place where Nanna had been pinned. Blood stained the flooring, only slightly faded by the rains and sun. It gave her an odd feeling to stand where she had inflicted so much pain. She'd had help in that horrible task: the white-faced Rand had been her main assistant, and the Reverend Donald had given himself over to Nanna, to shield her as he could. Vaguely Sylvan remembered a wet rag passing across her forehead and a dry one blotting the tears from her eyes, and later, when the job was done, she remembered someone holding her head. Obviously, the mill women had remained to give support to their friend, and they'd given her support as their friend's only hope. But . . . unwillingly she stared at the darker stain beside the great beam that so many men had had to struggle to move.

Shirley had died there. If Sylvan hadn't been so hesitant when the explosion had occurred . . . If she'd come to find Shirley instead of binding Beverly's ribs . . .

The ifs piled one on the other, and she knew that if she'd seen Shirley, she would have refused to move her for fear of internal injuries. Sylvan herself might have been kneeling beside her when the second big collapse occurred, and she might have died along with Shirley, or instead of Shirley. No matter how difficult life seemed right now, Sylvan couldn't bring herself to wish for death.

With almost painful resignation, she moved out of the mill and to the place where Garth's body had landed.

It was easy to find; someone had come here before her and marked it with stones. Not the large, worked stones that were used to build the mill, but small stones, smoothed by a stream or by the ocean and piled into a well-tended pyramid.

"Who has done this, I wonder?"

Rand had followed her, and she hadn't noticed.

He knelt and touched the little memorial. "I wish I'd thought to do it, but I would have put a carved marker, I suppose, something dignified and quite unlike Garth. This is better." He looked up, and his smile wobbled. "Don't you think?"

"Perhaps we should do something similar inside," she suggested tentatively.

"Where Shirley died?" He nodded. "Yes, if we're going to reopen the mill, it would be nice to honor our departed."

"I haven't been here since the accident."

"I have." He sat beside the pile of stones, his hand resting on them as if he could absorb the essence of his brother. "I've made several pilgrimages, and brought my mother and my aunt. It seems I've got the need to come and look, to get a grasp on the reality of it. He's gone, but I still expect to see him. . . ."

He faltered, and she looked at him. Tears slithered down his cheeks, tentatively finding their way.

"Sometimes I think I hear him." His tears flowed faster now, splashing off his dark lashes. "When Aunt Adela starts pontificating, I can almost hear . . ." Like a child, he wiped his cheeks on his sleeve. "I think she can hear him, too, because she half turns—" He choked on a laugh. "She looks so guilty, saying things she knows would make him furious, and him not there to respond."

Without volition, her hand reached out to touch his head. Then she caught herself. What would happen if she tried to comfort him? Wouldn't she reveal her own despair?

"I miss him. I spent the last months of his life in a wheelchair, making him miserable, when if I'd just told him, trusted him, treated him like my big brother, we could have found the bastard who did this." Great battering sobs began to punctuate his words, tearing at his coherence yet endowing him with eloquence. "Dammit, Garth didn't have to die."

His sorrow and guilt brought tears to her own eyes. Tears for him or for Garth, she didn't know, but she didn't want to sympathize. She didn't want to cry. If she started, she would cry for all the men lost or injured on the battlefield, for the women who died or were injured at the mill, for Rand in his agony and for Garth's memory. If she started her lament, she wouldn't stop.

Before her wavering gaze, she saw Rand's arms reaching out for her, begging her for succor.

Silently she fled, running over the hills to escape her grief, but finding it in every bank and hollow.

20

"*I'm fine now, Rand.* I just had a whim to run in the hills." Sylvan took a breath. "I've been inside so much, I just had an impulse to stroll in the grass before autumn stole the color . . . no, that's not right." She pressed her fist to her stomach and stared at the looming facade of Clairmont Court. *He* was inside, she knew. *He* would expect an explanation for her flight of the morning. *He* would want to know where she'd been all these hours, and *she* couldn't think what to say.

So she stood outside on the lawn in the shade of a hawthorn and practiced her lines. She had to get them right. She'd missed dinner and tea. It would be dark soon. . . . Oh, but she didn't want to see Rand. She didn't want to see any of them. Not anyone in the Malkin family, nor any of the servants, nor Jasper, nor the Reverend Donald. They all acted so kind and anxious about her, asking her what she wanted, giving her everything she needed. She felt like an ungrateful wretch to be so miserable.

Betty stepped onto the terrace and shaded her eyes against the westering sun. Sylvan wanted to hide, but that would be foolish, and when Betty waved in great sweeps of her arm, Sylvan waved back and started toward the stairs.

Betty met her halfway and ignored the pleasant smile Sylvan had practiced so ardently. "Your Grace, have you seen Gail in your ramblings?"

Feeling the fool, Sylvan realized she wasn't the center of at least one woman's world. "No. Is she gone?"

"Again." Betty sounded exasperated, but she looked worried. "She's going more and more, for longer and longer. I've tried to tell her she needs to let me know where she's going, but she says she'll be fine. I wouldn't worry, you know, if she were playing with other children, but it's solitude she seeks, and if she slipped or . . ." Digging in her capacious apron pockets, she drew out a handful of smooth rocks. "Do you think I'm being silly, Your Grace?"

"Not at all." Sylvan laid her arm over Betty's shoulders. "How long has she been gone?"

"She took a bit of supper in a rag and left in the late morning." Betty scattered the rocks around the base of the tree. "I hoped maybe she'd run into you and Lord Rand, but His Grace came back an hour ago and said no, he hadn't seen her, and now . . ."

Feeling as if she'd failed Betty in some way, Sylvan tried to comfort her. "Gail's fine, I'm sure, but I'll go back and look for her."

"Oh, you don't have to. His Grace has gone out." More rocks appeared out of Betty's pockets, and she threw these, one by one, as hard as she could. "I didn't ask him to, mind, for he's walking rather stiffly, but when he found you hadn't returned, either, he insisted."

"Did he?"

"That wasn't all, I don't suppose." Betty shook her head in disgust. "Him and Mr. James had another go-round, just like this morning when Mr. James arrived."

"A go-round?" Sylvan's old suspicions re-formed with Betty's lugubrious tone. "They fought?"

"Mr. James doesn't want His Grace to . . ." She trailed off. "Maybe I shouldn't be babbling, seeing as how nothing's actually decided yet."

"Mr. James doesn't want Rand to open the mill again."

"Oh, you know." Betty nodded, pleased. "I had hoped he would discuss it with you, but one never knows with a man."

"Where's Mr. James now?"

"Went to his room to sulk, I suppose. Childish as ever, that one is." Betty touched the painfully red tip of Sylvan's nose. "You'd best come inside and let me put vinegar on that sunburn. Where's your hat?"

"I lost it. I don't know where." With Rand gone, the house seemed a likely refuge where Sylvan could eat, rest, and gather her forces for the coming confrontation. But she, too, worried about Gail, for she'd spent time with the child and knew how desperately she missed her father. "I think I ought to go after Gail."

"I'll hug her to death when she gets back, then thrash her within an inch of her life." Betty tried to laugh at her own inconsistency. "But she really hasn't been out this long before, even when she wanders with you." With an exclamation of disgust, Betty turned her pockets inside out and shook them.

More pebbles rained at their feet, and Sylvan stared at them in sudden conjecture. "Where did you get those?"

"I went looking in Gail's chamber, just to see if she was hiding there, or if there was some clue to her whereabouts, and I found them and some other bigger ones, all piled in a corner. What the child wants with a bunch of rocks, I'll never know, but—Miss Sylvan, what's the matter?"

Sylvan had stiffened, staring at the stones, polished smooth from the action of sea or stream. "I know where she is."

"Where?"

"At the mill." A vision of the little pyramid of stones filled Sylvan's mind, followed by darker visions of crooked beams and hanging boards, of protruding nails and sharp machinery. "I'll go after her."

Apparently, the same visions filled Betty's mind, for she answered, "I'm going, too."

They started off at a run, following the path, but Betty knew the byways better than Sylvan, and she said, "This way. It's shorter."

They cut through the trees and down a steep bank into a ravine. Sylvan skidded in the soft dirt and landed on a rock, skinning the palms of her hands, and when she stood up again, Betty said, "This is stupid. We should have got the carriage."

"In the time it would take Jasper to hitch the horses, we'll be there." Sylvan blew on her stinging palms. "I'm fine now. We can go."

"Jasper's not at the court," Betty said. "He's off moping over Loretta again, poor sot. Uphill, now."

They started off, climbing as Betty directed.

"Jasper's in love?" Sylvan asked.

"For all the good it'll do him." Betty puffed hard. "Loretta's married and likely to stay that way. Nothing's wrong with Loretta's man that I can see, except he's mean as a boar and twice as stupid. 'Twould take a mighty blow to kill that one." They crested the rise, and Betty stood and panted. "See where we are now?"

"Yes." Betty's shortcut had eliminated half the distance

to the mill. "Hurry!" Sylvan started running again, only half aware of how Betty struggled to keep up.

"Stop, Your Grace!" Betty cried at last.

Turning, Sylvan saw Betty standing, hands on her knees, gasping for breath, and realized her exhaustion. "Betty, I'll go on without you. I've got to hurry."

"Your Grace!" Betty's cry stopped her in her tracks. "Why do you have to hurry? What do you fear?"

"The mill is a dangerous place. Gail might be hurt, bleeding . . ." Betty still stared, and Sylvan pushed aside her images of the inanimate dangers of the mill. Instead, she allowed her true fears to come forth. "The rumors will be all over the village, all over the district, that Rand is going to reopen the mill, and that could make someone very unhappy."

Betty comprehended at once. "Run, Your Grace. Run! I'll go to the village, or back to the house." Caught halfway between both, she tried to decide her best route. "I'll go to the village."

"Send help," Sylvan said, and ran again.

Too late.

When she was a child, Sylvan imagined herself a fearless heroine who responded to need without flinching. Instead, she ran each step aware of the blisters her shoes were rubbing on her heels, aware of her heart's pounding and the breath that burned her lungs.

Too late.

Gail probably wasn't even still at the mill. Maybe she'd never even gone there. And most likely, the man who pretended to be the ghost had left the district or didn't care about the mill anymore or wouldn't dream of harming a child.

But Gail was Garth's child, and Sylvan didn't dare slow for fear she would be too late.

Too late, too late. She scrambled up the steep hill that stood east of the mill and stood still for one wicked second. It helped her catch her breath, and she inspected the mill building. Its long side faced her, with Garth's intact office on the right and the vanquished wall on the left. She couldn't see any unusual activity, but the sun was setting and it blotted her eyesight.

She didn't want the sun to set. Not now, when she was here alone and a ferocious creature waited for darkness to prowl. But was she alone, or did Gail lie bleeding below?

She ran down the hill, jumping over the heather, skidding on the mossy stones. "Gail?" she called. "Gail!"

A small figure rose from beside the pile of stones and looked up at her, and Sylvan's heart pumped pure thankfulness. "Gail!" She waved like a madwoman, and as if responding to her rapture, Gail started toward her. They met on the grassy slope in front of the mill, and Sylvan wrapped the girl in her arms and hugged her tight. "Praise God you're well!" She panted, trying to get her breath. "You are well, aren't you?"

"Why wouldn't I be?" Gail asked belligerently.

"You frightened us." Sylvan dropped her head onto Gail's thin shoulder. "Your mother's worried sick."

"I was here when someone came." Gail patted Sylvan's head in quite an adult manner, but her reasoning was childlike. "I hate to be here when there's someone else around, so I hid until he left."

Sylvan's anxiety returned in a rush. "Who was it?"

"I don't know." Gail pushed Sylvan away, needling her with a scornful dismissal. "He was rummaging around. A lot of people rummage in the mill. Why can't they just leave it alone?"

Straightening, Sylvan wiped the perspiration from her forehead and scanned the mill site. They seemed exposed here, with the wind blowing so it would snatch away a woman's scream. "Why don't we go back to Clairmont Court?"

"Not yet." Gail marched toward the mill. "I've got things to do."

Keeping pace with her, Sylvan asked, "Put the stones on your father's marker?"

Gail whirled on her. "How did you—"

"Your mother found the rocks in your bedchamber."

"In my bedchamber?" Gail cried. "She knows I don't want her in my bedchamber."

"You were gone for so long, she thought maybe you were hiding."

"Oh." Gail's face worked, then grudgingly, she explained, "I fell asleep while I was hiding from the man. Did she take my rocks?"

"I'm afraid she did, but you should be grateful. I recognized them from the monument you built and knew where you were." Sylvan walked on toward the little pyramid, and Gail came to stand beside her.

A little abashed, the girl kicked at the stones. "It's not much."

"Rand saw it with me today. We both agreed your father would have liked it."

The quiver of Gail's lip matched the quiver in her voice. "Do you think so?"

"Makes us adults feel foolish not to have thought of it." Sylvan hugged Gail again, and this time the girl permitted it. "But you know, it is getting dark, and we should go back to the house before someone—"

"Is everyone coming after me?" Gail asked in disgust. "Because I'm tired of everyone acting like I'm a baby. There's you and my mother, and now Uncle James and I suppose—"

"Uncle James?" Sylvan turned to see James bearing down on them purposefully. His dark hair and towering stature reminded her suddenly of Rand and Garth and Radolf and . . . the ghost. Her earlier alarm came back, burgeoning with the appearance of this new target. She felt both prudent and absurd when she grabbed Gail's arm and said, "Where's your hiding place?"

Gail's amazement might have been funny if not for James's approaching figure. "What?"

"Go there. Hide. Hurry!"

"But Uncle James—"

"Now."

Something of Sylvan's trepidation must have struck Gail, for she fled into the mill, leaving Sylvan to face the oncoming threat.

"Damn the girl," James said as soon as he got close enough. "Where's she going? I've got to get my hands on her."

He started into the mill, but Sylvan grabbed him by the arm. "Why?"

"I'm going to lock her up. And you, too, Your Grace, the newest duchess of Clairmont. Haven't you any sense at all?" Grabbing her wrist, he dragged her toward the building. Setting her heels made no difference. He was a big man who refused to be gainsaid. He looked tired and exasperated, and when she wouldn't step up onto the floor, he put his hands at her waist and lifted her. "As soon as I heard the servants gossiping about the mill, I spoke to Rand. I swear, Rand doesn't know what a cesspool he's splashing around in, and he doesn't believe me when I tell him. Would you come *on*?"

Her fingers fastened on a heavy piece of machinery and clung, and he glared.

She glared right back, and his glance softened. "You look as ragged as I feel. The dukes of Clairmont play the tune, and we peasants dance." James glanced around at the demolished, now-shadowy interior of the mill. "Where's the brat?"

"She's hiding in Garth's office." Craftily, she asked, "Shall we go get her?"

"What's she doing in there?" James started toward the intact area.

Sylvan led for a moment, and when James followed willingly, she shook herself free of his grasp. The sun cast long shadows where it still reached through the open roof and the shattered walls, but the farther they went inside, the darker it became. "She's just playing. You know how children are."

"No." He kept one eye on her and one on his footing. "I've done my best to avoid them."

"I suppose it wouldn't do to get too attached to Gail." The closer they got to the office, the more Sylvan watched. If Gail really did hide in the office—a likely location—her presence there would be a disaster.

He frowned as if he found her words cryptic. "Oh, I'm attached. A man doesn't have a choice in a family like ours. But I just don't understand her. It's really a mess in here, isn't it? I haven't been back since Garth died."

She pretended astonishment. "You haven't?"

"No, I . . . no. I'm so guilty I can't stand myself anyway." He laughed sharply, in pain. "Why should I come here and torment myself more?" She stumbled, and he caught her. "Be careful," he admonished. "I don't need something else to feel guilty about."

Looking at him in the dimness, she saw the hollow of his eyes, the draw of his cheeks, the height of him. He looked like the ghost—like Rand, the ghost she'd seen the first night, and the real ghost who'd led her on a merry chase, and like the glimpse of the ghost she'd seen running from her room. Too many ghosts, too close a resemblance, and he'd admitted his guilt. James—pleasant, charming James—was the one, and he was smiling at her as if she were too stupid to comprehend.

"Are you feeling well?" he asked. "You look like you've seen a ghost."

He mocked, and fury shook her. He would not be sneering when she got done with him. She kept her gaze on him as she opened the door to Garth's office. "Gail, if you're in your father's office, come out right now." She hoped that if Gail were within, she would come out, and if she hid close enough to hear, she'd understand and stay in seclusion.

With his gaze on the opening, James said, "Are you sure she's in there?"

Taking a chance, Sylvan stuck her head inside and looked. She couldn't see Gail, and her heart leaped in relief. As if she were speaking to the girl, she said, "Gail, come on! Stop playing games."

"She *is* in there?" James sounded surprised. "Why won't she come out?"

"I don't know." Sylvan worked on looking and sounding disgusted. "Maybe you could talk to her."

"I?" James put his hand on his chest. "What would I say that would persuade her?"

Now Sylvan acted with the flair of Drury Lane's finest. "Young Gail misses her father, and while I cannot command her, I think perhaps your persuasions would bring her forth." Sylvan pushed him toward the office. "She's hiding under the desk. Just go in and call to her as if she were a babe, without seeking her. She'll come out for you, I know."

"Where are you going to be, while I'm making a fool of myself?" he asked in exasperation.

"Right here, cousin, waiting for you."

He believed her. The fool believed her, because he was a man and she was a woman, and women were stupid creatures who fell off of cliffs when they imagined unearthly groans—unearthly groans that were only an animal mating.

She hadn't realized how much she resented his patronizing her on the night he'd rescued her, but now, she wanted the blackguard to be James so she could absolve herself from the charge of simplemindedness.

Stepping into the room, James started talking, and Sylvan got a grip on one of the heavy metal machines. Taking a breath, she heaved. It moved a foot. She heaved again, and heard James say, "What in the—"

In a panic, she shoved it as hard as she could. It blocked the office door just as it swung out toward her, and James squawked when he smashed against the wood. "Sylvan?"

She leaned around the machine and looked, and saw James's three fingers grasp the doorframe. "No!" she said, and pushed again, and the machine skidded as if it rolled on wheels.

His fingers were trapped between door and frame. James howled in agony. Horrified, she tried to pull the machine back, but a man's voice said, "Don't!"

She gave a scream and spun around. The Reverend Donald leaned against the metal beside her; he had provided the grease to move the machine. Catching at her heart before it beat out of her chest, she said, "I've got him!"

"I know you do."

His stern face swam before her eyes, and she thought

she'd never been so glad to see another human being in her life. "James is guilty."

"Yes." The vicar nodded sadly. "He is."

"Sylvan," James yelled. "No, please, listen to me." With his free hand, he pounded on the door. "Please, Sylvan." Then she heard him mutter, "My fingers."

Sylvan didn't want to feel compassion, but she was never free of it. Gesturing wildly, she said, "His fingers are caught. We've got to—"

"No, we don't."

"He's hurt." She shoved at the machine, trying to pry it away from the door, but the vicar grabbed her shoulder and swung her away.

"No!" he shouted.

Hitting the spinning mechanism, she tripped on one of the legs to land sprawled on the floor like a dockside floozy. He loomed over her before she could catch her breath, and her overactive imagination made him appear dread and sinister. "Reverend?" she croaked.

"Leave her alone!" James battered the door with his body. "Don't you understand? If you touch her, you have to kill me, too."

James's words began to make sense to her, and she scooted backward. "Reverend?"

She was looking for reassurance in a suddenly skewed world, but the clergyman picked up a length of metal pipe. "I'm glad you shut him in there. It would have been much more difficult if I'd had to take care of you both."

Take care of. What did he mean? He couldn't mean . . .

Her skirts caught under her heels as she tried to scramble to her feet, and he kicked her foot out from underneath her. "No use trying to get up. You'll just fall down again."

Her ankle ached beneath the impact of his boot, and she grabbed it and rolled backward on her spine. "Dear God."

"I always bring them back to God." He smiled at her with the kindly insight he displayed at such moments. "They're always praying when I finish with them."

James was still shouting. "Run, Sylvan!"

Sylvan scarcely heard him. All her energy was concentrated on the Reverend Donald.

"You shouldn't have given succor to those who went counter to God's will." He chided her in a compassionate tone, but he held the pipe so tightly his knuckles and fingernails turned white.

"I didn't!" She groped for a weapon, but this part of the mill had been swept clean for machinery storage.

"How could you imagine that the hammer of the Lord would fail to find you and fell you?"

Still incredulous, she stammered, "Y-you're the hammer of the Lord?"

"Who better?"

His eyes also appeared deep and hollow in the dimness of the inner mill, but his blond hair glimmered. "You can't be the ghost. The ghost had black hair. He looked like Rand and Garth and"—she glanced at the office where James still hollered—"James."

"Oh, woman, thou art so foolish. You see only what you expect to see. Boot black does well to change a hair color."

"You're not related to them." She glanced longingly through the twisted metal and dangling wood to the still-sunny exterior. The sun was bidding farewell to the land with long streaking rays. "You don't look like them."

"Don't I?"

He chuckled with such gentle humor, she looked again at the length of pipe in his hand. She couldn't have made such an appalling mistake. She couldn't.

He continued in his soft, reproving voice. "But the first duke of Clairmont spread his seed liberally throughout the district, including a long-dead and easily seduced great-great-great-grandmother of mine. Others have told me I have the look of the family, and I think I pass for the duke quite well in the dark." He planted one large booted foot on her skirt as she tried to scoot into the open, and she looked up, up to his hands. He held the pipe firmly, with both hands on one end like a bat, and he smiled with gentle reproof. "The other women thought I was the first duke of Clairmont, but you know better, so I'm afraid I'll have to make the ultimate example of you."

21

No one in the village had seen Gail, no one had seen Sylvan, and Rand was tired and disgruntled. No wonder monks in early England took vows of celibacy. It most likely saved them years of suffering.

Grimacing, he limped toward the vicarage.

Of course, the monks probably suffered in other ways.

A fence encircled the neat cottage, and the yard inside was still fragrant with the scent of herbs and late-blooming flowers. Clover Donald, it would seem, was a gardener. Rand tapped on the door and waited irritably to have it opened. The vicar, with his everlasting nosiness, might know the location of Rand's niece and wife, although he'd also give Rand a lecture on maintaining control of his family.

The Reverend Donald had strong views on the proper roles of man, woman, and child. He hadn't yet come into the nineteenth century; Rand doubted he ever would, and that made the vicar uncomfortable to be around.

That was why Rand had exhausted all other sources before seeking his assistance.

Impatient, he rapped again, and Clover's quavering voice called, "Who is it?"

Surprised, Rand stepped back from the door. Country folk never demanded to know the identity of their visitors, but this was Clover Donald, the woman who feared not only her husband's judgment, but everything else in the world. "It's Rand Malkin," he said.

Nothing happened; she didn't open the door.

He sighed. "It's the duke of Clairmont," he said clearly and slowly. "May I come in?"

The door opened a crack, and her eye examined him. Cautiously, she swung the door wide. "Welcome, Your Grace."

It would seem his title gained him entrance where his name did not. As it should, he supposed. The clergyman for Malkinhampsted was in a position appointed and paid for by the duke of Clairmont since time everlasting. Clover Donald damn well should understand she owed her livelihood to Rand.

Then he took another look at the bashful woman who backed away from him as if he would take a stick to her, and began explaining before he stepped across the threshold. "I need to consult with the vicar about a matter of importance. Would you get him for me?"

"He isn't here right now, but I expect him soon." She didn't look at Rand when she invited, "Would you like to come in and wait?"

Obviously, she didn't want him, but he was weary and in need. "Thank you. I will."

The room he stepped into was the kitchen, bright with the westering sun and the smell of bread toasting by the fire.

"In here, Your Grace."

She indicated the door to a smaller, darker room, a parlor to impress the parishioners, most likely, and on impulse, he refused. "I'll sit here and you can make me a cup of tea, if you don't mind."

She gaped at him as he lowered himself into a chair by the table, then she whispered, "I don't mind."

Of course, what else could she say?

She put the kettle on to boil and stood watching it in such acute discomfort, he wondered how they'd ever get through this time together. "Won't you sit with me?" he asked, knowing she might be in too much awe of him to take a seat in her own kitchen.

"No!" She shook her head vigorously. "The vicar my husband wouldn't like it."

"Ah." He exhaled soundlessly, then suggested, "Maybe if we didn't tell him?"

She gasped audibly, her eyes opening so wide he could see the whites all the way around the iris.

He held up a hand. "Forget I suggested it."

She gulped and said, "I have to tell him everything. He says women lead men into temptation always."

If she hadn't been so pitiable, he would have laughed at the thought of being tempted by this limp, apathetic creature. "I think I'm strong enough to resist," he assured her.

She didn't seem to hear. "He says when a woman behaves in an unseemly manner, a man thinks she's a harlot, and whatever happens to her is a woman's fault."

A duke couldn't remove his vicar for being a pompous ass. If that were the case, there would be few vicars in all of England. But looking at Clover's tear-filled eyes, Rand was very tempted. "I can't say that I agree with that."

"Don't you?" She glanced around guiltily. "I have

occasionally thought it harsh, but only when I'm at fault, I'm sure. The sin of rebellion will surely send me to hell, the vicar my husband says."

Rebellion? Rand struggled to answer without vilifying her husband. "Your little sins could never drag your soul down. You'll reach heaven before any of us."

"Do you really think so?" Her lips parted, and she appeared to be thinking, then she said slowly, "The vicar says that when a woman doesn't stay at home and mind her hearth as the holy writ instructs, she lays herself open to all manner of discipline and castigation."

Studying Clover, Rand was inclined to say, *Madam, your husband is not worthy to sit in judgment of half the human race.* When he thought about Sylvan, and the anguish she'd found when she stepped out of the traditional role of women, he wanted to horsewhip the self-righteous ignoramus who called himself a clergyman. Reining in his fury, he said, "I think some things are better left for God to judge."

"I think"—she hesitated as if those words were radical—"you're right."

He might be right, but that wouldn't save her if she repeated this conversation to her husband. "When did you say you expected him?"

"Oh, a long time ago, but sometimes he doesn't come when he should." She jumped as if the shade of her husband stood over her. "I mean no disrespect. He ministers to many people, and sometimes he has to stay out all night to, um, minister to so many."

"I understand." The silence fell again, hard and dense as lead, and he tried to think of something, anything to chat about, that didn't involve sin or unpure women or punishment. Rubbing his aching calves, he said, "It amazes me that after three full months on my feet, I still suffer cramps in my muscles. The ones in my hip make it difficult to walk."

"When the pregnant women suffer leg cramps, we make them drink milk." Clover sounded sure of herself for the first time today. Maybe for the first time in her life. "Are you drinking milk?"

"I hate milk."

The kettle was about to boil, and Rand had been watching it longingly, but Clover whisked it off the fire. As he stared in astonishment, she took a mug from the cupboard, went to the bucket in the corner, and drew off the cloth that protected it. Brightly, she said, "I know what to serve you. Anne just delivered the milk, fresh from the cow, still warm and with the cream scarcely risen. Of course, there'll not be as much cream for my husband if I disturb it now, but—"

"Don't destroy your day's cream for me," he said feebly, but she dipped the mug into the bucket and drew it up dripping with foamy white.

She placed it on the table in front of him. "'Tis an honor to do it for the lord."

He wanted to gag. He really did hate milk, especially milk so thick it clotted in his throat before he could swallow it. But what was he supposed to do? Knock that hopeful smile off Clover Donald's face? She'd had too many smiles knocked off in her life. Grinning feebly, he lifted the mug, saluted her with it, and drank.

It was just as bad as he remembered, and he was containing a shudder when she said, "I'm surprised at Betty. Why hasn't she been serving you warm milk with honey and pot herbs mixed with your breakfast and before bed?"

"I haven't exactly told anyone about these cramps," he admitted. "They bother me less and less. I think it's just that I've walked so far today."

"Why?" She darted a frightened look at him. "If I may be so bold?"

"I've spent most of the afternoon searching for my niece, who has taken it into her head to explore the estate without her mother's permission, and my wife, who . . . well, I'm looking for my wife, too."

"Oh."

She was frowning as if uncertain of him, and he could almost hear the grinding as the conversation halted again. Unwilling to face the silence, he said, "I wouldn't be so worried, or so fatigued, either, but Sylvan and I walked to the mill this morning."

Clover Donald lifted her gaze full into his face. "Why?"

Smiling at her reassuringly, he said, "I'm surprised you haven't heard the rumors. Everyone in the village knows. We're going to reopen the mill."

Clover staggered backward as if she'd been struck by lightning.

"Clover?" He stood up, thinking she was ill. She certainly looked ill. "Clover?"

Her mouth worked, then the quiet, pitiful little woman shrieked, "You can't!"

"What do you . . . ?"

"You can't. He'll kill you. He'll kill you all. Don't you know you can't stand against his power?"

Confused and horrified, Rand asked, "*God's* power?"

"No, you fool. The vicar's. Merciful heavens, what have you done?"

The ghost never appeared in the daylight, but here he loomed with his foot on her skirt, and he frightened her more than he ever had in the blackness of night. Yet some corner of her mind still grappled to comprehend this—that the minister who had done so much good had also inflicted so much pain. That he waited to kill her with an anticipatory gleam in his eye. Sylvan whispered, "You can't do this, Reverend. The Bible says—"

Drawing himself up, he thundered, "How dare you tell me what the Bible says. You have not been at university, nor have you memorized Scripture nightly, with the threat of my father's stick over your head." Infuriated, he lifted the pipe—and a large something fell in the mill behind him, shaking the floor. He whirled, his attention distracted.

Sylvan jerked her skirt out from under his foot. He stumbled. She sprang up and ran.

Holding her skirt high, she leaped over machinery, over boards and piles of shale. Heart pounding, she stretched out her neck like a horse trying to win the most important race of her life. She had to get out of doors. She had to free herself from the shadow of the mill. The sun struck her in the head as she neared her goal, and as she ran the sun embraced her more and more.

She was Mercury, she was Triumph, she was the living embodiment of a goddess. She jumped off the floor of the mill onto the dirt and gave a hoot of victory.

She made it! She made it, and even in a race outdoors through the gathering darkness, she had a chance of success, for she knew what he did not. Betty was coming with the villagers.

Taking a chance, she glanced behind her. He wasn't following her.

He wasn't behind her. He wasn't anywhere near her. The mill stood as silent and dark as if it were empty, when she knew it was not. It held James, and the Reverend Donald . . . and Gail.

Gail, who had knocked something over to give her a

chance to flee. Was the vicar seeking the source of the
noise in the mill?

Would he find Gail? Valiant Gail, the girl he called a
child of sin?

Sylvan had to go back in. Her hands turned clammy
at the thought, but she'd faced worse things than a murderous preacher in her day. She'd faced the wounded at
Waterloo and watched them die.

Rage blew her fear away with the force of the ocean's
breeze. She had watched men die on the battlefield, for
Mother and country, and now a minister who styled
himself the hammer of God had killed Garth and Shirley
and crippled Nanna, and was trying to hurt her and Gail
in some maniacal desire to halt the march of time. She'd
seen so much of death, and like a plague, this clergyman
brought more.

Leaning over the monument Gail had built to her
father, Sylvan scooped up two large stones and weighed
them in her hands. She didn't want both her hands full,
yet she wanted to take all the stones with her and rain
them on the Reverend Donald. He deserved it.

If only she knew where he was and what he intended.

Taking her shawl from her shoulders, she laid the rocks
in the middle and tied them inside. Picking it up so the
rocks dangled like shot in a sling, she started to creep back.

Then she straightened her back and lifted her chin.
What use was creeping when the man either stood in the
shadows and watched her come or paid her no heed and
sought Gail?

"Reverend Donald," she called, trying to sound as
firm as Wellington himself. "I'm coming back in. I want
you to put down the pipe." She listened for laughter and
heard nothing, not even a yell from James.

That was worse than laughter.

She kept her eyes wide as she stepped back onto the floor she'd so cheerfully abandoned just a few minutes ago, but the sun's light had ruined her vision. She shuffled along, moving from the light to dark. A giant ridge beam, the main support of the roof, leaned from the cross ties in the still existing roof to the edge of the foundation, and she used it as a guide. With her hand on the smooth oak, she groped along. She stubbed her toe on a pile of heavy shale shingles. She was blundering into a trap, but she knew well what she sacrificed, and why. She would distract the minister from his quest for Gail.

"Reverend Donald," she called. "I can't believe that a man of the cloth could justify killing the duke of Clairmont." The wind whistled through the tumbled lumber. She walked on until the dark enveloped her, and she wished she could once again see the real ghost. She needed his intervention now. "You did blow up the mill, didn't you?"

"Not to kill His Grace!"

Although she expected him, she jumped. Quickly, she turned to face the vicar as he slipped in behind her, cutting off her escape route. Her elbow struck the beam. "Ouch!" She grabbed the tingling joint, and the rocks in the shawl banged the wood, making far too much noise and frightening her more than he ever could.

His body was in shadow, but the light formed a halo around his blond head, and he looked reprovingly at the lacy white thing she held. "What do you have in your hand, my child?"

She wanted to conceal her makeshift weapon like a boy caught with a frog in church. Instead she lifted her chin. "It's defense."

"What good will it do you? You can't use it. You're too compassionate."

His certainty made her stagger, and she wondered—could she? Could she ever inflict pain? "I would in defense of a child."

Lifting his head, he looked around at the pile of shingles behind him, at the oak beam. "So it *is* Gail who remains in the mill."

"No!"

He looked back at her. "You might as well admit it. What else would have brought you back when you had escaped?"

Through the mist of his lunacy, he saw too clearly, and she realized how desperately she wanted to save Gail. Gail had lost so much by this man's hand; she didn't deserve to lose her life, too. "Perhaps I returned to face a murderer."

"It wasn't murder, I tell you!" The jagged edge of the roof was right above their heads, and the vicar looked up into the dusky sky as if he sought divine assistance in controlling his temper. "It was God's justice."

A brew of anger and exasperation made her say, "I've heard a lot of nonsense in my lifetime, but saying that you sabotaged the steam engine and then that it was God's justice is the worst."

He seemed to grow taller, and in the deep, chiding voice of a minister, he said, "You have no understanding. I owe you no explanation." He stepped toward her. "And God owes you only death."

It wasn't anger that etched his face, but determination, and it chilled her to realize how firmly he believed himself justified in this duty. Her fingers clenched the shawl until they ached, and she battled to maintain her aplomb. "I think you should tell me, then, why you believe you're innocent, for if I die, I will fly to God's side and He'll ask why I'm there so prematurely."

"You're only a woman, and a wicked one at that. You'll not have a chance to speak with the Lord."

Rand's deep voice said, "Perhaps you could explain this to the duke of Clairmont, who is the lord to whom you owe loyalty on earth."

Sylvan staggered, her limbs abruptly losing vigor.

Rand had come. From beyond hope and prayer, he had come. Tears of joy sprang to her eyes, but what good were they? She might be a woman and an object of the vicar's scorn, but she wasn't a weakling. Swinging the shawl, she brought it up under the pipe he held and knocked it out of his hand. As it flew through the air, he grabbed for her, but she leaped back and his hand closed on thin air. She taunted, "You were right, Vicar. I couldn't use my weapon to hurt you."

He went for her again, but this time Rand jerked him around and clipped him under the chin with a punishing right. The vicar went down into a pile of slate roof tiles, scattering them and clattering them. James began a new barrage of yelling while Rand approached the floundering clergyman. "Tell *me* why you're not a murderer."

Sitting up, the vicar touched his swelling jaw with one finger. Harshly, he said, "I thought everyone would be at the wedding when that contraption of the devil exploded. That your brother was here, and the women, was God's work, not mine."

"Damn you!" Rand grabbed him by the cravat and half lifted him by the throat. "You killed him and you're too egotistical to even feel remorse." He hit him again and again, glorying in the crunch of tendon and bone beneath his fists.

But someone grabbed his arm. Someone said his name. "Rand, stop. Stop, Rand. You're hurting him."

"I know." Rand dragged breath into his scorching, deprived lungs. "I like hurting him."

Someone petted his face as he stood over that damnable assassin. "I know, but I can't watch it."

Rand looked into Sylvan's face, and the bloodlust began to fade beneath her anxious, loving expression.

"Rand?"

She was begging him, and he closed his eyes. "All right. I won't kill him."

"Thank you." She kissed his knuckles where the skin had swollen and burst. "Thank you."

Smiling with acrid pleasure, he stroked the place in her cheek where her dimple appeared. "If not for you . . ."

And pain exploded in his hip. He collapsed with a cry, and the vicar staggered to his feet and kicked him again with his hard, shiny boots. Rand rolled away from the agony.

"You dare contest the wrath of God?"

"You're not God!" Sylvan cried, flying at him with her fists, and the clergyman slapped her and sent her flying.

Rand shouted, "You're a murderer! A madman!"

The Reverend Donald paid him no heed, stalking after Sylvan with the vindictiveness of a man who'd heard the truth and abhorred it. Rand tried to rise, but his joints, worn and bruised, rebelled and he collapsed.

The vicar stood over the prostrate Sylvan. Rand wildly sought a weapon, then crawled toward the pipe the Reverend Donald had been clasping. His fingers curled around the smooth, cool metal.

But something dropped out of the darkening sky onto the vicar's back. He screeched and the creature hanging from his shoulders screeched, too.

Gail. It was Gail! Rand gripped the pipe, but he couldn't throw.

The Reverend Donald bucked like a mule, but Gail dug her hands into his hair and clawed at his face. Yelling at them, Sylvan came up and caught Gail around the waist. The vicar hung on to Gail's ankle. The little girl kicked at him with her other foot.

Rand brought himself to his feet. Relief swept him; he could still stand. Consternation rocked him; in this condition, he couldn't avenge his brother, and he desperately wanted to. Someone had to.

He concentrated on the Reverend Donald, scarcely noticing that the sun seemed to rise again. Then he realized flames moved within the mill.

The women had come. Their men stood behind them. From the village, the farms, and Clairmont Court, they came bearing rush torches. They held them high and moved deliberately, their accusing stares on their vicar.

He froze, looking at them as if amazed by their presence.

"Reverend," Betty said sternly, "let go of my child."

He released Gail, but only to draw himself up and say in a voice of disdain and command, "Stand back!"

Betty ran at them, and Sylvan pushed Gail ahead of her. Gail met her mother and Betty caught her in her arms as if Gail were a baby, swinging her up and away from the minister's madness. Sylvan wrapped her arm around Rand's waist, but whether to support him or to get support from him, she did not know.

The Reverend Donald spoke in a solemn tone. "You cannot halt the advance of God's justice."

Nanna stepped out of the crowd, a crutch under her arm and her amputated leg suspended. "'Tis not God's justice ye've meted out," she said. "But yer own."

Gesturing grandly, the Reverend Donald said, "How

dare you claim to know God's will—you, an ignorant woman who's never been beyond the boundaries of your own village?"

"How dare *ye* claim to know God's will?" Nanna countered. "It is not for a mere man to know."

The vicar stepped toward her. "*I* know, and you will all die if you resist."

"We'll all die eventually, anyway," Beverly said. "But when ye help us to heaven, it's called murder."

"Yes, it is." Clover Donald's tiny voice spoke from the back, and the women cleared the way for her. "Bradley, yes, it is."

The flames of the torches reflected in her husband's eyes. "I might have known you would betray me, Judas."

"Oh, Bradley." Clover blubbered, wiping at her eyes with a lacy handkerchief. "Don't you understand? It's over."

"It's not over!" he roared.

"What are ye going to do?" Loretta lisped slightly, teeth missing from his attack. "Kill us all?"

"It's the only way to bring this parish back into the fold." But the mighty vicar faltered.

"Kill us all?" Nanna repeated scornfully. "Not even *ye* can justify that."

James was still shouting and banging, but he stopped abruptly, and the scrape of metal sounded as someone moved the machinery back from the door. Then James, Jeffrey, and one of the village men stepped into the light.

Three more accusing faces, three more people the Reverend Donald had harmed. James cradled his fingers. Jeffrey returned to the shadows. The villager moved behind Nanna and she leaned against him.

The mill grew quiet. Only the Reverend Donald's harsh breathing broke the silence. Night had fallen, and the torches fluttered in the breeze. He did look like the ghost now—like Garth and the first duke and, Rand supposed, himself. He also looked sick, conscious of what he'd done and how hopeless his situation had become.

He put one hand up; everyone jumped back. He paused and stared, then rubbed his hand against his ear. "What do you plan to do?"

He sounded almost meek, but Rand didn't trust him. "What should I do with a man who betrayed the family who fostered him?"

"I didn't owe my loyalty to you, but to the Lord."

"You spied on me."

"It was God who brought you to your feet at night."

"And it was you who made me think I was mad."

"It was God's work I did." The vicar pleaded now.

"No." Sylvan stepped out of the shelter of Rand's embrace.

"It was. It was, it was!" In fury, he smacked the slanted oak beam with his fist. Lumber, nails, and heavy shale tiles slid off the shattered roof and rained down on them in response.

The flooring shook as each heavy tile hit and broke. The women drew back. Clover sobbed out loud. The Reverend Donald spread his arms wide and cried, "Don't worry, my children. The Lord speaks through me, and I say you are safe. Safe!"

"Safe even from you," Rand said. "It's a long, weary road to Bedlam, Donald, and we'd best start you on your way."

Still posed in his all-encompassing posture, the vicar hesitated as if shocked. "Bedlam?"

Clover Donald echoed, "Bedlam?"

"He'll go to Bedlam as a madman, or go to the gallows

as one who murdered a duke," Rand said relentlessly. "Perhaps in Bedlam they'll have a use for his delusions."

"Bedlam?" the Reverend Donald repeated again. "You cannot send the hammer of God to Bedlam. I will not go." He bowed his head and wrapped his hands together under his chin in a prayerful attitude. "I am innocent!"

And a shale tile slid off the roof and smashed into the back of his head.

22

Gentle hands took Sylvan by the arms and lifted her to her feet, away from the vicar's body.

The village men stood in small groups outside the mill. The women had remained inside, and now they closed around Sylvan, surrounding her with life, cutting her off from the finality of her latest failure.

"You can't save them all, Your Grace, especially not from a head wound like that." Betty sounded brisk and sensible as ever.

The flickering torches had been stuck here and there, chasing the night away, but Sylvan knew the dark still waited to pounce. Then the ghost of the clergyman and of all the others who had died would return, and right now, Sylvan didn't know if she was strong enough to throw off those clinging hands.

"Ye did all ye could." Loretta's face was puckered where the Reverend Donald's club had struck months ago, but she still stood tall and confident.

Tiny Pert edged close and patted Sylvan's trembling hand. "Not even Clover Donald stayed as long as ye have."

Rebecca jostled Sylvan and whispered, "It's better this way."

"Ye can't say it wasn't justice," Roz said strongly.

Sylvan nodded, still numb with the horror of losing another life. "I know it was. "

"It was almost as if Garth came back and handled it for us," Rand said.

"Or His Grace, the first duke of Clairmont." Beverly pulled Sylvan out from under the still-precarious edge of the roof.

Touching her aching forehead, Sylvan remembered how the ghost had once led her away from danger, then vanished before her eyes. "I felt that, too."

Loretta said, "It felled him like a hammer to the skull."

Gail had climbed one of the slanted beams and sat perched high above them. "He kept calling himself the hammer of God."

"Gail, get down," her mother commanded.

Scampering down, Gail stuck out her lower lip. "I guess he struck himself down."

"Gail," Sylvan rebuked.

"He deserved it," Gail insisted. "He hurt those women, he tried to hurt you, and he k-k-killed my . . . my . . ." She burst into loud sobs. "He killed my father!"

Mortified, she tried to hide her face, but Betty and the other women rushed to the girl, petting her and encouraging her outburst.

Only Nanna remained apart, seated on a block with her amputated limb outstretched. She watched Gail and said to Sylvan, "That's the best thing for the child. She needs to bring her grief out into the open, or it'll eat at her guts until she loses her vitality and ghosts stalk her dreams."

Sylvan, startled to hear her own symptoms described so accurately, slithered to the ground close against Nanna's seat. "Why do you think that?" She glanced at Rand. He'd watched Sylvan's frantic attempts to resurrect Bradley Donald without uttering a word, and she didn't want him to hear. But he leaned against a post, arms crossed, and looked out into the night as if he could barely tolerate the brew of anguish and sympathy that emanated from the women.

Beyond him stood the fellow who had helped release James from his prison, and all the way outside James paced and spoke to Jasper.

Of course, they were men. This flagrant display of emotion must frighten them.

It certainly frightened her. It might be catching.

Quietly, Sylvan said, "It's superstition, surely, to think that crying and sympathy helps ease the pain of a loss."

"Is it?" Nanna looked at her as if she saw more than Sylvan wished her to see. "When ye cut off my leg, my body had to heal. It was swollen, and it oozed, and it hurt so bad sometimes I'd just cry."

Sylvan winced.

"No." Nanna refused Sylvan's wordless sympathy. "It mended, and the pain's mostly gone. So my body's healed, but my mind still doesn't always understand. That foot's been there my whole life, and it's taking effort to convince myself it has departed. Sometimes I think the foot is there, and try to walk on it. Sometimes it itches, and I try to scratch it. It's the same way with Gail. Her da's been there her whole life, and she still hears his voice, still feels his presence, and she thinks she's going to turn around and see him."

"Poor child," Sylvan murmured.

"Lucky child," Nanna corrected. "It's well known to country folk that when a person dies, his soul is trapped on earth by ceaseless mourning. His Grace no doubt wants to come back and comfort the girl, and with each tear she sheds here, she's releasing her father to his grave. He'll rest now, and so will she."

They fell silent, watching the drama of Gail's tears and Betty's solace, and finally Sylvan asked, "What about you? Have you cried for your loss?"

Nanna sighed. "Not yet, Yer Grace, but it'll come in God's good time, and then I'll be healed through and through."

Hunching her shoulders, Sylvan said, "I'm so sorry."

"Fer what?"

"For doing that amputation. A doctor would have been better, but it had to be done immediately, and—"

"Why should ye be sorry? Ye saved my life." Nanna touched Sylvan once, lightly, on the head. "I guess ye don't want to hear it, and that's why ye avoided me so, but I have to tell ye one time. When I laid under that beam, I thought meself dead fer sure. I knew no one could move the beam without probably crushing more of me, and I thought I would just remain there and die in agony." Nanna lifted the stump and stared at it. Her voice quavered as she confessed, "I've got children, ye know, and as I lay there, I thought I would give anything to see them grow up, be strong, maybe hold their children in me lap. I've got a husband, too"—she pointed to the man who had released James—"my Mel. He's an ornery old mule, but he's my old mule, and I want to age with him. I'll never forget how I felt when ye said ye would free me from that beam. Ye cut off my foot, and ye gave me my whole life back."

Awestruck, Sylvan stared at Nanna. Nanna thought Sylvan had saved her life, and in a way, Sylvan had. It wasn't the life Nanna had had before, but Sylvan felt her gratitude like salve on an old, painful wound.

"God bless ye, Yer Grace." Nanna smiled through a tracing of tears on her cheeks. "If ye never do another thing, ye've earned yer place in heaven."

"Sylvan." Rand called her. "Jasper's ready with the carriage."

Mel came to help Nanna. "Ready, Ma?"

"Aye, Da, I am. Been a long, weary day." Nanna held out her hand to him.

He took it and held it as if it were more precious than diamonds, then turned to Sylvan and bared blackened teeth.

Sylvan flinched, then held herself still as he picked Nanna up and carried her out.

"Well, I'm in awe." Rand chuckled beside her. "I haven't ever seen that man smile, and he smiled at you. You've won a slave for life."

"I have?" Dazed, Sylvan let Rand lift her to her feet.

"You have." He kissed her once, lightly. "Let's go home."

The ride back to Clairmont Court would have been silent, except for James, who sat in the backward facing seat and railed without ceasing. "Told you opening the mill was a damn fool idea. All you could think about was the people of Malkinhampsted, their needs, their hungry bellies. Never even thought that the madman might take it in his head to kill you. Then you know what would have happened?"

"What would have happened, James?" Rand tucked

Sylvan tighter into his embrace and wished they were alone. Alone, he could have spoken, explained, and listened.

"*I* would have been the new duke of Clairmont, and *I* would have had to worry about the people of Malkinhampsted and their hungry bellies." James clasped his head in his good hand. "Couldn't have done my politics, couldn't have traveled, couldn't have dallied with the light skirts. Would have had to marry a proper woman, settle down, and produce a pack of brats to yip at my heels."

"A pack of brats." Rand thought that sounded rather pleasant.

"Realized some maniac was about when I searched for Sylvan and heard those stupid groans he emitted to frighten her."

Sylvan sat straight up. "You heard him?"

"Of course," James said.

"And you denied it?"

"Didn't want to alarm you!"

Leaning forward, she gave him a light slap on the cheek. "You fool. That was one of the reasons I locked you in that office. I thought *you* might be the ghost stalker."

"Oh." James touched his cheek. "That didn't occur to me."

She thumped her head back onto Rand's chest, and he massaged her shoulder.

Rand had been listening to Nanna, hearing the nuances of her comfort to Sylvan. Nanna thought Sylvan needed to grieve for some reason; Rand agreed, and he would never allow her to shut herself off from him again.

James shrugged. "Oh, well. No harm done. Just Jasper

and me stalking around like a couple of melodramatic dolts, trying to guard you both, bumping into each other and eyeing each other suspiciously."

Rand cackled, remembering Sylvan's apprehensions, remembering his own.

Even Sylvan shook under a slight gust of amusement. "So Jasper was guarding me."

"We took shifts once we realized. Made things easier, then." The carriage slowed, and James had the door open almost before it stopped at the terrace stairs. He stepped out. "Don't need to bother our mothers with the ugly facts until morning, Rand. I'll tell 'em. You and your lady come in when you're ready. No one'll plague you."

James's prescience startled Rand, and he once again realized his cousin was more than the graceful dandy he appeared. "How will you keep our mothers restrained?"

James poked his head back into the carriage. "Going to show them my hand." He held up his swollen fingers. "Going to tell them I'll never play the piano again."

"You never did play the piano," Rand answered.

"Should take ten minutes before they realize it." With a grin, James bounded up the stairs.

Jasper held the door as Rand helped Sylvan out of the carriage, and he grinned sheepishly when she said, "Jasper, I have wronged you. Were you protecting me all along?"

"Yes, and ye led me a fancy dance a good part of the time." Leaning into the carriage, Jasper brought out two of the carriage blankets and handed them to Rand. "I sure wished Lord Rand had married himself a meek and mild one, but as I told ye the first time I drove ye, the dukes of Clairmont aren't interested in good sense and comfort, only interested in struggle and challenge. Whole damned family's mad."

Rand leaned his head back and roared with laughter. "With a testimonial like that, I'm surprised Sylvan didn't turn back before she even got here."

"Ah, I knew she'd stick when she weathered that welcome ye gave her." Taking her tiny hand gingerly in his large paw, Jasper bowed over it. "If I may be so bold, ye're a duchess worthy of the Clairmont."

His servant and his lady made their peace, and Rand sighed in relief to see it. Then Jasper climbed back onto the carriage. Touching his hat with the whip, he said, "As Lord James said, 'tis a lovely night to sit on the terrace. Hope ye enjoy yerselves."

As he drove to the stables, Rand took the hand Jasper had so recently abandoned and kissed it. "You *are* a challenge."

"I don't know why Jasper says so." She freed herself with a little jerk. "Why do they think we want to stay outside?"

"Lovely night." He gestured up at the house where candles blazed from every window, then out at the grounds, where trees stretched beneath a gibbous moon. "Why not?"

"Because your legs are hurting you, and you should rest them."

"You needn't worry. The marble's soft stone, and we'll cover it with these." Rand showed her the carriage blankets he held tucked under his arm.

"But you—"

Laying his finger over her lips, he said, "Trust me."

He couldn't see her well, but he thought tears filled her eyes, and when she blinked and turned away, he was sure of it. Turning back to him determinedly, she took his arm. "I trust you."

"You'll need to," he said.

"What?" She tried to pull her hand free, but he caught it and led her up the stairs.

When they reached the terrace, someone—or a series of someones—extinguished all the lights in the lower story of the house. Was the entire household leaning against those windows, watching the drama they hoped would unfold, or were they tiptoeing away, leaving the married couple in peace to work out their problems?

"Eavesdroppers," he said to the facade of the house, and he ushered Sylvan to the most secluded corner of the terrace. There he spread blankets and gestured to her. She settled onto the blanket neatly, tucking her skirt around her ankles and sitting with her hands folded in her lap. He stretched out beside her, close enough that their hips touched, spread a rug over the two of them to keep out the chill, and propped his arms under his head. "Look at that," he said. "I've never seen a lovelier night."

The moon produced enough light for him to see her tilt her head back, but not so much light it obscured the stars. And there were millions of those.

"Millions and millions and millions," he said, "stretching across that blackness in patterns and paths. Where do you suppose they lead?"

"I don't know." She turned her head and looked from one horizon to the other, tracing the clustered length of the Milky Way with her gaze. "Perhaps we'll follow those paths someday."

"Someday," he echoed. "So many stars, we could never number them. One for each soul, the old wives say." He laid his hand on her spine. "Do you think there's one for Garth?"

She turned to him and smiled. "I hope so." Then her smile disappeared. "Do you think there's one for Bradley Donald?"

"Perhaps that is his punishment. Perhaps he'll be denied his star."

After thinking about that, she decided, "That would be fitting."

"Do you think there's one for each of the lads who died at Waterloo?"

She inhaled sharply. "Would that there were."

"I think there are. See how vigorously they twinkle? They're twinkling just for you, Sylvan, sending a message of thanks."

"For what?" She no longer looked at him, or at the stars, but at her hands as they smoothed the rug across her thighs.

"For trying to give them life, and for mourning them when—"

"When I killed them?"

He tugged her around until she faced him, and waited until she lifted her gaze to his again. "You didn't kill them."

"No." She shoved her hair back out of her face. "I know that. Really I do. Some of the soldiers came to me so wounded, it was a miracle they didn't die in the field. Some of them died because we didn't know what to do to help them. God called them to His bosom, I tell myself, but if God placed me there to help them, why didn't he give me the knowledge and the medicines for a cure? Why did they have to die like *that*?"

Her suffering was his, and he ached for her. He wanted to cure her, but he could only answer, "I don't know."

"Some of them cursed me. Most of them clung to me. None of them wanted to die. There wasn't any resignation, and there wasn't any dignity." Silent, she contemplated the stars, and he held his breath, waiting. Finally, she confessed, "There was one lad . . . I'll never forget him. His name was Arnold Jones. Strong as an ox, even with a bullet in his chest. Everyone thought him stupid as an ox, too, because he was nothing but a common soldier, but he wasn't stupid. Just silent, to keep the evidence of pain and fear inside him." She turned to him. "Not that he was a coward. He wasn't. He was just a boy. A cat could have licked the whiskers off his chin. . . ."

Rand realized words had failed her once more. She was too flustered to ask for succor. "Did you help young Arnold Jones?"

Now she did more than shake her head. She laughed, and laughed, and laughed, a hysterical note in her voice. He sat up in alarm. Scooting back, she raised her arm as if she expected a blow, and he conjectured that she'd been treated for hysteria before, and in the most brusque manner possible.

He clasped his hands to keep them at his side and watched as slowly, painfully, she regained control.

"Help him?" Her voice shook. "If keeping a man alive is helping him, then, yes, I did. He took an infection in his lungs. Well, the doctor who removed the bullet said it nicked one lung, so it wasn't surprising that he . . . well, Arnold just wanted a soft hand to hold occasionally. He had no family, had brought himself up in the streets of Manchester, and only survived with his wits. That's why I knew he wasn't stupid, because he . . ."

She was edging away from Rand, and edging away from the story. Gradually, trying not to startle her with sudden movement, he lay down again. "So you held his hand?"

"He was so sick. I was the only one who could control him, because he was strong as an ox." She hesitated. "Did I already say that?"

"Strong as an ox," Rand repeated. "But you could control him with the touch of your hand."

"And my voice. I used to sing to him." She chuckled, but the sound cracked. "There's no accounting for taste. The other men in the ward used to ask me to stop, but Arnold liked the lullabies and the rhyming songs you sing to a baby. It was like having my own giant baby to tend." Drawing her knees close to her chest, she wrapped her arms around them and began rocking back and forth, back and forth.

"How long did you tend him?"

"Weeks. He was in hospital from the moment I stepped in until the moment I left."

Rand was startled. He had thought she was going to confess a tragedy. "He was alive when you left, then."

Tucking her knees in tight, she rocked harder. "I left one evening because I . . . I had to rest sometime. As soon as I came back to the hospital, I went immediately to examine Arnold. If I didn't, no one else would, so I always made him my priority." Her breath quivered as she sighed. "And they'd covered him with a sheet, all the way over his eyeballs. Those fools. They thought he was dead."

He stiffened. What was she talking about? "Wasn't he dead?"

"No, he's not dead. Nanna was right. I see him every night, begging me to sing the rock-a-bye song." Dropping her face into the cradle of her knees, she hid it from any chance sighting. "I don't really remember what happened. They tell me I went a little crazy."

Her muffled voice tantalized him. He had to know, and she needed to tell him. "Crazy?"

"I tried to revive him. Sang to him, talked to him, crooned to him."

He thought she must be crying, but she looked up and her cheeks were dry and her chin was set.

"He'd been dead over four hours. He was already cold."

He could scarcely restrain his horror.

Now she looked directly at him, and said, "That's when Dr. Moreland sent me away. I was no help to him after that. I came back to England and went to my father's house and thought about what I'd seen and what I'd done . . . and I wanted to kill myself. I probably would have, if Garth hadn't come and rescued me."

He wanted to speak, but he still had no words. How could he express his rage at her pain, his admiration of her bravery? Like a eulogy spoken over a new-made grave, any speech he might make would be barren, lifeless, inadequate.

"Now that you know, do you want me to go?"

"Go?" He croaked, then spoke more fully. "Go where?"

"Back to London or"—she shrugged—"back to my father's house. It doesn't matter."

"Doesn't matter? You want to leave me, and you say it doesn't matter?"

"I don't *want* to leave you, but I understand if you're repulsed—"

He found himself on his feet. "Don't you ever say that again! I am not repulsed by you or your actions. With your courage and your strength, you're more than I deserve, but I have you and I will keep you."

She just stared up at him as if she didn't believe him, and he knew what he had to do.

He didn't want to tell her. When she'd first come to Clairmont Court, he'd been at the mercy of his emotions and his disability. Then he'd stood and walked, and had become the duke of Clairmont in one dreadful event, and he thought it a sign that he had to be all the duke of Clairmont should be.

Like all the dukes before him, he'd had to be strong, in charge of everything, and most important, impregnable. He admitted to no weaknesses, because the duke of Clairmont wasn't weak—and he'd lost Sylvan. She was sitting at his feet, but the essence of her had escaped him. He had laid a claim to her, but he knew one day he'd turn around and she'd be gone, unless he shared with her his pain and his fear. Quickly, before he could change his mind, he confessed, "I have nightmares, too."

"You do?" Bitterly, she asked, "But what could you possibly have nightmares about?"

"Every night, I have nightmares of being confined to a wheelchair again. And every day, I wake up and think, 'My legs won't work.'" His heart began a slow steady thump, a thump so loud it no doubt shook the ground. He couldn't get enough air, sweat coated his palms, but he fought to speak. "Because you know what? I never know when that paralysis will return. We don't know what caused it, we don't know what cured it, and we *don't know* if it will return."

"It won't."

He recognized her bravado from another time. From the time she'd found him holding Garth's body. She didn't know what she was talking about, but to comfort him she pretended knowledge. Savagely, he struck the marble wall beside him. "Pray God, it won't! I walk too far, and my legs cramp, and I'm happy for the pain. Grateful for the ground beneath my feet. All my life I'll live with uncertainty, but damn! It's made me savor each step, each moment." Squatting down, he took her by the shoulders and shook her gently. She was crying now, and he urged, "Mourn for the lads you lost. Grieve for them. Cry for them, and cry for you, too, and all the innocence you forfeited on that battlefield. Then let them fly up to the stars—Arnold, too—and twinkle. They don't want to haunt your nightmares, Sylvan. They want to go."

Her slow seepage of tears became a deluge, and he drew her down onto his chest and wrapped the rug tightly around her. His shirt got wet, his handkerchief got used, and he encouraged her to persist until all her sorrow was discharged. When the sobbing slowed, he said, "Sylvan, do you ever think about the people you've helped? The ones who walk with a limp, but they walk? The ones who can't see, but they can speak and hear?"

"Ye . . . es." Her voice wobbled pitifully.

"Do you really?"

"I try to."

"Remember Hawthorne and Sagan? Remember how they watched over you at Lady Katherine's house party?"

"They were nice."

"Nice." He snorted. "They would have killed me if you'd asked them to."

She dug her fingers into his shirt. "I thought about it."

"Yipe." Carefully, he disengaged her hand, freeing his chest hairs to curl another day. "I'm glad you didn't." Lifting his head, he kissed her ear. "I heard what Nanna told you tonight. She's grateful to see her children grow up. Can you imagine how grateful her children are that they still have her?"

"Maybe." This time he nipped her ear. "Probably." She was silent but not relaxed, and finally she stirred and asked, "Don't you blame me for all the deaths?"

Honestly bewildered, he said, "Why would I blame you?"

"Those society women despised me so much, and I don't think I'll ever wash all the blood off my hands."

"You are a fool, Sylvan Miles Malkin." He picked up her hands and kissed each finger. "Don't you know the newest duchess of Clairmont is following a tradition that reaches back to Jocelyn, the first duchess?"

Warily, she watched him. "What tradition?"

"Jocelyn had the mind and soul that inspired everyone, especially despicable old Radolf, to an eternal love." Rand turned her head up to his. "Won't you stay with me and, every morning, touch me with your healing hands? With you, I'm not afraid."

She stared at him, trying to see the truth behind his words, but she couldn't. The truth couldn't be seen, only felt, and she felt the strength of his body, the profundity of his soul, the perception of his mind. They formed the whole of Rand, and Rand restored the whole of her.

She broke into a smile. "I'll touch you in the morning if you'll hold me in the night."

"I promise," he said fervently. "On your command, my duchess, I will move heaven and earth."

"When are you coming home, Radolf?"

It had been a very long time since Radolf heard that voice, but he recognized it immediately. "Jocelyn?" He turned, and there she stood, looking as lovely, as healthy, as impetuous as ever.

"I've been waiting for you, and been very patient, too." She belied her words with the restless tap of her foot. "I knew you wanted to assure yourself that our family will prosper, but haven't you done enough? Don't you think they can take care of themselves now?"

Radolf tore his gaze away from the miracle of Jocelyn

to glance at Rand and Sylvan. "They can, but what about their children?"

"Their son's already forming in her belly—can't you see him kick?" She smiled fondly at Sylvan. "He'll be the best of his father and the best of his mother. He'll be fine." She looked back at Radolf. "After that, who knows? We have a strong and fecund bloodline, we've proved that, with men and women who survive, regardless of the challenge. Now can't we go home?"

She held out her slender hand, palm up. He looked at it, then around at Clairmont Court. He'd been here so long he'd almost forgotten he should be somewhere else, and it took the sight of Jocelyn to jolt his memory.

"We'll be together always," she said.

The promise of Jocelyn convinced him. Reaching out with his broad hand, he laid it in hers. A light began to glow where spirit met spirit; it dazzled him as it grew. "What is it?" he asked.

Jocelyn laughed, showering silver notes of joy throughout eternity. "It's you and me—together at last. Hold on. We've got a long way to go."

Sylvan stirred in Rand's arms. "Did you hear that?"

"Hm?" He pulled her closer, trying to absorb her into his bones.

"It sounded like a lady laughing."

"Yes, I heard it." Propping himself up on his elbow, he smiled at Sylvan. "It was the angels laughing because we're together at last." He clasped her hand; their palms kissed. His lips touched hers; their souls kissed, and through closed eyes, he saw a glow as two stars shot from horizon to horizon and formed bright new lights in the heavens.

Thanks to all the nurses who served in Vietnam
and saved the boys I knew.
No one who lived through that time
will ever forget.

WAR CLOUDS!

Joel smiled. "If I were you, Garth, I'd make plans for new employment. A dead boss doesn't pay much."

"You ain't got a chance in hell, Hollings!" The puncher turned his horse and rode off down the street.

The smile remained on Joel's face, but inside he wasn't smiling. He was wondering how he'd spot the extra guns Will Pickett was sure to bring to the party. When the time came, he'd have to locate them fast if he expected to leave the street alive. . . .

ACROSS THE MESAS

Moore Moran

BALLANTINE BOOKS • NEW YORK

Library of Congress Catalog Card Number: 85-90759

ISBN 0-345-32769-1

Manufactured in the United States of America

First Edition: November 1985

To Frederick Faust
(1892–1944)

Sun smolders in the upper peaks,
leaking its glory from the spill;
once more your simple ethic speaks
across the mesas, dry and still.

M.M.

1

IT WASN'T FAR now. The ranch lay in a sheltered valley ahead, just beyond the ridge where two pines embraced above a giant boulder. The sun was climbing to its noon perch, searing everything below, and Joel Hollings for the third time that morning pulled in his mustang and sat motionless, studying the terrain behind him.

Near-barren hills fell away to the gray desert floor. Occasional mesquite bushes grew there, but no other form of life showed itself. The land was dry and still. No rising dust . . .

As he shifted in the saddle, the nerves in his arms twitched, as they often did lately—ever since his decision to return home from the silver fields outside Virginia City. He'd left the old boom town in a hurry after a card-game shooting—some were going to see it as murder no matter what—not even pausing to collect his prospecting gear at the rooming house.

Early afternoon on the first day out, he'd spotted a posse a dozen miles back; it troubled him some, because he knew the sheriff, Jake Barnes, who was sure to be leading the search. A scrappy bulldog of a man, Barnes never let go once he got his teeth into something or someone. There was no love lost between them, so with his own jaw set a little tighter, he'd kept his black mare at that swift, effortless trot mustangs never seem to tire of. That was a week ago, and he'd seen nothing of the posse or any other rider since.

Though he'd lingered in the north, hoping to uncover a workable ore vein, he found no silver. In fact, he had little to show for his time and travels but a dwindling poker stake and a deep scar along the chin of his hard, rather handsome face.

He thought now how his father and brother Jason would greet him—with righteous anger over his sudden departure more than a year ago. He wasn't looking forward to the reunion. He relished even less the prospect of an angry posse piling after him into the valley, cornering him in the house of his father.

Satisfied that his backtrail was clear, he turned his horse and headed for the two pines that stood alone together on the ridge.

He topped the summit exactly at noon, and a sudden dread crawled in his chest. Far below to the southwest, in a grove of cottonwoods where the ranch should have been standing, he saw a column of smoke twisting skyward. The main house was gone, as were the barns and bunkhouse, and the horses, too? Through the trees in the distance, he spotted the brick chimney, the only familiar sign left of the house where he was born.

For more than an hour Joel scanned the valley for reflections or movement. Nothing. Then, warily, he began his descent into the valley that his father had worked thirty years to reclaim from the desert. A small wheat field to the south stood ripe and expectant. To the west fat cattle grazed, occasionally snapping their heads to scatter the flies.

He moved slowly, using trees and rocks for cover as he descended. At the creek, a quarter mile from the house, he dismounted and led his horse through the stands of scrub oak and cottonwood.

Where the barns had stood, he found a scramble of tracks left by unshod ponies. Apache! Seven, eight? Skirting the barns, he broke into a run toward the house.

2

Jason, a Winchester still in his hands, awkwardly sat on the ground, one shoulder pushed against the stoop as though he were trying to stand up. Five cartridge belts lay across his knee, all empty save one. An arrow was sunk into his neck, two more in his chest, another in his stomach. On his lips he wore a sneer of disgust, in his eyes a frozen stare of accusation.

Joel looked away, anger gathering in his eyes. They had never been close, yet Jason was a worthy man—big temper but a big heart to match. Often he'd wished he had Jason's dogged loyalty and simple outlook on things, but nature never seems to deal the same hand twice.

He noted the Winchester with satisfaction, and the four belts of spent cartridges. Much as the Apache covets rifles, he does not steal from people he admires—and he admires only gods and fighters. He must have counted a good many coups before they got him, though only bloodstains here and there in the grass told of the raid.

Inside the still-smoldering walls, neither his father nor Silverfoot, the Apache girl, was to be found. He looked again, lifting each piece of rubble to be sure. The bunkhouse gave up no remains, either. Where was Mouse, Ike, Caldwell? Slowly he returned to his brother's body, laid it out gently, then dug the grave among the nearby cottonwoods. By the time he laid on the last shovel of dirt, it was getting dark. He sat down on the steps of the porch, tired to the bone and lonelier than he'd ever been in his life.

A whispering of leaves sat him bolt upright, his gun already clear of the blankets and cocked. Through the trees, stabs of morning sun pierced the curtain of sleep in his head. He waited and listened. Then he heard it again. He tossed a stone toward the sound and flushed out a small rabbit, which sprang directly at him. On reflex, his gun spoke, and the rabbit dropped twelve feet away.

As he rolled his blankets, he remembered he had not

eaten for two days, and the thought of roast rabbit set his stomach growling. He made a spit from two Y-shaped branches, trimming them down to size, then went after kindling under the trees.

He skinned and cleaned the animal quickly. When the fire crackled with a good flame, he put the rabbit on and went up to the gutted house to see what was left. He found a tin of ground coffee that had somehow escaped the inferno. From the icy creek he filled his tin pot and returned to the fire to make coffee. From time to time, he turned the browning rabbit on the wood spit, and the aroma of roasting meat filled the morning air.

Another sound turned him toward the house. A slender Indian girl of about twenty stood on the charred porch. She made no move to hide herself but stood quietly staring at him.

"Silverfoot!" Joel rushed to her. "What's happened here?" The girl's eyes welled with tears; still, she could say nothing. He rocked her in his arms, dreading the answers she would give him.

"Apache raiding party," she stammered. "They took your father—"

"Where are the hands—Mouse and the rest?"

"Only Mouse is here. The others left a month ago. Mouse was with the cattle when the—the Apache came." Joel saw she was still fighting for control.

"Come on; I have food and coffee at the fire."

From his saddlebag he produced two tin plates and served up the roasted meat. They ate in silence, drinking the scalding coffee from the same cup.

"Where's Mouse now?"

"He went after the Apache, after your father."

"Why did the Apache attack us? My father was their friend."

"I don't understand. It was a horrible thing. I heard them

4

come down the mountain, yelping like dogs. I hid myself in the trees."

"You saw it all?"

"Jason fired forty, maybe fifty times. He hit many. They took away their dead and wounded. Your father they shot in both legs, taking him, too. I watched them till they disappeared over the ridge. But it was strange . . . a white man riding a roan waited on the ridge, then disappeared with the Apache."

"White man? Did you recognize him, Silverfoot?"

"No, but he was very large—too large for his pony."

There was a crashing and cursing in the brush, and Joel's gun was out. A moment later Mouse's familiar figure stepped into the clearing. He was hatless and had the look of a wild animal. Blood from a shoulder wound had turned his sleeve scarlet to the cuff. He focused on Joel a minute; then his face broke into a grin.

"Well, if it ain't the prodigul son!"

Joel went to his saddlebag and tore a spare shirt into strips to dress the wound. It was more than a nick, but the bullet had passed clean through. As he worked at the little man's shoulder, he put the picture together.

"Ambushed on their backtrail?"

Mouse nodded. "They must'a spotted me followin' and left one brave on the ridge to finish me. But I finished him instead." A light danced in Mouse's eyes.

"Did you see a white man with them?" asked Joel.

"They was too far away to tell color, but I could see they carried four dead across their ponies."

After the wound was dressed and a chunk of sizzling roast was placed on Mouse's plate, the three sat down by the morning fire with their coffee and their private demons.

No use starting after them alone, Joel thought. Apart from the sheer numbers stacked against him, there was the heavily shaled terrain on the outer slopes. Even professionals could not successfully track for long on that surface. Besides, he doubted the oversized white man Silverfoot had seen lived with the Apache. Find the white man, he guessed, and he'd find his father soon enough. And probably alive.

Joel decided to pay a call on Brenner Falls, the closest settlement, eighteeen miles to the south. There he'd report the attack and see how big they grew their white men in that neck of the woods.

As he cinched up the black and readied a packhorse, he carried on a running argument with Mouse, who was bent on riding with him to Brenner Falls.

"That's Indian country," Mouse protested. "A man travelin' solo out there's got his hands a whole lot fuller than he needs 'em to be. Even with one good shooting hand I can boost the odds considerable."

"No. Rest the shoulder and be ready when I need you, which from the look of things is going to be soon enough. By the way, what happened to Ike and Caldwell?"

Mouse looked off at the hills. "Couple of months back things started goin' wrong here. First the fences was cut; next some'a the best horses was scattered or stolen. Then one night the big barn burned to the ground.

"There was notes left each time, threatening anyone who stayed on. Your pappy, like ya' know, doesn't scare easy, but Ike an' Caldwell looked at things different an' pulled up stakes."

"Did you keep those notes?" asked Joel.

"I got one. Your pappy kept the rest." Mouse rummaged in his saddlebag and came up with a scrap of yellow paper that had been folded and refolded many times. He handed it to Joel, saying, "This was the first one. I found it nailed to a post where the fence was cut."

Joel read the childishly rendered letters.

6

THIS RANCH IS DOOMED. CLEAR OUT
QUICK IF YOU WANT TO GO ON
BREATHING.

That was all. The note was on long prelined paper, the kind school kids or sometimes business people use.

He put the note in his pocket and looked at Mouse. "I see you lost your hat; I'll pick one up for you in town. Anything else we need fast besides food?"

Mouse shook his head. "Maybe me and Silverfoot kin do somethin' about a roof fer the kitchen; them walls is still intact."

"It's better you rest."

Joel turned the horses and started the climb out of the valley.

As he neared the pass, the tracks left by the raiding party grew less distinct. At one point they were joined by the prints of a shod horse. They were deep prints, as if the animal were carrying great weight. The tracks continued for about a mile. There the shod horse had abruptly left the others, headed due south—toward Brenner Falls!

2

BY THE TIME Joel approached the lights of town, it was nine o'clock. As a boy, he came here with his father from time to time, packing in wire for the fences, winter feed for the livestock, dry goods, and other supplies. But that was a long time ago, and he could see, even from this distance, that the town had more than doubled in size.

At the head of the main thoroughfare he turned the horses and began circling the town from the back streets, watching and straining to pick up any bits of conversation that came his way. All seemed normal for that time of evening. The number of lighted windows in the old hotel told him the place was nearly full. From the saloon he heard a muffled piano and laughter. There would be at least one card game in progress.

Finishing his reconnaissance, he steered the mare down the main street and brought the packhorse alongside. He found the livery stable across from the bank, which stood dark and still in the shadows. What was there about the inscription plaque, *Brenner Bank*, that seemed so familiar? A bell tolled somewhere in his memory but he could not place it.

The stable was deserted except for a boy about twelve who took his horses to a vacant stall and asked, "Oats?"

"Oats will be fine," Joel said.

"That's fifty cents for the night."

Joel reached in his pocket and handed the boy a coin. Then he said, "Son, I'm looking for a large man—large enough to dwarf the horse he rides."

The boy shot Joel a glance, measuring him. Finally, he said, "We got three of them. The Picketts—all big, all brothers."

"Good men?"

The boy looked away. "You a friend of theirs?" he asked.

"No, not a friend. What about you? I mean, are you a friend of theirs?"

"Gad, no," said the boy. "They're a mean bunch, 'specially Will, the oldest. They run the teamster company west of town."

"What's your name, son?"

"They call me Gilly mostly."

"I appreciate the information, Gilly." Then, handing the boy another coin, he said, "And I'll appreciate it even better if you forget I've been here asking questions."

Gilly looked deadpan. "You been asking questions?"

Joel gathered his gear and rifle and started toward the street. At the door he turned. "Who's sheriff here now?"

"Tom Sweeney."

"Thanks."

The hotel was a block up. They had a room, so Joel checked in and took his gear up to the third floor. He didn't stop to arrange things but went straight down the back stairs that let out on an alley. When he rounded the corner onto Main Street, it was deserted.

A half block down stood the jail and sheriff's office, and he headed for it. From the saloon two doors beyond, the piano was simpering:

> O Leave a kiss within the cup
> and I'll not look for wine . . .

9

Joel scanned the WANTED posters in the sheriff's window. The faces all looked the same—brutal and aimless men who'd been on the run most of their lives. His picture wasn't among them. Not yet. He wondered absently if his printed face would be like others.

A voice sounded behind him. "See anyone you know, puncher?"

Joel turned and faced a tall, able-looking man of middle age with the leathery face of the land, friendly eyes, and a star on his chest.

"Sweeney?"

The sheriff nodded, unlocking his office door and firing a lantern on his desk. He waved his guest to an overstuffed chair that was on its last legs.

"My name's Hollings." Joel looked for a reaction. Seeing none, he recounted the details of the Apache attack, his brother's death and his father's kidnapping. The sheriff listened, making pencil notes. Joel did not mention the white man who'd waited on the ridge or the note he had in his pocket. When he finished, both men sat silent a moment.

Then Sweeney asked, "Where were you during the raid?"

"Riding in from the north. I'd been away."

Sweeney rose. "Sorry to say, we haven't had much luck about the Indians. And that far away—I doubt we'll be of much help. Course I'll record the incident and report it to the military at Fort Briggs. Maybe they can get a line on your father."

Joel stood up, "Thanks, sheriff. I wanted the kidnapping reported. Nothing anybody can do about the rest."

Tom Sweeney watched the closed door for a full minute after Joel departed, his brow gathered like a man expecting trouble and not liking it one bit.

* * *

On the ride to town, Joel had eaten hardtack and wasn't hungry. But his thirst had been building. He stepped up the street toward the sound of the music and entered the saloon.

There were a few farmers and punchers drinking at the bar that reached the length of the room. At a table to his right, a stud game was in full swing, capturing the interest of a handful of bystanders.

One of the players was an enormous man, slightly drunk, who spoke in a thick voice. "Come on, Burgess, you know a flush beats a straight. What are you tryin' to pull!"

"But you don't get that fifth card, Pickett. You didn't call the bet." Burgess, a spare figure, wore his hat pulled low and tight on his head.

"I called. I called," said the burly man. Then, looking up at the gallery for support, he said, "I called the bet, didn't I, gents!"

Joel stepped to the bar and ordered a beer. In the mirror he could see the argument was getting out of hand.

The man named Burgess was standing now, shaking with fury.

"Damn you, Pickett, you've cheated me for the last time!" he shouted. The saloon was suddenly quiet.

Pickett placed both hands flat on the table and slowly rose, a sneer on his lips.

"I said I called. Maybe you'd like me to ventilate that closed up brain of yours!" he said, drawing his .45. Silence deepened in the room.

"He ain't wearing a gun, Jack," someone called out.

Jack Pickett grinned, swaying a bit. "Well, ain't that too bad," he said in a whisper. "Then maybe instead of shootin' it out, Mr. Burgess would like to do some dancin' for us!"

The .45 barked, and a bullet crashed into the floorboards at Burgess's feet. The little man jumped as if he'd been hit by lightning. The gun spoke again, sending Burgess into the air, flailing.

Three, four, five shots.

There were whistles and guffaws from the other players as the helpless man reeled, crashed through an empty table, and scrabbled to get to the door. Then he was gone.

Pickett gazed around the room, the grin still fixed on his face. "I like to play poker with people what know the rules and pay attention to the game," he said, and sat down.

"If you're good at rules, you ought to know the rules about gunplay, Pickett." Tom Sweeney stood just inside the door. "It's against the law to do your shooting in town."

"Whose law!" growled Pickett. "I ain't heard of that law."

"My law," said Sweeney. "I'm fining you a hundred dollars."

Pickett got up, his face red with anger. "You can go find yourself some green kid to fine, sheriff, but you ain't finin' me!"

"It's that or jail."

Before anybody saw his arm move, Jack Pickett's gun was out and pointed at Sweeney.

"Now sheriff, I don't want no trouble, but I'm walkin' out of here, and you ain't doin' nothin' about it, right?"

"Wrong."

The crowd turned to see who spoke. Joel stood quietly at the bar, his .44 leveled at Pickett's stomach. Sweeney stepped in quickly and took the big man's gun.

"That was stupid, Jack," said Sweeney, slapping the cuffs on. "Now it's assault with a weapon, and there ain' no fine for that. Just jail."

Pickett glared at Joel, a mixture of hate and bewilderment in his fast-sobering eyes.

"I don't know who you are, puncher, but I'm gonna make a point of finding out. You watch for me, hear!"

The sheriff led his prisoner out. As they passed by Joel, Sweeney said, "Thanks, Hollings." Pickett suddenly stiffened and cast a look at Joel over his shoulder. The confusion was gone from his eyes. Only the hate remained.

It was late, and Joel figured that with Jack safe in a jail cell, the news of his identity wouldn't reach the other Picketts till morning. He turned back to the bar and finished his beer.

3

NEXT MORNING JOEL rose early. In the hotel washroom at the end of the hall, he toweled down till his skin tingled, marveling at the freshness a bona fide bath could bring. For more than a week he'd had to make do with occasional splashings in creeks and water holes he'd come across on the ride south.

He buttoned on his last clean shirt and with the hotel comb made a few passes at his coal-black hair, which shone now from the washing.

He finished dressing, pondering the events of the previous day. How did the Picketts figure in the raid on his father's ranch? The kidnapping? What could profit a clan of teamsters in such a remote valley? It didn't make sense unless they were working for somebody else. But who? And why? His family had no enemies he knew of. And his father wasn't the sort of man one easily disliked.

He pictured the tall, gentle figure of Shad Hollings, resolute, slow to rile. If he had a fault, it was probably his refusal to fear the things that needed fearing. Where was he now? Lying wounded in an Indian village somewhere? And again Joel felt the nerves running wild in his arms, the hate gathering deep inside. Hang on, old man. I'm coming!

Famished, he left the room and headed down to the lobby. The hotel dining room was empty, so he took a seat at a corner table by a window that gave out on the street and hotel entrance. His back was to the wall. A vintage waitress with a limp and a young face spotted him, gathered a setup of water, menu, and butter, and came over.

"You're the early bird this morning."

"It's a bad habit I have." He smiled, waving the menu away. "Steak and eggs, if you've got 'em."

"Best this side of Winters."

"Where's Winters?"

"Eight miles east." She grinned.

Joel liked her face and laughed, "Two steaks rare, eggs straight up. *Papas fritas*, too?"

"You've got it." She poured out the coffee, left the pot on the table, and disappeared through the room into the kitchen.

He noted, across the street, the general store where hats and other apparel were displayed in the window, touched now by the first reach of morning sun. He thought of the hatless Mouse and his own need for some new things. He'd stop there later and see what they had.

His eye drifted to the corner of the street. A nondescript puncher stood brushing down his pinto and from time to time looking over at the hotel. Joel got the feeling the man was more interested in the hotel entrance than in his work. As the minutes passed, he was doing more looking and less brushing.

The waitress arrived with the rib-eye steaks still sizzling, the eggs standing tall—whites hard, yokes soft. There was even corn bread and honey.

"Here you go, handsome. Enjoy. If you need anything else—like a wife or mother, say—just ask for Lucy. I'm the only one here till seven."

Joel laughed again. "Careful, Lucy. I rarely turn down invitations from people I like!"

He started in on the platter, wearing it down evenly. Honeyed corn bread crumbled in his mouth and stuck to his fingers.

A short time later, he pushed the empty dishes aside and

poured a third cup of coffee. From his shirt pocket he took out the makings, rolled a cigarette, and lit it. Pulling deep, he thought of his next move. The sheriff seemed straight enough, but experience told him nothing's for sure. If Tom Sweeney was bought and paid for, Joel didn't want to play into his hands. And what was his own position with respect to the law? It was only a matter of time before he'd have to reckon with Sweeney about a certain shooting in Virginia City. The best solution, he concluded, was to work alone— to find Will Pickett and take him aside for a chat.

Gilly was sweeping out the stalls and changing the hay when Joel arrived at the livery stable. Putting his broom aside, the boy hurried over to the black-haired owner of the black horse, his face calm but his eyes betraying excitement.

"Gad, you don't believe in wasting time, do you?" said Gilly. "It's already around how Jack Pickett's spending his nights in jail!"

"There's a note for you." The boy was breathing faster. "Came last night. I heard somebody fumbling around your saddlebags, but by the time I got the lantern fired, whoever it was had gone." Gilly reached in his pocket and handed Joel a dirty sealed envelope.

Tearing it open, Joel recognized the juvenile scrawl awkwardly spaced on the yellow paper.

IF YOU WANT TO SEE YOUR FATHER AGAIN,
STAY AWAY FROM BRENNER FALLS. THIS
HERE'S THE ONLY WARNING YOU GIT!

Looking into Joel's tight-lipped face, the boy ventured, "Don't guess it's any good news, huh?"

"I reckon not." Joel pocketed the note and took his saddle from the rack, swung it across the black, and cinched up. He set the bit and brushed a few strands of hay from the

16

mare's mane. "Where do I find the Picketts' place of business, Gilly?"

The boy walked Joel to the stable doors and pointed up the street to the edge of town. "It'll be about a mile past the church on the left," he said. "But if I was you, I'd think twice about taking that bunch on alone. They're poison, and they ain't used to taking water."

"Depend on it."

With a single move, Joel was in the saddle. He turned his horse and started up the street.

As he passed the hotel, he noted the cowboy still grooming his pinto. The man looked down as Joel went by, seemingly engrossed in his work.

At the edge of town, the dusty street played out into a narrow trail that wound its way toward the baked foothills. Around the second bend, where a clump of scraggy trees strained to give shade, stood a long building with wooden walls bleached by time and sun. A sign hung from the corral gate, announcing:

PICKETT BROTHERS
TEAMSTERS FOR HIRE.

Still a hundred yards away, Joel pulled up and studied the scene. No movement, no sound except the cawing of a magpie that vented its temper at the sky. Joel left his horse out of sight in the trees and approached the building on foot. On the door was another message to the world at large:

GONE ON A HAULING JOB.
BE BACK FRIDAY.

W & B PICKETT

He entered the corral where a half-dozen horses bunched in one corner dozing in the sun, their tails kept busy by a scribble of metallic blue flies. He moved quietly, hugging

17

the side of the building. At an uncurtained window he stopped and peered in, cupping his eyes to cut the darkness inside.

He looked into a storeroom filled with long wooden cases, several of which were splintered open. Rifles. Six to a crate—maybe twenty cases in all.

Convinced now the place was empty, he moved quickly to the back door. It was locked. He began on the windows, and finally one gave under the thrust of his arm.

Once inside, he moved from room to room without pausing, letting quick glances tell him what he needed to know. When he reached the office up front, he tried the rolltop desk. It was open. Tucked into a far corner was a ribbon of cloth with an opal inset at the middle. Joel recognized it immediately—the dressy headband that Apache braves wear into battle! He pocketed the cloth and closed the desk.

A horse neighed out in the corral, and Joel froze. He heard nothing. Then, four feet from where he stood, he saw the doorknob slowly turning under key! Swift as a cougar, he fled through the littered warehouse to the back door and let himself out. Without pausing for breath, he hit the ground and skirted the corral on all fours. Not until he was well into the trees did he chance a backward look. There at the hitchrack in front of the building stood a well-groomed pinto snorting and pawing ground and casting a wild eye in his direction.

Taking a roundabout route back, Joel entered the town from behind the general store. He steered the black down an adjacent alley to the main street, which lay mostly empty in the heat of approaching noon.

If he was going to get food and supplies back to the valley before nightfall, there was little time to waste. Besides, with Will and Barney Pickett gone and brother Jack in jail, he saw nothing to be gained by sticking in town. He

18

doubted the rider of the pinto was anything more than a paid flunkie.

The general store was well stocked. Joel made his selections quickly—beans, flour, coffee, sugar. The clerk stacked the purchases outside on the boardwalk. Moving to the dry goods corner, Joel gathered up two pairs of denims and a cotton shirt long in the sleeve. A muslin dress the color of sunset hung on a nearby post. Silverfoot? Looked like a fit—why not? He gathered that up, too, and began trying on the different styles of cloth and leather hats piled on a shelf. His head and Mouse's were about the same size, he guessed. So, with a leather-trimmed model still on his head, he moved to the cash register at the front counter.

He paid the total from his poker stake and was about to leave when he heard a woman's voice.

"Like *that* one—that's a hat he'd love!"

He turned to face a handsome girl in her mid-twenties pointing an insistent finger at him. Stylishly dressed, she wore her honey-blond hair long and smiled directly into his eyes. The clerk scurried off to the hat section to find a duplicate.

"Don't you know it's rude to point?"

The girl instantly dropped her hand, "Oh, I'm sorry, I—"

"You're late for a birthday."

"My father's. And he's not an easy man to please."

Her eyes traveled the length of Joel's six foot frame, coming back to rest on his dark blue eyes.

"You're not from around here."

"North about twenty miles. I don't get to town much."

"You don't *look* like you get to town much."

Together their eyes went to the brush scars that covered his jeans from the knees down.

The clerk returned empty faced and empty-handed. "Sorry, Miss Brenner. That hat seems to be a oner," he said.

Joel took off the hat and held it out to the girl.

19

"Take it. There's others I liked as much."

"No, I can't," she protested. "You picked it—"

"Take it."

The girl looked at him evenly. "You're used to having your way, aren't you?"

"Sometimes. And you don't do badly yourself, I'll bet."

She laughed and reached out a steady, fine-boned hand. "All right—I'm Whitney Brenner."

"Joel Hollings."

"Thank you, Mr. Hollings—and my father thanks you." She turned to the clerk. "How much?"

"It's paid for, ma'am." The clerk was uneasy.

Throwing a despairing look at Joel, she said, "You'll at least let me pay for it!"

"I won't hear of it."

"Why not?"

"Because I'm used to having my way."

At this they both laughed and made a polite good-bye. She paused at the door without looking back and said in a clear voice, "I hope, Mr. Hollings, your future plans might include visits to town more often." Then she stepped lightly into the street and was gone.

Joel went to the shelf, pulled on another hat, paid the clerk, and walked over to fetch his packhorse from the stable. Suddenly, the town of Brenner Falls had a little more shine to it.

4

As THE NOTE on their office door said, Will and Barney Pickett were on a hauling job. Fifty-five miles to the northeast, they wound their way up the side of a mesa where Jerama, the Apache chief, had pitched camp. Each led a pack mule weighted down with cases of new rifles. The trail was steep and the going slow.

From a cloudless sky, the sun burned down, and sweat ran freely from behind Barney's ears into his shirt.

"This ain't hardly a trail at all," he complained to his brother. "You sure we got the right tabletop?"

"It's okay; we're almost there." Will kept his eyes fixed on the treacherous path. Loose rock, kicked free by the horses, rattled down the slope behind them. Now and again a larger rock broke loose, leaving a charged, expectant silence till it was heard crashing and splintering on the boulder reef far below. A lone brave stood on the ridge above, watching their progress.

At the top, they were quickly surrounded by six Apache, who looked longingly at the rifle cases and escorted the climbers the last three hundred yards to the camp. The wickiup of Jerama stood near the north ridge of the mesa, wrapped with skins and brightly painted with symbols, sending its cryptic message to the gods.

Jerama sat alone studying the ground as the teamsters dismounted and stood before him. At length, he raised his eyes, revealing a face battered by time and battle. It was

21

hard to tell where the wrinkles stopped and the scars began. He looked from the brothers to the burdened mules, then back again.

"How many long guns?"

"Eight crates, Jerama. Forty-eight rifles." Will nudged at a rock with his boot.

The chief's eyes were steely slits. "The agreement was for one hundred rifles, was it not?"

"True chief, true," Will hastened to agree, "but half now, the other half when old Hollings signs that paper."

Jerama rose and walked to the mules. A brave quickly pried open one of the cases and handed him a shaft of blue oiled steel. He looked the rifle over carefully, testing the bolt action, sighting through the barrel for trueness of bore.

"Ammunition," he demanded.

Barney dug into a second crate and passed Jerama a handful of .30-caliber shells. The chief disappeared into the wickiup and emerged with a small eating bowl. To a brave he said. "Take one of their mules to the blue rock and place this bowl on its head." The teasmsters looked at each other in astonishment as the mule was led away.

Two hundred yards across the mesa, the brave signalled that the bowl was in place. The mule stood calmly staring into the afternoon.

"The long guns you bring me are not as many as you said." The chief's voice was cold. "Now we see if they are as *true* as you said. For the sake of your mule, I hope so!"

Jerama loaded the rifle and raised it to his shoulder. For a moment the weapon trembled in the old warrior's hands, slowing to a stone steadiness. Then he fired.

The bowl exploded like fireworks above the mule's head. Turning to Will, Jerama said, "The rifles are good. I accept them. . . . We will talk." The chief led Will Pickett into the wickiup where animal skins were scattered two and three deep as a floor. Jerama waved Will to a seat, and both men reclined. The air was close and pungent.

"Hollings is a brave man," said the chief. "He has endured much and still will not sign the paper."

Will looked cautiously at Jerama. "But our agreement was that he must sign, chief. My principal says no paper, no more rifles."

Jerama fell silent and bowed his head. Finally, without raising his eyes, he spoke. "For now, I believe it is better that you speak to Hollings. Perhaps he will respond to White Eyes' reasoning. He does not respond to our persuasions. There is no fear in his heart."

"All right, Jerama. Where you holding him?"

The chief rose and led the way out. Many squaws and their children were busy at chores as they passed through the village. The women paid them no heed, but the children paused to glance after them. At an unmarked hut, Jerama stopped and pointed. "In here."

Will looked at the chief, who made no move to enter. Shrugging his shoulders, he bent to the opening and stepped inside. Shad Hollings was lying flat on the ground, his fevered head propped up by a saddle blanket. His shirt was torn and bloodstained, and there was dried blood in his long sandy hair. Below the waist he was covered by a blanket. Though his eyes were fixed on the entrance, he appeared not to see the man who had entered.

"Hello, Hollings."

There was no response.

"The chief tells me you're a mighty brave man. 'Zat so?" Still no response. Pickett continued, "Says you won't sign over the deed. 'Zat right?" Only the eyes of Shad Hollings moved, settling on the face of the big man.

"What is it you want from me, son?" The old man's voice was rusty with disuse.

"I'm here for the deed to your ranch—that is, if you feel up to signing."

"I don't as a rule sign over ranches."

Will's face turned suddenly ugly.

"Well, we was hoping in this case you might make an exception."

"What is your interest in my ranch?"

Will took a step closer to the old man. "I have no interest one way or another," he said, "but the people I work for do."

"What people?"

Will didn't answer but moved to a wooden stool covered with leather where a pen, ink container, and some printed papers rested. Gathering these up, he bent over the wounded man and said in a fierce whisper, "Sign, old man, or I'll put your light out now!"

The fever glistened on Shad's forehead as he looked into his tormentor's eyes. Then he turned his face away, saying nothing.

Will Pickett stiffened and threw the papers to the ground.

"Maybe Jerama is right; maybe some White Eyes' reasoning is what's needed here. . . . Let's have a look at those legs!" With one hand, Pickett grabbed the stool; with the other, he snatched away the blanket covering the rancher.

Shad's legs were bare and streaked with dried blood. Two scabs the size of silver dollars showed where the bullets had done their work. Pickett raised the stool above his head, and uttering a savage grunt, brought it down on Shad's legs with all the force he could muster. Only a moan issued from the wounded man as he slipped into unconsciousness.

Pickett stood a moment, breathing hard, watching the flow of blood begin again under the broken scabs. Then he tossed the stool aside and strode from the hut.

Outside, a scout had arrived on a lathered roan and was speaking to Jarama in low tones.

"Three remain at the ranch. One they call Mouse, the Apache girl—now a second son who rode in yesterday."

The chief, seeing Pickett had joined them, said, "If this

is a concern, it is yours, not mine. My business is with the father, and I have taken him as agreed."

"It's not a concern, Jerama," said Pickett. "In fact, it may be our trump card! This other son could be just the bait we need to change old Hollings's mind about signing."

When the scout departed, the chief looked steadily at the big teamster.

"I heard well your white-man reasoning a moment ago." Jerama nodded toward the prisoner's tent. Then he laughed loudly. But there was no mirth in his laugh, and his eyes were as cold as the new rifle he carried under his arm.

Piano music drifted from the rambling yellow house on the hill just north of town. On the wisteria-covered veranda, the short, compact form of Cyrus Brenner reclined, staring into the twilight. From time to time, he pulled on a glass cradled in his hand.

When the music stopped, a slender girl in riding clothes emerged from the house and joined the banker in the gathering dark. "Another whiskey, Dad?"

Brenner smiled at his daughter with pride. "Your piano is the best tonic for this old banker's cares," he said.

From the shadows down on the lawn came a stir followed by the call "Cyrus, that you? Tom Sweeney here. Can we visit a minute?"

"Of course, Tom; come up."

Into a circle of light stepped the erect Sweeney and mounted the veranda stairs.

"Evening Cyrus . . . Whitney. Hope I'm not disturbing you."

"Not at all, sheriff." Whitney had moved to the stairs to greet their visitor. "But you have to drink to father's health. It's his birthday, you know."

"I'd like that." Then, noting Brenner's glass, he said, "Whiskey will be fine."

As Whitney went for the drinks, Sweeney settled into a wicker chair next to Brenner.

"What can I do for you?"

"Well, Cyrus, it's a long chance. Last night a young fellow from up north stopped by to report an Indian raid on his family's ranch. They killed his brother and took his father off prisoner. The name was Hollings. Since you've been banker here a long time, I wondered if you ever had dealings with a family of that name?"

Brenner stroked his short beard. "Seems I recall that name—yes, Shad Hollings, I think. Came to me some years back for a crop loan. He had two sons, both shavers at the time. I made the loan, and as I remember, he paid it back before the note fell due. It's Shad's ranch you speak of?"

"Seems likely. But the thing gets more complicated. Today I received a WANTED poster in the mail. Looks like Joel Hollings, the son I talked with, is wanted for a shooting in Virginia City."

Whitney was setting the drinks down when she heard the name.

"Hollings!" she exclaimed. "Why, he's the man with the hat I told you about, Dad. A little brash perhaps, but Joel Hollings is no murderer."

"Sorry, ma'am. I don't read him as a killer, either. In fact, he helped me put a muzzle on Jack Pickett last night— Jack was drunk and punching bullets around the saloon. . . . I suppose now I've got to pay a call up Joel's way. Anyhow, here's cheers; happy birthday."

Cyrus waved his glass in acknowledgement. "How did you suppose I could help you in this, Tom?"

"Thought maybe if you knew the Hollings you could vouch for the name; it would make it easier."

"Sheriff, this may surprise you, but in this part of the world I couldn't honestly vouch for the name of half the people I loan money to!"

When Tom Sweeney had gone, father and daughter sat

side by side on the veranda, looking at the star-spiked sky. Whitney was the first to speak.

"How well did you know the Hollings?"

"Not well. It was a long time ago."

"Do you remember Joel as a child?"

"Just a quiet boy, standing beside his father."

"Well, I have a notion about Joel Hollings," Whitney said, "and you know my notions usually prove out. . . . He has a hard look, all right, but it's not born in him. It's the kind of hard that comes from living wary. I've seen the same look on other men that life's dealt a difficult hand to."

5

As HE PASSED the summit and entered the valley, the ink-stained clouds that had dogged Joel all afternoon opened, and rain began to fall. Large drops slapped at the leaves of the poplars, and grateful for the sudden cool, the black mare bunched and wound herself through a bone-rattling shake from mane to tail. Then the deluge came. All business.

He pushed on as sheets of rain blew through the still-warm air, rapidly building a wall of fog from ground to sky. Mist and the steady sound of the rain in the trees wrapped horse and rider in a world of slow and silent motion.

When he reached the valley floor, the air turned colder, dispersing the fog. Soon he had the ruins of the ranch in sight where a flicker of light played in the paneless kitchen window. He picked up the aroma of pot-simmering stew.

At the crumbled walls of the barn, he dismounted and stored the supplies in a cellar locker. He rubbed down the horses with handfuls of the driest straw he could find. Then he gathered his gear, turned the animals loose, and started for the house.

Silverfoot turned from the open fireplace as he entered, her eyes dark and bright. Was there the trace of a smile? Relief? With a quick motion of her head, she tossed back her long hair.

"We have a roof of sorts," she said, "and none too soon. Get dry clothes and come to the fire."

Joel looked up. Between the walls, fence wire had been

strung across the room in rows, then covered by tarps from the buckboard and securely tied. Another canvas was fitted to form the far wall. No water showed anywhere.

"Couldn't have done it better myself," Joel said, watching the girl's shoulders rise with pride.

"Mouse mostly did the roof." She turned back to her fire, stirring the olla that hung there. "I made a privacy room behind the screens." She nodded to one corner.

Joel took his things behind the screens and pulled on dry denims and a soft shirt, then went to the fire and kicked off his boots.

"Silverfoot," he said, "I hope you find a man soon, somebody worth the time and trouble you spend on us."

The Indian girl said nothing.

Moments later, Mouse clumped in with an armload of deadfall piled up against his good shoulder and marched past Joel to the holding bin where he dumped the logs with a clatter.

"Ya certainly took yer time! Probably spent the night in a fancy hotel an' et in one'a them dinin' rooms with silver coffeepots!"

"That's exactly what I did, Mouse, and I was sure glad you weren't along to embarrass me by picking your teeth in front of the ladies."

Mouse wasn't faking anger now. "Why, I pick my teeth discreet just like any other gent! And what do you know about tooth picking, anyway. Ya' ain't hardly old enough to get in out'a the rain by yerself!"

"You did a fine job on the roof," Joel said.

Somewhat appeased, the little man looked at the make-shift covering over their heads. "Well, I ain't much of a carpenter, but it's holdin'." Then he focused hard on Joel. "So, are ya' going to tell us about Brenner Falls?"

"We'll eat now," said Silverfoot, and placed the steaming platters of stew on the table. The men sat down, their eyes telling the girl how empty their stomachs were. The sound of the steadily falling rain, the hissing and popping of the fire, and the clatter of forks against dishware filled the room with a drowsy warmth that bound them firm and close.

Joel related the events of the trip, pausing now and then to stoke in another mouthful of boiled potatoes and stew meat.

As he described his search of the Pickett warehouse, he pulled out the Indian headband and laid it on the table. The girl's eyes widened, recognizing the battle talisman of her tribe, its rough beauty glowing in the firelight.

"The brothers look to be part of it," Joel said, "and I suspect they're working for somebody who wants this ranch mighty bad. I aim to find that somebody when Will Pickett checks back into town."

"Ya think the Indians are holdin' Shad, then?" asked Mouse.

"Seems that way. Why else would they take him alive? And why would they leave good horses and cattle? The main motive here was kidnapping, not stealing."

When they finished dinner and pushed their chairs back, Joel went to his gear behind the screens and returned with two bags. He handed one to Silverfoot, the other to Mouse.

"Mementos from town," he said.

Mouse pulled out his new hat, slapped it on his head, and grinned. "Perfect! Thank ya kindly, Joel."

Silverfoot was more tentative, looking into the bag a moment before removing the orange-dappled dress. She stood up, holding the full length of the garment against her, as women will do to judge the look and fit. The delight of a child showed in her face, but she managed to say only, "It's beautiful."

Long after Joel had rolled in his blankets on a mat in the far corner and Mouse was asleep nearby, Silverfoot sat at the fire, holding the new dress. Now and again she raised the material to the light and ran her fingers over the soft

30

colors. Presently, she stood and unfastened her belt, letting her doeskin shift fall to the floor. Firelight played on the rich dark of her waist and shoulders. She stepped into the dress, buttoned it up the back, and turned to face Joel where he slept. As a slow smile formed on her lips, Joel began snoring in earnest.

The northeast slope of the valley was rugged and steep, and a mixed growth of brush and pine grew there. For two hours Joel scoured the area without luck for stray horses scattered by the Apache. Handpicked by his father, these animals were a long-legged Arabian breed that over the short haul could run down anything in the West, and they accounted for a good piece of the ranch's income. Across on the west slope, Mouse was wrangling, too, and from time to time his faint cries reached Joel in the still morning air. Mouse, it seemed, was having better luck.

Joel pulled up in a stand of pines to let the black rest and cool off. He loosened the cinch and was walking her toward a grassy clearing when he saw the big man reclining under a tree, smoking a cigarette. Propped against the trunk, the fellow had the neck of a bull and was looking in his direction. Joel made no move to conceal himself. Instead, he opened his holster and approached the stranger with an easy stride, his hand resting lightly at his side.

"You're a bit off your trail, aren't you, partner?"

"Not at all," said the big man. "Matter of fact, I've been waiting for you."

"And what would be your business with me?"

"My name's Will Pickett. That mean anything to you?"

Joel's eyes turned hard. "It means you saved me a trip into town tomorrow. Seems I've been looking for you, too."

"Well, this simplifies things, don't it?"

Joel looked Pickett over carefully, noting the strong resemblance of the brothers. Bunched muscles filled his shirt to the splitting point. He wore two guns, but his hands were well away from them. He looked relaxed, too relaxed.

"Where's my father?"

"Aw, I'll do better than that. I'll take you to him if you like." Pickett's face spread in an ugly grin.

Gilly was right; this wasn't the sort of man to take lightly.

"Where's Shad?"

"In due time," Pickett said. "First put your gun on the ground and step back." Pickett's hand remained well away from the authority tied at his hip.

"I don't think so," said Joel.

Like his brother Jack, Will Pickett knew how to move a gun. Suddenly, his hand was full, but it wasn't quite fast enough. With his muzzle still on the way up, Will stared down the barrel of Joel's .44.

"Your 'due time' is up, Pickett. Dump the guns!" Amazement stood in the eyes of the big man; then he gently laid down his irons and smiled.

"I should'a know'd better," he said, "I saw your brother shoot once. . . . We'll have to try this again sometime when I ain't forgotten my business posture."

Joel spread Will Pickett against the tree and searched him. In his boot he found a knife and tossed it into the trees.

"Now, what's this all about?" Joel demanded.

"You'll know soon enough—one way or another."

"I think I want a better answer," said Joel. He spun Pickett around and buried the muzzle of the .44 deep in the teamster's neck.

"Easy! Your father's safe enough for now."

"Why was he taken? And why was my brother killed?"

"I ain't got all the answers, Hollings, I just do what I'm told to—when the money's right."

"Whose money?"

"Like I said, come with me and you'll get your answers."

32

"All right, let's go."

Silently, Barney Pickett stepped out of the trees on the left, his rifle leveled. "Drop it, Hollings!"

For a split second Joel considered his options. None of them seemed very good. He let the .44 fall at his feet.

Barney Pickett looked much like his brothers. What set him apart was the bright red hair that pushed out from under his hat.

"We thought your pappy would enjoy some company about now, so we planned a surprise party."

The brothers worked fast. They tied Joel's hands tight behind him with rawhide strips, then shoved him up on the mare and tied his feet underneath. Will retrieved his guns as Barney went for their horses.

The three riders started south along the slope toward the east rim, keeping well back in the trees. At one point jagged granite took over the mountainside, and they had to descend and cross a short reach of meadow on the valley floor. During this stretch, the ranch was in sight, but there was no trace of Mouse. As they passed the rock flow and started back up into the trees, Joel threw a last look at the ranch. The air was clear, and the adobe walls shone in the sun. In the kitchen window he thought he caught a glimpse of the Indian girl's dark hair, but he couldn't be sure. Then they were swallowed again by the trees.

Though matters weren't moving in the direction Joel had planned, maybe it didn't matter. This way might prove even better. If he was headed directly for a reunion with Shad, which looked to be the case, a good deal of time and probably some bullets would be spared. He wished he'd been able to somehow alert Mouse, but Mouse would figure things out fast enough once he discovered Joel was not in the valley. Joel knew his chance would come.

As they neared the rim, he heard Will Pickett say to his brother, "We got the situation in hand now. Just make sure he don't get near a gun and the deed's as good as signed over."

"Lucky I tagged along, ain't it?" said Barney. "Otherwise, you'd be hanging out to dry about now." Will's face showed annoyance, but he said nothing, and the three rode in silence as they topped the mountain and set a trail to the northeast.

6

A̲T̲ ̲T̲H̲E̲ ̲R̲E̲A̲R̲ of the lobby in the Brenner Bank, two marble columns rose from the oak floor, forming the entrance to the private offices of founder and president Cyrus Brenner. Behind the door, the banker sat at a burnished desk, plainly irritated by the loud tones of his visitor, Jack Pickett.

"Keep your voice down!"

"But this other son, Cyrus. We didn't count on him—"

"I knew about him, but he wasn't expected back." A frown rode the banker's face.

"Where is he now?"

Pickett shrugged. "I been in jail."

"Any news from your brother?"

"They was supposed to be back yesterday."

Brenner rose and went to the window. "Send Will to me as soon as you see him. I want to know the situation with Shad. Understand?"

"Sure, Cyrus." Pickett turned a greasy hat in his hands.

"In the meantime, find out more about Joel Hollings. There's a WANTED poster over at the jail; see if you can get a copy."

"Got it right here." The big man reached in his shirt and produced the notice. "There's a stack of them in Sweeney's office." Brenner sat down and studied Joel's face, carefully reading the charges.

"Say he's wanted by Sheriff Barnes in Nevada. You know Jake Barnes, Pickett?"

"Heard tell of him—tough to fool in a manhunt, they say."

"Send a wire. Tell Barnes that Joel Hollings has been seen in Brenner Falls. Then leave it unsigned." Brenner thought a minute and added, "It's possible we can use Joel for our own purpose. If not, we'll see that Sweeney and Barnes add another heroic capture to their records."

The door opened, and Whitney's blond head poked in. "Are you busy, Dad?"

"Come in. Jack here was just leaving." Cyrus turned to Pickett and murmured, "Remember—as soon as Will gets back!"

Jack rose, and still turning his hat in his hands, said, nodding to the girl, "Miss Whitney," and left the room.

Whitney sat down with a puzzled look. "You didn't tell me about the raid on Hollings's ranch—about the kidnapping of Joel's father."

"I guess you were getting the brithday drinks when Tom gave us the news. Quite a story, isn't it?"

"It's grim," said the girl. "What do you suppose Joel will do now, with his ranch gone and a price on his head?"

"If I were he, I'd take the earliest opportunity to leave this part of the country, if it's not too late already."

"Just meeting him once, I doubt his mind works that way. . . . Speaking of jail, who let that teamster out?"

"I posted bail." Cyrus pulled a stack of papers in front of him. "Pickett and I have some business together, and I need him free."

"Who do you think's behind the raid? Tom now says the motive was clearly kidnapping."

"Indians, probably."

"It's possible. Apaches do kidnap for ransom." Whitney picked up the WANTED poster that still lay on the corner of her father's desk. Studying Joel's face, she went on. "But if you're dealing direct—and the extortion is for money, or even guns, burning a ranch is self-defeating, and the Indians know it. I think it's more complicated than that."

Brenner had been watching his daughter closely as she spoke. He got up and came around the desk, extending both arms to her as she rose.

"Whitney, I wish I knew the answers to a lot of things. If I did, you'd be playing your piano for me in the senator's mansion! As it is, I'm just a small-town banker trying to get by.

"You run along now and let me finish my work. I'd like to get home to dinner on time just once." He kissed the girl lightly and returned to his desk. Whitney smiled as she watched her father settle into his characteristic "business" frown. Then she left the room and the bank.

It was, in fact, Silverfoot's face Joel had seen in the kitchen window as the Picketts led him captive from the valley. But it didn't stay there long. Even as the trio disappeared into the trees, she was running to the barn. Halter in hand, she topped the corral railing with a graceful leap and moved in on the bay mare that was closest. Talking softly in Apache, she slipped the halter on. Seconds later, she streaked along the valley floor to where she last heard Mouse's calls directing the stray horses.

She found him in a small canyon where he'd herded the strays and was riding out to look for others. Mouse saw her coming and put his horse at a trot to meet her.

"Ya ride that animal better'n most whites with saddles!" he said, "*Que tal?*"

"Joel's gone. Two men took him out." She pointed northeast. "One was the man I saw on the ridge during the raid—same size, same horse."

"How long ago?"

"A half hour at most."

Mouse looked up at the rim where Silverfoot pointed, his

eyes hard slits against the sun. Then he saw the movement he was looking for. High on the slopes above the timberline, three dark specks moved slowly across the rocky terrain.

"I have 'em!" Mouse said softly. "And this time, by God, I'll keep 'em!"

"Your shoulder's hardly started to heal."

"I'll be fine."

"You'll need food and water. I'll get some things and catch up."

"No, Silverfoot, this is man's work."

"Man's work, maybe, but I know this country. You know the valley." She spun her horse and was gone.

For a moment longer, Mouse watched the progress of the tiny raiders on the bald mountain. Then he turned to the horses quietly bunched in the canyon and said, "You people stay put. I'll be back for you."

Before Mouse was halfway up the mountain, the Indian girl overtook him. This time she rode in a saddle with full bags and blankets rolled behind. She fell in beside Mouse, and the two moved on, picking their way upward through the rocks and trees. At the east rim, the girl pulled up, and they dismounted. Ahead lay the outer slopes that dropped away to canyons and arroyos below. In the distance, tall mountains half clad in pines reached as far as the eye could see, and the clearness of the morning put an edge on things, bringing the whole land into focus.

Silverfoot watched and waited. Then her arm went up, pointing to a faint column of dust that rose near a canyon several miles to the north.

"Good girl!" Mouse was climbing back on his horse.

"Wait—another few minutes will tell us their direction better." They watched the dust cloud, which seemed to hang motionless. Then, little by little, it snaked off toward the east.

They remounted and began a slippery descent across the shale that hugged the mountain like an overcoat. Then the horses got the feel of the surface and lowered their heads to the business of the downward climb.

Mouse looked at the slim figure of the girl with new respect. "How come ya know this land so well? I thought ya grew up among whites."

"Until I was fourteen, my home was with the Apache, and the Apache is never still. We cover great distances each year in search of food and wild mustangs. Yes, I know the land—all of it that you saw back there from the mountain."

They rode on in silence till they reached the canyon where the dust was last seen. Their eyes now scanned the softer ground and quickly located the tracks put down by Joel and his captors.

They followed till the canyon ended and the trail veered right—across an expanse of desert—toward a series of sun-drenched mesas far to the east.

"Jerama's land," said Silverfoot. "He favors the high mesas since the white man came."

"Do ya know this Jerama?"

"I saw him once. My people range farther south."

"Fort Briggs is south," Mouse said. "We might find some help there if they still keep a garrison."

The girl nodded and looked at her companion. She seemed to wait for his descision.

"How many Apache run with Jerama?" Mouse asked.

"Not as many braves as before. I don't know."

Mouse removed his new hat where a sweat stain was already showing through at the hairline. Drawing a sleeve across his face, he muttered, "The odds ain't good—even without the Indians."

She looked again at the distant mesas. "If the army cannot help, I think I can find Jerama."

That seemed to settle it. Mouse replaced his hat and picked up the reins. "Come on, Silverfoot. Let's pay a call on the U.S. Cavalry; we'll see if them fellas is half as good as folks claim."

The two started south over a desert that gave off heat and silence in about equal measure. Here and there scrubby mesquite and ocotillo struggled for existence, and the giant saguaro lifted a warning finger to all who ventured into the precincts.

Sun drained the blue from the sky, and the heat came at them in waves. Sweat ran freely down Mouse's face and shoulders, funneling into a column that turned his shirt black the length of his spine. The girl seemed less affected. A few beads of moisture had formed on her upper lip; otherwise, she showed no effects from the furnace that held them.

Several hours passed before Silverfoot drew Mouse's attention to a small flight of birds above an arroyo that gaped on their right.

"There is water," she said.

They turned and descended. Tucked back in the canyon, half hidden by an outcropping of red rock, stood a pool left by recent rains. Five cactus wrens hopped about on the rim in a delighted commotion of feathers and song. After Mouse and the girl drank, they brought up the horses, who plunged their noses deep in the cold water, their sides heaving relief.

They ate hardtack and some jerky in the shade of the overhang and rested. Mouse seemed to be wrestling some tough questions. Finally, he said. "It was them Picketts that took Joel."

"Yes, I think so. They fit the description."

"We got to make this thing happen fast—with or without the soldiers."

"Speed is good, but help might prove better. Neither the Apache nor the Picketts are cowardly."

Mouse rose, then refilled the canteens from the pool and cinched up the horses. As they picked their way out of the canyon, he took a last look around, as if wanting to fix the place in his mind for the future. The pool lay as still as they'd found it, a patch of desert sky etched on its glass surface.

An hour later, Silverfoot pointed to a range of lavender hills in the distance. "Fort Briggs is there. If we keep the pace, we'll be inside by nightfall."

These words seemed to pick up Mouse's spirits. "Sorry to be nosy,"—he winked at the girl—"but how'd ya get a handle like Silverfoot?"

She flashed a smile. "On special days, Apache children run races. I always won, even against the young braves. After that, they called me Silverfoot, and I judged the races, but they wouldn't let me run anymore."

Mouse beamed to have this bit of privileged information. "I'd like to've seen them races, and the looks on the braves' kissers—gettin' whupped by a girl!" He chuckled again and again as they rode toward the shadows that were starting to lengthen from the lavender hills ahead.

7

TWENTY-THREE MILES northeast of Fort Briggs, Joel sat on the ground, his hands and feet tightly bound with rawhide. With his back against a boulder, he watched Will and Barney Pickett pour coffee from a dented black pot. The brothers had eaten and were letting the fire settle down as they rolled out their blankets. Barney was saying, "What d'ya think? Shall we give him coffee?"

"Naw. That means untying' his hands or feedin' it to him. Leave him be. He'll survive till we're done with him."

"Ain't you just a bit edgy, Will? This here junket weren't part'a the plan." Will looked over at Joel.

"He made it part of the plan by showin' up. It's gonna turn out even better this way. You'll see."

Joel studied the two men silhouetted again the fire. They were big, all right. Mean for sure. But both had ample beer guts, and he could feel his fist sinking into that sea of flab. Or was it flab? He couldn't imagine those bellies being as hard as the rest of their huge frames.

Joel said, "You gents must be drawing awfully good wages for this caper. . . . How much are they paying you?"

Will and Barney looked at each other and grinned.

"Though it ain't none of your business," Will said, "I'd venture that we was gettin' adequate wages for our work."

"For your sakes I hope it's more than adequate. Kidnapping is one thing; murder's another."

"Murder?" Barney looked genuinely surprised. "We ain't murdered nobody." Joel looked at Will.

"You were with the Apache when they killed my brother. There was a witness."

"There weren't no witnesses," said Will. "Besides, I never been at that ranch of yours till today."

"You were close enough. And the law will see that as conspiracy. You'll swing for it."

It was plain that Will Pickett didn't like this sort of talk. He got up from the fire and came over to Joel.

"What d'ya mean there was a witness, Hollings?"

"You were seen on the ridge during the raid. Then you left with the Apache."

"I ain't askin' you where I was. I'm askin' you the name of this so-called witness."

"It wouldn't do any good if I told you. You're finished—it's just a matter of time."

Will lashed out with his boot, catching Joel on the side of the jaw, slamming his head back hard into the rock. Joel recovered saying, "Pickett, I've known your kind all my life. You all wind up the same eventually. At the end of a rope."

Will didn't seem to like these words any better. He reached down with both hands to pull Joel off the ground.

Barney jumped to his feet. "For God's sake, Will, that's enough! He's no good to us dead."

For a moment Will froze. Then he slowly relased his captive.

"Don't crowd me, Hollings," he said. "I'll give you nothin' but bad road!"

"Come on, Will. Bed down," said Barney. "It's still a fair piece to the village. We got to keep him in 'bargaining' shape till then."

The brothers turned in, and a few minutes later their snores cut like ripsaws through the night air. Joel watched the dying fire with mixed emotions. Though the day, and

43

the miles covered, had brought him nearer to Shad, his rawhide bonds severely troubled him. There was dried blood on his wrists now where the thongs had cut deep.

He wondered if Mouse, with his bad shoulder, was up to tracking. And if he was, could he follow such a faint trail as they had left? Deciding to keep things simple, he focused his thoughts on Shad. When his chance came, he would be ready. He wriggled his shoulders, trying to get a fit with the rock behind him. Then he lowered his head to his chest and slept.

Dawn broke like a rainbow tide, washing over the mesas to the east and staining the desert sand with green and gold. Joel was awake, watching Barney make the coffee. The latter had rekindled the fire, stoking and blowing. Will, still under blanket, lay in a heap, his hat covering his face. When the fire was leaping and the coffee hot, Barney filled a tin cup and came over to Joel.

Squatting, he said, "Here. I'll hold it." Joel leaned forward and sipped the steaming brew. It was strong but good. Then the redhead offered a string of jerky. Joel chewed off a section and washed it down with more coffee.

"I thank you, Barney."

"It's little enough."

Joel looked at him a minute.

"You don't seem like your brothers."

"How d'ya mean?"

"I think there's a good man in you somewhere trying to get out."

Barney stood up and went back to the fire. About then, Will woke with a growl and sat up.

"I ain't never seen rocks that was so determined to punch holes in my hide," he said. He pulled his boots on and got up.

As Barney readied the horses, Will opened a canteen and splashed water on his face, still puffed with sleep, slicking his hair back at the same time. He filled a cup from the

44

coffeepot, drank it off, and poured another. Then he looked over at Joel. "Well, let's get this show over with. On your feet, Hollings."

A few minutes later, the three riders crossed the last stretch of the flatland before the mesas took over. The morning air was cool in the shadows, and Joel felt strangely elated as they began the climb.

Off to the north stretched the spectacular wilderness that many called the heart of the mountain desert. There were few, Joel guessed, who really knew this land, and even fewer who had charted its lonely reaches. Ahead, sun smoldered in the upper peaks, leaking its glory from the spill. And they rode on into the mesa country where the land was still and dry.

The squaw who brought Shad a bowl of cornmeal mush and now sponged his legs with warm water bore an uncanny resemblance to Silverfoot. Though somewhat older, she had the same boyish figure, the same widow's peak, and the same haunting softness of voice. She worked gently and thoroughly. When the last traces of blood were cleaned away, she took strips of bark and firmly bound them around his legs from the ankle to a height well above the knee.

Shad watched as he savored the contents of the bowl. When she finished, he said in Apache, "I won't forget your kindness."

The woman looked up, a faint smile in her chestnut eyes. She nodded at the bowl in his hands and said, "I'll bring you water after."

"What do they call you?"

The smile spread to her lips. "I am Siki."

"You look much like an Indian girl who works for me. Her name is Silverfoot, but she's not of your tribe."

"Silverfoot!" Siki's eyes widened. "She works for you?"

"You know her?"

"Yes, yes—she is my sister's firstborn. She was taken years ago from our tribe by the White Eyes."

"How is it you are with Jerama's people?"

"I belong to a brave here."

She took Shad's blanket outside and shook it. When she returned, she brought water in a deerskin bag. She arranged the blanket on Shad's legs and handed him the water.

"Drink this now. You will feel better."

"Siki, why do they want my ranch?"

The woman shook her head as she straightened the rest of the wickiup. "They do not speak of these things to the women."

She refolded the saddle blanket and placed it under the wounded man's head. "Was Silverfoot well when you left her?"

"I can't be sure. The attack was sudden, and they hit us hard."

The hut opening darkened, and Jerama stepped in. With his head he motioned the woman to leave. Then he looked about as if inspecting the place. Apparently satisfied, he sat down near Shad and spoke in a matter-of-fact tone.

"I think it is better if you sign the paper. Either way, I doubt if the White Eyes will let you live. But you may die easier."

"I don't make sense of this, Jerama. For years we have been neighbors. Your braves have watered at my creek and hunted animals in my hills. We've been good neighbors, have we not?"

"This is true."

"My son is dead. Why?"

"Good men and bad are in all colors, and I count you among the good. But this does not change the future for my people. The White Eyes are slowly killing our nation. The only course for us is to fight and continue fighting. For this we need powerful long guns, the weapons your people use against us."

46

"You did this thing for rifles?"

"For rifles, yes, and the spirits of our ancestors who haunt our camps. I do not believe we will win the fight, but our heritage demands that we persist. . . .

"You hear of friendships between whites and Indians. It is true that these exist. But the times are bigger than we who live them. Eventually, the Indian must fight *all* White Eyes to survive. And you must understand that our will to survive is as strong as yours—perhaps stronger—for we fight for our own land.

"It is not a personal thing. . . . My braves did not come to destroy your son but to take you. Your son, like his father, was very brave. He did what he had to."

"I see what you are saying, Jerama, but you know I hate you for it."

"So it must be."

"Who gives you the rifles?"

"The teamsters bring them."

"They're working for someone, Jerama. Who?"

"They talk of one who is higher, but it is they who make the agreements."

"What is it they're after?"

"They want your mark on this paper." The chief picked up the deed that lay by the stool. "For this, we receive one hundred rifles—enough to fight for two, maybe three more winters. So far they bring only forty-eight long guns. . . . I know nothing more of the matter."

Jerama rose and looked at Shad. "In the next life, we may well be brothers, and that would please me. For now, we must carry the burdens we have geen given." He stooped, picked up the waterbag, and placing it in Shad's hands, quietly left the hut.

8

THE INDIAN CAMP was alive with activity when the Pickett brothers rode in leading their captive. Beyond the wickiups, thick-backed braves readied their ponies and traded jokes in loud voices as the women scurried here and there, helping with the blankets and ammunition and sacrificial meal bags. The children, their eyes shining with excitement, stood clustered at the edge of the camp, watching their fathers and smiling at what jokes they could understand. The raiding party was almost ready to leave.

Will Pickett spotted Jerama, who was sliding a new rifle into his buckskin sheath, and rode over.

"Chief, we've got Hollings's other boy!"

Jerama threw the teamster a hurried look. "There is a battle planned. We will be gone until sundown."

"We should proceed without you, then?"

The chief looked over Will's shoulder at Joel. Then he mounted his horse and turned away, saying; "Do what you have to do."

Seeing the three alien riders enter the camp, the braves went suddenly quiet. They stared at the white men with open resentment but continued their preparations for departure. When the band was ready, Jerama joined them and led the way out of the camp and down the mesa.

In the brief moment he and Jerama exchanged glances, Joel saw the indifference in the old chief's eyes. The battle lines were drawn then. Except for the overworked strength he drew from deep inside, he could expect no help from any human soul.

The brothers led Joel to the wickiup where Shad was held and dismounted. Untying Joel's legs, Will grinned.

"I said I'd take you to your father, Hollings. Here we are."

Single file, the three entered the hut and stood letting their eyes get used to the dark. Shad lay as Siki had left him, but now hope flashed in his sunken eyes as he recognized his son.

Will Pickett said, "We brung you a surprise, Shad . . . Lookie here; your prodigul son's come back!"

"Will you leave us alone a minute?" Joel asked.

"Why sure—we want this homecoming to be warm and friendly. . . . C'mon, Barney. Let's get us somethin' to eat while these two visit a spell."

When the brothers were gone, Joel walked slowly to the shell of a man he knew to be his father and took his hand. Tears stood high in his eyes as he knelt.

"My God, what have they done to you!"

"Joel—it's really you?"

"It's me, Shad."

The old man tried a smile and got half of it. "Sorry to greet you so rudely . . . on my back—"

"Shad."

"When did you get home?"

"Four days back."

"The ranch is gone?"

"The buildings are gone, but we saved most of those long-legged horses of yours."

"We?"

"Mouse and Silverfoot made it through."

Shad tried the smile again. This time he got all of it. "How did you find me?"

Joel raised his hands, showing the rawhide cuffs. "I

49

suppose I'm insurance. . . . Do you know what this is all about?"

"Must be something on the ranch besides the wheat and livestock. Something we know nothing about. But this I'm sure of—the Picketts are running somebody's errands."

"Any idea whose?"

The old man shook his head.

"You know about Jason, Shad?"

"Yes."

Father and son looked at each other; then Joel spotted the papers on the stool. "They want you to sign these?"

Shad nodded.

"Looks to me like a losing proposition." Joel said. "Nobody's going to take the ranch and let us live. They'll have to get rid of us either way. But what are the Indians doing in this?"

Shad related the events surrounding the raid and his captivity. He told of Will Pickett's first visit and the rifle talk with Jerama. When he finished, his eyes were closed, and Joel could see he was feeling the pain in his legs again.

"We have to buy time, Shad. If it comes down to it, we'll go ahead and sign over the deed. Till Jerama gets the rest of his rifles, he'll try to keep us alive. If we die, his leverage goes with us."

The Picketts returned, chewing on jerky sticks, and sat down inside the wickiup entrance.

"Renewed ol' acquaintance?" asked Will, grinning. Joel wondered if the older brother had any other facial expression.

"Now folks, the reason we're all here is to get some paper work done. Shad's got a deed to sign, and we're hopin' his boy might be of some help in that regard . . . We don't have a lot of time, so are there any suggestions as to how we can move this meeting along?"

Joel said, "We'd like more time."

"How much more?" Will glared.

"An hour, maybe two. We're talking thirty years of a man's life and sweat here."

"What's there to discuss? You got no alternative." Will flashed that grin again. "Still, I'm a reasonable man. . . . Let's try it your way first—but if that deed ain't signed today, you won't be around to see the sunrise tomorrow! C'mon, Barney." The brothers got up and left the hut.

Shad lay strangely quiet, and Joel sensed the conflict going on in his father's head. Will was right about one thing—as long as the Picketts held the guns, there were no options. The best they could hope for was to put off the signing until Jerama returned. To sign before would be certain suicide.

Again Joel tried the rawhide that bound his wrists for any give. It wasn't there. Watching his son, Shad said; "I could try—"

"We'd need an ice pick for the knots, anyway," said Joel.

"Where are Mouse and Silverfoot?"

"She's likely at the ranch. Mouse, too, unless he. felt strong enough to track. He took a bullet in the shoulder. By the way, Mouse made a fast-patch roof for the kitchen. Those walls survived the fire."

"They're good walls. Two-foot-thick adobe."

"Shad, let's try to make this happen—we'll stall the Picketts till Jerama gets back. Then you sign the deed. If my guess is right, the Picketts will want to finish us then and there. Jerama will oppose them.

"At that point, the Picketts will leave to deliver the deed to their boss. I'm hoping by then to slip these ties and follow them to the spider's nest."

Shad said, "Jerama is all Apache. You can't tell what he'll do."

The hut faced east, as most wickiups will do in respect to the Holy People, and through the opening Joel watched the sun already starting to burn itself out on a jagged peak that rose like a bear claw in the distance.

"Maybe so," he said, "but it's our only chance."

When Mouse and Silverfoot arrived at Fort Briggs, they learned the garrison was in the south, quelling a Chiricahua uprising led by Nana. The troops weren't expected back for at least a week. The sergeant on duty, though of little help, was friendly, so they spent the night as guests of the government and were on the trail again long before sunup.

That was nine hours ago. Ever since, they had held a steady course to the northeast toward the mesa country, stopping only once to water and feed the horses at a drying creek that played out in the sun-scalded bedrock of a lonely arroyo.

Most of the trip had been covered before the heat of the day, and now the vast tableland was sharply rising on either side of them. They moved slowly, keeping to the shadows that thickened as the sun cut its westering path well to the south.

Soon they left the flatland and began to climb. A trail, faint with disuse, wound its way upward through the shale, slowing the pace still further. Silverfoot's eyes remained fixed on the giant butte that towered above the others a mile or so to the north.

"Puma Mesa," she said. "From there we can see many miles. It is possible we will see Jerama's camp."

Mouse looked at the girl in wonder. He wasn't used to this sort of trek—even less to having his life ride in the hands of a woman. He could only admire her confidence and straight thinking.

"If we get out'a this alive," he said, "ya got my marker for life!"

What growth there was at the base of the butte thinned as they climbed, leaving only the barren and treacherous rock.

Still, they found some cover in the shadows, and the trail held.

An hour later, they reached the summit and dismounted well back from the rim, away from any eyes that might be probing the tabletop from below. Silverfoot checked Mouse's shoulder. Signs of blood still fought to get through the bandages. From her saddlebag she brought pieces of fresh linen, and with water from her canteen, set to work cleaning and redressing the wound.

The sun was low in the sky when they crawled side by side to the south rim and looked out over the desert and mesas below. For long minutes they lay there, bodies still, eyes tracking the scene for signs of movement. They were about to pull back when Mouse, gazing down and westward, suddenly nudged his companion.

"Riders," he said.

The girl focused on a column of horsemen beginning to ascend a mesa half hidden by others in the waning light.

"Apache." She murmured. "Twenty five, maybe thirty." Another minute passed, and she said, "Jerama and his braves returning from a raid. They lead seven stolen horses."

One by one the riders disappeared into the shadows that were clustering on the slope. From where they watched, Mouse and Silverfoot could hear the chorus of loose rock skittering across the shale long after the band was gone from sight.

"We can't foller on horse," Mouse said. "Them loose rocks could wake the dead. . . . We got to go up on foot."

They waited a few minutes longer, then pulled back and led their horses down the north face of the butte to the desert floor. It was almost dark as they turned west, staying in tight against the cliff to cover any sounds the horses made. They quickly crossed a patch of open desert to the foot of the mesa where the Apache had begun their climb.

Silverfoot said, "It is better I go up alone. My feet are silent, and the climb will need both hands." She looked at Mouse's hobbled shoulder.

Mouse considered this a moment, but the eagerness in his eyes was rejecting the idea. She continued. "I am dressed like the Apache, and I might slip through unnoticed in the dark."

Mouse bowed his head under the weight of this reasoning.

"If you remain here with the horses," she added, "I will see if I can find Joel—then signal by throwing a rock."

Mouse smiled wanly, "*Vaya con Dios*, then. I'll be waitin'."

Silverfoot moved swiftly up the side of the mesa. Less than ten minutes later she neared the summit and paused for breath. When she looked over the rim, fires were already burning in many of the wickiups, flickering through the loose walls of brush and poles.

Near the center of the village, a half-dozen squaws readied the ceremonial fire where the victory dance would take place. They laid down armfuls of dry mesquite and retreated into the darkness to gather more. Silverfoot crouched when she saw one of the women coming her way. There was something familiar in her walk. The woman stopped at a clump of shrubs not twenty feet away and began breaking and gathering the larger branches. As she turned back, a reach of firelight fell on her features, and Silverfoot recognized the face of her mother's sister.

"Siki!"

The woman stopped in her tracks and flashed a look in Silverfoot's direction. Then she casually stepped out into the full darkness of the night.

The two women stood inches apart, facing each other. Suddenly, they embraced, swaying in each other's arms. Siki's smile turned to joyous tears as she stepped back, still grasping the younger woman's hands.

54

"Five winters—is it six?"

"Siki, I can't believe it's you—more beautiful than I remembered!" The two moved farther back in the shadows, whispering away the years that had come between them.

"But you are in great danger here," Siki said, "You must go immediately. Jerama is holding the father and son captive. I fear they are marked for death."

"I have come to free them, Siki. Can you help me?"

"What can I do?"

"Show me the hut where they keep them; then get me two horses. Also, I will need two riding blankets."

"The father is sick. He cannot sit a horse."

"Then one horse and one blanket."

"Jerama must not know I helped in this."

"You will not be named, even if we fail."

Again the squaw took the girl's hand and looked skyward as if asking guidance.

"The hut is third from the end on the west side." Siki pointed, one, two, three. "Can you see?"

Silverfoot nodded.

"Do nothing till the ceremony begins and all eyes are on the dancers. Then you must take great care, child. Joel's black mare will be waiting on the west rim."

Silverfoot hugged her aunt once more.

"Can you care for Shad till we return?"

Siki smiled. "He is already in my care."

9

Shad was asleep, but Joel heard the excited voices that greeted the raiding party's return. The entire village, it seemed, had turned out to welcome the warriors. Above the din he heard Jerama's brittle tones directing the handling of the new horses and questioning the braves who had remained as lookouts when the party left earlier in the day.

As the clamor subsided and the men dispersed, carrying gear and spoils to their wickiups, Joel recognized Will Pickett's drone.

"Looks like you had a fine day, chief," he said. "We was just about to conclude the signin' ceremonies. I think it's a good thing if you're with us."

The weariness in Jerama's voice was unmistakable. "As you wish."

"Soon as it's over, we'll be leavin' to deliver the deed and bring the rest of your rifles."

The Picketts and Jerama entered the hut and faced the captives. Shad was wide awake now, sitting up. Will walked directly over to Joel, drew his gun, and pushed the muzzle against the young man's throat.

"Games are over, gents," he said. "Time for business."

Barney picked up the papers from the stool and lay them in Shad's lap. He opened the ink, dipping the quill several times, then handed it to the old man.

Joel said, "Remember this scene, Will. You, too,

56

Barney. When I catch up with you and shoot you down, I want this moment fresh in your minds."

The gun sank deeper into Joel's neck. Standing by the entrance, Jerama's face was without expression. Shad looked questioningly at his son, and Joel nodded.

Although his hand badly trembled, Shad's scrawl was swift and sure. Then he let the quill fall. Barney snatched the paper and handed it to his brother.

"Chief," said Will, "why don't I save us both a lot of trouble and finish these two off now?"

"First the guns, then do with them what you wish." There was a note of finality in Jerama's voice that discouraged further words on the matter.

Will scowled but holstered his .45. From his vest pocket he brought out the rawhide thongs and again bound Joel's ankles tight. Stepping back, he said to Jerama, "Then keep a close eye on 'em—the young one 'specially. Him I don't need on my trail right now. . . . We'll be back in a day or two."

When the brothers had gone, Jerama remained a moment, looking at father and son.

Joel said, "I get the notion you don't care for those two any more than we do."

These words seemed to puzzle Jerama. Finally, the old Apache spoke. "I care for no White Eyes. But if you do as I say, you will not be harmed further at my hands."

The children laid claim to the two front rows when the village assembled and the victory dance commenced. Their voices lifted in anticipation as the costumed dancers appeared, donning their animal masks and shouting for attention. They invoked the Holy People in thanksgiving, and the drums began their ceremonial beat. Soon watchers and dancers were caught up in the hypnotic rhythm. Firelight glistened on the dark legs of the dancers and flashed from the bangles that adorned their symbolic clothing.

A ripe persimmon moon hung in the sky, absorbing the

primal incantations that rose from Puma Mesa in waves to appease the hearts of whatever gods were watching and listening.

Inside the prisoners' hut, Joel continued to work on the bonds that held his hands. Suddenly, his gaze went to the wall of the hut where a section of the filigreed brush was crumbling, creating an opening that steadily widened in size. Joel signaled his father, and the two watched in fascinated silence.

Several minutes passed. Then Silverfoot's face appeared at the opening, her dark eyes taking in the scene before her.

"Come," she motioned to Joel, "we have a horse." Joel turned and started for Shad.

"No. Your father must remain for now. He will be all right."

Shad nodded. "Hurry along—see to it the rest of that rifle shipment is delayed."

Silverfoot said to Shad, "Siki will care for you." As they bolted through the opening, she produced a knife from somewhere inside her clothing, and Joel's bonds fell away like ribbon.

Outside, she broke into an easy lope, Joel close on her heels. Behind them, the dance was nearing its climax, the chanters' voices rising in unison to a monotone roar. They would hold that pitch, Joel knew, for another half hour at least. Under the moon, the mesa lay bright and empty before them, and soon the voices and drums began to subside as they raced through the night.

The black mare stood alone and untethered on the west rim, a riding blanket across her back. A filled waterskin lay on the ground nearby.

Scarcely breaking stride, Joel took the reins as he ran by, and the startled animal fell into step behind him. Silverfoot snatched up the waterskin. Within seconds, they were at the rim where the girl halted. She picked up a stone, handing it to Joel.

"Throw this as far as you can," she said, pointing into the darkness on her right. "Mouse is below. He waits for the signal." Then they were over the rim and skating crazily down the shale that fell away to the desert.

Mouse was waiting with the horses as they reached the bottom, his eyes questioning, but he said nothing. At that moment, fire opened up high on the mesa, and suddenly bullets sang and richocheted everywhere. The guard had heard them and sent for help!

As they ran for their saddles, Joel counted five rifles blazing toward the fading pink hem of sky that was still settling over the mountains to the west. The horses, eager for the run, needed no urging and covered the miles quickly.

Into the faces of the riders, the night air streamed, bearing the smells of the desert—spicy cereus, pungent creosote. When the mesas behind them began to shrink, Joel slowed his animal to a trot.

"Another few miles and we'll be clear," he said. "They're not likely to follow at night."

Mouse glanced over his shoulder. "They say the only thing about Apaches ya can count on is that they'll do what you don't count on everytime!" Joel tried to unscramble this piece of Mouse wisdom. Then, for the first time since leaving the wickiup, he looked at Silverfoot.

"That was quite a show," he said, "If I didn't know better, I'd say it was impossible. . . . how did you kow where to find us?"

Again Joel saw the pride rising in the girl's shoulders. "I had a friend," she said simply.

"I hope to meet your friend one day." She seemed satisfied to let it go at that, so Joel quickened the pace, saying, "We'll dry camp in those hills ahead."

The hills turned out to be a series of dunes formed by the winds that blew there. Still, they were tall enough to give cover, and the riders dismounted and rubbed down the horses as best they could.

Without a fire, they huddled close together, sharing a meal of hardtack and jerky. Joel considered the situation. He leaned toward a direct showdown with the Picketts in Brenner Falls. If he survived it, he'd soon know who was behind this nifty piece of ranch rustling. If he went down? He didn't let himself think about that. He had trouble enough right now without wandering into the world of "ifs."

He watched Silverfoot, unwrap the last of the hardtack, and thought he'd never seen a woman with such poise. Was it her confidence in him that inspired her calm manner? More likely her Indian blood and training. She cut the remaining loaf in halves and passed one to each man.

"We can't leave Shad up there much longer," he said. "There's no telling what Jerama will do now." His father had been through too much already. What the old man needed now was home and bed care. He needed things back to normal in a hurry.

"Silverfoot, maybe it's best if we split up in the morning. Can you get back to the ranch and tend to things?"

"Of course."

"Mouse and I have to settle it with the Picketts. With any luck, we'll soon have the answers. In any case, that rifle shipment must be stopped."

Mouse said to the girl, "I got most of the horses together in the north canyon. They shouldn't of strayed far by theyselves."

"I'll bring them in the rest of the way." Then, looking at Mouse's shoulder, she said, "The ride has reopened your wound. I'll dress it again now." Taking the last strips of linen from her saddlebag and water from her canteen, she worked at the shoulder till the skin was clean. Then, pressing what looked like dark herbs directly over the wound, she bandaged it tight and dry.

"The wound is in a bad place. You must go with care; any movement could start the bleeding."

Mouse, looking grateful but edgy, rose and stepped out into the night to inspect the terrain. Still admiring the girl's poise and skill, Joel closed his eyes, letting the warmth of his weariness wash over him. "Wake me when Mouse gets back," he said. "I'll take the first watch."

At dawn the sky was clear and cool, and the mountains to the west stood out so sharply one could almost count the needles on the piñon pines that grew there. The desert, under the new light, stirred with hidden life as once more the cycle of day began.

Down low between the dunes, Silverfoot had started a small smokeless fire of dry wood, and the coffee now bubbled and hissed as runover dripped from the pot into the flames.

The three ate quickly as Joel studied their backtrail. He took the desert in sections, starting with the land that lay farthest away, closest to the mesas, and working westward to their present position. They had covered the better part of twenty miles during the night, and the only movement he could detect was a lone turkey vulture, its bald purple head and white beak stark against the morning sky.

They finished eating, and Mouse readied the horses as Silverfoot packed up. Joel doused the remains of the fire with sand and brushed out their tracks with an uprooted rattleweed that lay nearby.

By the time the sun cleared the mesas behind them, they were already four miles to the west, starting the gradual climb out of the desert into the rolling foothills. Silverfoot rode up to Joel and touched his arm.

"I'll leave you now," she said, and pointed north toward a pass that cut between a huddle of taller mountains in the distance. The sun shone on her fine head, drawing a blue highlight from her midnight hair. Joel wanted to say something, but he wasn't sure what, so he simply nodded. "Go carefully."

She flashed a smile.

Very carefully, he thought, as he watched her disappear over a rise.

Whitney Brenner had not been the same since meeting Joel that day in the general store. Normally, hers was a lighthearted spirit, unruffled by circumstance. Of course, the circumstances of her life had been mostly favorable with a good home and well-to-do father. Though she had a disposition that leaned a little too close to vanity, she also possessed a humble streak that ran to her soul. She had a high regard for people in general, and it showed.

But lately, her mood was detached, and her handsome face carried the hint of a frown. In her jacket pocket she kept the folded poster that demanded Joel's capture, offering a thousand dollars to the person who could do the job.

Now, on a large buckskin gelding that she kept at a trot, she rode alone toward the Hollings valley. Her pace was hurried, but she had her mount in control, and her chin was set. Not used to riding such distances from town, her keen eyes showed measured fear from time to time as she crossed the series of ridges that led north to her destination.

When a strange rider appeared briefly on the skyline a mile or so ahead, her face showed no surprise. Her only reaction was to slow the buckskin to a walk and shift her trail closer to the trees that bordered the mountain on her left. A minute later the rider came into view again. She followed, staying in the shadows.

Suddenly, the rider shifted course and started up the bald mountainside. Something silver flashed on the wrist of the stranger, and she could see plainly now. A girl—an Indian girl. Whitney pulled the gelding to a stop and waited for the figure to clear the ridge before tackling the slope herself.

Atop the summit, the gelding pumped for air, and the

banker's daughter dismounted. She peered into the valley before her as a voice came from the trees. "What do you want here?"

Without turning her head, Whitney said evenly, "I come with a warning for Joel Hollings. Is this the Hollings land?"

"What is the warning?" Silverfoot stepped into the open, a rifle in her hands.

Slowly, Whitney turned and studied the Apache girl. She appeared fascinated by the other's primitive clothing. Finally, she said, "Are you Joel's friend?"

"I am his friend."

"Then you must tell him he is in danger. He is wanted by the law." Whitney reached in her pocket and handed Silverfoot the notice.

"This poster hangs in the sheriff's window in Brenner Falls."

Silverfoot studied the paper. "You come a long way to deliver your warning. Why?"

"I'd like to think that Joel is my friend, too. . . . . My name is Whitney Brenner." She extended a hand to Silverfoot, but the Indian girl ignored it.

"Joel is away now. I cannot help you."

"Will you give him the poster, then?"

"Yes, of course " Silverfoot looked into the white girl's face a moment, then lowered her eyes. "You are very beautiful. Do you know Joel well?"

"I saw him only once—when he came to town for supplies. But he's not somebody you easily forget, is he?"

Silverfoot said nothing, her eyes still fixed on the ground between them.

"Do you live at the ranch—or I should say, what's left of it?" Whitney asked.

"We will rebuild it."

"Has there been any word of the poor father?"

Once more Silverfoot looked into Whitney's eyes. Then, suddenly, she reached out her hand. "You must forgive

63

me," she said. "I am Silverfoot, and I have been rude to you. I see now you are a friend. It's just that—"

"Oh, I know! Who can one trust in such circumstances? You were not rude, Silverfoot. I understand perfectly!"

In what looked like sheer relief, the two women embraced. Then Silverfoot asked, "Are you returning to Brenner Falls today?"

"I plan to. Why?"

"Joel will be there before nightfall. He'll be looking for the brothers named Pickett. Perhaps you can find him before the sheriff knows he's in town."

"I'll do what I can," said Whitney. She gave a small laugh. "Isn't there an old Indian saying 'Sometimes you can go faster by staying in one place'?" Silverfoot nodded and smiled. Whitney swung herself up on the gelding. "To our mutual friend," she waved. "And till we meet again, Silverfoot!"

10

Cyrus Brenner paced the floor in his office and blistered the air around him with exclamations of disgust. In his hand he waved the deed to the Hollings ranch. The three Pickett brothers stood before his desk, heads down, nervously enduring the tirade.

"The damn deed's no good to me as long as Shad and Joel are alive!" he hissed. "What were you thinking of? Why didn't you finish them on the spot?"

"We wanted to, Cyrus," said Will, "but the old chief said no. He wants the rest of his rifles first."

"Then why didn't you give him the damn rifles?"

"We gave him half. Like we all agreed. We thought he'd trust us for the rest—"

"What do you mean, 'you thought.' Fact is, Pickett, you don't know how to think. . . . Where are the rifles now?"

"We got 'em stored in our warehouse. We'll be taking them up directly."

"You bet you will—before I pay you a cent more!"

The Picketts' faces all held the same expression of surprise and anger.

"We want the rest of our money now," said Will, raising his head. "Either that or you run the guns up there yourself."

These words turned the banker's face crimson with rage. "Who do you think you're talking to!" he bellowed. "You live up to our agreement, or the Pickett Teamster Company will be out of business before the sun goes down today. I'm calling in your loans!"

"Then pay half of what's owing us now and the rest later," said Will. His tone had lost some of its starch.

"Get out of here, all of you—and don't come back till you've put the Hollingses six feet under!"

There was a tense silence in the room. For a moment nobody moved.

Then Will said, "It's a mistake to threaten us, Cyrus." He slowly put on his hat and turned to leave. The brothers followed, and a moment later the banker's door clicked behind them.

Brenner walked to his desk and sat down. There was a guarded but triumphant smile on his cherublike face as he opened the deed papers in his hand and studied them.

Through the bandages, Mouse's shoulder was showing red again, and Joel was worried as the lights of town came in sight.

"We'll see the doctor here if they've got one; maybe sew in some stitches."

"It's all right," the little man grinned. "First things first—this shoulder'll be around long after them Picketts is pushin' up petunias."

"Still we better have a look," Joel insisted. They crossed the last rise and descended into the town where a few late shoppers were scurrying home from the stores that still showed lights. Across from the bank, Joel saw Gilly in the entrance of the livery stable, sweeping out the last of the day's dust.

"Hey, Gilly," he called.

"Joel!" Gilly's face showed amazement.

"Got a stall for two tired ponies?"

Gilly urgently waved them into the stable. "Don't you know your face is plastered all over the sheriff's window!"

"It was just a matter of time."

"They're offering a grand for you?"

"Dead or alive?"

"No, alive."

"Who said the law is heartless."

When the ponies were bedded down, Joel said, "We've got a bad shoulder here, Gilly. This town have a doctor?" The boy looked at Mouse, then at the wet stain near his armpit.

"Doc Bowman—he's mostly retired, but he still lives here. Want me to fetch him?"

"I'd appreciate that, Gilly—but don't say any more than you have to, all right?"

"The doc, he ain't nosy, if that's what you mean. I'll be back—you can put your friend in my room if you like."

"Thanks. He can use the rest."

Mouse went up to the tiny room at the back of the stable and stretched out while Joel unburdened himself of hat and vest, rolled a smoke, and stood in the thick shadows of the doorway, watching Main Street close down for the night. He wondered where the Picketts were and what they'd done with the ranch papers. They couldn't have started back to the mesa, he knew. He'd had their backtrail blocked all day.

At that moment, the front door of the bank opened across the street, and a small man in a tight suit stepped out. He looked up at the sky. Joel knew that face. From where? The man turned and locked the door. Then, halfway across the street, he spotted Joel in the shadows. Smiling tentatively, he peered forward, trying to see who it was.

"Evening, puncher. Nice night for walking after a day behind the desk."

At the sound of the man's voice, the picture came back. He was a small boy again . . . standing beside Shad . . . looking over a desk at this man . . . the banker, Brenner . . . Sidney? Cyrus? He remembered Shad didn't like him, but the loan was necessary to develop the ranch.

"Couldn't be nicer," Joel agreed.

Brenner tipped his hat and walked on. Several minutes later, Gilly returned with the doctor, a fat, disheveled man permanently bent forward at the waist. Without introductions, they moved to the back room where Mouse lay. The doctor set down his bag and went to work.

"How long have you had this?" asked Bowman when the bandage was off.

"Couple of days, I reckon."

"These herbs are a nice touch. They've kept most of the infection out and greatly stemmed the bleeding. You must have Indian friends?"

"Now and again." Mouse winked at Gilly. The doctor continued, working in silence. When he finished, he drew Joel aside.

"This man shouldn't ride for at least a week. The wound needs a start at healing."

"Thanks, doc." Joel handed him several pieces of silver. When Bowman had gone, he said to the others, "I don't know about you two, but I could eat the bark off a cottonwood about now."

"I'll fetch some grub from the hotel," said Gilly.

"You know Lucy over there?"

"Sure—nice lady."

"Tell her it's for the puncher who needs 'a wife and mother.' She'll understand." Gilly left, smiling and shaking his head.

Joel sat down in a chair and looked at the little man who had fallen asleep and was now breathing easily. Mouse couldn't be much help to him, he knew. Anyway, it wouldn't be right to ask him. He'd already given all he could—and without complaint. No, it began to look more and more like Joel Hollings against the world—against the Picketts, the sheriff, and the man behind the attack on his family. . . . That was the lineup of players. Well, hell, he'd faced these sorts of odds before and somehow got through. He'd damn well do it again.

When he opened his eyes, Lucy was standing in front of him, two covered trays under her arm. She was saying, "What'll it be tonight—wife or mother?"

Joel grinned. "Right now, how about 'mother.' I'm starving."

Mouse and Joel ate like a couple of grizzlies in springtime, hardly pausing to pull on the scalding coffee that Lucy poured from one of the silver pots from the hotel.

"You see, Mouse," said Joel. "You're eating in style at last—silver service and everything."

Mouse hadn't noticed but now inspected his gleaming fork with a mixture of awe and curiosity.

"I suppose it's purdy," he said, "but it don't make a pork chop taste no different—dresses things up a bit, is all." Still, Mouse continued to admire the utensil, turning it over in his hand.

Lucy studied Joel; her gentle eyes were serious. "Did you really kill a man in Virginia City?"

"I'm afraid so."

When the inevitable question didn't come, he filled in for her. "It was self-defense. The poster doesn't say that."

"Over a card hand?" Lucy persisted.

"Guilty again."

"What will you do now?"

"The only sensible thing to do is clear out of here as fast as possible. I don't want you and Gilly implicated."

"Don't worry on my account," the boy offered. "I never go near the sheriff's office. Besides, I can't read, anyhow."

Lucy gathered up the trays and dishes. She was plainly troubled.

"I read character pretty good," she said, "My business is people, and this doesn't wash. If I can help further, you let me know."

"I'll do that, Lucy. We're very grateful. Maybe we can drink some beers sometime?"

"I'd like that," she said. Then, with the service wrapped carefully in a linen tablecloth, the crippled waitress let herself out the back door of the stable.

Joel walked to the entrance and once more studied the activity on Main Street. Full darkness had settled in, and the chalky thoroughfare lay deep and silent under the new moon. Time for action.

He turned, saddled the mare, and went back to check on Mouse. His feisty companion had fallen asleep again. Joel said to Gilly. "I'm going out for a while. Look after Mouse, will you?"

"No problem, Joel. I'll tend to him. And there's a cot I'll set up for you."

"You use the cot, Gilly. I'll sleep with the mare. The hay's fresh. . . . We'll be moving out before dawn."

Using his horse to shield him, he stepped out into the street and moved quickly to the corner, turning into the darkness at the mouth of an alley. There he mounted and took the back streets to the west edge of town where he cut across a rise and joined the main road leading to the teamsters place. He said to the mare, "Let's see what the brothers Pickett are up to tonight, girl."

The warehouse sat dark and quiet under the trees, a single shaft of moonlight illuminating the corral and three dozing horses that bunched there. As before, he approached the building on foot, stepping noiselessly from window to window. At the storeroom he paused and looked in. Over his shoulder, the moon poked just enough light to show that the room was empty.

The rifles were gone!

Joel heard a voice whisper his name. The sound seemed to come from the trees across the road. He drew his .44 and stood motionless.

"Joel Hollings!" The voice came again. "Over here— you don't need the gun. I'm a friend!"

70

Out of the shadows, the slender figure of Whitney Brenner appeared, her honey-blond hair aglow in the halflight, the buckskin at her heels.

He put up his gun. "Miss Brenner. What brings you out here?"

"Whitney, please."

"Whitney, then."

"I suppose you know about the poster?"

"Yes—the timing couldn't be worse."

"Silverfoot told me you'd be coming to the Picketts', so I rode here directly."

"You've been at the ranch?"

"I went there to warn you about the notice."

Joel said nothing, and the girl continued; "You missed the brothers. . . . About an hour ago, they loaded up two mules with rifles and went out through those foothills heading east."

"All three of them?"

"Yes, all three."

"Why are you doing this? Helping a wanted man, that is?"

"I don't believe the poster. Besides, I'm not known for my rational behavior. . . . My father may be a banker, but I'm afraid practicality in the family stopped with him."

For a moment Joel studied the girl. "How did your father like my hat?"

"He loves it! Won't take it off." Whitney's eyes turned suddenly serious. "Joel, I'm sorry about your brother and father. I didn't know—"

"No way you could know. But thank you."

"You'd better get started if you want to catch up to the teamsters. By the way, where are they going with all those rifles?"

Joel could see the girl knew nothing. "No telling where they're headed." Wasn't any use feeding the tongue of the town till he knew who the enemy was.

"You take care of yourself," she whispered. "We'll talk about Joel Hollings the outlaw next time."

As she climbed on her horse, she threw him a last quizzical look.

"Self-defense?"

"Self-defense."

11

AN HOUR'S RIDE on horseback is a long head start to give anybody, but Joel knew the Picketts' mules would slow things down and he'd overtake them long before they reached the Apache camp in the mesas. He had another edge: the teamsters didn't know the chase was on.

So he took his time walking back up the road to the black mare who stood in the trees, nibbling loose bark that peeled from the cottonwoods. He mounted and chose a northern course where he could ride with the grain of the land, staying in tight on the shoulders of the ridges, well down and out of sight of the skyline.

Once under way, the sure-footed mare moved quickly and silently, trotting most of the time but loping whenever the trail dipped to the flat land in the valley bottoms. The Picketts were somewhere ahead and to the south, he guessed, proceeding along the main road that led east.

He thought about Whitney as he rode, traces of her cologne still in his head. She was an exciting woman, all right. In fact, she had it all. What was troubling him, then? In her childlike frankness there was a kind of sadness, a vulnerability. He wrestled with it awhile, and coming up with no answers, put the matter on a back burner.

Sometime later, he was certain he'd outflanked the teamsters. He pulled up and climbed on foot to the summit of a rise off to his right. The moon was new, and from somewhere in his childhood memories came the lines:

73

I saw the old moon with
the new moon in her arms.

He'd guessed right. Below and a mile to the south lay the central route used by stagecoaches and the settlers' wagons moving west. Two miles east, the trail snaked into a pass, and Joel decided to wait for the Picketts there.

The pass was narrow, with red rock abruptly rising on either side. Thirty feet up on the north slope, he picked a niche that offered good cover and an unlimited view. Then he led the mare farther into the pass around a turn and dropped her reins to the ground. "Good girl," he said. "Stay here and keep your voice down."

Joel hadn't long to wait. From his perch on the slope above the pass he heard the shambling click of horses' hooves and strained to pick up any silhouettes that offered themselves. Then he saw them—three riders, five animals. They plodded steadily into the pass, expecting nothing.

When they were directly below him, he called out, "Hold it right there! The first man to draw a gun is dead."

One of the Picketts' horses reared, nearly dumping its rider, but the caravan instantly halted.

"Get off your horses and stand away," said Joel. "I'm coming down."

Maybe it was the darkness, or maybe Joel got careless. In any case, he didn't see the rifle barrel, still in its sheath, rotate upward. He heard only the crashing and ricochet of the bullet as his hat was cleanly lifted from his head.

When he looked again, they were scattering, scrambling for cover up the opposite slope. Another bullet crashed on the rock in front of him, stinging his face with a spray of granite.

So much for a bloodless coup, he thought! It would be all business from here in. Spotting a figure climbing frantically toward the ridge, he raised his rifle and hurried a shot. Too high! He fired again, but the man was over the top and

74

running, hunched low, giving him little to aim for. Again a bullet slammed into the rock that shielded him, loudly echoing down the canyon walls. They had their shooting angles now and were neatly pinning him down!

In the pale light he saw an exposed leg and pumped a whistler in that direction. There was a muffled cry and the sound of rocks breaking loose, then silence.

A voice came from the left—his side of the pass!

"Hollings!"

It was close. Too close.

"Come out of there peaceful or we'll cut ya to ribbons. I've got ya in my sights!"

Joel crouched still lower, looking for a shape to go with the voice. Then he saw his man, above and to the left, standing erect, rifle at his shoulder, not a hundred feet away! From the hair bushing out under the hat, Joel recognized Barney Pickett. Sick inside, he waited for the rifle's bark, the impact of the bullet.

But the shot came from a different direction—from somewhere near the mouth of the pass. He saw Barney recoil, then topple sideways down the slope in a clatter of rocks, coming to rest against a shrub that poked out of the hill. Barney's rifle continued down the slope without him, skittering and banging all the way to the bottom.

For a moment, the only sound to be heard was the crickets. Then Will's voice came tentatively through the darkness. "Barney? You okay, Barney?"

A second shot flashed from the floor of the pass, sending a figure leaping from cover on the hill opposite. Joel heard the cry of Will Pickett. "Gawdammit, how many are out there!"

Joel responded, "Enough to take you down, Will. Barney's dead. You want to join him?"

There was a scrabbling sound and muttered curses. Then Jack and Will Pickett emerged from the rocks, making a run for the horses. Jack was limping badly.

When Will veered to grab the reins of the mules, Joel buried a shot at his feet that changed his mind. Then Will had both revolvers smoking to cover their retreat. As their horses streaked on through the pass, Joel picked up Will's roar above the commotion.

"If Barney's dead, Hollings, you'll wish you'd never heard the name Pickett!"

Joel started down the slope at a dead run, leaping the last six feet to the trail. There he slowed up. Hell with it, he thought. The Picketts could wait. First, he'd find out who was behind the extra gun that broke up the crossfire.

"Who's out there?" he called.

"It's me, ya piteefull excuse fer a gunfighter!" Mouse appeared around the side of a boulder. "I figgurd I better trail along 'n wet nurse ya, seein's how ya got such a nose fer trouble!"

Joel rolled his eyes and turned away. "Mouse, I'm not sure I ever met a man like you." He managed to hide the smile.

"There ain't probably another man stupid enough to foller' ya around 'n wipe yer nose fer ya!"

From the hill came a groan. Barney was up on one elbow, attempting to rise. He didn't make it and sunk back against the shrub that had broken his fall. They went to where he lay and tried to ease his pain. Joel removed and folded his jacket, slipping it under the big man's head.

"Don't bother, Hollings. I ain't gonna make it."

Joel saw that the bullet had passed through the chest just below the heart.

"I'm sorry, Barney. We both did what we had to."

"I ain't complainin'. I just want ya to know it warn't nothin' personal—"

"Easy."

Small bubbles of blood formed at the corners of the wounded man's lips. That was it, then—the bullet had found a lung.

76

"I always wanted to bust loose of them two. . . . Couldn't never seem to do it. . . . I'm big but not so strong of mind. . . .

Barney's eyes began to congeal. "Hollings, will ya bury me here—away from the others?"

Joel nodded.

"I'll tell ya everythin', Holl—"

But the teamster was gone.

Joel slowly walked to the mules and removed a folding military shovel. He found some soft ground under an outcropping of rock well back from the trail and began to dig. Mouse located a flat stone and began carving the letters. When they finished, Joel took the marker and set it in over the head.

BARNEY PICKETT
A rite-harted man
SLEEPS HERE.

The Brenner house was dark except for a living-room lamp that poured light out on the veranda. The banker sat alone, sipping brandy. He called to his daughter, but there was no response.

"Whitney!" he called again. "Not feeling up to playing this evening?"

Presently, the girl appeared at the filigreed screen door. She looked at the back of her father's head in silence. Finally, she said, "I'm tired tonight, Dad—if you don't mind."

"What did you do today? You hardly said a word at dinner."

"Oh, shopped a little, then took the buckskin out for some exercise."

"Go anywhere special?"

"Nowhere special. We found an old trail in the mountains and followed it awhile."

77

"Whitney, come sit with me. Something's on your mind." The banker was alert, his small eyes searching his daughter's face. Whitney came out and took a chair, but her head was turned away toward the garden.

"Since I'm a banker," he said, "I suppose I'll have to offer a *dollar* for your thoughts."

"Dad, what is the business you're doing with the Picketts?"

"What do you mean?"

"In your office the other day you said you bailed Jack Pickett out of jail because you two had some business together."

"Oh, that. We're selling some rifles, is all."

"Who's buying?"

The father darted a glance at his daughter. Her eyes were still on the garden. "Whitney, can I ask what all this is about?"

"I'm just curious. Who's buying the rifles?"

Brenner's face reddened in the shadows, and his tone seemed a bit stiffer than normal. "I honestly can't say. I picked them up cheap at a sale. The customer was Pickett's, not mine."

"Do you know that Joel Hollings was in town tonight?" Whitney asked. With these words she turned her eyes full on her father.

He looked as if he'd been shot in the back. Recovering too quickly, he tipped his glass, and brandy sloshed on his pant leg.

"Holl—oh, the young man wanted by the sheriff. No, I didn't know. How is it you know?"

"I saw him on my way home," said Whitney.

"Way home!" Cyrus was on his feet. "You mean that killer is running around loose in the vicinity of our home?"

Whitney looked to be smiling, but her eyes were cold as stone. "I think he's gone now. Besides, he's not a killer. He's wanted for questioning."

78

"Killer or not, I don't want him near my house or in my town! He has some nerve showing up here again. Why, his picture's pasted in practically every shop!"

The girl rocked back in her chair and stared at the sky. "I think the Picketts are somehow mixed up in this thing—and the rifles, too," she said.

"Mixed up in *what* thing! What are you talking about, girl?"

"The attack on Joel's ranch—the kidnapping of his father."

"Poppycock!"

"You said yourself you don't know who's buying those rifles. Could be it's the Indians . . ."

Suddenly, Cyrus straightened his coat, smiled, and sat down. "Lord a'mighty, Whitney, you'd make some sleuth. I'm just glad you're not on my trail! But in this matter you're quite wrong. The Pickett boys are a bit rough-and-tumble, but they're good boys at heart. Why, remember last Fourth of July? They put on the fireworks show for the whole town. No, the Picketts are all right in my book."

Whitney had risen as her father talked and was headed inside. As she passed through the screen door, she said, "And what book is that, Dad?"

Inside the sheriff's office at Brenner Falls, Tom Sweeney listened quietly to the harangue being delivered by his early-morning visitor—a jaunty, wound-up spring of a man who reeked efficiency in a large dose. Like Sweeney, he wore a star on his shirt. Between them on the desk lay the WANTED poster of Joel Hollings.

"Look, Sweeney, 'wanted for murder' means WANTED FOR MURDER. You know the routine, and I got a job to do—with your help or without it!"

"Simmer down, Barnes. I didn't say I wouldn't help. I merely asked about the shooting—card game, wasn't it?"

"Like it says on the poster," Barnes snapped.

"Mind telling me about it?"

Barnes impatiently raised his eyes to the ceiling but after a moment said, "All right. I wasn't called in till after, but this is the story the marshal bought: Hollings was in a game where stakes were high. He has a way with cards and was winning, like he mostly does. The game thinned down to Joel and this miner. Both were bidding their hand up when the miner ran out of silver and Hollings wouldn't take collateral.

"So the man folded with three tens. When Joel reached for the pot, the miner flipped Joel's hand over, showing a pair of sixes. Course it wasn't his right to do this, but naturally he was bitter to be forced out of the game with a winning hand, and he said some things to Hollings.

"Apparently, Joel punched him through the table, drew and fired. . . . The most damning thing was that the man wasn't wearing a gun."

"There'll be a trial, of course," said Sweeney.

"Of course, but we've got to catch him first!"

Tom thought a minute and said, "Like I told you earlier, I only met Joel once—when he reported that Apache raid. No one's seen him since, so I suppose the logical place to start is at the ranch. It's north of here. Brenner, the banker, knows. He's lent the family crop money."

Jake Barnes rose. "You coming along? It's just me, and I could use the help."

"I'll get some men together. We'll ride with you."

12

JOEL AND MOUSE started back to the valley with the rifle-ladened mules in tow. For more than an hour Joel was silent, thinking. Since he couldn't take on Jerama and the Apaches alone, he decided the best course was to consolidate his small forces at the ranch and wait out the Picketts. He knew it was just a matter of time till they came after the rifles. Whoever they were working for wasn't likely to settle for a job half done—not a job this size, anyway. Well, he'd be ready for them.

Mouse, too, was strangely silent. Brooding silent. Finally, the little man said; "I never killed a man before."

"It's not a good feeling—but it couldn't be helped."

"Dead's fer eternity, ain't it?" asked Mouse.

"Depends on how you see it," Joel was amused by Mouse's philosophical turns of mind.

"How long is eternity, anyhow?"

Joel thought a moment, then replied; "The Indians have a way of describing it—it's the best I've heard so far."

"So?"

"So, picture a mesa a thousand miles long, a thousand miles wide, and a thousand miles high. . . . Once every million years a hummingbird comes and for a few minutes sharpens it bill on the side of that mountain. When the entire mesa is worn away, one moment of eternity will have passed."

That seemed to do it. Mouse gave a shrug of resignation and let the matter go.

Joel went back to his earlier thoughts. In addition to the Picketts, he knew the law would soon be heading north, looking for him. All the more reason to be on familiar ground when the crisis came.

"How's the shoulder?" Joel asked.

Mouse looked at his wound. "No more blood—I guess she's startin' to heal, awright."

The mountains ahead loomed larger and Joel picked up the pace.

"With luck," he said, "we'll be inside the valley by morning." They could see piñon trees now high above them, and off to the left, the moon, its persimmon bleached out, was starting a last descent to the western horizon.

They arrived at the pass before dawn, and by the time they crossed the creek below, a new sun was easing over their shoulders.

Silverfoot stood in the corral, feeding the horses, her slight figure moving from trough to trough. When she saw the riders emerge from the last line of trees she waved and started for the house.

Joel went to the cellar locker in the floor of the burned-out barn and stowed the rifles down deep below the sacks of staples, out of sight. He closed and covered the door with some half-burned boards. Any searchers would have to be good and know what they were looking for, he thought. Then he stripped the packsaddles from the mules and shooed the animals into the trees, where they began grazing.

"You found two good mules." Silverfoot smiled as the men stamped their boots and entered the kitchen.

"Funny thing," said Mouse, "they was standin' alone, abandoned in a pass to the south. . . . My gawd, Silverfoot, I never in my life smelled bacon'n coffee any better'n that!" Mouse went to the fire, got down three cups, and passed the steaming brew around. The girl heaped bacon and biscuits onto their plates, and they all sat down at the oak table.

As they ate, Joel was piecing together a plan. "We'll have visitors soon, and it won't do for them to find us bottled up here in the house. . . . I don't know who'll show first, the Picketts or the law. Either way, we'll need a vantage point."

"There's a cave on the south slope, up high near the ridge," said Mouse. "We could hole up there out'a sight— it gives a bird's-eye view'a the whole valley."

"Good. But we'll have to act fast. Silverfoot, get some grub together and be ready to move out in ten minutes. We'll need enough supplies for a week or more. Mouse and I will load up the ammunition, then strip the place of clues."

When they finished eating, the three moved quickly, like a precision team that had been together a long time. Minutes later, the smell of fried bacon in the air was the only sign the place had been recently inhabited.

They crossed the creek where Silverfoot filled three waterskins, then headed south along the border of a rocky meadow. From time to time, Joel cast a look at the main pass to the east. Soon they were climbing under the cover of trees. They passed within feet of a doe and her fawn, which looked up from their gazing—calm and curious—before lowering their heads again to more serious matters.

Presently, Mouse, who'd taken the point, signaled and the group halted. Off to the left, partly screened by pines, the mouth of a cave gaped over the valley below. Joel studied the location, the paths of access and retreat. The setting was just about perfect.

Turning to Mouse, he said, "Is there anything like this spot on the east slope?"

"There's a small hollow just below the pass."

"What's the view to the valley?"

"Good, if I 'member rightly," said Mouse.

"You set up over there, then. Take supplies and firepower. That way we'll control the pass—who gets in and gets out." As Mouse departed, Joel said, "Signal when you get settled in—and remember, the aim just now is not to be seen. If any shooting is necessary, I'll give the sign."

Morning moved across the valley, swallowing the last of the shadows and filling the sky with tiny plum-colored clouds. Far below and to the west, Joel could see the ranch house and the corral that held the Arabians. To the north he saw the cattle standing quietly in the fields. He went to the lip of the cave and set up shop among a cluster of rocks that gave good cover. There he leaned his two rifles and spread a half-dozen cartridge belts on the ground beneath. Then he sat down to wait.

Minutes later, Mouse appeared in a rocky clearing below the pass. He waved his rifle and Joel raised his arm, acknowledging the signal.

Inside the cave, Silverfoot had finished setting up camp and came out and sat by her companion. After that there was just silence and the whine of insects. A circle of gnats found Joel's ear, which had started to sweat under the thickening heat of day.

An hour passed, then two and three. Just before noon, Silverfoot touched Joel's shoulder and nodded to the tree line at the foot of the east slope. In single file, nine horsemen slowly emerged from the trees and made their way across the meadow toward the ranch house. Joel spotted Tom Sweeney in the lead; he seemed to be studying the hillside beyond the ranch.

Just behind Sweeney rode another familiar figure. Joel's heart sank—Jake Barnes! So now it was all business, and Joel knew it would take the best thinking he could muster to outwit that bulldog.

Long before the riders reached the corral, Sweeney signaled a halt, and the group spread out on foot in all directions. In the absence of cover, Sweeney and Barnes crouched and proceeded toward the house.

Through the morning air, Joel heard Sweeney's faint cry. "Hollings!" The sheriff cupped his hands to his mouth. "Hollings! Step out if you're in there. We've got charges to discuss!"

After a few minutes, the two lawmen straightened up and boldly walked into the ruins. The other seven converged on the building like ants on a dead bee. There was much shouting among the men as they combed the site for anything that might suggest Joel's whereabouts.

Sweeney stepped out on the porch and stood there for a long while, scanning the walls of the valley. At one point, his eyes settled on the rocks where the fugitive lay hidden, and Joel felt a tingle in the small of his back. Then the sheriff's eyes moved on, completing their round of the valley.

Suddenly, one of the posse who had joined Sweeney on the porch excitedly pointed toward the east ridge.

"Jesus!" Joel muttered, "they've spotted Mouse."

Then the men were shouting and running for their horses. Joel grabbed Silverfoot and scrambled back from the ledge.

"Let's go!" he said. "I hope to God Mouse left himself a back door."

The posse was still pounding across the meadow when Joel and Silverfoot topped the south ridge heading west. They didn't stop or look behind but spurred everything they could get from the horses that carried them. Joel ached to know how Mouse handled it after being sighted. He was probably doing just what they were, but no telling which direction he'd pick for his escape. At least he wasn't on the law's WANTED list and should be all right even if Sweeney and Barnes caught up with him.

They rode all out toward the denser, younger mountains to the west; the Indian girl held her own just off the black mare's flank as rise after rise sank away behind them. They climbed on the shoulders of the foothills and turned south, following the north-south line of the range. When sweat began to lather on the necks of the ponies and they were blowing hard, Joel cut the pace back to a trot, then, minutes later, to a walk.

Soon they were high in the mountains, moving through a forest of piñons that crowded up to the edge of a sheer cliff. Getting down from their horses, they moved to a perch above the wall where, for miles, they could see their backtrail. The trees gave off the cool scent of pine, and they heard a creek somewhere in the forest behind them.

They both saw the rider at the same time. Below, maybe two miles back, the unmistakable silhouette of Mouse had just come over a rise. Silverfoot was smiling. And then she wasn't smiling.

Three miles back of Mouse, a small band of riders in a hurry kicked up a shaft of dust that said they, too, were on a trail.

"Do you think he knows?" asked Joel.

"He knows," said the girl. "See how he picks only the rock to ride over."

Silverfoot moved closer to the cliff and stood in the open. Suddenly, Mouse was waving. She waved briefly, then stepped back.

"He sees us." She said. "We can wait and still have time enough."

But it seemed an eternity before they heard Mouse's horse in the trees. When he came in, he was lavishly cussing.

"They must'a picked up the glint from my rifle back there. I took the chance ya'd come west, what with all these mountains to hide in."

Joel's tone was somber. "Who's wiping whose nose now?" The words had the desired effect. Mouse started cussing all over again, but this time not at himself. Silverfoot and Joel mounted up, and the trio left that place.

The Apache girl took the lead and was urging her horse up a steep incline where the pines thinned out. Still ruffled,

Mouse called out from the rear, "I suppose ya know this land, too, missy!"

She smiled and without turning her head answered, "If it's still standing, there's a miner's cabin in a valley to the north, but we must hide our tracks."

Joel showed surprise at this unexpected source of local lore.

"From here in?" he asked.

"No, when we come to the creek."

The sound of water grew louder as they came over and passed down the inner slope. Between the trees they caught sight of the silver ribbon that was the stream; it was alive with determination as it swept among the stones. When Silverfoot pointed upstream, he knew what had to be done and wasted no time getting started.

How many times had this ploy been worked—to plant false track leading out of the water a short distance, hoping to fool would-be pursuers? More than once Joel had been foxed by it, but he knew Barnes too well to believe he'd be taken in. The common pattern was to show a false trail going in the opposite direction from one's true course. Joel decided to add a new twist.

He waved Mouse and Silverfoot into the creek behind him and plodded against the current for a quarter of a mile. At a sandy patch along the east bank, they left the stream and headed east, covering another quarter mile before pulling up under trees where the earth wore a mantle of pine needles. Here he dismounted, removed a blanket from his saddle roll and began cutting it in squares. Twelve in all. He wrapped and tied the sections around the mare's hooves. With the remaining squares, Mouse and Silverfoot did the same. Then they moved north through more trees. When he was satisfied about the distance, they veered left, back to the creek, and high-stepped across in shallow water. On the far bank, he waited for the others to get clear, then brushed away any sign of the crossing with a pine branch. They rode for another mile before removing the hoof covers.

The last shafts of sun were gone, and the sky was darkening with clouds and approaching night when Silverfoot pointed to a small cabin high on the mountain before them. Half hidden by the trees, the structure was canted sideways, as though it could tumble off the hill at any moment. They made their way up and came in at the site from behind. From the looks of things, nobody had used the place in years. The roof was caved in at one corner, but the door stood tight and locked. Mouse tried a window at the side, and surprisingly it gave.

Inside, an army cot sagged above a frayed hook rug. Two rough-hewn chairs were stacked in one corner near a cast-iron stove, and a few pans, clean but rusty with disuse, were piled there. An old hat hung from a peg on the wall.

Outside, there was precious little flat space for the horses—no barn at all. As dark settled in, the cold came with it, and the two men stripped and fed the horses, lightly watering them from one of the skins they emptied into a cooking pot. Then, leading the animals a short distance back in the trees, they hobbled them on long leads and returned to the shack.

Silverfoot had gathered some deadfall and lit a fire in the stove, which began to groan and pop as the metal expanded with the first waves of heat. She wiped out two pans and began preparing a dinner of *refritos,* fried potatoes, hardtack, and coffee. Before going in, Joel checked the small chimney that pushed up through the roof. The dry wood gave off little smoke, and what there was of it burned white—scarcely visible.

Mouse unstacked the chairs and sat down, his eyes softening to the heat and firelight. Joel took blankets and spread them on the cot.

"Lay down here, puncher, and give that shoulder some rest."

"Silverfoot gits the cot," Mouse said. "My patch is still holdin':"

Presently, the smell of coffee and *papas fritas* filled the cabin with the promise of full stomachs.

Joel's boot struck a loose floorboard. He tossed back the tattered rug, revealing a trap door. With his hunting knife, he pried at the opening and lifted the board free. Inside was a shallow cellar with earth walls about three feet square. Reaching down with both hands, he pulled up a sack of badly decomposed onions and a dusty bottle of wine.

"Lookee here, Mouse. Some fancy trimmings for your dinner! First silver service from Lucy, now vintage wine all the way from California!

Mouse looked at the bottle suspiciously. "They got any beer down there?"

13

JAKE BARNES GOT down off his horse and knelt beside the creek where three sets of horse tracks were visible in the soft earth. Abruptly, they disappeared into the wake of white water. For a long time he squatted there, deep in thought. Sweeney and the other men had pulled up in the trees behind him, giving their horses a blow. They'd been moving fast for the past five hours, and the men were grateful for a rest. Finally, Barnes stood up.

"Which way would you go, Sweeney, if you were the fox in this chase?"

Sweeney looked tired but patient. "I suppose I'd go upstream," he said.

"I would, too," said Barnes. "Let's you and me go have a look. Meantime, send a couple of men to check the downstream, just in case."

It didn't take long for the two sheriffs to find what they were looking for. Barnes smiled as they spurred their horses onto the east bank and began to track the sign left by Joel and his party. When they reached the trees where Joel had muffled the horses' hooves, the wiry Barnes again dismounted; this time his face showed irritation.

"What the hell's going on here? Tracks don't just disappear unless those ponies have wings!"

He got back on his horse, rode out about two hundred feet, and began tracing a circle around the area.

Ten minutes later, he returned and said to Sweeney, "If

they covered their ponies' feet, it was a good job—but a little patience is all that's needed here. we'll pick up the traces again."

"It'll be dark soon," Sweeney said. "Maybe we ought to make camp and go after it again in the morning."

Barnes grunted reluctantly, and Sweeney called down to the others.

Later, over coffee at the fire, Barnes said, "I never liked Hollings, and don't ask me why—a bit too arrogant, maybe."

"You heard about the attack on his ranch and family, I guess?" Sweeney unbuckled his guns and poured more coffee.

"I heard, but that's got nothing to do with me." Barnes said.

"No, it doesn't," Sweeney agreed. "But there's a lot of things going wrong in that kid's life right now."

"Life's tough on all of us now and then; ain't that right?" Barnes turned his face up and coldly smiled at the older man.

Sweeney's eyes tightened. "You're a hell of a tracker, Barnes. I'll give you that. But I wouldn't give two dimes for the heart that beats under that badge of yours."

Barnes merely shrugged and took another pull at his coffee.

Tom Sweeney was awakened by a rough hand on his shoulder and a voice at his ear. It was Barnes.

"Rise and shine, Sweeney. It's hunting time. I found their trail!"

Sweeney opened his eyes, taking in the unfamiliar landscape around him. He nodded to the Nevada sheriff and climbed out of his blankets. One of the men had a fire going, and some of the others were gathered around, tin cups in hand, waiting for the coffee.

"There's rain on the way," said Barnes. "Let's get moving before the tracks wash out."

91

Sweeney looked at the threatening sky and felt the sharp night air that still clung to the ground in pockets.

"You found sign in this half-light?" He was impressed.

"It's not a matter of light. It's knowing where to look."

With the news that tracks had been found, the men came fully awake and moved quickly. They finished their coffee and saddled up the horses. Within ten minutes they were mounted and ready to ride.

Barnes led the way north along the creek and crossed over where the flat stones formed a natural bridge.

"Here's where they came out!" he called back to the others. "Now keep it up close. Nobody fall behind." To Sweeney, who rode beside him, he said, "Can you guess where they might be headed?"

"There's no settlements up this way I know of. Only thing I remember is a miner's shack north of here somewhere."

"That's a good bet," said Barnes, "If the trail washes out, we'll go to the cabin. . . . Think you can find it?"

"I reckon I can," said Sweeney.

The sky had steadily been gaining weight, and the first spatters of rain fell on the small column of men that twisted its way north through the trees. Then the sky opened up and pounded them, and Barnes began to curse. Within minutes, nothing on the ground or in the air looked the same. The earth turned black and silver slick; the pines looked hysterical, groaning and swaying under the force of the storm.

Barnes signaled a halt and rose in his stirrups, watching the last of the tracks melt away. His face was dark with anger.

"Okay, sheriff," he said, "show us that cabin you're talking about!"

Sweeney signaled to the men and turned his horse west through a meadow where the grass stood three feet deep in places. He climbed a small rise and turned north again, proceeding along the shoulder of a mountain until the level places gave out. Here he paused, then spurred his horse upward, straight at the peak of the mountain.

It was slippery going. Already rivulets had begun to form and gather momentum on the hillside, and the horses were having a bad time of it.

Two hundred yards from the top, Barnes caught up with Sweeney.

"What the hell are you doing!" he yelled through the flattening wind. "This is no goddamn trail in *any* weather—a man and his horse are down back there!"

"We'll cut the distance by an hour or better," roared Sweeney. He didn't try to say more but kept spurring his pony, scrambling and sliding, till he reached the summit. One by one the men came in after him, their faces white. They couldn't believe they'd made it.

Sweeney strained to make out the valleys below. The rain came thick and hard, blurring all but the general contours of the land. Still, he saw what he needed to and waved the men on. The down-trail slope was gentler, and sensing the worst was over, the men exchanged smiles of relief. Barnes rode just behind Sweeney, saying nothing.

A half hour later the rain eased up, and the cloud cover split apart, letting sun shafts through to stand in the grass of the countryside. A rainbow, preposterously bright, arched over them, and they wound their way off the mountain.

Sweeney kept a course north by northwest for the better part of the morning, crossing over canyons and arroyos still alive with water from the sudden rain. Then, from a stand of second-growth pine that covered a valley bottom, he spotted the shack high above. Silverfoot was out front washing shirts in a wooden tub, her black hair mirroring the brightness of the new sky. He signaled Barnes, who rode up quickly. When the Nevadan saw the girl, he froze.

"Apaches!"

"I don't think so. They say the Hollings have Apache girl help."

"That's the cabin?"

Sweeney nodded. "But now I see it again, I think we'd do better coming in from above."

"How long will it take?"

"Hour, maybe."

Barnes fixed his eyes on the cabin.

"If a few of us could get up there quietly, we might box them in . . . What do you think, Sweeney? Will they give us a scrap?"

"Hard to say. You know the boy better'n me."

The Nevadan drew his revolver and checked the cylinders for the third time that day.

"Well, if it's the same kid I knew in Virginia City, I'd say he'll come out shooting." Barnes turned his horse back and began organizing the men.

A few minutes later, Barnes and three of the posse made their way from the trees and skirted the northern base of the hill. They moved cautiously, staying to the needle beds that lay deep under the piñons.

While the two sheriffs had talked at the foot of the mountain, Joel and Mouse watched from a rock cluster just above the shack. Then, as the four men below started their approach on the north slope, Joel said, "I'll set up over there, right above them. You stay here and watch for movement from the others. If they start to climb, let them have it hard and fast!"

Joel draped several belts of cartridges across his shoulders and crawled away. The noon sun stood hot in the sky, and the only sounds on the mountain came from two jays disputing territorial hunting rights. Joel crossed the hill directly above the cabin, noting the silence there; Silverfoot had disappeared inside. He continued on till the shoulder of the hill turned. There he set up and waited.

The face of Jake Barnes was first to come in sight, and Joel, rifle raised, had a bead on his two front teeth.

"That's far enough, Barnes!" he yelled. The four men scattered as though dynamite had been tossed in their midst.

"Hollings!" yelled Barnes. "I have a warrant, and I'm taking you in!"

"You're welcome to try, sheriff!"

Joel squeezed off a whistler that slammed into the tree where the Nevadan crouched. There was some scurrying and the sound of branches breaking. Then Barnes's voice again. "This isn't helping your cause, Hollings."

"And just what is my cause, sheriff?"

A bullet sizzled by Joel's ear. He responded with three shots into the thicket where the rifle had flashed. There was a grunt and more snapping branches.

"Gawdammit, Hollings, you're shooting at a sheriff! Come to your senses, will you?"

"What makes sense to you, Barnes?"

"Let me come up and talk—just the two of us. I'll send the others down."

Suddenly, shots broke out from Mouse's position, and a full-scale volley thundered from below.

The lid was off!

One of the posse cropped up from behind a swale fifty feet away. Out of the corner of his eye, Joel saw Silverfoot raise a Winchester and fire. The man screamed and fell, grabbing at his leg. The three fugitives were firing rapidly now, almost in unison. As Barnes turned for his horse, a bullet creased his backside, taking a furrow of blue jeans with it. Then the posse left their horses and started a run for it straight down the mountain, slipping and sliding and hollering at their own men below not to shoot at them.

Joel put up his rifle and waved his companions toward the horses behind the shack. As they passed the cabin, Mouse and Silverfoot grabbed up their things and were in the saddle a split second behind Joel. They streaked into the trees above, pushing hard but skirting the clearings. To the north, they found a pass leading out of the valley and raced on through at a dead run.

They kept the pace stiff and the direction northwest till the valley was far behind, then eased up the horses as they crossed a small mountain meadow. A band of elk grazing at one end looked up, ears back, and trotted stiffly to the bordering trees.

From time to time Joel turned in his saddle, his eyes sweeping the skyline behind them. "Barnes seems as good as they say."

"Maybe so," said Mouse, "but he won't be settin' much saddle for a while. I believe I nicked him on the ass."

The others laughed and congratulated him. Still, Joel was troubled. They were moving ever north, ever west—away from Shad. Time could be running out for the old man, and Joel knew they'd have to make the turn soon. He'd have to reckon with Jerama far to the east if he wanted to see his father again—alive.

By late afternoon the trio had climbed even higher mountains that stretched unbroken to a northern horizon lost in the miles and the mist.

As daylight weakened, they set up camp in some trees behind a ridge that faced south. From there they'd be able to see anyone following from that direction—the way Barnes would be coming if he still had the starch. They scanned the lower reaches of terrain till dark closed in, seeing nothing, then ate sparingly without a fire. Silverfoot took the first watch, and the others rolled in their blankets.

Joel was up when first light crossed the sky, scattering the few clouds that hung there. Below, the land lay like a fallen giant, all elbows and knees. Soon the last pools of dark drained from the hollows, and he could see clearly for twenty, maybe thirty miles.

Far to the south there was movement. Horses? He

couldn't tell yet, but something was out there, all right. So much for a morning fire and coffee, he decided.

Fifteen minutes later, he could distinguish the horses. No mistaking them—it was Barnes and the posse! They were studying sign and moving steadily north over the tracks put down by the fugitives. Joel woke the others, and after a hurried breakfast they broke camp.

Casting a last look at the distant posse, with Barnes out front, Mouse shook his head.

"He's a tough bird, all right—from one end of him ta the other."

The threesome turned their horses and proceeded north, into the mountain labyrinth that stretched before them.

14

CYRUS BRENNER LOOKED worried. He hadn't heard from the Picketts in two days and now prowled the floor of his office like a caged animal. Between trips from his desk to the window that looked south to rolling hills, he signed the routine papers that make up a banker's work. After two hours of this, he tossed down the quill, grabbed his hat, and started out of the bank. As he passed through the lobby, he nodded to his cashier.

"I'm borrowing your horse for an hour."

"Sure, Mr. Brenner." The cashier's eyes followed his employer in mild inquiry.

Out in the street, he broke a small roan loose from the hitchrack, mounted, and steered the animal west through town. He rode past the church where a parish lady was sweeping dust off the stoop. She went after it with sharp, determined strokes, as though the reality of temporal dirt were yet another unpleasant consequence of the fall. When she saw the banker, she called out. "Morning, Cyrus! New horse? Mighty pretty."

But Brenner didn't turn his head or acknowledge the greeting in any way. His jaw was set, and his eyes were focused on the air three feet in front of his nose. The woman shrugged and went back to chasing her dust devils.

When he reached the teamsters' warehouse, he rode up to the door but remained on his horse. The silence was heavy.

"Pickett!" he yelled.

From inside came the sound of boots scraping on a wooden floor, and a moment later Jack Pickett appeared in the doorway, an open bottle of whiskey hanging from the end of one arm.

"Why, hullo, Brenner. What brings ya' out here slummin'?" Jack's face wore the patented Pickett grin. The banker was wary.

"Where's your brother?"

"Which one? Will's inside. Barney's dead."

"Barney's dead!"

"Hollings ambushed us."

"Where are the rifles?" Brenner's face was turning white. Jack limped out on the porch.

"Hollings got 'em."

"Jeezus H. Chr—"

"If ya want them guns, you're gonna have to git 'em yerself. We ain't working for ya no more."

"You've decided to retire from business, then?" Fury was gathering behind Brenner's eyes.

"I don't think we decided anythin' that drastic," said Jack. He took a pull on the whiskey bottle and grinned up at the banker.

"You get Will out here pronto, you hear me!"

It was Will Pickett who stood in the doorway now. "Who could keep from hearin', you dumpy little windbag!"

For a moment Brenner studied the brothers. Then he scrounged up a fragile smile. "Hey, what's wrong with you two? When did you start hating money?"

"You know better'n that, Brenner. We just want what's due us."

The banker's smile dissolved. "But you haven't kept your end of the bargain. You haven't finished with the Hollings!"

"No, we haven't," Will growled. "But we've finished with you!"

"I'll have you in jail, then—soon as the sheriff returns!"

"It's your word against ours. Besides, I told you once it's a mistake to threaten us."

A look of something like panic flooded the banker's face. "Awright, awright!" he said hurriedly. He reached in his vest pocket, producing a checkbook.

"What is it, Will? Two thousand, isn't it? I'll write a check if you promise to finish the job with no more screwups!"

The brothers exchanged glances.

"I'll even throw in a five-hundred-dollar bonus, okay?"

Again the brothers exchanged looks.

Will said, "I been wonderin' since we started this thing just what's so valuable about the Hollings place. Is there gold buried out there or somethin'?"

"That part of it's none of your business."

Brenner made out the check, tore it from the book, and handed it to Jack, who was nearest.

"There! Now the first thing you do is get those rifles up to Jerama."

"No," said Will Pickett quietly. "The first thing we do is blow Joel Hollings away."

"That sheriff from Nevada is already after Hollings. You concentrate on finding those guns and delivering them."

Jack handed his brother the check. Will glanced at it and stuffed it in his pocket.

"Okay," he said. "We'll give it another try." He turned and started back into the warehouse.

"Wait a minute!" Brenner called. "This time I want to be kept informed. I want reports, hear?"

"Don't worry, you'll git your money's worth." Will disappeared into the building. Jack tipped his hat to the banker and followed close behind.

From where he stood on the mountain, Joel could see the nine tiny riders that made up the posse still following far below. He estimated the distance at six miles. Seven at most. Although they'd taken care to cover their tracks all morning—moving across rock wherever possible and frequently changing direction—it wasn't working. Barnes apparently had the nose of a bloodhound and the eyes of an eagle. A new tack was needed, and fast.

He motioned to Silverfoot. "Is your horse strong enough to carry two of us?"

"For some distance, I think." She looked at Joel's mare. "Is there something wrong?"

"Nothing wrong except that infernal Barnes behind us! We've got to try something different if we're going to shake him."

"What'cha got up yer sleeve?" asked Mouse.

"A tracker like Barnes notices things you and I don't see. For example, he knows my horse's prints from yours.

"When we reach that open space ahead, we'll turn east. I'll slide over onto silverfoot's pony and send the mare flying north with an empty saddle. Since I'm the one Barnes wants, he may take the bait long enough to buy us time."

The girl smiled. "It is not a new trick, but I have seen it work."

"If it slows up the posse an hour or so, it'll be worth it." said Joel. Then he pointed off to the right. "You see that river below?"

Several thousand feet down, a string of water looped lazily across the floor of a canyon.

"We should have time to work some real deception there. The last thing Barnes expects us to do is turn back towards town. . . . Ready!"

In the center of the clearing, Joel climbed up on his saddle, then leaped to the girl's pony while giving the black a resounding swat. The startled mare shot forward as if she'd been fired from a cannon—ears back, reins dragging, stirrups flapping at the sky.

It worked well. The mare was showing no signs of stopping as she crashed through the brush that lined the trees in the distance and disappeared into the forest. Minutes later they could still hear her, far to the north, the sound of straining leather and snapping branches clearly audible in the mountain air.

They approached the river at the canyon's shallowest point and spent the next hour laying down false sign in every possible direction. Satisfied he'd left no ploy unused, Joel motioned, and they left the river at a point three miles south, heading in the easterly direction of Brenner Falls.

When they'd covered several miles of terrain marked mostly by dips and swales in the granite flatbed, Joel turned to a hill on the left crowned by a cluster of red rock. It was a good position from which to check the trail ahead and whatever action that might be gathering behind them. They brought the horses up the rise slowly, and Joel walked the better part of the last mile to ease the load on the girl's pony.

Behind the rocks they found shade and loosened the horses' cinches. Joel removed his hat, dark with sweat, and poured lukewarm water from a canteen through his dusty hair. From here the view back to the river was unobstructed, and they settled in to watch what effect, if any, their multiple tracks would have on the progress of the posse.

Almost immediately, Barnes and his men emerged from the trees beyond the river and stopped in the clearing. Joel could see Barnes and Sweeney exchange words as they studied the ground. Then Barnes took three men and turned north, while Sweeney waved the others on to the river. When Sweeney's group reached the water, confusion set in. Some of the men pointed up the river; others were already plunging their horses into the stream. The rest pulled up and looked at the sheriff for direction. From the jerking of heads and waving of arms, Joel could tell the men were shouting in their bewilderment, but the distance was great, and no sound reached him.

Joel chuckled. Maybe the pursuers wouldn't be fooled for long, but long enough possibly for the fugitives to set a new trail, all but impossible to follow, across the rockland that lay open to the east. Keeping the rise between them and the river, they led their horses down the back slope, mounted, and rode away into the first shadows of the dwindling afternoon.

Gilly was standing inside the doors of the saloon, drinking a bottle of pop, when the Pickett brothers entered and walked to the bar.

The barkeep left a conversation with a group of men down at the end and hurried over to take their order.

"Whiskey," said Will.

Jack nodded. "The same."

It was just before sundown, and the room was starting to fill up with thirsty punchers. A few merchants gathered, too, to enjoy a cooler before starting home to their families. Soon all the standing places were gone except for some space on either side of the Picketts, and the tables took the overflow. Everyone was hot from the long day, and voices were raised in anticipation of the first cold beers.

Still, nobody seemed quite relaxed. The men threw quick glances at the brothers, who stood at the middle of the bar like twin towers. Then Jack Pickett said, loud enough for most of the room to hear, "I think we ought'a bring Barney back to town and bury him proper, don't you, Will?"

A voice from one of the tables called over, "Barney's dead? My God, what happened, Jack?"

The brothers turned together and faced the room.

"Yeah, Earl, Barney's dead, all right. What d'ya think of that?"

"I don't believe it. Barney ain't the dyin' type, 'less somebody got him from behind!"

Then Will joined in. "That's just what they did—shot him in the back when he wasn't lookin'!" The room suddenly went quiet.

Another voice came from the tables. "Who done it, Will!"

"Why, Hollings done it a'course! Joel Hollings! You all seen his pitcher on the WANTED poster down to Sweeney's office. He ambushed us. Barney never had a chance!"

The room responded with a growl of disapproval, and Will held up his hand for silence.

"Don't y'all worry about it none," he said. "Me and Jack here are goin' after that bushwhacker, and when we meet up with him, he's gonna die slow and painful!"

Gilly's voice snapped the silence like a broken fiddle string.

"Joel Hollings ain't no bushwhacker! If Barney's dead, he likely had it comin'!"

The brothers turned to see who was speaking, their faces hard as granite.

"And just who the hell are you, kid?" hissed Jack.

"Just somebody that knows Hollings a lot better'n you!" Gilly shot back.

The room started to laugh but swallowed it.

"If you know Hollings so well," said Will, "maybe you can tell us where to find him."

"If I knew, you two baboons would be last to get it from me!"

This time a ripple of laughter got out, and Jack made no attempt to hide his rage.

"Git your punk face out'a here before I push my fist through it!"

But instead, Gilly did a peculiar thing for a twelve-year-old. He walked up to the brothers, looked them in the eye a moment, then spit on Will Pickett's boots.

The room gasped.

Will raised a meaty paw, and there was the sickening sound of bones breaking as he slammed the youngster across the saloon into a wall. Gilly went down in a heap, unconscious. His cheek was caved in, and blood ran from his nose and mouth.

For a moment nobody said a word. Then the man named Earl yelled. "Somebody get Doc Bowman. The kid's hurt bad!"

Another puncher raced for the doors. "I'll get Lucy from the hotel; she's done some nursin'!"

Then it seemed every chair in the place was scraping hardwood as the room came to its feet and crowded around the boy. People were all talking at once.

"He ain't moving."

"I think he's dead."

"That was a brutal blow!"

"Lordy, the boy ain't but twelve!"

The crowd was angry. Still, nobody turned to face the Picketts, who stood alone at the bar, their faces blank, chests heaving.

Behind them the barkeep whispered. "You two'd be smart to clear out'a here. I seen a crowd of men mad like this once before, and what happens next ain't pretty to see."

As if they'd been awakened from a hypnotic trance, the brothers set down their beers and moved quickly from the saloon.

The doctor arrived and pushed through the crowd that still huddled around Gilly. He knelt and began rubbing the circulation back into the boy's neck. He turned Gilly's face upward, probing around the shattered cheekbone with gentle arthritic fingers.

"Jesus," he said, "looks like this boy's face stopped a train!"

"The 'train' was Will Pickett's fist!" someone said.

But Bowman didn't seem to hear. The old doctor picked Gilly up in his arms and started out to the street. At the door, he walked into Lucy, who was out of breath from running.

"I'll take him, doc," she said, "We have an empty room at the hotel. . . . Oh, God! Look at his face, will you!"

Tears formed in the waitress's eyes as she lifted the boy to her arms and started back across the street. The doctor was close behind, followed by some of the crowd from the saloon. A current of outrage still buzzed from the men.

Lucy didn't stop in the lobby where a scatter of old men filled the easy chairs, reading month-old newspapers. She went straight upstairs to a corner room on the second floor and gently laid Gilly out on the fresh linen of a sagging brass bed.

Gilly had one eye open; the other was swollen shut. He tried to speak, but the words wouldn't come. Terror poured from his one good eye. The doctor entered the room, telling the crowd behind to stay clear. Then he closed the door.

15

RIDING DOUBLE WITH Silverfoot stirred up feelings in Joel that were new to him. He'd been among women before—and a good deal closer than now—but somehow this was different. The only thing he could liken it to was the feeling of coming home after a long absence, a feeling of familiarity and rightness that fed a hunger he'd kept deep inside.

A wind sprang up out of the west, lifting dust from the rockland around them. Mouse pulled his hat on tighter and squinted into the distance.

"Another ten mile an' we'll be in shoutin' distance of the ranch."

Joel looked behind them. There was nothing to see but billows of orange grit rising in the darkening sky. He raised his voice against the wind.

"I'll be going into town," he said to the girl. "My hunch is I'll find the man we're after this time."

Silverfoot turned, her breath warm, her lips close to his ear. He saw the lineup of her fine white teeth.

"Perhaps I can reason with Jerama about your father."

"Alone? I don't think it's likely."

"You forget I am Apache."

"You forget Jerama is very angry about the rifles. No, our best chance is to find the man behind this. We'll let *him* reckon with Jerama—and the law."

But find him how? Joel's gut feeling told him to locate

Will Pickett and call him out. But suppose he killed Pickett? He might never find the man who set him up. Still, if he handled it right . . .

Silverfoot's hand casually found his and the feeling struck anew. Could she be sharing his emotions of the past few hours? Impossible! But he left his hand where it was all the same.

The wind died down as darkness came and the sky filled with stars. Some looked as big as the nuggets he'd dreamed of finding in the silver fields. The bay that carried them moved easily over the land, and Joel felt a new and strange peace nudging at the old anger in his soul.

Soon the familiar ridge of the valley loomed ahead. The two pines, marking the pass, stood etched against a sky that hummed with the closeness of stars.

Mouse signaled, and the three pulled up.

"We'll head south from here," said Joel, sliding to the ground. He looked up at Silverfoot. "You'll go to the ranch, then?"

"Unless you want me with you."

Joel wanted her with him very much but said, "We'll go on and finish this matter. . . . Watch the passes and stay out of sight if intruders come."

He started to climb up behind Mouse, and she said, "You'll need the horse, I can go on foot almost as quickly."

"That town owes me more than a horse," Joel smiled. "I reckon I'll find one along the way!"

Silverfoot sat in her saddle erect and motionless long after the men moved down across the flatland and disappeared into the darkness. Then she turned the bay, not up the slope to the valley but toward the high mesa country that lay to the east.

The figure that rode through the night was headed straight toward them, and Joel instinctively opened his holster. As

108

the distance closed, he heard the familiar voice of Whitney Brenner.

"Joel? Joel Hollings, is that you?"

"Hello, Whitney! Are you alone?"

"Alone and a little scared, if you must know!"

When she drew close enough to tell their faces, she laughed self-consciously.

"You must think I'm crazy, forever running around in the dark after you!"

Joel grinned. "Anyway, Whitney, it's a good kind of crazy."

"I was hoping to find you up in the valley."

"Something's happened in town?"

"You bet something has! The Picketts are steaming your trail over the shooting of their brother Barney."

"I'm not surprised."

"Not surprised! You mean you shot him, *too*?"

"I shot 'im, Miss Brenner," said Mouse. "He was fixin' to kill this lummox."

"They say you ambushed them."

"That's true," said Joel. "Look, maybe we should talk."

Whitney seemed embarrassed. "You don't have to justify yourselves to me. I'm sure you had your reasons."

Joel nodded toward a clump of trees. "We were looking for a rest, anyway. Let's drink some coffee."

Inside the tree cover, Mouse collected some dry wood and dug a hole. They kept the fire small and out of sight. It didn't take long for the coffee to boil, and soon they all held steaming cups, the fire pressing a welcome blanket across their shoulders.

Whitney waited for somebody to speak, and after a moment Joel took the cue. "The Picketts were taking those rifles to the Indians," he said. "The guns were payment for kidnapping my father. But it turns out neither the Indians nor the teamsters are the brains behind this thing." Then he told the story, leaving out nothing.

Whitney listened, her gray eyes wincing from time to time, her handsome head nodding in wonder as the unlikely scenes unfolded. When he finished, Joel rose and poured more coffee all around.

Whitney sat deep in thought, and Joel noted the sadness already beginning to carve faint lines on the girl's beauty.

"And you have no idea who's behind it?"

"Soon. Very soon." Joel's words were more of a promise than a statement.

"What will you do about Barnes and Sweeney?"

"I'm hoping they'll be busy in the mountains awhile."

"I want to know about the charges in Virginia City," said the girl. Joel heaved a sigh but didn't try to dodge it.

"There was a poker game—and an argument."

"They say the man you killed wasn't carrying a gun."

"He carried a gun, all right—a small pistol tucked away in his boot."

"And nobody saw it?" the girl persisted.

"He had a friend at the game who should have seen it. All I know is I saw it—pointed at my heart."

"What was his friend's name?" Whitney asked.

"Carl, I think." Joel looked at the girl. "What difference does that make?"

"None, I suppose." she said. Still, she looked as if it made a difference.

Mouse hadn't heard this part of the story and was leaning forward, fascinated. "Sounds to me like his friend covered up fer 'im."

"I don't know," Joel said.

Whitney rose and filled her cup again. Then, putting her back to the fire, she said, "Do you know Gilly, the livery boy?"

"Yes. Nice kid."

"He's been badly hurt. They say he might not live."

Joel rose in disbelief. "Hurt . . . how?"

"Will Pickett hit him—crushed part of his face. They've

110

got him at the hotel. Doc Bowman and the waitress, Lucy, are with him."

Joel didn't wait to hear more. "C'mon, let's go." He began kicking dirt over the fire.

"May I ride back with you?" asked the girl.

"Of course—but it might not be good if you're seen with us."

"I'll take my chances on that," Whitney said.

With no wasted movement, they broke camp and pushed on through the night. Joel led the way, Mouse riding double behind.

"What was Pickett's beef with Gilly?" Mouse asked.

"I've only got hearsay. Apparently the boy spit on Will's boots."

"Oh, God," said Joel, and pushed the horse faster. Somehow he couldn't picture the boy hurt. All he saw in his mind's eye was a sunny twelve-year-old looking up at him, trusting . . .

It was nearly three in the morning when they reached Brenner Falls. Main Street lay quiet under the late moon that scattered its chill on the sleeping town.

"I'll be heading home," said Whitney. "Where will you go?"

"We'll hole up at the livery stable till morning." As the girl turned to go, Joel added, "Thanks, Whitney."

She waved. "I'll be close by. Let me know if I can help." Then she was gone.

Except for a pack mule and a carriage team, the stable was empty. Mouse put up the horse, and Joel went to the entrance to check the hotel lights. A solitary shaft of yellow from the lobby stood in the street. That was all. Mouse finished with the horse and came out to join him.

"Looks like we got a job cut out fer us," the little man said.

"Several," said Joel, and offered Mouse the makings. They smoked for a minute in silence. Finally, Joel said,

"The poor kid. He was probably taking our part . . . The more I see of this town, the less I like it."

They heard a soft tapping at the back door, and Mouse went to check.

"Who is it?"

"Lucy—from the hotel. Is Joel with you?"

Mouse unlatched the door, and Lucy stepped in, her face drawn, her eyes busy, never resting.

"I saw you ride in from my window. You've heard about Gilly?"

Joel had joined them. "We heard. How is he, Lucy?"

"Unconscious again. The doc says it's a bad concussion. He says he might not make it." Joel saw her fighting back the tears and held her.

"He'll come through it, Lucy. . . . Can we go to him?"

The waitress nodded and pulled away. "Come along, then."

Entering the hotel from a side door in the alley, the three made their way up a flight of stairs that moaned and complained at every step. At the end of the hallway, Gilly's door stood ajar. They entered softly and made out the form of the boy lying motionless in the bed. His face, heavily bandaged, was turned toward them. Joel sat down at the foot of the bed and removed his hat. For a long while he looked at the floor between his boots, saying nothing.

Finally, Lucy whispered. "His breathing seems better."

Mouse, who had sat down on the floor in a corner, said, "There's a good prayer I got—an' I'm sayin' it now. . . . Sometimes it works; other times it don't."

Gilly's one good eye began to flutter, then slowly it opened.

"Joel . . . is that you?"

Joel's heart leaped inside him. "It's me, Gilly."

"Oh, Gad, Joel, I'm a'hurtin!"

"Easy, Gilly. I'm staying right here."

"I told them Picketts where to get off for ya."

"I heard, Gilly—they say you were magnificent."

Then the boy's eye closed again, and in a minute they could hear his breathing, steady and even. A smile had formed at the corners of his mouth.

16

THOUGH IT WAS after three in the morning, Whitney made one more stop before going home to bed. She cut across town to the telegraph office, that still operated full-time at the railway station—a facility used mainly in recent years for nonscheduled shipments of freight. The main passenger line now avoided the mountains and went west through Latham and Barker Flat, thirty miles to the south.

A light burned in the office, but no one was in sight. Whitney rapped on the counter, then rapped again. At length, a door at the back opened, and a sleep-ridden clerk appeared, smoothing down a white thatch of hair. He squinted into the night to see who it was.

"Why, hello, Miss Brenner. Up kinda early, ain'cha?"

"It's the other way around, Tony, I haven't been to bed yet." The man arched his eyebrows but said nothing.

"Who's the marshal at Virginia City these days?"

The clerk scratched his head. "Believe Harley Craig still runs the territory."

"I want to send a wire."

The clerk nodded and slid a form and pencil stub across the counter. Whitney thought a moment and wrote:

HARLEY CRAIG, U.S. MARSHAL
VIRGINIA CITY, NEVADA

HAVE REASON TO BELIEVE JOEL HOLLINGS IS
INNOCENT STOP QUESTION DEAD MINER'S FRIEND

CARL WHO SAT IN AT CARD GAME STOP DEAD MAN
CARRIED SMALL GUN IN HIS BOOT, DREW BEFORE
HOLLINGS STOP ADVISE.

WHITNEY BRENNER

She pushed the paper to the clerk and said. "See this gets
on the wire immediately, will you, Tony?"

"I'll send it right away, Miss Brenner. Shall I bill the
bank?"

Whitney turned it around in her head a minute, then
smiled. "Yes, Tony, do that—bill the bank."

When she reached the hill north of town, there were no
lights burning in the house above. Talking softly to her
horse, she took the path that rose through a grove of oaks.
As she passed under her father's window, she looked up. It
was dark and quiet. At the stable behind the house, she
bedded the horse down and made her way to the kitchen
door, letting herself in without a sound.

In the dark, she felt for the kerosene lamp on the table,
found it, and struck a match.

From a chair at the far end of the room, Cyrus Brenner
looked at her through stone-grey eyes. He didn't signal any
greeting; he didn't move.

"Dad!" exclaimed the girl. "Why are you sitting here in
the dark? It's almost four in the morning!"

"Where have you been?"

"I couldn't sleep. I've been riding."

"You've been with Joel Hollings, haven't you?"

"What if I have! He's not what you think he is—he's not
a criminal!" Tears stood ready in Whitney's eyes, but she
was too angry to cry.

"Good Lord," she said, "I'm twenty-four years old! Do
I need permission to leave the house?"

Brenner didn't take his eyes from his daughter's face.

"I told you I didn't want Hollings in this town. He's
poison. . . . What did he say to you?"

"I was right about the rifles. And about the Picketts, too." Her glance fell to the floor. "They're hired killers."

"You're a fool to meddle in things that don't concern you."

"Joel's in trouble, and he's innocent. The man he shot in Nevada *was* carrying a gun—and tried to use it, too!"

"Maybe so, maybe not. It's his business, not yours."

Whitney cocked her head, as if seeing her father in a new light. "Aren't you a bit too concerned about *not* being concerned?" she asked.

Brenner shifted positions in the chair. "I don't want to see you hurt."

"Nobody's been hurt. Besides, if you were in Joel's position, wouldn't you welcome any help you could get?"

The banker's face tightened. "I'm not in his place," he said. "But if I were, I wouldn't stoop to playing on a young woman's emotions."

"It's almost dawn," said Whitney. "I'm going to bed." She walked over to her father, kissed him lightly, and left the room.

The sky was gray when Joel gave up the effort to sleep and pulled on his boots. Outside, a cold Saturday half-light was gathering momentum in the street, and from the livery window he could see a block or two in either direction.

He stood at the window, thinking about the Indian girl whose presence he had taken casually for so many years. He tried to picture her asleep up at the ranch but couldn't. No, she'd be up by now, tending to the stock or sweeping the floor in the makeshift kitchen. He saw the gentle curve of her throat, the shy smile lurking at the back of her chestnut eyes, her long legs, smooth as madrona . . .

At that moment, a pinto carrying a familiar rider passed the window. It was the puncher who'd followed him to the Picketts' warehouse his first morning in town. The rider proceeded up the street and stopped across from the hotel where Joel had first seen him—through the dining room window—currying his horse.

As Joel expected, the man took up his old watching post, dismounted, and began working the pinto over with a currycomb. But this time the man's guarded glances were not directed toward the hotel; they settled on the livery window where Joel stood.

So his presence in town was no secret. Somebody knew exactly where to find him. What somebody? Whoever it was didn't waste his sleeping time.

Joel strapped on his guns, dropped his hat on his head, and stepped out into the street. The puncher saw him approaching and looked away. Joel walked up to the pinto's head and scratched the animal between the eyes.

"Nice horse you have here," he said. The man's face showed embarrassment under his weather-beaten hat.

"Nice enough, I reckon," the man said.

"Why are you tailing me?"

"Tailin' you? I don't even know you, puncher." The man turned his back and started dressing the pinto's hindquarters. There was nobody on the street but the two men.

"I think you're working for the Picketts—or the Picketts' boss. What's your name?"

Without turning, the man answered, "I don't know what you're talkin' about. My name's Garth."

"Turn around!" Joel commanded. The puncher slowly stiffened, letting his free hand settle near the revolver on his hip.

"Don't try it, Garth. Turn around!"

The man turned his head slightly, but it was enough to show him the .44 Joel held in his hand.

The puncher scowled, then dropped the currycomb in the dust.

"You're crazy," he said. "I ain't done nothin' to you."

"Who are the Picketts working for?"

"Why, nobody. They got their own business."

117

"That's not what I mean. Who's behind the ranch rustling?"

"Look, mister, I do a little scoutin' for the Picketts now and again, them being cousins, but they don't tell me nothin'."

"I want you to take a message to Will for me."

"Why should I run your errands?"

"It's your choice." Joel cocked his gun.

The man stared at the .44, and the red in his face segued to white.

"What's the message, then?"

"I'm calling Will out. It's family business."

"I'll tell him. But I'll tell *you* somethin', too, for what it's worth. Will Pickett ain't never been beat in a fight—guns or otherwise!"

"That makes it simple. I'll be the first and the last. Tell him he can pick the place and time."

Joel leathered his pistol and turned away toward the stable. The puncher glared at his retreating back, and from the look in his eyes you could see he was tempted. But he picked up his currycomb, climbed on the pinto, and rode off at a gallop toward the foothills west of town.

Up in Gilly's room, Doc Bowman and Lucy kept watch over the boy. He seemed to be sleeping, but the doctor wasn't pleased and said as much to the waitress. "His breathing is ragged again. Can you hear?"

Lucy nodded her already lowered head. "What are his chances, doc?"

"I've done all I can," he said. "Things are back in place. Now only time will tell."

"I'll stay with him. If there's any change, I'll send for you." The old doctor rose and placed his hand on Lucy's shoulder.

"These head wounds are the worst kind, but he's strong, and that's in his favor."

When the doctor had gone, Lucy raised the blanket to

cover the boy's shoulders and tucked it in. Then she sat down at the window to watch day lighten in the street below.

Presently, there was a tap on the door, and Joel entered, followed by the tiptoeing Mouse. Lucy's face told them what they'd hoped it wouldn't.

"You need sleep," Joel said. "Mouse and I will stay a spell." But Lucy's eyes had already closed in the chair where she sat.

Mouse kept his voice low. "You didn't say what happened in the street."

"Pickett had a lookout waiting."

"The yegg with the pinto?"

Joel nodded. "I called Will out. The puncher's delivering my message."

"Where an' when?"

"I left it to Pickett."

"Suppose the posse returns."

"We just have to hope they don't—not till it's over, anyway."

The little man rose and covered Lucy with a blanket. "Jeez," he said, "I hope ya start shootin' straighter than what I been seein'."

"I'm good enough when I have to be."

Mouse snorted and took up a post at the window.

An hour passed in silence; then Mouse began frantically signaling.

"What is it?"

"The feller on the pinto," he whispered. "He's ridin' in!"

Joel got to his feet. "I'll be back." He looked at his gun belt lying in the corner, decided against it, and quietly left the room.

The pinto and its rider pulled up across from the hotel as before, but this time the puncher made no show about grooming his pony. He just sat in his saddle and waited. Joel emerged from the hotel, checked the street in both directions, then crossed over to where the man waited.

"Will says he'll take time from his busy schedule to meet you here at four o'clock today. He says be sure to wear the clothes you want to be buried in."

"Four o'clock will be fine," said Joel, "unless Gilly, the stableboy, dies first—in which case he can look for me sooner."

The puncher sneered.

"You talk a good game, Hollings. Let's see how you handle it in the pinch."

Joel smiled. "If I were you, Garth, I'd make plans for new employment. A dead boss doesn't pay much."

"You ain't got a chance in hell, Hollings!" The puncher turned his horse and rode off down the street.

The smile remained on Joel's face, but inside he wasn't smiling. He was wondering how he'd spot the extra guns Will Pickett was sure to bring to the party. When the time came, he'd have to locate them fast if he expected to leave the street alive.

17

THE REASON JAKE Barnes hadn't found the tracks he was looking for was because he only went two miles down river instead of three. This was due partly to the bullet crease on his rump, which had him standing in his stirrups most of the time, and because, in his foxlike mind, he was sure Joel would choose any direction but the one that led back to Brenner Falls.

The posse had been stymied at the river for a full day now, and the men were losing their taste for the hunt. Barnes seemed to sense this and waved Tom Sweeney over.

"We've got to stay on this thing—even if it means starting over from scratch. The tracks are here someplace, and we're going to find them!"

"The men are tired. They've been out a long time," said Sweeney.

"That's what I mean. It's your job to keep them fired up. They're your posse, not mine!"

"Face it, Barnes. Hollings has outsmarted us."

The Nevadan's eyes narrowed. "Nobody outsmarts me on the trail—nobody!"

"We all do our jobs best we can, but aren't you stretching pride a bit tight?"

"Look, Sweeney, the reason you're a podunk sheriff and I'm respected in four states is because I don't accept defeat!"

"That's good to know, Barnes. I'd been wondering about that."

"Wondering? What are you talking about?"

"Forget it."

"Okay, take your men and go downstream again. I'll spend the rest of the day on exits to the north."

"For what it's worth," said Sweeney, "I think Hollings went east toward town—or toward the mesas where his pappy's being held."

"That would be foolhardy. Fugitives don't go places where there's a price on them—not unless they're soft in the head."

"All the same, I think that's what Hollings has done."

Barnes stared at the mountains to the north. "Well, I think he's up there somewhere, and I'm turning over every stone till he's found! C'mon, get your group together. Let's move out."

"Last question, Barnes. What happens if Joel is in town? Brenner Falls at the moment is without a sheriff."

"He's not in town. C'mon; move the men out."

Sweeney shrugged and started down to the river where the men sat in a circle on the ground. They were weary and spoke little. When Sweeney called to them, they groaned and got up slowly.

"Hey, Tom," one said, "ain't we beat the bushes enough? If Hollings laid real tracks out of here, he didn't leave us much!"

"We're going back over it one more time," said Sweeney. "Barnes still thinks the sign is here."

Again the men groaned. It wasn't a popular decision.

"If Barnes is so sure," said another, "why don't he do the backtracking?" There was a mutter of general approval from the men.

"He's going over the ground to the north again," said the sheriff. "Weaver and Radley, you two join him."

The man called Radley got on his horse, and standing in

122

his stirrups, pranced a circle around the others, mimicking the Nevadan.

"'Jake Barnes is the name and trackin's my game!'" he said, "'Course I ain't settin' down just now, what wif a bullet hole in my ass an' all!'"

The other men liked this touch and loudly guffawed.

Sweeney stifled a smile. "Get along, Radley," he said. "You, too, Weaver!"

The rest of the morning and most of the afternoon, Sweeney and the posse scoured the stream. They found nothing but occasional tracks of the bighorn sheep and several deer. Still they pushed on, and by the time the sun started its slide behind the canyon rim, the men were exhausted from traversing the slippery stones on the river bottom and from frustration.

Finally, Sweeney raised his arm. "That's enough, men! Let's head back to camp. We'll be starting home in the morning."

There were smiles here and there but no cheering. The men were bone tired.

When they reached the camp, it was almost dark. Some of the men gathered wood and lighted a tall fire against the chill in the air that spilled off the mountains. There was no sign of Barnes or his deputies.

The fire caught quickly, sending its flames licking at the sky. As it settled, the men skewered chunks of deer meat and began roasting their dinner. Soon the coffee was hot, and a cheerful buzz arose from the group that was now thinking and talking of home. Sweeney exercised a toothpick and was arranging his blankets when he heard the watch.

"Barnes and the others—coming in from the north!"

The men at the fire turned their heads but nobody got up. Moments later, a bedraggled Barnes approached the circle of firelight, leading a black mare. Behind, to his left and right, rode Radley and Weaver. The Nevadan's face was covered with scratches, his shirt and chaps in tatters. Weaver and Radley looked almost as bad.

"Evening, boys," said Sweeney pleasantly. "I see you got a horse for your trouble."

Behind the cuts, Barnes' eyes flamed. "It's Hollings's mare, Sweeney! Can't you see!"

"Why, I believe you're right, sheriff! Where's its owner?" A chuckle came from the men.

"Damn you, Sweeney, this isn't cause for humor. It's important! It tells us Hollings rode double with one of the others."

Sweeney put on a sober look and nodded politely. "Come down, boys. We've got coffee and venison steak."

Radley and Weaver jumped down and headed for the coffee pot, but Barnes stood a moment longer in his stirrups.

"Find anything downstream?" he asked.

"Zero. Sorry."

"We'll try again in the morning. There's got to be tracks!"

"I'm afraid not, Barnes. We have to leave it. We're headed home at dawn."

"But you can't quit on me now! I got a reputation to think about!"

"And these men have families to think about. We've done all we can. I wish you luck."

Will Pickett sat in his office at the teamsters warehouse, putting together a battle plan for that afternoon. Across the desk, Jack lounged in a chair, pulling from time to time on the whiskey bottle still hanging from the end of his arm. Garth paced the floor chain-smoking and nodding as the big man's voice droned on.

"It'll be the three of us, then, and we'll work together. Zat right?"

"Hollings'll never know what hit him!" Garth laughed.

"Okay," said Will. "Garth, I want you out of sight on top of the bank—just behind Hollings and to his left."

"I'll settle in up there about three—before word'a the showdown gets around."

"Good." Will turned to his brother.

"You'll be across the street, at a second-floor window in the hotel. Make sure the window's open. . . . And for Christ's sake leave the booze home. We'll need straight heads for this one! I'll enter the street from the saloon—"

"You ain't partic'ar'ly popular at the saloon right now," said Jack.

"Just let one of them cross me!" Will scowled at his brother, then continued. "Like I was sayin', I'll come out from the saloon. When Hollings shows, he'll probably have his runt friend along, so I'll go toward them slow. At this point, I want your guns out and ready. The minute you see Hollings's hand closin' in on his hip, you fire—and keep on firin' till your guns are empty. Understand?"

"Suppose he's faster'n we think?" asked Jack.

'It ain't gonna matter how fast he is. He'll never touch leather if we do the job right."

"What about the law?"

"What about it?"

"He means what if the law sees it as murder," said Garth.

"How can they? It's one side against the other—that's fair, ain't it? Besides, Hollings'll be goin' for his gun first."

"Maybe we should tell Brenner the plan." Jack still seemed wary.

"What for?" said his brother. "He don't care how the job gets done."

"He might not like shootin' in the streets. Maybe he wants it done quiet."

"Look, on the surface of it, this beef don't involve Brenner at all. It's a personal thing. Hollings killed Barney, didn't he?"

125

"I guess you're right."

"What happens after?" asked Garth.

"We track down those rifles and finish the job with Jerama and the old man."

"Sounds slick, Will—slicker'n snot on a doorknob," Garth said approvingly.

"Gimme that whiskey." Will grabbed the bottle from his brother.

"Here's to the end of a pain-in-the-ass job!" he said, taking a deep swig and smiling benevolently on his associates.

18

FROM THE DINING room, Lucy beckoned to Joel as he passed through the hotel lobby on his way upstairs. "When did you eat last?" she asked.

"I don't remember exactly."

"Follow me." She led him to a small table set back in an alcove near the kitchen. When he was seated, she took his hat.

"You won't be bothered here. The breakfast crowd doesn't come down for another hour. Steak and eggs all right?"

"Better than all right! Thanks."

"*Papas fritas?*"

Joel glanced up. "You've got a memory, too. I thought you just had looks."

The waitress flushed. "Mouse is with Gilly. I had to open the dining room." She took the order to the kitchen and returned.

"Who's the man you were talking to outside?"

"Says he's Pickett's cousin. Name's Garth."

"I know it's none of my business, but mind telling me what's going on?"

"Will and I have some business to take care of. The cousin's been passing the messages."

"What kind of business?" The waitress's hand trembled slightly as she poured the water.

"You know the kind, Lucy. You've seen it before."

127

"I'm afraid so." After a moment she added, "You know of course, Will Pickett won't come alone. . . . They say he won't go near a card table unless the deck is stacked first."

"I'm not taking him lightly."

"What will you do when it's over, Joel?"

"Go after my father and bring him home."

"And then?"

"Drink some beers with you."

The waitress's shoulders suddenly relaxed, and she laughed. She had a beautiful smile. "Seriously," she said.

"I am serious."

Two guests entered the room and took a table by the window.

"Let me get their order. Then I'll bring yours."

Joel reached in his vest for the makings, rolled a smoke, and started building his plans.

He figured Lucy was right. Pickett wouldn't be easy, and he wouldn't be coming alone. He tried to climb into the teamster's boots and get a feel for his brand of thinking. Whoever Pickett brought along for help would likely be concealed, so he'd better get on the hotel roof and check out the surrounding buildings. He'd look for possible sites that could hide a man and still give him an open look into the street below.

What about Mouse? He wanted Mouse out of it. The thought of him taking another bullet on the Hollings's behalf was out of the question. If he himself had stayed at the ranch where he belonged—instead of burying his head in a mine shaft, Mouse probably wouldn't have been shot in the first place.

No, when the time came, he'd say nothing to Mouse. Meantime, he'd put down some breakfast and do his scout work.

Lucy brought the plates, and everything was as before,

hot and cooked to perfection. As she set down the tray, she nodded sideways toward the two men at the window table.

"We've got a distinguished guest this morning—Cyrus Brenner, the town's namesake and banker."

Joel's view was partially blocked by the kitchen doors, which stood ajar. But by leaning forward, he could see one of the men clearly—a chunky figure with short arms and a wide mouth tucked back in a close-cropped beard. It was Brenner, all right, and he was doing the talking. Of the other man, he could see nothing. Brenner's words easily carried across the empty room.

"I'll be ready to start excavation in a day or two. Think your company can handle an operation this size?" The other man spoke low, and Joel couldn't pick up the response.

Lucy filled his coffee cup again. "Anything else?" she asked.

"Who's Brenner talking to?"

She glanced at the man. "Owns a mining company over in Winters. I don't remember his name."

Joel ate slowly. Today was not a day to rush. He would savor it and use the time well. Perhaps sleep a bit if he could manage it.

When he finished, Lucy was busy in the kitchen, so he rose, took his hat from a wall peg, and left money on the table.

No point calling attention to himself by sneaking out, he thought. Given his position in the room, he'd do what any other casual breakfaster would do—take the shortest route to the door that led into the hotel lobby. So, pulling his hat on low, he walked past Brenner's table and smiled. "Morning, gentlemen," he said pleasantly.

The banker looked up blankly and returned the smile without losing a stroke in his conversation. As he left the room, Joel heard Brenner say, "About twenty miles north . . . two days probably to get your equipment in place . . ."

He remembered that voice from his childhood and didn't like it any better now than he did then.

Using the back stairs, he started up to the roof. At the top, he unbolted the fire door and stepped out onto a tar surface crisscrossed by loose-board walkways. To his left, a water tank loomed another eight feet into the sky. Moving slowly, keeping his silhouette back from the roof line, he studied the buildings below that flanked the street on both sides.

Across and several buildings down stood the bank, a portly structure, like its owner, built close to the ground. On its roof, Joel noted a small shack of the sort bird lovers keep pigeons in. A good place for a man to hide, he thought. When the time came, he'd remember the shack.

With the exception of the bank and the hotel itself, there were no other bona fide roofs in the area. The rest of the buildings sported facades that shot high above humbler structures behind. A man could get no purchase on these stucco edifices without being seen from below. That narrowed the choices down considerably.

He remained on the roof the better part of an hour, checking the parallel streets and alleys for access. The overcast had dried away, and a new sun, still low in the sky, was headed toward town.

As Brenner Falls came awake, the sound of voices reached him from the street below. Merchants had begun to open their shops, calling greetings to each other and rolling out their awnings against the heat that would soon be gathering there.

It was going to be a good day for many, he thought. The largest concern of the merchants would be a decent showing in their receipt drawers at the close of business. For others, like the regulars at the saloon, the pressure was even less. But where would *he* be when the indifferent sky that covered them all began to darken under a retiring sun?

Again Silverfoot stepped into his mind with her proud,

130

quiet ways, belief in him shining from her eyes. He thought, too, of his dead brother, Jason, who lay in the earth, never to know the love of a woman, the trust of a son . . .

But this was the day he had wanted, a day he had waited and planned for, and he'd play out the script as written. He cursed the nerves that were singing falsetto in his arms, yet noted with satisfaction that his hand was rock steady. When four o'clock came, he would be ready.

He left the roof by the same stairs and descended to the second floor, where Gilly was fighting for his own life. Entering the boy's room, he found Mouse still posted at the window.

"I'll stay with him awhile," Joel said. "Go get some eats."

"What about Pickett?"

"It's not settled. I'll let you know."

Mouse wore his suspicious look but left the room, saying, "I think that prayer'a mine's startin' to work. He opened 'is eyes once an' smiled at me!"

When Mouse had gone, Joel took the chair by the window, and for the first time since he could remember, wished he, too, knew something about prayer. It wasn't that he didn't believe in God; he'd just never had much cause to trouble Him before. He was too used to going it alone. As he sat there looking at the sleeping boy, a voice somewhere inside him said, "Let him live, God, please let him live. . . . This town's got few enough good people!"

It was twenty minutes to four on the bank clock when Joel awoke and saw Gilly staring at him from the bed.

"Hey, Joel," the boy said weakly. "Looks like you been sleepin', too. I'm glad you're here."

Joel squinted into the sun that streamed through the open casement and tried to get his bearings. Then he was on his feet.

131

"Hey, Gilly!" he said, pressing the lad's shoulder and stepping to the window.

"Feeling any better?"

"I'm powerful tired, is all."

"You lay back, hear?"

"Yes, sir."

"Gilly, is that clock on the bank mostly right?"

"I think so, but I don't pay time much heed."

Joel left the window and came back to the boy. "Look, I have to go out for a bit. If Lucy or Mouse come looking for me, tell them I'll be back. There's an errand I have to run."

"I'll tell 'em, Joel. . . . What kind of errand?"

"Just a favor that needs returning."

"Don't be long," said the boy.

"It's a promise."

He turned, silently lifted his gun belt from the floor, and left the room. In the washroom at the end of the hall, he splashed away the last traces of sleep from his head and checked his guns. They were ready. Then he proceeded down the back stairs that let out on the alley.

As the door clicked behind him, he stood in the shadows. From there he could see the bank across the street and the clock that hung there. Seven minutes to four.

A movement from above caught his eye. It was the door of the shack perched back on the roof of the bank. Had the door just closed? For a minute longer he stood motionless, watching. Again the shack door quivered, as though it were stuck. From his angle he could see only the top third of the lean-to. Someone was up there trying to get in or out. Joel backed farther into the alley to get a better perspective. Then he saw the silhouette of a man and the flash of sun on a rifle barrel. It was the cousin, Garth, crouched low, peering down into the street. So his hunch had paid off! He was glad he'd taken time to scout the area.

At one minute past four, he moved to the mouth of the alley and stepped out into Main Street.

It was empty.

The doors of the shops stood open, but there were no shoppers. At the grocery on his left, crates of apples were stacked out under the awning. Next door, he could see the barbershop, its white-clad proprietor sitting alone in his cutting chair, eyes busy jumping between his newspaper and the street outside. When he spotted Joel, he dropped the paper and scurried to the back of the shop.

Joel stood quietly in the center of the street, facing west. The sun was dropping but still ranged high enough not to bother his vision. He felt the pointed rifle on the bank roof behind him, and the hair above his collar tingled like an arm asleep.

Okay, Pickett, where the hell are you?

19

THE HINGES ON the guest-room portals of the old hotel must have been well oiled, because Jack Pickett, standing at the window of room 216, didn't hear a sound when the door he thought he'd closed opened partway behind him from a draft in the hallway.

Mouse, carrying hot tea and sandwiches to Gilly, noted the door standing ajar and peered in on his way by. When he saw Pickett, he kept walking a few paces before setting down the tray. Then he drew his revolver and returned for a better look. Pickett, his pistol out, used the curtains to conceal himself from the street below. Mouse silently entered the room and stepped up behind the teamster.

"I'll take the gun," he said.

Pickett froze. "Hold on. I'm turnin' around."

"Yer handin' me the gun first," said Mouse.

For a moment Pickett hesitated, then slowly raised his arms. Mouse grabbed the pistol from Pickett's hand and stuck it in his belt.

"Now, let's have a look at ya," he said.

Pickett turned and faced the little puncher, his eyes ugly with hate.

"Yer Will Pickett's brother, ain'cha?"

Pickett said nothing.

"Git in the corner an' face the wall."

Stiffly, the teamster complied.

"Who was ya' layin' for?" Mouse demanded.

"To hell with you," said Pickett.

"So this is how ya Picketts do yer fightin'—from behind curtains like the cowards ya are!"

"You'll see who's the coward when Will gets here."

Mouse went to the window and looked out. Joel stood alone in the street, waiting. From time to time he glanced down at his boots, then looked up, squinting against the blast of sun that filled Main Street end to end.

Turning back to the teamster, Mouse said, "Maybe this'll even up the odds a little."

"It won't make no difference. Hollings is a dead man."

"That, Mister Pickett, remains to be seen."

"You must be Hollings's runt friend Will talked about."

Mouse smiled to himself. "Yes, indeedy," he said. "In the flesh."

At six minutes past four, the music coming from the saloon abruptly stopped. The doors pushed open, and the hulk that was Will Pickett stepped down into the street. He looked as big as Asia. Ignoring Joel, he gazed up at the sun, removed his hat with one hand, and swept back his long dusty hair with the other. Then he pulled the hat on again and turned to face his enemy.

Joel could see Pickett's eyes as they settled on him. They looked like bees searching for a place to sting.

"Afternoon, Hollings! Nice day for dyin', ain't it?"

Joel said nothing. But once more he was amazed at the man's girth. He wondered if a bullet, even at close range, could make it through that stomach, front to back.

Pickett had found his position and was digging in. He wriggled his shoulders and licked his bottom lip in concentration. . . . Faces began piling up in the window of the saloon.

"I'm givin' you the first move," said the teamster.

"Who are you working for, Will?"

"Hey, we been over that before."

135

"It's different now," said Joel. "One of us is going to die. If it's me, I won't be telling anybody; if it's you, what more have you got to lose?"

Pickett's face struggled with the thought, but either he didn't like it, or it didn't get through.

"Make your move, Hollings!"

"Call your man off the roof."

"Call what?"

"Call your man off the roof of the bank."

Will lifted his eyes to the roof in question and smiled. "I always carry a little insurance. You got no insurance?"

"I won't be needing it," said Joel.

Still, he didn't move, and Pickett's fingers began to twitch. Suddenly, Joel threw himself to the left, twisting clockwise in the air, and fired down the street behind him. Before he hit the ground, his .44 had spoken twice. At the same instant a bullet from Pickett's gun cleanly picked the holster from his hip. There was a shriek down the block. On the roof of the bank, cousin Garth was standing straight up, clawing at his throat. Then he tumbled off his perch, ripped through an awning, and crashed to the boardwalk. Joel continued his roll to the side of the street, bullets spitting dust as they chased him. Pickett hadn't moved except to close one eye for aim as he emptied his gun, trying to fix the enemy in his sights. Joel came to his feet, returning the fire, but Pickett had stepped behind one of the horses tied at the saloon hitchrack.

Something hard struck Joel on the forehead, wobbling his knees and sending a sheet of flame across his brain. From what seemed a great distance, he watched the revolver fall from his own hand to the street. In the dust next to it lay Will's .45.

So that's what had hit him. Will's gun was empty!

He looked up in time to see the giant barreling in, his hamlike fists screaming for a target. Joel stepped quickly to the side and planted his heels. Will's eyes showed they knew what was coming, but he couldn't stop.

Joel got all his weight into the punch, but the big man's stomach was made of India rubber. He didn't so much as grunt. Instead, he made his turn and charged again, this time keeping his arms out and his head low. He caught Joel in the chest, lifting him high in the air and sending him through a support post on the walkway. Part of the overhang came down in a clatter of boards and tar paper. Pickett spotted Joel's gun and dove for it. At the same time, Joel grabbed a section of four-by-four and leaped on the teamster's back, flailing at his head with every ounce of his strength. Gun in hand, the big man rose from the dust and shook off his tormentor like a rag doll.

Someone yelled from the saloon. "Hollings, here's a gun!"

Joel picked the weapon out of the air, but Pickett already had him in his sights and was squeezing the trigger. Pain stabbed at Joel's ear as a spatter of red descended on his shirt. Lying flat on his back in the street, he jerked up the revolver and fired into the hulk that loomed above him. The bullet entered Pickett's stomach on the right side. He fired again, then again. The three holes formed a neat pattern across the teamster's belly, and all began to leak blood at the same time. . . . One for Jason, one for Shad, and one for the prodigal son . . .

Pickett's face hadn't changed expression. He stood there, grinning down at Joel, his eyes fixed, his fist frozen around the gun. He didn't seem to know he'd been hit.

Then the big man turned away and started for the saloon. He was walking easily as he mounted the two steps and passed through the swinging doors. Inside, a sea of spectators parted, leaving a path open to the bar. Pickett set one boot on the rail, said, "Whiskey," to the barkeep, and crashed to the floor like a poled ox.

Joel entered the saloon and knelt beside him. "Who you working for, Will? It can't matter now."

Pickett's eyes were busy with something on the ceiling. Then they began darting around the room in a frenzy, as if he'd lost something of great value and wanted it back.

Finally, his eyes slowed up, and without looking at his enemy, he said, "You're right, Hollings. It don't matter anymore. . . . Your man is Cyrus Brenner."

"Brenner! He put you up to this? The Apache, too?"

"Seems you got something at that ranch he wants awful bad. He'd of had it, too, if you didn't come back when you did."

"You still want that whiskey?"

"I'd take it kindly."

Joel signaled to the bartender, who filled a shot glass. He lifted Will's head and helped the amber liquid down his throat. The teamster eagerly gulped.

"Brenner wrote the notes, too?"

"Naw, Jack handled that part of it—used the banker's scratch pads."

That accounted for the legal-size paper.

Joel said to the man closest, "Get Doc Bowman over here."

Mouse pushed Jack Pickett ahead of him into the saloon, a gun firmly planted in the teamster's back.

"Look who I found, Joel—fixin' to bushwack ya from a hotel window."

The brothers looked at each other. Then Jack cried out, "I don't believe any of this! Will, what the hell ya doing down there on the floor? Git up, will ya! Fer Christ's sake, git up!"

But Will's eyes were already closing for the last time.

"So, here goes nothin'!" the fallen giant muttered. Then a shuddering sigh left his body, and Will Pickett was dead.

Joel eased Will's head to the floor and rose. He searched Jack's face, but nothing save hate lived there.

"Take him to jail. We've got work to do," said Joel.

Four or five punchers, more than pleased to help with the task, stepped up and took charge. Joel and Mouse moved out to the boardwalk and gazed up at the white-trimmed yellow house that stood alone on the hill.

20

FROM THE VERANDA of the big yellow house, Cyrus Brenner heard the gunshots in the town below. The oaks filtered his view of Main Street, but he saw Garth's figure topple from the bank roof and moments later caught a glimpse of Will Pickett unsteadily entering the saloon.

Something was wrong. Very wrong. Quickly, he moved to his den inside and removed a small revolver from the desk drawer. He checked the cylinder, loaded in more shells, and slipped the weapon in his belt. He buttoned his jacket and returned to the veranda. For a few moments he stood watching, listening, but the streets were quiet now, and nothing moved in his field of view. He went back inside to the foot of the staircase and called up to his daughter.

"Whitney! You up there?"

Silence.

"Whitney?"

The house was ghostly quiet.

With a countenance several shades paler than normal, the banker returned to the den and sat down behind the desk in his leather wingback chair. Framed in the great chair, he looked tiny, almost childlike, except for the beard and the cruel lines about his eyes.

He heard the knock at the front door but didn't move. Again the knock sounded—almost a banging this time.

He heard a man's voice calling his name. "Brenner, open up!"

Still he didn't move.

He heard the door handle being tried. Then the sound of wood giving and splitting under some great weight. The portal slammed open, quivering like an arrow.

Joel and Mouse stepped into the foyer, their boots ringing on the Spanish tile. Separately, they swung through the downstairs, checking the rooms, finally converging on the den. They passed through to the veranda without seeing the man who watched from behind the desk stacked high with papers.

As they came back inside, Brenner spoke. "Looking for me, gentlemen?"

Joel spun around, but it was too late. The banker had his revolver out and pointed.

"Please remove your gun belts."

Anger and frustration were plain on Joel's face, but there was nothing else to do. He let his guns fall to the floor, and Mouse followed suit.

"Now sit down in those chairs behind you and tell me what it is you want—why you come breaking into my house like runaway bulls."

"Cut the sham," Joel said. "You took my ranch, killed my brother, shot my father, and sent him off with hostile Indians. I'll do the asking why!"

"So you're Joel Hollings?"

"Yes."

"What was the commotion in town?"

"We thinned out the Pickett clan, is all—your friends, I believe."

Almost imperceptibly, Brenner winced. "It's too bad you returned when you did, Joel. You might have had a long and happy life."

"Get on with it!"

Brenner was quiet a moment, then shrugged his shoulders. "You might as well know, since you won't be passing the information along."

141

"Don't bet yer safe deposut box on it," said Mouse.

Brenner smiled wanly and continued. "Years ago, when your father and I were starting out, there were copper strikes all over the state. Many young adventurers like us were getting rich overnight. For more than a year, Shad and I were partners, putting a little money and a lot of sweat into finding and working likely copper sites. It was our efforts that founded this town.

"Then Shad tired of the search and decided to put his efforts into ranching. Just after he bought that spread of yours, a young assayer came to me with the story of vast copper deposits under your ranch. The assayer had done his work privately, and no one else knew. I paid him to confirm the find, which he did. Then I tried to buy the land from Shad—"

"What happened to the assayer?" asked Joel.

"I had to kill him, of course. Then, over the years, I continued trying to buy that land on the pretext of using it to create a watershed, which was badly needed in this part of the state. But Shad wouldn't be moved. He wouldn't sell under any conditions.

"As you see, I'm getting old, and time is running out for me, so I hired the Picketts for money and the Indians for rifles to kidnap Shad and force him to sign over the deed."

"Of course you planned to kill Shad, too, after the signing."

"Of course. What I didn't plan on was your return."

Joel marveled at the glacial ambition of this man, at the twisted nature that would let him so casually take lives and so easily talk about it. If only he could get his hands around that pudgy throat . . .

"By your brand of thinking, I suppose it's necessary for us to die, too."

"That would be the thinking of any man in my position, wouldn't it?" Brenner rose. "Now if you'll oblige me by stepping outside to the garden . . ."

142

Nobody had heard Whitney as she entered the foyer. Noting the broken front door and hearing strange voices in the den, she had approached the room cautiously. For the past several minutes she'd been listening outside the door. When she heard this last remark, she cried out and rushed into the room.

"No! You can't! You mustn't!"

The astonished banker drew back, but the girl was already grabbing at the revolver with her leading hand. She got part of it. Brenner tried to wrestle the weapon free, but Whitney fiercely clung to it, wailing, "No! No!"

The shot sounded muffled, almost as though it came from another room. The girl straightened up slightly, then went to her knees. Clutching both hands to her breast, she lowered her head and knelt there, rocking in silence. Horrified, Brenner threw down the revolver and rushed to his daughter.

"Whitney! It can't be . . . What have I done!"

She continued to rock, as if she held a baby in her arms, then she slipped to the floor, making hardly a sound.

Mouse stepped behind Brenner, retrieving the pistol. Joel joined the banker at the girl's side. Looking into her eyes, he could see the pain there, but he knew the tears were for him and her father. Whitney Brenner wouldn't know how to cry for herself.

Her gaze found Joel, and she extended a trembling hand. In her clenched fist was a wadded piece of paper stained now with her blood.

"For you . . ." she said, "Seems we can cancel our talk about Joel Hollings the 'outlaw.'"

Joel took the paper and weakly smiled. "There you go, chasing me around again! Doesn't a beautiful woman like you have better things to do with her time?"

"I suppose not, after all."

Noting the wet stain that was rapidly spreading toward her waist, he said, "Can I bring you—"

143

"Not a thing, puncher. Just promise me you'll take care of yourself. It's a job I would dearly have loved."

She turned to her father. Again tears glistened on her cheek. She held his hand tightly but could say nothing. A moment later her eyes closed, and it was over.

Brenner remained kneeling, still clutching his daughter's hand. Joel opened the paper. It was a telegram.

PER YOUR WIRE REGARDING HOLLINGS
CASE STOP UNDER LENGTHY REQUESTIONING, THE
WITNESS CARL ADMITTED MINER CARRIED
CONCEALED GUN AT TIME OF SHOOTING &
TRIED TO USE IT STOP ALL CHARGES
AGAINST HOLLINGS BEING DROPPED STOP
OFFICIAL CORRESPONDENCE FOLLOWS TO
SWEENEY & BARNES.

HARLEY CRAIG
U.S. MARSHAL

He handed the paper to Mouse and looked again at the face of the dead girl. The ache he felt inside widened. He thought about the balance of good and evil that was man's nature and how most souls, for their makeup, receive a liberal measure of each. But in the case of this father and daughter, the balance was missing, the rules broken. Here, somehow, a dedicated, uncompromising evil had begotten an equally obstinate good. He lowered his head in wonder and in sorrow.

Brenner's voice was strangely loud, his face animated. "It's okay, boys. She's just sleeping—had a mighty tough day, she did! We'll let her sleep awhile. Then, after supper, she'll play for us—either of you ever hear Whitney play the piano? And she sings like an angel!"

Mouse and Joel exchanged glances. Neither said a word. Just then Tom Sweeney entered the room and stood by the door. From his quiet manner, Joel guessed he sensed what had happened there. Mouse handed him the telegram. Sweeney read it slowly, nodding his head as though he were reading something he already knew.

"I'll put her to bed," Brenner was saying. "She'll be more comfortable in bed, don't you think?" He lifted his daughter in his arms and started for the staircase. "She'll be up by dinner, boys. . . . I've never known her to miss her dinner. . . . You'll see!" And Cyrus Brenner disappeared up the winding stairs.

"Let them be for now," said the sheriff. "I'll bring them along in a while." A few moments later, when the three men left the room, it was Sweeney's voice again that broke the silence.

"By the way, Hollings, I brought your mare back with me. She's outside."

21

THE RESCUE PARTY, formed to find and free Shad Hollings, was made up of fourteen men in all. Not a heavy force by frontier standards but a group that had some history with guns and the men who use guns.

Many had been part of the posse that just days before had tracked Joel and now eagerly joined forces with him. There was general admiration and respect for the young puncher who had faced the Pickett clan and bested them at their own game. No one was sorry to see the Picketts go down. Sweeney led the way, with Joel and Mouse riding close on his wing.

"You say you were at Jerama's camp and saw your pappy?" the sheriff asked.

"Yes, but at the time Shad was too sick to ride."

"Where are the rifles promised to the chief?"

"Barn cellar up in the valley. But I don't think they'll buy us much at this point. Besides, once in Apache hands, they'd just fuel more hate for the White Eyes."

"I agree," said Sweeney. "It's likely we'll have a fight on our hands either way."

The morning sun on the rim of the mountains to the east was quickly climbing into a virgin sky.

"What will happen to Brenner?" Joel asked.

"He'll stand trial for murder and probably hang. . . . In this state, the choice is death by shooting or hanging."

"Is his mind still off?"

146

"Seems so. He wouldn't let us take the girl's body—had to pry him off of her. A sad thing."

Joel nodded and looked away.

"The West does funny things to a man, Hollings. It seems to bring out more of what we are to start with. I mean, if a man is basically good when he gets here, he seems to only get better. If he's bad, he just turns worse. I get the feeling it's all born of the brand of freedom we enjoy here.

"In the beginning, I'm told, Cyrus Brenner did a lot for this country. He built the town almost single-handed. He even helped create new watersheds for the land, mostly at his own expense, but the flaw was there all the time. We were just too busy being grateful to see it. . . . Why is it that most men with one million dollars somehow think they'd be better off with two?"

It was a good question, and Joel didn't have an answer.

Throughout the morning and into the afternoon the party rode on toward the mesa country. There were few words spoken by anybody. The men understood the danger of the mission and seemed to be counseling themselves, getting prepared for the worst. They were eager for the chance to square things with Joel, but there was the natural element of fear.

As the sun began to settle into the western hills, Joel directed Sweeney to the spot where he'd spent the first night as the Picketts' prisoner. He knew they had to be wary of Apache anywhere in this corner of the mountain desert, and the spot in question gave good line of sight in all directions. When the men had pitched camp and eaten, Sweeney took Joel's cup and his own to the fire for a refill. Handing Joel the coffee, he said, "We'll need a plan for tomorrow. Any ideas?"

"Might be best to split up," said Joel, "We could make the approach from two directions. It'll give them more to think about."

147

"I'll take a group up the backside?"

"Yes. We'll leave ourselves time to get in position and set our arrival for the same moment. . . . Do you carry a timepiece, Tom?"

The sheriff produced a fob watch from his pocket.

"I'll need one, too." Joel called to the men for a pocket watch. The man named Radley came over and handed him his. "My pappy's," he said. "It's never failed me yet."

Then Joel picked a stick from the ground and traced the tabletop in the dirt.

"Jerama's hut sits here, close to the rim where you'll be coming up. If you can take Jerama quickly and let them see you do it, it will help. Apaches lose their fight when their chief goes down. . . . The place they're holding Shad is here. I'll clear him off the hill; then we'll be on our way."

"How many guns do they have?" the sheriff asked.

"Not many, I think, but don't count on these people to be easy. They're scrapping for what little they have, and we're the intruders."

Sweeney nodded and sipped his coffee.

Then Joel changed the subject. "What do you make of Jake Barnes?" he asked.

"He's all right, I guess. A hell of a tracker for sure—awful stiff, though."

"Where is he now?"

"Still scouring the mountains, I suppose." Sweeney looked up and smiled. "He could be there for weeks."

The morning light found the rescue party well into the mesas, and the face of every rider wore the same uneasy expression. Since leaving Brenner Falls, they'd seen no sign to tell them an Apache was within a hundred miles. About noon, Joel signaled the men, and they drew up in the shadow of a cave that was hewn in the base of a cliff.

"There's our hill," he said, pointing to a mesa that looked like a Stetson hat with its lid blown off. "Go quietly from here on and stay below the rim till Tom and I give the signal." They adjusted the watches to agree to the second, and the men watered down. Then they left in two groups, hugging the base of the cliff.

When Joel and his men reached the mesa and started their climb up the west face, the loose rock started its commotion. They slowed the pace, carefully picking their way along a well-worn path that Joel guessed was the one used by the Indians. But not a single track, human or otherwise, showed there. As they neared the rim, they halted in the sun and waited. Now and then a horse jerked its head or stamped its impatience; otherwise, nothing moved.

At exactly 12:45 P.M., Joel drew his .44, motioned to the others, and spurred the black up over the rim onto the mesa.

A quarter mile to the east, where the Butte abruptly ended, he saw Sweeney and his men rising into view. It was like looking into a vast mirror and seeing their own reflection as the two wings of the attack party closed ground and approached each other. In between, the mesa lay empty. There were no Indians there, and no leavings of Indians anywhere in sight. The men in both groups began to mill around, murmuring their relief. Joel and Sweeney continued toward each other, coming together at the center of the tabletop.

"What do you make of it?" asked Sweeney.

Joel felt a hollowness in the pit of his stomach. It never occurred to him that the Apache would move on, taking Shad with them. The reality of the empty mesa hit him hard. Still, he should have been ready for it. He should have known . . .

He raised his head. "Like most chiefs, Jerama probably carries an ancient schedule in his head," he said quietly. "The Apache doesn't remain anywhere for long."

They turned their horses and together searched the mesa more closely for sign that could tell them the direction of the Apache march.

An hour passed, then two. But they found nothing. No tracks. Not a remnant of clothing. Even the thin grass that the wickiups had covered was standing tall again in the light breeze. It didn't seem possible!

Mouse rode up and joined them.

"When we was lookin' fer you," he said to Joel, "Silverfoot took us up there." He pointed to the towering mesa off to the north. "Ya kin see half the world from up there."

Leave Silverfoot to think of it! Joel mused. But he and Sweeney liked the idea immediately and called the rest of the men over.

"Hollings, Mouse and I are going up on Puma Mesa there for a better look. Keep at it here, boys. We'll be back."

And the three departed down the north face where the footing was tricky but saved them the better part of a half hour.

Atop Puma Mesa, under a blue sky that stretched all the way to Mexico, Joel and the others looked out on the steppelands and desert below. He estimated the line of sight at thirty miles or better and wasted no time starting to scan the outer reaches of terrain. Far to the south, a lone covered wagon struggled west across the blazing desert.

Suddenly, Mouse called out. "I think there's somethin' out there—due southeast."

Joel and Sweeney followed Mouse's line. Maybe twelve miles off, a black dot made a period on the sweltering land. The distance was great, and Joel wasn't really sure he saw it at all. Then, by looking beyond and just above the area for some minutes, he was sure.

Almost imperceptibly, the dot seemed to move toward them, but that could be merely the heat that busily rippled its waves skyward. They kept the speck in sight and finished their survey.

"Probably a stray lost out there," said Sweeney. "Still, it looks bigger than an animal. . . . What do you think?"

It was all they had, and Joel said, "Let's have a look."

At the foot of Puma Mesa they were joined by the rest of the party and rode into the desert, following the bearings Joel had taken while above. The sun fell farther and farther behind, flattening its rays against the earth, growing each shrub into a tree of shadows.

Before dark, they passed among a stretch of sandy dunes that offered their first elevated view since entering the desert. Joel urged his mare up the side of the tallest mound and looked out into the gathering dusk.

Sweeney had been right. The object of their interest was larger than an animal. Less than a mile away now, he saw a man on horseback being led by someone on foot. The travelers looked oddly familiar as they proceeded across the darkening sands. Then he recognized them. It was Shad and Silverfoot!

Joel spurred the black, coming off the dune at a dead run, and reached them in minutes.

"Shad!"

His father looked frail and tired as he clung to the pommel of his saddle, but his eyes held their old humor.

"I suppose I'll have to give this girl a raise in pay now?"

Silverfoot's shoulders arched once more in the gentle expression of pride Joel had come to know so well. The hint of a smile played on her lips.

"Aren't you supposed to be at the ranch?" he asked.

"It's better that we all go together."

She carefully looked him over. She saw the blood clot at his ear, the gash on his forehead.

"You found the man you were after?"

"Yes, I found him."

He took the reins of Shad's horse and she climbed up behind him on the black.

151

"How did you do it?" he asked. "How did you get Shad and yourself out?"

"The Apache was moving on, and Jerama changed his mind. He didn't want Shad killed. He gave him to me. He told me to take him home."

Joel gazed up at the mesas but said nothing.

"You are all right?" she asked, lifting a hand to the angry nick on his ear.

"I'm fine, Silverfoot. I'm just fine now."

22

THE GROUP THAT rode out from town in Tom Sweeney's wagon to help lay the new adobe walls for the ranch included Lucy, Gilly, Doc Bowman, and the sheriff himself.

Except for the doctor, who sat with Shad, sipping beer under a cottonwood, the others were busy lifting and setting the large bricks in place. The work went easily, and everyone sniffed hungrily at Silverfoot's open fire where white billows of smoke carried the aroma of roasting beef.

Two weeks had passed since Shad's homecoming, and though he still spent most of his time resting and watching the antics of his prize Arabians, the old rancher was getting visibly stronger each day.

When the food was ready, the group sat down at the long oak table that the men had moved outside. Joel handed Lucy a beer and raised his own in salute.

"For being there when it counted, Lucy—"

She winked at Gilly. "So kids and outlaws get to me."

Joel faced the others in turn with clumsy toasts delivered in half phrases. But everyone was too busy putting down steak and squash and potatoes to pay him more than an occasional polite glance.

"Yer steak's gettin' cold," said Mouse. "Clam up an' eat."

Silverfoot sat down next to Joel, and he felt the softness of her shoulder against him. Her presence held a thrill he'd never known. It could have been the beer or the sun, but he felt slightly faint. Then a look in her eyes told him all he needed to know. A man could spend three lifetimes searching for a woman like this. . . .

Gilly, whose face was healing nicely, was the first one up for seconds. "When I grow a bit, Joel, kin I git a job helpin' here on the ranch?" Joel looked over at the section of wall the boy had laid.

"You've done some growing, Gilly. And some helping, too. Anytime at all you want to start."

Then Sweeney rose. He had on his peace officer manner. "I'd like to just say I'm mighty pleased to know you people and in a sense be working for you. . . . Our town's had its troubles lately, but all that's over now. There's a lot of decent folks in Brenner Falls, and you're looking at a few of them right here." He glanced at Lucy, the boy, the old doctor. "Plus new 'uns it seems are arriving for a fresh start almost every month . . . What I'm trying to say, I guess, is I hope you Hollingses won't harbor any bitterness towards us—though, God knows, you got every right to feel it. . . . Well, that's my piece," said the lawman. He sat down, his ears bright red. Then he raised his glass and drained his beer in a single gulp.

In the days that followed, the ranch was gradually restored to its former eminence, while Joel and Silverfoot patiently led Shad back to health and each other into a love that would endure.